WHAT DEATH FORGETS

THEA VERDONE

ISBN ebook: 979-8-9899748-2-5
Paperback: 979-8-9899748-3-2
Paperback alternate cover: 979-8-9899748-5-6
Hardcover: 979-8-9899748-4-9

Copy editing by Alona Stark
Cover design and title typography by Novel Hounds Designs @novelhounds
Cover illustration by Anniris @anniris
Character illustrations by Amanda @legendsofaukera
Key and lock illustrations by Olga Kamieshkova

*For anyone haunted by a past they wish they could forget,
and for anyone afraid to forget what they lost.*

CONTENTS

CONTEST

1. Icarus 3
2. Every Painting is a Portrait 7
3. Macabre Doppelgänger 19
4. My, What Sharp Claws 29
5. Shackled Muses 34
6. Come Along, Snake 41
7. The Tide Returns 45
8. Never Lie About Art 54
9. Through a Painting 63
10. Footprints 75
11. A Parting Gift 79
12. Fever Dream 86
13. Spate of Tempests 90
14. Apathy is Worse 100
15. Two Halves 107
16. Lick the Plate Clean 113
17. Purple on a Blank Canvas 123
18. Inky Darkness 131
19. Signing His Name 135
20. Paint Everything Black 140
21. Maelstrom 144
22. One of the Best 150
23. The Ghost of His Sigil 161
24. Art That's Honest 171
25. Spun a Tapestry 180
26. The Huntress and the Trap 187
27. Effigy 198
28. Strong Enough to Bow 206
29. No One's Prey 211
30. Tangled Thicket 220

31. Like an Ancient Oak   234
32. Open to You   242
33. Feel You Everywhere   249
34. Amelie   261

MENTORSHIP

35. Beautiful Cage   269
36. Tracing Lines   275
37. Premonitions in Reverse   284
38. Guilt Manifested   292
39. Cursed Heirloom   300
40. Ghost Story   310
41. Only Now, Only Me   320
42. Love Too Much   327
43. When a Mind is Lonely   335
44. Mourning in the Shadows   345
45. A Shrine to You   356
46. Ouroboros   363
47. Cathedral of His Chest   378
48. Passion to Doldrums   386
49. Salt and Damp Earth   393
50. Tempest   405
51. Art Will Remember   414
52. The Closed Door   422
53. No More Secrets   433
54. Swimming in the Shallows   440
55. Those Forgotten   448
56. Paper Boat   462

Epilogue   468

Afterword   481
Acknowledgments   485
About The Author   487
Also by Thea Verdone   489
Content Warnings   491

AUTHOR'S NOTE

The book you hold in your hands has been part of my life for nearly two years. Most days, I struggled to complete a single paragraph, let alone write the poetic prose I find creative fulfillment in.

But with the help of family, friends, readers, and my mental health team, I not only finished, but rekindled my love for writing.

In the end, Lichenmoor became my sanctuary, and Asher and Lev my family, but as Lev said,

The painting is no longer yours once you give birth to it. It's for the viewer, and the emotions you evoke in them.

This story is yours. I hope you enjoy it.

Lichenmoor (lai·kn·mor) is a fictional place on the North East England coast.

Listen to the playlist on Spotify. Visit theaverdone.com for the link.

Content Warnings

The mental health of my readers is very important to me. *What Death Forgets* explores darker themes, including sexual assault and death.

Please consult the content warnings and mental health resources in the back of the book. They may contain spoilers.

CONTEST

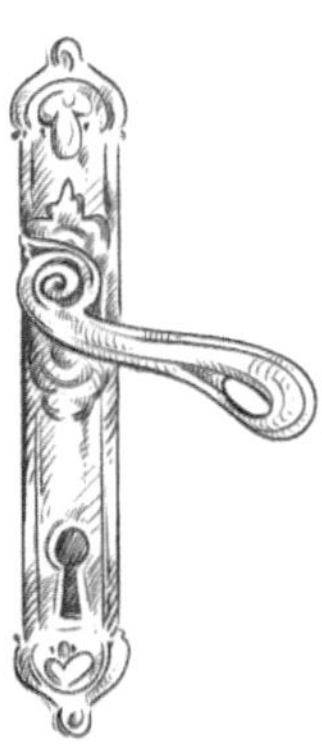

Every portrait that is painted with feeling is a portrait of the artist, not of the sitter.

— OSCAR WILDE, THE PICTURE OF
DORIAN GRAY

ICARUS

ASHER

OCTOBER 1

The gates of Lichenmoor were open, but fog obscured what lurked beyond them. A man guarded the gate, arm lifted, finger pointing through the mist.

Was it *him*?

A flock of butterflies launched into flight inside Asher's chest and disappeared as the luxe SUV slowed to a stop in front of a life-sized statue shrouded in scarlet ivy and mottled with moss.

Leather creaked. The gray-haired driver unbuckled his seatbelt and turned around. "This is as far as I'll take you, Mr. Blakely."

"I don't mind paying." Asher reached into his wallet and pulled out one of four remaining twenty-pound notes. Lugging his clothes and six months' worth of empty sketchbooks uphill sounded exhausting after a long day of traveling.

"All guests are to walk the remaining distance. His rules."

Him. His. He. Too big to refer to by given name, like he was a god or something—the God, which was only fitting.

Leviathan Marks might as well have been a god to Asher,

and this journey was as much a pilgrimage as a chance to win a prestigious mentorship under the artist he idolized so much he'd turned his body into a living shrine to him.

Never meet your heroes. They'll only let you down. Asher knew the adage well, but he would risk flying too close to the sun if he could witness a moment of Leviathan's mastery before he plummeted like Icarus.

"Don't worry, lad." The driver smiled, deepening the wrinkles on his face in a way that reminded Asher of a bulldog. "Stick to the road and you'll be right as rain. Let me help you out."

"No thanks," Asher rushed to say. The last thing he wanted was a man well into his sixties standing in the drizzle while he retrieved his bags.

Asher slipped a rain jacket over his lucky black hoodie and pushed the door open, then heaved his oversized duffel bag out.

Salt and decay stung his nose. Waves rumbled somewhere unseen.

"Remember what I said, Mr. Blakely. Mind the tide too. It sneaks up on you."

Lovely.

The driver tapped the steering wheel with his thumbs. "Speaking of which, I'll be off now. My wife won't be happy if I'm trapped here overnight."

Asher didn't blame him. Lichenmoor Hall lorded over miles of boggy moors from its perch atop the bluffs. When the tide was high, the ocean swallowed the land around Lichenmoor, cutting it off from the mainland until the tide went out again.

"Good luck!" the man said.

"With what?"

Finding the castle, winning the mentorship, or surviving Leviathan? But the driver had already rolled up his window, and the quiet soccer game on the radio now blasted from the speakers.

Fog swallowed the taillights in seconds, and the engine fading in the distance was the only proof he hadn't gotten lost inside a daydream.

The back of his neck tingled with awareness. Was someone there? Maybe Leviathan?

His pulse sped as he whipped his gaze over his shoulder to find a monstrous aquamarine eel arcing over the gate, glaring at any who dared enter with rows of sharp, needle-like teeth.

What a warm way for Leviathan to welcome his guests. Shaking off a shiver and his paranoia, he passed through the gate.

"Creepy."

A blast of briny wind snatched a fistful of leaves from the trees, twirling and tumbling them down the path as if a malevolent force had shown him the way.

Chasing the trail of breadcrumb leaves, Asher hurried up the cobblestone driveway. His vision only ventured a few feet into the fog, and he had no choice but to put faith in the driver's directions and the castle's existence, like God or Santa Claus or Leviathan Marks.

Nobody had heard from the aristocratic playboy and celebrity artist in five years, but his reputation was legendary.

Asher had feared him dead, or at least the muse inside of him. He'd already mourned the loss of the greatest artistic genius of the twenty-first century—until he'd received a wax-stamped envelope bearing the Marks family crest.

Leviathan had selected Asher and six other artists to compete for one month at the Marks Family Artists Retreat, the first held since Lucian Marks had died. The prize? Six months as Leviathan's protégé.

Asher had to win. Learning from Leviathan would be a dream come true, and help relaunch his art career.

His calves burned as the path sloped upward through a tunnel of interlocking trees. An ancient oak groaned, clawing long branches over the path. *Widow makers.* That's what his dad called them. Heavy branches that grew too greedy, and broke easily, thirsty for death.

The sun hung lower in the sky. He checked his phone again. Still no service. He'd been walking through a fugue of fog for twenty minutes without a clue whether he headed toward his destiny or his doom.

Anxiety bubbled in his blood. If he couldn't find the castle before the sun set and high tide swept in, Leviathan would assume he'd asked the driver to take him back to the ferry. To have his hero believe him a coward and a quitter was a fate far worse than being lost on the moor until the sea dragged him to death.

A rock clattered. Blades of seagrass crunched. Was someone in the fog?

"Who's there?"

Footsteps clicked on the cobblestone in the staccato of a hurried pace. Asher swirled around, but the mist was so thick, and… Fuck. Now he couldn't remember which direction to go.

He took a deep breath. *Calm down, Asher.* If he met the ocean, he'd turn around and go the other way. He trudged off in the direction that felt most right.

"You're going the wrong way," a voice called, velvety low and laced with a British accent.

"Who said that?"

Asher spun with stuttering footsteps, thoughts spiraling with his field of vision as he scanned the haze, searching for a silhouette.

The fog grew denser, shifting, coalescing into something darker, more defined, and then a man stepped out onto the road. But not just any man.

Leviathan Marks.

EVERY PAINTING IS A PORTRAIT

ASHER

There was no mistaking him.

Faded copper hair and a close-cropped beard, freckles like paint splattering every inch of his skin, or at least every inch that Asher had glimpsed while scouring the internet. And those eyes—blue-gray like stormy waters midwinter, like a sleeper wave.

Even at forty, Leviathan's towering frame and stocky build harkened back to his rugby roots, making him every bit as imposing as his disposition.

His features were so symmetrical, drawing him was a study in perfection. Perhaps only Leviathan would be up for the challenge, but he'd never released a full self-portrait—only one with the eyes scribbled out.

Asher should know. He had a copy tattooed over his heart.

"Are you alright?" Leviathan said, casting a cloud of mist from his lips. "I'm Leviathan."

"I know who you are," Asher said in a voice that sounded nothing like him, terrified and awestruck, like he'd stumbled upon an angel and couldn't decide if he should fall to his knees and beg for his life or worship at his feet.

Leviathan drew closer, extending his hand, fingers trailing towards a handshake.

Asher had studied those hands in motion and at rest, covered with paint, pastels, and charcoal.

Leviathan wielded his paintbrush as masterfully as if he'd sharpened his craft over hundreds of years and traveled through time after outgrowing the Renaissance Age.

Remembering his manners, Asher met Leviathan in the middle, and shook his hand. Leviathan had a powerful grip, not in a show of force, but quiet confidence, which made sense.

After all, Leviathan had nothing to prove. He was art royalty, a prodigy born from a prodigy, interred in the hallowed halls of lauded artistry before he'd turned eighteen. A predator completely comfortable at the top of the food chain.

Asher's body warred with his head, wanting to catalog every sensation to reminisce over later and scour his hand with soap until he erased any trace of him.

Because Leviathan ruined every man he touched.

He'd left no shortage of brokenhearted artists over the last twenty years, plying them with compliments and his cock, and after he was through with them, they were too heartbroken to paint.

Maybe that was why he was so talented. He'd stolen everyone else's muse.

Leviathan released his hand. "Asher Blakely, I presume?"

How did he know?

"You're our last straggler," Leviathan added, as if he'd read his facial expression, if not his very mind. "The others have been drinking for hours, so I volunteered to fetch you, lest I wind up with more than one pupil lost amongst the moors. I'm sorry I frightened you."

"You didn't." Asher hid his trembling hands in the pockets of his jacket.

Leviathan tracked the motion and clicked his tongue. "You

must be cold. That rain jacket is hardly warm enough. Let's get you inside."

Before Asher could protest, Leviathan snatched up his duffel bag. "Christ. Did you fill this with bricks?"

"I packed to win, sir."

Fuck. Fuck. Fuck. He hadn't meant to flirt or say *sir*.

Almost three years had passed since he and Ben broke up, but Asher's submissive tendencies still lingered.

"Sir?" Leviathan's eyes widened, then glinted with mirth as his face stretched into a smirk. "Please. I'm not *that* old. You may call me Lev."

Asher's cheeks burned. "Look, can I just have my bag back?"

Leviathan clutched the bag to his chest. "Of course not! No guest of mine will slog up this wretched hill with a bag that weighs more than him."

"My bag does not weigh—"

Leviathan strode off, calling over his shoulder, "Come along, pretty American." Mist engulfed him, and he disappeared like a mirage.

"Don't call me that," Asher said, hurrying after him.

Leviathan slowed. "Oh? What shall I call you then?"

"My name."

"I couldn't possibly. Asher strays my mind to what your skin would look like with charcoal on it."

Leviathan was just playing his rakish role, but the suggestion that his hero had thought about drawing on his bare skin tantalized him.

What would Leviathan think if he knew Asher had already transformed his body into his canvas? Not that Asher would ever give him the opportunity.

"Call me Blakely, then."

"I'll try my very best." Leviathan flashed a conspiratorial grin.

A wave crashed behind them. Asher jumped.

Leviathan rested a staying hand on his shoulder for a second before lifting it.

"Fret not, Mr. Blakely. The ocean sounds closer than it is. High tide is still a few hours away."

Asher didn't reply, thoughts swimming with the surreality of meeting Leviathan Marks. His hero had flirted with him, had worried about his warmth, and consoled him when the waves startled him.

God, Asher was so fucked.

"You know, I was frightened too when I first moved here," Leviathan said.

Asher's elation wilted like the waterlogged thistle lining the path. Leviathan had moved to Lichenmoor with his family after doctors diagnosed his mother with terminal cancer. "You were seven, and I'm not scared."

"How do you know how old I was?"

Asher shrugged. "I'm a fan."

Leviathan gasped. "You are?"

Asher resisted the urge to say, *obviously*. How often did he meet an artist who wasn't a fan of his work?

"I must admit, I'm a fan of your work too," Leviathan said.

"Really?"

"Of course. Why else would I have invited you?"

As much as Asher wanted to bask in Leviathan's praise, it was hard to believe. No matter how many paintings he sold within hours of listing, imposter syndrome told him he wasn't good enough.

"I've been dying to know where you get your inspiration," Leviathan said. "Who influences your work?"

Asher cleared his throat. "You do, sir."

"Ah-ah," Leviathan chided. "If you keep calling me that, I may start calling you *lad*."

Yes, please, especially if he put *good* in front of it.

"I'm sorry. It's a habit."

"How very polite of you." Leviathan stroked his ginger

beard. "Where were we? Oh, right. You were saying I was the reason you became an artist and that I should thank myself for creating you."

Asher rolled his lips inward. He wouldn't let Leviathan charm him, or make him laugh, or seduce him.

With the feigned nonchalance of a jealous lover, Leviathan said, "Well, I can't be your only influence."

But Leviathan *was* his only influence. No one else's art gave him that burst of dopamine that had his pulse thrumming, his skin buzzing, saliva filling his mouth. Not even Leviathan's father, Lucian Marks.

"It's not a pop quiz," Leviathan prodded.

"I have as many influences as there are color combinations. Tears turning hazel eyes green, soft moss blanketing a tree, the sharp angle of a paper cut, the look on a mother's face when she can't afford food *and* formula, so the person behind her pays for both. That's what inspires me."

Leviathan slowed his pace and turned toward him. "Were you the person who paid for her groceries?"

"I paint portraits of other people, not myself."

"Ah, but every painting is a portrait of the artist regardless of the subject. That's lesson number one." Leviathan's gaze raked over him. "I paint in textures and emotions, too."

Asher's lips tipped up. "I mean, is there any other way?"

"Not if you want to make art."

"And you're the gatekeeper?"

Leviathan scoffed. "The only gate I keep is the one to Lichenmoor. Anything can be art, and any person who picks up a paintbrush is an artist, whether they're any good or not."

"And here I pegged you as an art snob."

"Interesting word choice."

"For a dirty mind."

Leviathan's laughter boomed across the moor. "You're not the meek dormouse I was expecting."

Asher bit back a smile. "And you're exactly as I imagined."

"Oh? What did you imagine?"

"Big and loud. Insatiably flirtatious."

But that only scratched the surface. Leviathan was a Russian doll of a person. Beneath the layers of old money and bad boy socialite, bohemian artist and humble philanthropist, the man was deeply lonely. Asher saw it in his art.

Leviathan clutched a hand to his chest with a sharp gasp, startling the hell out of Asher. Was Leviathan having a heart attack? Forty wasn't old. Then again, Asher's bag *was* heavy, and Lucian had died unexpectedly.

"Words hurt, Blakely." Leviathan pushed perfect lips into a pout.

The fist around Asher's own heart unclenched. He exhaled a nervous laugh. "You scared me."

"Don't worry, lad. I'm made of sturdier stock."

Okay, so Leviathan calling him lad was going to haunt his wet dreams for weeks—no. No wet dreams. He was here for art and art only.

Asher loped ahead. They had to be almost there. He just needed to keep his mouth shut until then.

Leviathan caught up quickly. "Please stay close to me. I'd hate for you to get lost again." He lowered his voice, drawing Asher's ear closer. "Not to mention, some say the moors are haunted. Tell me, Blakely, do you believe in ghosts?"

Asher shook his head. "If ghosts existed, we'd have video evidence by now."

Leviathan clucked his tongue. "Your generation has no imagination."

"Or we had less lead poisoning."

"Touché." Leviathan laughed. "Once we're out of these woods, the road hugs the cliff's edge closely. I assume you believe in gravity?"

"Hilarious," Asher deadpanned.

The path snaked around tree trunks Asher could barely see.

The scent of pine and macerated leaves competed with the salty breeze. He wished he'd arrived in better weather.

Lichenmoor's forests appeared almost enchanted in the photos he'd found online. Old-growth pine, alder, and birch trees towered over the Fuilteach River, intersected by a series of medieval arched bridges.

"What about curses?" Leviathan asked next. "Folklore claims centuries of battles and bloodshed once lured the ocean onto land, giving it a taste for man, and that's why the tide is so hungry. When the ocean retreated, it left behind a curse that all who die here will spend an eternity walking circles in the mist."

"I read about that."

"Where did you learn these things about me and my land?"

"I'm not sure if you've heard, but there's something called the internet."

"Hm."

"What does *hm* mean?"

Leviathan inclined his head toward him. "*Hm* means *hm*. I was simply acknowledging that I'd heard you."

"Okay, because it sounded like something someone would say if they didn't know what the internet is."

Leviathan laughed. "Your sarcasm is delightful."

A gust of wind slipped under Asher's jacket, sending a shiver down his spine.

"Take my coat," Lev said. "I run hot."

Asher eyed the lined olive coat. It probably smelled like him. The idea of wrapping himself in the ghost of Lev's body heat was difficult to resist, but the last thing he needed was to accidentally pop a hard-on for Lev's jacket.

"I'm not cold."

Leviathan's eyes narrowed. "If you aren't cold, then why are you shivering? Unless... Are you scared? They're only stories. I think." He bent his lips to Asher's ear and stage whispered behind his hand. "I'm approximately forty-eight percent certain I don't believe in ghosts either."

Asher laughed. He couldn't help it. "The only thing scary is that you noticed me shivering in near darkness."

"Observation skills are a must for any artist. Lesson number two, Mr. Blakely."

The path curved.

"We're by the cliffs now. Let's switch sides," Leviathan said, then, like a total fucking gentleman, guided him away from the ledge with a light hand pressed between his shoulder blades.

Asher was in trouble. Sure, he'd nursed a nerdy crush on Leviathan, but he hadn't expected to be so smitten with him in person.

Was their chemistry real or imagined? Not that it mattered.

Even if Asher had a chance, which he didn't, he refused to be chewed up and spat out like gristle by a man fifteen years older than him. Not again.

Leviathan drifted nearer, like the tide chasing the moon. Asher tripped on the lip of a buckled brick and lurched forward. Great. He was going to fall on his face in front of Leviathan Marks.

Except he didn't.

Leviathan reacted faster than gravity and yanked him back. "Alright there, Blakely?"

"Yeah, thanks."

It was a wonder Asher could talk at all because Leviathan's hand was still on his shoulder, thumb sweeping back and forth in a soothing rhythm.

Asher looked down at his freckled hand and back up, a mouse caught in a snare.

"I'm sorry. Did I hurt you?" Leviathan asked, lifting his hand. "My mum always said I was like a Great Dane, clumsy and overexcitable, unaware of my strength. You look a wee bit like a gale would knock you over."

Asher scowled. He wasn't skinny. Leviathan was built like a giant who bench-pressed tree trunks, and the only thing Asher lifted was his paintbrush.

His snarky response fell from his head as the castle materialized the same way Leviathan had, like the fog had taken shape, coalescing into a limestone fortress whittled by wind and stained with algae.

Sepia light made murky by fog glowed anemically from the lower windows. The upper floors were dark, save for a few lit windows carving the face of a jack-o'-lantern.

A riot of red and orange ivy climbed the eastern facade, gargoyles peeking from the foliage like phantoms. Laughter and music curled out, whispering *come hither.*

"Welcome to Lichenmoor." Leviathan led him up the grand front steps, and opened a massive iron door. "After you."

A glittering chandelier illuminated a double staircase. Framed art—most of it Lucian's—hung on a grid of walnut wainscoting. The metallic screech of Leviathan sliding an iron drawbar over the door grated against Asher's frayed nerves.

"Sorry. Most of the doors and locks protest. It's all the salt and mist in the air. Stay here long enough, and you'll learn Lichenmoor's language. She's always talking."

"She?"

"Whomever. I've always felt a maternal stewardship, but perhaps that's Luna."

Asher opened his mouth to ask who Luna was, but then Leviathan removed his parka. The knitted cables of his sweater strained over stocky shoulders and a well-muscled chest. If he looked that good in thick wool, what did he look like underneath?

Leviathan flung his parka onto a coat rack. "May I take your jacket?"

"Oh, sure."

Asher unzipped his jacket, but before he could slip out of it,

Leviathan's fingers dipped inside the collar at the back of his neck and slid it down and off.

"Thank you," Asher said, mouth dry. Leviathan Marks had undressed him. Sort of.

Leviathan smiled and hung Asher's thrift store jacket on the rung below his own. If Asher was lucky, the spicy jasmine in Leviathan's cologne would settle in the fibers of his own jacket.

"Who's Luna?" Asher asked.

"She's been with my family for ages, and has mothered me longer than *my* mum, truth be told."

"Been with your family?"

Leviathan laughed. "Sorry. She started as my child minder and served as head of house. Now she's my only family."

Asher didn't know what to say. Poor Leviathan.

Loud voices and laughter called down a wide hall on the left.

"It sounds like the others have continued drinking in my absence. Care to join them?"

That sounded like a nightmare. "It's been a long day."

"Are you a teetotaler?"

"Would it be a problem if I were?"

"Of course not. *Teetotaler* is a seldom used word, and I don't want it to go extinct." He shielded his mouth with his hand. "I'm so relieved you didn't think I was talking about golf."

Condescending snobbery shouldn't have been so charming.

"Come, Blakely," Leviathan said, and started up the grand staircase with Asher's duffel.

Pheromones. That had to be it. Only a chemical reaction could explain why two words and Leviathan's ass filling out his slacks sent Asher's blood southward.

He steered his eyes away from Leviathan to the gothic majesty surrounding him. Thorny rose vines lined the carpet runner. A large stained glass window overlooked each landing they passed, depicting an emerald dragon and a griffin fighting over a bouquet of thistle. The battle progressed as they ascended, and by the time they exited the stairwell, Asher was out of breath, and the dragon was winning.

"It's a bit of a climb, I'm afraid," Leviathan said without a hint of strain. He slowed his pace to match Asher's as they walked down a wide hallway with stained glass on one side, and tapestry-lined walls on the other.

They passed five doors, each with a tarnished brass lock depicting a figure from Greek Mythology, before Leviathan slowed in front of Poseidon's door.

"That's my room." Leviathan stopped in front of the next door. "And this room is yours."

They'd share a wall.

Medusa watched over Asher's lock, crown of coiled snakes so alive he had the absurd impulse to close his eyes.

Leviathan plunged an old key into her mouth and opened the door with an eerie shriek. "After you."

The bedroom wasn't the dreary tomb of stone and dark wood he'd expected. Periwinkle curtains framed large leaded windows. Pale oak floorboards and carved wood paneling brightened the space. A matching four-poster bed leaned against the tapestry-lined wall separating their rooms.

Was Leviathan's bed on the other side?

"Are the accommodations to your liking?" Leviathan asked from the doorway.

Asher turned. "I'd sleep anywhere in the castle for the opportunity to learn from you, but this room is so beautiful I want to paint it."

Leviathan said nothing at first, appraising Asher until his cheeks turned warm, then responded with a total anticlimax. "Lichenmoor Hall is not a castle. It's an estate."

"If it has turrets and more than one suit of armor, it's a castle."

Asher knew it technically wasn't a castle. With all the research he'd done on Lichenmoor, he could give a docent tour. But Lichenmoor Hall was too much of a mouthful to say and too sprawling to call a home or a manor.

"Americans, always so intent on being willfully ignorant." Leviathan pushed off the doorframe and handed him the key.

Their fingers grazed. Static sparked.

"Sorry," they both said.

Leviathan cleared his throat. "You must be knackered. You'll find water and snacks in that basket." He tipped his head toward a small table by the lit limestone fireplace. "I should nip back down to check the others haven't destroyed anything."

"This is perfect. Thanks, Leviathan."

"Please call me Lev. If I'd had any choice in the matter, I would have picked something more sensible."

So, Lev hadn't been trying to be flirtatious or force familiarity when he'd asked Asher to call him Lev earlier.

"Lev," Asher said, testing the word on his tongue.

"Good lad."

Fuck.

3

MACABRE DOPPELGÄNGER

LEV

Leviathan Marks collected people like paintings, but it wasn't as sinister as it sounded. The trick was to search for that haunted look.

Broken souls made the most beautiful art, and lovers. With any luck, Asher Blakely would be the crown jewel of his collection.

Lev had discovered Blakely after stumbling upon a portrait of an older man looking at his hands. The man's face was leathered with wrinkles, and the artist had etched guilt and self-loathing into each weary crease. Even the way he wrung his hands captured his regret.

The painting of the guilty man had been like looking into a mirror, because Lev was guilty. He wasn't a martyr mistakenly blaming himself for a death he had no control over. He'd killed a man.

There was so much blood on his hands that every time he painted with red, he thought of *him*.

After discovering Asher Blakely, Lev had devoured every painting. The lad was brilliant, a rare, once in a lifetime find, talented with oil and acrylics, his watercolors as alive as the ocean.

His pieces ranged from erotic to ethereal, but Lev fancied his darker work, the grim pieces burdened by fear and loss, as if he'd used shadows for paint, and bled melancholy and rage from his brush.

There was something dark and sad and broken inside of Blakely, and Lev wanted to poke it with a stick and see what happened next. Would he bite?

Lev couldn't wait to knock down Asher's walls and rummage through his thoughts until he figured out where such haunting art came from.

Lichenmoor Hall still slept. Lev sat at the dining table with his sketchbook open in front of him and a cup of tea beside it.

The lit crystal chandelier turned the world outside the windows black. He sensed the man hiding in the darkness on the other side of the window in front of him more than he saw him.

"Go away, Silas."

A figure appeared behind his reflection in the window. He spun in his chair and found Asher, hazel eyes wide, black hair tousled, one hand clutching the doorframe as blush bloomed on his cheeks.

Asher's hands and feet were too big for his slender frame, like a puppy that hadn't grown into his paws yet. Yum. He wore the same black hoodie from the night before over gray joggers.

Bloody hell. Those joggers left nothing to the imagination. He lifted his gaze from the imprint of Blakely's cock. He had no business looking at him that way. Shagging a twenty-five-year-old sounded exhausting.

Lev closed his sketchbook. "You're up early, Mr. Blakely. Couldn't sleep?"

"I'm sorry. I didn't mean to interrupt you." Asher rubbed the back of his head.

Lev stood. "I'm delighted to be interrupted. You must be hungry. Come, let me feed you."

The blush on Blakely's cheeks flushed a darker rose against his light brown skin. Lev's mouth salivated at the prospect of crafting his color palette.

"This way."

Would Asher follow? Most people worshipped Lev like a vengeful deity, the art god everyone claimed him to be. But not Asher. The clever exchange they'd parried last night was the most fun he'd had in ages.

Lev strode toward the kitchen, and there it was—the creak of a floorboard, then footsteps ghosted behind him. At one time, an entire squadron of staff had toiled away to prepare food for lavish parties in the kitchen, but it was far too large for Lev's solitary existence.

He passed Asher a glass of fresh orange juice from the fridge. "Start with this. The damp and mildew are murder on the immune system. Not to mention all the bubonic plague knocking about."

At Asher's horrified expression, Lev laughed and added, "I was joking."

"What a relief." Asher yawned once, twice, and thanked him, then brought the glass to his lips, and tipped his head back, stretching the column of his neck.

Lev busied himself with the kettle. His only interest in Asher was artistic, regardless of how seductive the rise and fall of his Adam's apple was as he drank.

Asher was far too talented an artist for Lev to consume like the others. Coaxing raw *je ne sais quoi* from his shell would be Lev's sacrifice to the art gods.

"How do you take your tea?" Lev asked.

Blakely's nose twitched. "Not at all."

"How woefully stereotypical, pretty American."

Blakely rolled his eyes. "There's nothing more stereotypical than an Englishman with a penchant for tea." His tongue was sharp but his tone was playful.

"I have espresso. How does a Caffè Americano sound? It's espresso diluted with water."

"I know what it is."

"Forgive me for assuming." Lev crossed to the shiny espresso machine. "Allow me to introduce you to Desiderio. He's a persnickety fellow, but makes the finest espresso I've tasted this side of Italy."

"You named your coffee maker?" Dimples winked at the corner of Asher's mouth. Not a smile, but Lev would take it.

"Desiderio is far more than a coffee maker." Lev removed the beans from a ceramic canister and dumped them into the grinder. "Naming the appliances keeps the loneliness at bay. The refrigerator goes by Frederick."

He pressed the button on the grinder.

Asher startled. "Why are you up so early?"

"I do my best work before the day begins."

Blakely nodded. "Me too."

"Milk?"

"Yes, please."

"Such manners." Lev passed him the mug.

Asher took a small sip, and hummed.

"It's not too hot, is it?"

Asher swallowed. "No. It's perfect. Delicious, actually. My nonna brews espresso for the family every morning, but it's very strong."

"I imagine tending cattle requires more caffeine than painting."

Asher's brows lifted.

"I told you I'm a fan," Lev said. "Though I must admit I mostly follow you for your animals."

While Asher had never shown his face on social media, in between art-related posts, he'd shared photos of cows frolicking in the daisy-dotted fields of his family's cattle ranch, a black and white American Paint horse named Holstein, and his Italian grandmother's cooking.

"Is there anything you'd fancy for breakfast?" Ordinarily, Lev lost himself in art for hours without need for food and drink, but he'd have to be careful not to burn Blakely's candle from both ends. "Luna's filled our larder to the rafters, so I likely have whatever you fancy."

"I'm not hungry."

"Nonsense. No one should tour my studio on an empty stomach."

"Your studio?"

"Yes, but you mustn't tell the others. Early birds and worms and all that." Lev pulled a jar from the fridge. "You can try my current fixation—vanilla bean yogurt from Iceland."

Whenever Lev discovered a new favorite, he consumed it until he hated it. The same was true for men. He channeled all of his passion into one man until he couldn't stand to look at him.

He spooned the yogurt into a bowl and topped it with pomegranate pearls and granola.

"I don't need all this."

"Let me treat you." He plunged a spoon into the bowl and pushed it toward him. "Go ahead and give it a taste."

Asher slid the spoon between his lips. Lev was jealous of a spoon.

"Well?" Lev asked.

"Thank you, sir."

Asher dropped his gaze, cheeks turning scarlet. Christ, he was a delicious paradox—bratty one moment, and blushing in deference the next.

"Sorry," Asher said. "I've studied you for so long it's going to take me a while to get used to calling you Lev."

"That's alright, *lad*." Lev winked. "I wasn't asking for gratitude, by the way. I wanted to know if you like it." He nodded to the bowl in Asher's hands.

"Oh." Asher licked his lips and lifted his gaze. "It's really good."

"I think so too. Take it with you." Lev led the way before he licked the yogurt Asher had missed on the corner of his mouth. "My studio is this way."

Father's studio took up the top floor of the north wing. Arched windows flanked the two exterior walls and stretched toward a ceiling of herringbone stone.

Lev stepped aside and held one of the double doors open. "Guests first."

"Thank you." Asher squeezed past with plenty of distance, yet Lev felt his presence as if he'd grazed him.

Asher's hair stuck up in the back like he'd slept fitfully, or been fucked all night in missionary. He didn't get very far across the paint-spattered hardwood before he stopped.

"Where are your paintings?"

"This is Lucian's old studio. I've kept it the way he left it."

"You paint in your father's studio, surrounded by his work?" Asher asked, though not with derision.

"It gets the most sunlight." Which wasn't saying much. The brightest light at Lichenmoor most days was a melancholy shade of gray.

Asher walked along a wall of Father's paintings and paused in front of a portrait Lev couldn't bear to look at, yet couldn't take down. Lev clasped his hands behind his back and joined him.

Silent seconds passed while Asher examined the painting, gripping his bottom lip between his thumb and forefinger as he mused.

"This one isn't Lucian's."

"How can you tell?" Lev asked in shocked wonder.

An art critic Lev despised had claimed that the same bolt of lightning had struck the Marks bloodline twice. His work matched Lucian's so closely, even the most devoted collectors guessed incorrectly.

Lev wasn't an artist. He was a copy machine.

After Father died, Lev's work had fetched even higher prices, and he hadn't kept a single coin, pouring it all into philanthropy. So how on earth had Asher Blakely been able to tell?

Asher handed Lev the empty bowl, and traced the painted line of Silas's clavicle with a hovering finger.

"Your shapes are sharper." His finger climbed Silas's neck and paused over his jugular. "You're more playful with color, filling veins with indigo instead of blood."

His focus moved to Silas's face. "Such bright eyes could easily look flat, but you've embedded emotional depth without losing their iridescence, and forced so much vibrance into pale paper skin, it's like light scattered through a prism."

Beautiful words. Lev wanted to believe them, but he couldn't accept praise on a painting that was meant to be his punishment.

"You certainly are a fan," Lev said.

"Sorry." Asher's gaze dropped again, long lashes casting shadows on the apples of his cheeks.

What would those lashes look like clenched together in pleasure, or wet with tears? He wanted to count each strand, draw and paint them, feel them brush against his skin.

"I'm impressed you noticed such small details," Lev added. "Let me show you what I'm working on now."

Lev abandoned Asher's bowl on the counter along the way. Asher approached Lev's easel like a deer that might run off.

"I'm afraid it's still in the ugly stage," Lev said.

An ugly stage was perfectly normal. Every good painting had one. What wasn't normal was how much Lev wished he'd been further along. What wasn't normal was how much he wanted Asher to like his attempt at Silas's neck.

Lev had spent years in therapy learning to disconnect his self-worth from his art, a task made more difficult when Lucian had raised him to be a successor, not a son.

The Marks family couldn't help but repeat the same mistakes, passing the same baggage on to generation after generation like luggage on a carousel. Lev's grandfather had tried to force Lucian into a corporate box, but he'd rebelled. Lev, on the other hand, had climbed right into Lucian's art-shaped box and remained there, desperate for his approval.

Asher surveyed the painting quietly. His gaze shifted to the floor where Lev's last three pieces leaned against the wall.

Each painting was a snapshot of what remained of his memories of Silas. Never the full picture. Only a hand fisted in bed linen. The tight cage of ribs beneath skin. The sharp edge of a tilted chin.

Every studied artist knew their anatomy as well as they knew their geometry, but Lev had mapped the landscape of Silas's body with his hands and tongue, been inside of him, scented his blood.

Nearly two decades later, that knowledge was slipping through his fingers, especially when Silas had come back all wrong. He looked the same—obsidian hair, pale blemish-less skin, high cheekbones, and powder blue eyes—but it wasn't him.

The Silas who haunted him was a macabre doppelgänger.

That was why Lev continued painting Silas no matter how much it hurt. It was the punishment he deserved, and the only way to preserve the real Silas's memory.

"You've never painted anything like this before," Asher said.

Lev raised his eyebrows. "Is that so?"

"I'm sorry. It's just, I've followed you so closely, I thought I'd seen everything."

"This is a new series. I've never dabbled in something so…"

"Vulnerable?" Asher suggested.

"Precisely."

"This is the man from the other painting. Who is he?"

"Come now, Blakely, you don't expect me to tell you that, do you?"

Returning his attention to Lev's work-in-progress, Asher gestured along the sinewy strands of muscle and tendon in Silas's neck.

"You've captured him clearer here. The man in your first portrait," he swiveled to the one on the wall, "looks like he's holding his breath, but in this one you caught him mid-gasp.

"The shadows under his eyes are a moodier purple too, and the lavender freckles give it movement. This isn't a gasp of pleasure, but of despair, maybe even the last breath of death. I can almost hear it."

Lev's stomach dropped. How did Asher read his art so acutely?

"I'm afraid to tell you, Blakely, but like any other uninspired art critic, you're inferring more meaning than the artist intended."

"But it doesn't matter what you intended, right? *Art is what's inferred. The painting is no longer yours once you give birth to it. It's for the viewer, the emotions you evoke in them…* You said that."

"That was a long time ago."

"Hm," Asher replied with a cheeky smirk and walked back to the wall of Lucian's paintings.

A handsome man with black hair frequented most of Lucian's portraits—Wendell Morrigan, noted poet, Lucian's romantic partner, Lev's surrogate father, and Silas's father by blood.

Asher pointed to Wendell's neck, his clavicle, his Adam's apple. "Lucian's work is beautiful, but it isn't fluid. It's too heavy-handed. Too static."

Lev said nothing, watching the genius of a lad with rapt attention.

Lucian had once said that his art was stone, while Lev's was water. At first, Lev thought water meant weaker, until Lucian clarified that water carved through stone if given enough time, while stone would only gather moss.

Blakely's tongue peeked out between parted lips. A tic when lost in thought. An intimate thing for Lev to witness. His tongue dipped back into his mouth.

"It's all subjective anyway, isn't it? I prefer your style, but it doesn't make Lucian's any less."

"Don't worry, Blakely. You haven't offended me. In fact, you've enchanted me so thoroughly that I fear I'll die if I don't watch you paint immediately."

Lev exchanged his still-drying painting for a fresh canvas and placed it on the easel.

"Sit." He patted the stool he'd spent so much time working from.

Asher nibbled that plump lower lip again. Lev bit into his own and turned his gaze heavenward.

"I don't have any of my equipment."

"Use mine."

"I couldn't."

"Come now, Blakely, you know you want to."

"He *is* rather pretty," said a saccharine voice.

Silas.

4

MY, WHAT SHARP CLAWS

LEV

Silas prowled on spindly legs, dressed in black like a splotch of spilled ink, playing every bit the part of a stain Lev could never erase. Pale, near-skeletal fingers trailed toward Asher's flushed cheek.

"No wonder your little protégé enchants you so."

Lev fought the urge to tackle him, but he couldn't touch Silas, because he wasn't real.

"He almost reminds me of me. Beautiful. Haunted. A half-empty glass waiting to be filled." Silas moved behind Asher and toyed with a curl at the base of his neck. "Entirely unaware that you have nothing to give him, that you'll leave him more empty than before, then dance on the shards of the trust you broke."

Silas buried his nose in Blakely's hair, sharp shoulders rising as he inhaled. "What does he smell like, Levvy? Does he smell like ours?"

Lev steered Asher by the shoulders to the stool.

"He is young, though..." Silas crossed his arms and leaned against the wall beside a painting of his father. "I never knew you were that kind of predator."

Then, he disappeared.

Blakely was staring. Fucking Silas.

"Please begin," Lev said. "I need to see to breakfast and shall return shortly."

Lev sped from the studio and into the washroom. His hand shook as he twisted the dial of the faucet, and while he waited for the pipes to clear, he searched his reflection in the tarnished mirror. Aside from the black spots of mirror rot and guilt that ate at him, he found no predator there.

The crimes Lev had committed against Silas were many, but he'd never preyed on him. He splashed water on his face, and forced Silas from his thoughts.

When Lev returned to the studio, he found Asher engrossed in his work, sketch finished, a few colors mixed on a saucer he'd stolen from beneath one of Lev's forgotten teacups. A battered notebook lay open on the ancient utility cart he stored his paint in.

On his canvas, Asher had sketched a narrow river surrounded by trees, the Bolton Strid, according to the page in his sketchbook. Curious choice. A man clung to a granite boulder on the bank, his lower half already engulfed by the Strid, but the man's face was as serene as if he were a water sprite returning home after nearly drowning on dry land.

"You're making yourself at home."

Asher turned. "I'm sorry. I was only..."

Lev lifted his hand. "I was teasing, Blakely. I want you to be comfortable at Lichenmoor."

Asher moved to take the sketchbook from the stool, but Lev plucked it up first.

"I'm not finished with that." Asher extended his hand, attention still fixed on his painting, a perfect picture of ambivalence belied by the subtle twitch of his jaw clenching. "Give. It. Back."

Yummy.

"Come now, Blakely." Lev hoisted the sketchbook just out

of reach. "Surely you can paint without your reference while I have a quick peek."

Looking at another artist's sketchbook was like peeling back their skin and flaying their soul. Lev wanted to make things even, to see Asher as much as Asher saw him.

In a flash of motion, Asher leaped from the stool in an ineffectual, if not adorable, attempt to wrest it from his grip.

Lev lowered the book, intending to return it, but in the melee, the book fell from his hands.

Pages fluttered as the sketchbook drifted to the ground, flashing snapshots of blurry sketches and Asher's notes to himself. One drawing gave him pause.

Four crescent lines that could have been turbulent waves, blades of snipped grass, vertebrae trailing down the center of a back. But it was familiar. Uncanny.

His long arms were no match for Asher as he plucked the book from the floor and opened it—a freight train barreled into his chest.

Using Lev's foot as a step stool, Asher vaulted up Lev's body, and snatched the sketchbook from his hands, then stuffed it into the front pocket of his hoodie. His cheeks were, if possible, an even darker shade of red.

"My, what sharp claws you have, little dormouse."

Blakely scowled. "Don't call me that. I won't let you bully me."

Lev saluted him. "Noted. But you misunderstand. I wasn't bullying you. It was sheer curiosity that carried me away."

"*Right.*"

Baring his palms, Lev turned on the puppy-dog eyes that had gotten him out of many a quandary. "Please forgive me."

The wrinkle between Blakely's brows smoothed, but not entirely. "Would you have let me look at yours?"

"No. I suppose not." Lev stroked his beard and snapped his fingers. "But it's only fair. I'll trade you…"

What were those four marks?

He retrieved his notebook from the top drawer of the utility cart. "Here."

Blakely stilled, eyes glazed with want, looking very much like a lover who'd been told he could come. His lips parted on a soft inhale caught in his chest. Blood fluttered in the pulse point of his neck.

Lev wanted to taste him there, count his heartbeats with his tongue. If he were as villainous as Silas claimed, he would have.

But he wasn't, so he stepped back and gave his sketchbook a little shake like a lure on a line. What would Asher think of the sketches Lev had already drawn of him?

"No. I couldn't." Asher pushed the sketchbook away.

"You disappoint me." Now he'd have to steal Blakely's sketchbook later.

Curiosity would drive him insane if he didn't find out what those four lines made up. He could ask, but something about the lines filled him with foreboding. He'd take it only long enough to look.

"Please continue." Lev gestured for him to sit.

Asher's eyes narrowed on the stool as if it were rigged with a shocking device.

"It's not a trap. Go ahead. I promise to behave."

Asher scoffed, but finally sat. He stretched his neck, tilting his head backward, and rolling it to one shoulder, and then the other like he wanted to taunt Lev with an Adam's apple so anatomically perfect only some sculptural deity could have constructed it.

Before Silas had died he'd once said, "You know it's just glands strewn over cartilage. I cannot fathom why you're so obsessed." With a pop of suction broken, Lev had lifted his mouth. "It's living art, an architectural landmark." Lev had ended the sentence with a bite to the spot. Silas had laughed and pushed his head away. "Easy there, Van Gogh. You need some fresh air." Lev had clucked his tongue. "Perhaps you're right. Forgive me whilst I steal the breath from your lungs." Sealing his lips over Silas's, Lev had done exactly that, kissing him until they both were breathless. Things between them hadn't always been bad.

The swirl of Asher's paintbrush on his palette brought Lev back to the present.

Lev memorized the way Asher gripped the brush between his fingertips with nary a tremor despite his audience, how his tongue darted out between his teeth again, resting on his lower lip as he surveyed his progress, the sharp glint in his eye as he layered confident strokes on the canvas.

He'd slipped into that liminal space where art bled into reality, where the outside world faded away, and all that was left was emotion, memory, sensation—the scent of wet paint and linseed oil, the nearly inaudible scratch of bristles against canvas.

Watching someone make art was like watching them get off, the closest Lev could get to reading someone's mind, to knowing what they looked like on the inside. If he sank his teeth into Asher, what would he taste like? What would he bleed?

5

SHACKLED MUSES

ASHER

An artist's sketchbook was supposed to be sacred, a private vessel for ideas newly birthed. It was a first draft —a zero draft, really—a place to repurpose pain without fear and let his thoughts run amok.

Stealing a glance inside an artist's sketchbook was like reading their diary. In Asher's case, the sketchbook *was* his diary. He recorded his version of events there every day through sketches and notes to later refer to.

His sketchbook was his lifeline to the truth, to knowing who he was, and Lev had rifled through it.

"Forget I'm here," Lev said, as if such a notion was even possible.

Asher paused his paintbrush and shivered, inhaling the earthy scent of tea and the same hint of jasmine in his cologne. Did he always smell that good?

Breathing through his mouth, he dipped his brush into blue and mixed it with burnt umber before adding the faintest hint of titanium white until he'd created the murky gray of the Bolton Strid, a fatal stretch of river hidden beneath an idyllic stream.

The Strid looked shallow enough to traverse on foot, and

34

narrow enough a single leap could bridge the gap, but that was a lie. One misstep on the slippery stone, and the Strid would claim another victim.

Destruction lurked beneath disarming charm and enigmatic magnetism. Even with warning signs, and crosses marking lost lives, the allure was too strong for some, coaxing victims into a watery grave with a single question:

What if? What if he stepped a little closer? What if he dipped his toes in? That wasn't so dangerous, was it? What if he jumped?

That's what men like Leviathan Marks and Ben Swarthing were.

Asher wouldn't fall for it again. He would ignore the call, just like he had when he stopped at the Bolton Strid on his way to Lichenmoor. He knew better. He knew if he jumped, Lev would drown him.

"If I may..." Lev's words caressed Asher's neck as he reached for his hand, easily eclipsing it.

Asher stiffened. Ben had courted him similarly. Maybe they'd trained together and compared notes on breaking hearts.

There was a subtle difference, though. Ben's flirtation had made Asher uncomfortable from day one, whereas Lev's touch was *too* comfortable.

Highjacking Asher's hand, Lev led the brush across the canvas like a debutante across a ballroom.

The tattoos beneath Asher's clothes tingled, each mark a brand buzzing with recognition. Their creator was near.

Could Lev hear his heart racing?

Asher swallowed thickly. He wanted to lose himself in the professional ecstasy of making art with Leviathan Marks, but he'd rather forfeit the mentorship than implode his career again.

Besides, what kind of cocky bastard thought so highly of himself that he took control over another artist's work? Was this a test? Surely Lev lusted for artists confident in their craft.

Asher jerked his hand free, slashing his canvas with gray paint.

"Forgive me." At least Lev had the grace to don a mask of roguish embarrassment. "I have an issue with control."

"Clearly," Asher muttered.

Lev laughed. "You're oh so prickly, little dormouse, just like the thistle and rose vines on the moor."

"I told you not to call me that."

"But Blakely is so dreadfully boring." Lev harrumphed and slouched onto his stool with boyish playfulness.

"Not all of us can be named after sea serpents." Asher picked up a new brush and feathered viridian fern fronds between rocks on the river's edge. "What about calling me by my first name—or do you call it a Christian name here?"

He'd stretched *Christian* into three syllables with a sharp T sound, as he imagined Lev might say in his accent.

Lev waved his hand airily. "I want to have a name for you that no one else has. I think I'll call you Ash."

Asher snorted. "Last night you said Asher reminded you of charcoal on skin, and now you'd rather call me Ash?"

"Did I say that? How wantonly slutty of me."

"You said a lot of wantonly slutty things."

"Are you certain? That doesn't sound like me. You're very cute when you smile like that, Ash."

Asher bit into his lip. "I'm not smiling."

Lev tapped the side of Asher's mouth. "Your dimples betray you."

The briefest touch of Lev's finger on the side of his mouth nearly compelled Asher to turn his head and suck.

"Has anyone ever told you that you're orally fixated?"

"What?" *Oh my God.* Had he said that out loud?

"You rake your teeth over your bottom lip, roll your lips

inward, wet them with your tongue, pinch them and rub them with your fingers. What about Ashy?"

"Fuck no." Asher paused his paintbrush and added, "Sir."

Lev boomed a laugh that startled Asher so sharply a splotch of paint fell from his brush. Asher refused to laugh too.

"If I may propose a solution..." Lev said.

Asher rolled his paintbrush as if to say, "You may."

"If you let me call you Ash, I'll let you call me Lev."

"But I already call you Lev."

"You're very cute. Are you sure you don't want to be called Ashy?"

Asher scowled.

"You're even cuter when you're cross," Lev said.

Asher added a final stroke, and rested his paintbrush on the palette. It would take days more to layer details, but he was content with what he'd started, and he'd had enough of this discussion.

Lev clicked his tongue. "Come now, Blakely. Have you finished already?"

Did Lev have any idea of the effect *those* words said in *that* accent did to a man? Probably.

Asher should have called him out on it, but words escaped him. His dick hardened down his right pant leg, impossible to miss in sweatpants stretched tight over his thighs.

As if lured by a spell, Asher turned his face toward Lev, and froze, locked in the depths of azure irises made of shards of lapis. Ginger lashes flashed downward to cheeks dusted with cinnamon freckles. Lev was looking at Asher's lips.

"If I chose you, what kind of art do you think we would make?"

Asher wet his bottom lip. Not on purpose. His mouth was dry. What had Lev asked? What even *was* art?

A bell sounded, a hollow tinkling, like one pulled on a string. Asher jumped and turned back toward his canvas, saved by a literal bell.

"Ah. That would be breakfast." Lev's footsteps retreated.

Servant bells? It was almost as if they resided in a timeless realm. At least that explained the faint ringing he'd heard last night.

"While I'd love to stay and explore the delicious sexual tension brewing between us, we should go."

Asher's jaw dropped. "I don't know what you're talking about."

"Little dormouse, lying doesn't suit you."

"Neither does that nickname."

Irritation drained the blood from his dick. He couldn't make it one day without falling for Lev's wiles. He gathered his brushes, dropped them into the cup of water, and brought them to the sink, then scrubbed the bristles with far more aggression than necessary.

"Oh, don't sulk. You look so much prettier when you sulk."

"Don't wait up," Asher said when Lev made no move to leave.

"Nonsense. You'll never find your way out of the labyrinth without me to escort you. Besides, I don't want the others to think you aren't taking this seriously if you arrive late again."

"You can tell them I'm jet-lagged."

"I couldn't possibly. I can't show favoritism, even if you're my favorite." Lev leaned his elbows against the counter and held out a clean towel for him.

"I don't want to be one of your *favorites*." Asher emphasized the word with air quotes, flinging diluted paint against Lev's forearm.

The muscles in Lev's arm twitched, but he made no move to clean it.

"I'm not sure if you're aware, Blakely, but I've instituted a new policy. No fraternization with prodigies, protégés, and other such p-words. I was just having a little fun, but if I've made you uncomfortable, I apologize."

"Right."

Lev raked derisive eyes up and down Asher's body, then rubbed his beard, sending paint droplets tracking lines down his forearm. As Asher watched the paint descend, he had the strangest urge to lick it from his skin.

"Not to mention, you're practically an infant."

Asher snorted. "Then you're practically ancient."

"You still haven't answered my question. What kind of art do you think we could make together?"

Asher turned off the tap and watched the water spiral around the paint-stained porcelain sink before slipping down the drain.

"Best-case scenario, we'd make the kind of art that hurts in all the right ways. Worst case..." Asher took the towel and wiped his hands. "You've said it yourself, haven't you? That it's better not to learn under others, that in doing so you shackle your muse and what you make isn't art, but a charade of what your art should have been."

Lev frowned. "I don't recall saying that."

"I'm not surprised. You looked pretty blitzed in that interview. It was back when you were in your bad-boy artist phase."

Lev pouted. "I thought I never left that phase."

"Nope. You're in your mysterious recluse phase. Sorry." Asher smirked.

"Is that so? Is there some sort of fan club that votes on these things?"

"I don't know if you have any fans. I think the only followers you breed are fanatics."

"Are you saying you're a fanatic, Blakely? Please tell me this isn't going to turn into some dreadful *Misery* sort of situation?"

Asher had just been about to confess that, yes, he was president of the fanatics, that he'd paid thousands of dollars and hours of pain to etch his art into his skin so it would always be with him, but he couldn't say that.

Lev would lose all respect for him.

Because Lev was no narcissist. Beneath the facade of condescension and bloated self-importance was a man who hated himself.

6

COME ALONG, SNAKE

LEV

Ting. Ting. Ting. Lev clinked a spoon against his champagne flute, dispatching dozens of bubbles to the surface of his mimosa.

"As tradition dictates, you have four weeks to impress me with art inspired by each of the Seven Deadly Sins, but only one of you shall remain on for six months as my protégé."

Lev was bored. Less than an hour had passed, and he already longed to see Asher at the canvas again. The lad had breathed life into Father's hollow studio. For the first time in decades, an artist had painted for the joy of it, rather than penance.

Lev stifled a yawn. "Excuse me. After last night's debauchery, I've decided today's theme will be Gluttony."

Asher had hardly touched the traditional English breakfast Luna had prepared. He'd wrinkled his nose at the bacon and sausage, eaten a few spoonfuls of beans, and spent the rest of breakfast pushing fried eggs around his plate.

Lev would learn his tastes in due time. Perhaps he was a light eater, still full from the yogurt Lev had served him.

Still, he couldn't help but worry about why he wasn't

eating. Was it because of something Lev had said or done? Finally, Asher's hazel eyes met his.

"Right, then." Lev sipped his mimosa. "I'd like to get to know you all a little better with a series of questions, starting with why you create art. Blakely, you may answer first."

Asher lowered his fork to his plate. "Art lights up all the dark spots inside my mind. It's magic in a world that has none." Then, he shrugged as if he hadn't answered the question with poetry.

Silas appeared in the flowerbed, hands pressed against the window, black hair damp from the drizzle, dark clothes stark against the fog. He cocked his head to the side and mouthed, *He's perfect.*

Lev looked away. He couldn't afford to lose time with Silas now that he had an audience. The other artists still waited. Asher had twisted toward the window, following Lev's gaze, almost as if he could see Silas too.

But that was impossible. No one else could—not Luna, or his groundskeeper, or the lad he paid to muck the stables, or any of the other staff he employed to battle Lichenmoor's decaying facilities.

Silas haunted him alone.

"Yes, well..." Lev cleared his throat. "Blakely, I quite agree with you."

Instead of smiling or blushing at the praise, Asher still stared at Silas, who waved and grinned.

"What about you?" Lev asked an artist with bushy blond brows and the temperament of someone who'd been told how special he was ever since he'd made *papier-mâché* with wet wads of toilet paper and the contents of his nappy. "Remind me of your name again."

Forgetting the man's name wasn't an overplayed attempt at a power move. Remembering names was one of his weaknesses. Father's too.

"Chuck," the blond said in the public school drawl he'd

expected from the youngest son of a new money Tory politician.

"Ah, right. Chuck, I apologize. Please continue."

"I feel like a god when I create," Chuck said.

Lev officially hated him.

Julian answered next. The barrel-chested photographer and occasional painter wore corduroy overalls and a brown tweed jacket, looking all the part of a bear wearing the costume of an Oxford librarian on a field trip.

"Anyone can paint or take a picture," Julian said in a rumbling timbre. "But not everyone can paint something so alive it breathes, or capture the extraordinary of something mundane."

The remaining artists' answers were more of the same. Melody, the pastel artist seated at Julian's right, answered last, explaining that she made art because she could get away with saying things through art that she would never be brave enough to say otherwise.

With wavy blonde hair and dark eyebrows shaped over giant eyes, a most striking green, Melody was a modern-day Botticelli painting. Objectively speaking. Lev wasn't interested in women.

"Let's move on to housekeeping. The grounds are free for all to explore, but please mind the cliffs, the fog, and above all else, the tide. The ocean moves swiftly. You'll find the weather is rather tempestuous in autumn; best not to stray far from the Lichenmoor Hall."

He took a swig of tea and lowered the cup to his plate. "Do note that the third floor is off limits. The framing is too unstable, and I'd hate to have one of you fall through the ceiling. Any questions?"

Melody lifted her hand, flashing rainbow fingers stained with pastels.

"Please don't raise your hand, love. We're all equals here."

"Why now?" she asked.

"I beg your pardon?"

"I mean, why are you holding the retreat now?"

It was a valid question. He'd shown little interest in Father's retreats, only making a brief appearance to appease him. Nor had he voiced a desire to continue his legacy after he died.

"At the Marks' household, art was our religion," Lev said, repeating the answer he'd prepared. "Lucian taught me that those gifted with talent are responsible for stewarding the next generation, passing on techniques, and craft secrets. But after he died…"

Lev's thoughts scattered as Silas stepped through the window and crept toward Asher. What was he playing at?

"The truth is, it gets rather lonely out here all by myself, and I thought I'd give it a go," Lev said in a rush and clapped his hands twice. "I have horses to feed and matters to attend to. Please meet me on the first floor in front of the main staircase at ten."

Asher pushed his chair back first, just missing Silas.

"The audacity of the living," Silas said, shooting Asher a scowl.

Lev ignored him, only breathing again once Asher and the others had filed out of the room.

"Was that necessary?" Lev asked.

Silas crossed his arms and jutted his chin upward. "You can't blame me for being curious." He spun on his heel, issuing a sharp whistle like one would summon a dog. "Come along, Snake. Let's go look for my body."

7

THE TIDE RETURNS

LEV

High tide had only left shells and a wavy line of white polystyrene sprinkles behind.

"How many times must I tell you, *you're wasting your time?*" Silas sang, leaving no footsteps in the sand as he traipsed ahead. "The tide won't return me to you."

Lev had long ago stopped questioning whether Silas was a projection of his guilty conscience, something supernatural, or something far worse.

Before Silas died, he'd promised he would never leave Lev, or Lichenmoor again. Was that what made ghosts? A love so ardent not even death could part them?

"What's tossed into the sea around Lichenmoor always comes back," Lev repeated the local lore, the hypothesis of which he'd tested and proved time and time again, tossing from Lichenmoor's cliff dozens of paintings, sculptures, moth-eaten rugs wrapped in twine and weighed down with bricks.

The ocean took them, but it always returned them like a possessed doll that wouldn't stay dead.

"My bones are long gone, probably used for toothpicks by a giant squid."

Silas bit a sliver of nail off his index finger and spat it

toward a tide pool. Lev resisted the urge to drop to his knees and sift through the water.

"The next storm could dredge the ocean."

There'd been hundreds of storms since Silas had died, but Lev clung to it year after year. There was always that chance, that flickering hope like the ghost of a lighthouse beam swinging through fog, that if he found Silas's bones, he'd set him free.

"I don't know why you bother. It makes no difference to me if you find my body. I'll still hate you, regardless."

Lev kicked a clump of sand snatched by the wind and stalked off toward the path.

"Oh, don't be cross," Silas called after him.

How could Lev not be upset? He may have killed Silas, but he'd still loved him. He'd still lost him.

As long as Silas haunted the moors, Lev would keep searching. He had to find Silas and lay him to rest before his memory died with him.

Asher joined the group at the front stairs six minutes after ten.

"Nice of you to show, Blakely."

"Sorry. Jet lag," the cheeky bastard teased.

"See that it doesn't happen again."

"Yes, sir."

"Good lad," Lev said, delighted that they already had an inside joke.

Asher's eyes narrowed. His lips pursed, not with loathing or distrust, but determination. Asher was plotting a retaliatory strike and Lev couldn't wait. Nor could he hide his smirk.

Chuck and Lars chortled as if they were in on the joke. Loathsome twats. They'd already identified Asher as the outlier to beat, the art genius with inherent talent others could barely scrape at, even with years of practice.

Giftedness was a lonely existence. Jealousy masqueraded behind reverence.

"This way, please." Lev led them away from his father's studio. He didn't want to share that sacred space. Only he and Asher would step foot inside it.

Lev hesitated on the threshold of the decaying ballroom Father had converted to an atelier for group instruction. Awe-laced gasps rippled through the group. The ballroom did possess a certain appeal.

Ivy crept through arched windows and climbed to the top of the stone cathedral ceiling, raining down scarlet leaves that swirled around their feet with the hushed rustle of whispers at a funeral.

Asher weaved past the art stations, silhouette blurred by trespassing fog and damp wood-smoke.

"Time to go," Lev hissed to Silas, who'd stuck to his heel all morning, like a wad of gum he couldn't scrape off.

"A little please and thank you goes a long way," Silas said. *"Please fuck off so I can flirt without you cock-blocking, Silas. Thank you very much. See."*

"Go."

"Fine." Lifting both his middle fingers, he backed into the massive fireplace, and disappeared. Arsehole.

Lev exhaled the tightness from his chest. Every time he vanquished Silas was a victory, proof he hadn't lost all control yet.

He shook out his shoulders, and stepped onto the stone subfloor spider-webbed with cracks, then followed Asher to one of the windows overlooking the ocean.

"We really are trapped here," Asher said, gesturing to the soggy moor and rocky beach.

Cumulus clouds loomed on the horizon.

"It feels that way, but it's an illusion. We do have boats, after all." Boats rendered useless during a storm surge, but Asher didn't need to know that.

"Why paint in your father's studio when you could paint here?"

"What makes you think I don't?"

Asher turned. "None of your things are here."

"The moisture is bad for the canvases."

"But good enough for ours?" Asher arched a brow. "The logic of your lie is flawed, *sir*."

Being caught in a lie by a twenty-five-year-old shouldn't be as hot as it was. "My reasons are too nebulous to explain, and they're private."

"Hm."

"I wish you wouldn't use my own *Hm* against me."

Asher rolled his lips inward and returned his attention to the scenery. Long seconds passed, during which Lev mixed colors in his mind's palette to match the faint purple shadows under his eyes, the—wait—was that inky black line a tattoo peeking out from his neckline?

Lev fought the urge to slip his fingers inside Asher's collar and peer down his chest. What art had he loved enough to immortalize on his skin? How many tattoos did he have, and where? But a good mentor wouldn't ask his protégé such questions.

"Come," Lev said. "Let me show you to your station."

Lev guided Asher to a spot with good light near the warmth of the fireplace. He'd already moved his painting to the easel.

"I brought your things here after breakfast." Lev stroked the top corner of the canvas. "Unless you wish to abandon this?"

Regardless of the answer, Lev would see that Asher completed it.

The muscles in Asher's jaw tightened.

"What's wrong?" Lev asked.

"I don't like people touching my art before it's finished."

"I see. More of a lone wolf, are you?" How sharp were his teeth?

"If anyone's a lone wolf, it's you."

"You speak as if you have any idea whose company I keep." Lev cleared his throat and traced the graphite trunk of a tree. "If you can't bring gluttony into this piece, I'm happy to provide you with a fresh canvas…"

"No."

"Splendid. Good luck, Blakely. May the best artist win."

Before Asher could answer, Lev turned and walked away. Best not to piss the morning away flirting.

Over the next few hours, Lev roamed the room, stopping at each canvas. Melody's project was a hot pink nightmare. A young girl with eyes too big for her face clutched a teddy in a wrecked bedroom. Wardrobe tipped over, rainbow clothes spilling out. Disemboweled stuffed animals bleeding fluff. A monster drawn on the wall in black crayon.

"It's the death of the inner child," she explained with a smile that looked like she'd spent years practicing in a mirror.

An art critic with his head stuck up his arse might have said her work wasn't all that inspired or different. How many artists over the centuries had editorialized the death of their inner child?

But Lev didn't care about originality. He didn't care about technique. She could have drawn a stick figure for all he cared. What made it art was the piece of herself she'd embedded in it.

An honest artist flayed open their veins and painted with their pain, and carved a piece of their soul out and put it on display.

Melody's message was clear; her inner child hadn't died from natural causes. It had died suddenly and under suspicious circumstances, had an entire autopsy performed before money disposed of it.

"This is fantastic. Well done."

Melody beamed.

Lev felt Asher's eyes on him like a spell chanting, *look at me, look at me, look at me.* But Lev didn't need to. He'd already synchronized his peripheral vision with Asher's paintbrush.

"Alright there, Lars?" While Lar's work with ballpoint pens was novel and exquisite, the thrashing bodies of a gluttonous circle of hell a la *Dante's Inferno* rang a touch too literal.

Julian was off somewhere snapping pictures, and Lev refused to look in Chuck's direction after being the captive audience to what was, essentially, a self-masturbatory monologue.

"Daria." Lev stopped at her canvas.

"Lev," she answered in a husky voice without pausing her brush.

She'd been at it for hours, and Lev still hadn't the foggiest notion of what she painted. Thus the peril of examining surrealist works in progress.

"May I ask what message you hope to convey with this piece?"

She tossed her head, shaking long, midnight curls from her face. "You'll know when I'm finished."

"I've no doubt."

Daria's self-taught and somewhat bastardized methods worked incredibly well for her. He didn't impart any words of wisdom. She didn't need them.

At each canvas, he heaped praise intermixed with the occasional suggestion, because Father said he always left his artists in a better place than before they'd met him. Lev would save his hard edge for the one he'd selected, exactly as Father had done to him.

Saving the best for last, quite intentionally, Lev made his way toward the dangerous and depressing rendition of the

Bolton Strid brewing in Asher's painting. Except, somebody else was already looking at it—Theo Laurenti.

Asher leaned toward Theo, his lips moving as he told him something Lev couldn't hear. When Theo laughed, Lev's eyes narrowed. He wanted all of Asher's words, even the ones he spoke to someone else.

Forcing a casual gait, he strode over and rested a hand on Asher's shoulder like a toddler claiming a toy.

"Blakely, I see you've met our very own modern day impressionist." Lev nodded toward the handsome French oil painter with warm brown skin and bright eyes. "Has he shown you his glass?"

"No?"

"Theo works with molten glass, takes these photos all sweaty, and covered in soot. He's talented too." Lev released Asher's shoulder and extended his hand to shake Theo's calloused one.

"Thank you, Lev," Theo said, peppering a clean-shaven kiss to both of Lev's bristly cheeks.

"It's the truth." Lev pulled his phone from his pocket and showed Asher the photo he'd saved of a pale glass hand sinking into a pool of murky black. "This one is my favorite."

Rather than step closer as Lev had hoped, Asher took the phone from his hand. Theo's arm grazed Asher's as he sidled closer and hovered at his elbow.

"Theo, this is beautiful." Asher's voice took on a reverent hush as he traced the glass tendril fingers reaching through obsidian depths for the scattered stems of a wildflower bouquet drifting on the surface. "It reminds me of Millais's *Ophelia.*"

"That was exactly my intention!" Theo smiled, lowering a lingering hand to Asher's forearm.

Asher zoomed in on the petals. "I love the dichotomy. It's so delicate, but if you don't give it the respect it deserves, it cuts sharp, almost like the fledgling first days of the tragic love story that inspired it."

A frisson of chills erupted all over Lev's body. Watching Asher view fine art was even more beautiful than the art itself.

"Are you speaking from experience, Blakely?"

Asher shook his head and returned the phone without making eye contact.

"Lucky for you, then," Lev said, pocketing it.

"Have you worked with glass before?" Theo shoved his way back into their conversation.

"No. I don't have the finesse for it."

"Nonsense," Lev said. "There's no finesse required. Theo all but fights with the glass, wrangling it into shape. Hell, he even blows a metal rod."

"Oh, stop." Theo swatted Lev's arm.

Asher followed the motion. Was his pretty American as jealous of Theo as Lev was? Good. Best to keep things on an equal footing.

"Doesn't Lichenmoor have a forge?" Asher asked.

"It does," Lev said slowly.

"Maybe you can give me a private lesson?" Asher suggested to Theo, then trapped his bottom lip between his teeth.

Lev didn't like that. Not one bit.

"Come now. Private lessons?" Lev clicked his tongue. "That wouldn't be very fair. We're far more into voyeurism at Lichenmoor."

Theo's lips curled into a seductive smile. "I brought my tools."

"Did you now?" Lev asked.

"I was hoping to make art with that famous forge."

Lev *could* lie. He could tell them he didn't have any raw glass in stock or that the forge was out of order, but he wasn't entirely sure if a forge could break.

"I look forward to seeing you in action," Asher said.

This fucking walking sex on a lacrosse stick wanted to hook

up with Theo? Lev could acknowledge that Theo was offensively handsome, resembling a young Alain Delon, but how could Blakely reject Lev's advances, given their chemistry, and then fall for Theo's sophomoric attempt at getting into his pants?

"Careful, Blakely. At this rate, you're going to have to buy Theo a drink before he demonstrates his lips wrapped 'round the old blowpipe." Lev placed a hand on Theo's back. "Come, Theo. I'll give you a tour of our forge."

Asher rolled his lips inward, nearly suppressing his scowl.

"It was a pleasure to meet you." Theo took Asher's hand and squeezed, not a true handshake, more an intimate goodbye.

"You too," Asher said.

"Happy painting, Blakely." Lev guided Theo away and winked over his shoulder in time to catch Asher's face fall.

Lev felt a bit shite, then. Silas materialized, matching Lev's stride. Impeccable timing as always.

"Well, *that* was embarrassing," Silas said over Theo's droning monologue about medieval glass blowing.

Lev ignored him.

"Your little dormouse doesn't know it yet, but he's in the early days of a doomed love story like dear Ophelia." Silas sighed melodramatically and lifted the back of his hand to his forehead. "If only I could warn him."

8

NEVER LIE ABOUT ART

ASHER

OCTOBER 5

Lev bent before the man-sized hearth in the ballroom and added another log to the fire. The charred logs beneath cracked, sending sparks skittering up the chimney.

Asher dragged his eyes away from Lev's muscular ass and returned his attention to his canvas. He shook his head and swirled his brush in the midnight blue he'd mixed, irritation growing.

Lusting over Lev was the last thing he should be doing. The other artists had already advanced to the next sin, and finished for the day, while Asher still toiled away at his painting of the Bolton Strid.

Lev brushed his hands on his pants and leaned against the stone wall, arms crossed over his chest. His gaze raked over Asher, and lingered, examining him like a modern art piece he didn't understand.

What was he looking for?

Why couldn't he leave Asher to paint in peace? Asher hated painting in front of other people, except for that time in Lucian's studio, but Lev hadn't invited him again. Which was probably for the best. Lev's fickle favoritism had fucked with his head enough.

Asher knew better, but he'd still deluded himself into believing he was special up until Lev had shown off photos of Theo's glass sculptures like they were baby pictures.

Aside from the occasional praise for his use of color and light, Lev had remained otherwise silent. Without further guidance, Asher was rudderless.

Anxiety had stolen his muse and stalled his paintbrush.

He'd overworked his painting to the point that he didn't know if he was making it better or worse, or if he should throw it out the ballroom window.

He added more black to the midnight blue on his palette and took another stab at blending depth into the water's surface.

"Alright there, Blakely?" Lev said from behind him.

Asher flinched so hard his neck cracked. The log Lev had added had nearly burned out. How long had he been painting?

"I'm fine, but you should wear a bell if you're going to keep sneaking up on me." Asher pressed his palm to his chin, and leveraged the angle to crack the other side of his neck.

Lev laughed, and joined Asher's side. "No one's ever complained about me being too quiet before. You'd have heard me if you weren't so busy glaring at your canvas. Are you two having a row?"

"I don't argue with inanimate objects." Asher's nose wrinkled.

"Really? You've never had an argument with a toaster that somehow manages to burn and undercook your bread at the same time?"

Asher rolled his lips inward. "Can't say that I have."

"Hm." Lev inspected Asher's painting, drawing closer before swiveling to face him. "I'd be in a foul mood too if I'd worked on a finished painting for as many days as you."

"It's not finished."

Lev lifted the canvas before Asher's paintbrush made contact and leaned it against the stone wall beneath the window.

"Hey. What are you—"

"You finished two days ago, Blakely. It's some of the finest art I've seen in some time, but it's teetering on the edge of becoming an exhibit on self-flagellation."

Asher discarded the compliment and clung to the critique. "You're saying I ruined it?"

"God, no. Your Bolton Strid is a glutton for death. Hunger ripples beneath the surface of your babbling brook, and the man climbing into it fills me with dread, almost as if he's been possessed and called into the depths so the monster beneath could be fed."

"Wait. Really?"

"I never lie about art, Mr. Blakely. Surely a lad as clever as you must know that by now," Lev said. "When I look at your art, I feel as if you're speaking to me directly, as if you're keeping me company. Remember that the next time you doubt yourself."

Lev's praise flooded his bloodstream like a drug, and the fact that he'd understood Asher's message so clearly made his feedback even more meaningful.

Asher lowered his brush onto his palette, and tried to get a hold of himself before he popped another easel-adjacent boner in front of Lev.

Lev's lips curled into a sphinx-like smile as if he knew how much his words had affected him. The sun hovered just above the ocean in the window behind him, highlighting the rare gold and silver strands in his hair.

"You missed a drop of paint, here." The scars on Lev's forearm shimmered as he swiped his thumb over Asher's temple.

He pulled his hand back to reveal the steely blue paint

Asher had used to highlight the subtle turbulence simmering beneath the water's surface.

"This color reminds me of something," Lev mused, rubbing the paint between his thumb and index finger.

The color was probably familiar because it resembled Lev's irises. When Asher crafted a color palette, his subconscious often pulled inspiration from the colors around him. Lev's eye color paired perfectly with the way Asher felt about the man, and the painting's theme of destruction hidden behind charm.

Sometimes art was magic.

Lev's eyes darkened to the ocean at night the longer Asher stared, lost in his irises. Lev inhaled, shoulders lifting as his chest expanded, pressing his pecs against his dress shirt. Had Lev made the connection? Was he as affected as Asher?

Lev cleared his throat, severing the silence. At least one of them was strong enough to stop their sexually charged staring contest.

"In any case, Blakely, it's time to put your canvas out of its misery, and move on to the next sin. I'm desperate to see what you'll do for lust. Erm. I mean to say because lust is your specialty." Lev winced. "As in you often paint more erotic pieces."

Was *the* Leviathan Marks blushing and stumbling over his words? Adorable.

No. Not adorable, especially when Lev had let him struggle with that painting for days.

"If this painting is finished, I'm done for the night." He carried his palette and brushes to the sink. Lev followed.

"Allow me." Lev took Asher's palette plate and scrubbed it with large hands that Asher wasn't at all thinking about wrapping around his...

Asher cleaned his brush with more aggression than necessary. "If you thought I finished days ago, why didn't you say something?"

"It was a teachable moment."

Asher scowled.

"I'm serious. Don't try to please me when you already have. Focus on pleasing yourself, hm?"

Asher quirked an eyebrow. "Pleasing myself?"

Lev laughed, and elbowed him gently. "Freud would have enjoyed dissecting that."

They fell into a comfortable silence as Asher cleaned his remaining brushes and Lev rinsed them.

"You've done very well, Blakely. Trust your instincts." Lev turned off the tap. "The best art you make is the art you make for yourself."

But Asher had always painted for Lev, even when he painted for himself.

OCTOBER 8

Lev watched Asher over the rim of his teacup from his place at the head of the table.

"What?" Asher bit into his third cinnamon bun. Luna had baked them that morning and sprinkled them with orange zest.

"I envy your ability to consume that much sugar," Lev said between bites of bacon he ate with a fork like he was an alien pretending to be human.

Asher shrugged. "They taste like Christmas." He washed down the dusted sugar with coffee.

Lev's eyes lingered on Asher's face for a few seconds before he returned to his tea without further comment.

Julian, a married gay man with big dad energy leaned over and whispered, "Did you see the way he eats his bacon?"

Asher rolled his eyes.

Theo leaned over Asher's plate, covering his mouth in the least subtle way possible, and hissed, "What are you two talking about?"

"Bacon," Asher said at full volume. "Do you want to sit next to each other?"

After leaving art school, Asher had sworn off friendships with other artists. Betrayal hurt more than loneliness did, but Julian and Theo had adopted him like an aloof dog at an animal shelter.

The therapist he'd seen for a few months after he and Ben broke up said he wasn't a solitary creature. He was afraid of getting hurt. Well, yeah. Obviously.

He should have saved the money he'd spent on therapy for paint. Art was the only therapy that had ever helped him—that and horses.

Lev wiped his mouth with a cloth napkin. "Now that we've wrapped up Lust, I thought we could start the day with a discussion on seduction in art."

For Lust, Asher had painted a woodland scene of malevolent fairies with black eyes hidden behind masks, luring unsuspecting humans to their secret garden of poisonous plants with the promise of sex.

Armed with Lev's blessing to paint for himself, Asher had switched from oil paint back to watercolors, his preferred medium, and challenged himself with a richly pigmented, concentrated watercolor palette and liberal use of black.

One wrong move or hurried misstep would ruin everything, just like the Bolton Strid he planned his series of sins to revolve around.

Melody raised her hand, jingling the rainbow of bangles on her wrist.

"Melody, what did I say about raising hands?"

"I think you said it made you feel old," Asher said. The urge to brat was automatic.

Lev's eyes narrowed. Asher bit into his bottom lip, and

when Lev's gaze fell to his mouth, butterflies fluttered behind his sternum.

"Can I go first?" Melody's blonde waves swished as she stroked her hair like a rope.

"Please do." Lev sipped his tea, eyes still on Asher.

"My art doesn't feel like art until other people see it. I'm not making a statement. I'm pointing a finger. I want to pull people across a gallery, and through cell phone screens to spread my message." Melody's bright eyes dimmed. "I've found that sex sells, but sex paired with naïveté sells even more."

Asher's stomach twisted. Melody's candied color choices and ethereal textures were the naïveté to the sharp edge of sensuality and darkness in her paintings.

"Mel..." Daria's dark eyes turned tender.

Asher traded glances with Theo. Daria was scary in a probably-bit-the-head-off-a-raven sort of way, but apparently she had a soft spot.

"Well, you've navigated that line between seduction and accusation excellently," Lev said. "Anyone else?"

"I just make pretty things and hope for the best." Theo laughed.

"It seems to work for you," Lev said.

Jealousy burned inside Asher's chest.

"I don't care about seduction." Daria eyed the curtain of hair blocking the side of Melody's face. "But all good art is inherently seductive."

Asher lost interest a few minutes into Chuck's long and pedantic response. Lev cut his answer short not long after.

"Lars?"

"Huh?" Lars lifted his head from his sketchbook, flashing sun-bleached hair, and tucked his ballpoint pen behind his ear.

"Seduction," Chuck said.

"I don't go out of my way to add sex appeal. When I draw with a ballpoint pen, my goal is to amaze with my skills. It's like a fuck you to all the teachers and critics who called them doodles."

Julian snapped a piece of bacon in half, and shook his head. "Seduction doesn't cross my mind at all. I'm focused on the visuals."

"I'm surprised we haven't heard from you, Blakely," Lev said. "Many of your paintings are sexual, though still quite nuanced."

Asher's cheeks heated. "I just find sex interesting."

His more erotic pieces *had* gathered a lot of attention on social media, and in the art community, but he hated talking about his art, or having it discussed within earshot.

"That's it? You find sex interesting?" Lev said.

"Yeah. The French call an orgasm *la petit morte* for a reason. There's so much conflict to explore, power granted and surrendered."

Lev said nothing, eyes still on Asher, but disconnected and distant. Asher had that uncanny feeling again that there was someone behind him, but when he looked, he only saw fuzzy shadows of fog-filtered trees through the window.

"But I will admit," Asher continued slowly, waiting for Lev's attention to return to him. "I prefer my art to be viewed, and seduction leads to that. I require that external validation, as pathetic as it is."

"I don't think it's pathetic," Melody said. "I think it's human."

Asher smiled. "Maybe. But it's a dangerous thing. If I give people the power to pass judgment on my work, and let myself think my art defines my worth, it hurts when a piece flops."

"You want to be perfect?" Lev asked.

"No. I want to please everyone."

"But you can't," Julian said.

"I know that objectively. But it's hard for me to apply."

"When people hate my art, it feels like a win," Daria said.

"They can hate it all they want, but that means it worked. Whether good or bad, my art influenced their emotions."

"I used to feel that way too, Blakely." Lev held Asher's gaze. "It took a long time for me to shake it, and even now, I struggle with it on occasion."

The revelation transformed his hero into man.

9

THROUGH A PAINTING

ASHER

OCTOBER 15

Firelight scattered shadows on the faces of the other artists and cast an amber glow over Theo as he battled the glass, melting and pulling it like saltwater taffy, turning raw matter into technicolor cotton candy.

Watching Theo was no hardship. Sweat shimmered on his bare skin. His forearms flexed deliciously while he worked.

Asher's fucked up brain was the problem, intruding with images of Lev's bulkier frame in Theo's place, his freckled cheeks turning ruddy the longer he worked by the flames.

It had taken Lev two weeks to find all the equipment required—a task made more difficult because Lev kept forgetting where he'd left things, or to look at all.

In a shadowy corner, the man himself leaned against a pillar, arms crossed over his chest, glacier eyes turned black save for the flames flickering in their depths.

Centuries of survival instincts whispered *predator*, whispered *run*, but Asher was a moth pinned to a board by a hypnotic gaze so intense it was like Lev wanted to see inside his brain, like he wanted to cut him open so he could taste the blood inside his veins.

The wind shifted, funneling rain through the columns of the covered courtyard. Asher shivered and took a sip of the scotch he'd been nursing all night.

He should have sat closer to the forge, but he hoped to leave early without notice.

Lightning forked outside the arches to his right, followed by a crack of thunder that made him flinch. Lev had warned that tonight's storm could make the tide surge over the seawall.

Asher felt more claustrophobic during high tide inside Lichenmoor's cavernous rooms on a good day than when Ben had restrained him. Sleep wouldn't come easy tonight.

Whoever had built a castle this close to the ocean, and then dug a half-moon moat to guard the land-facing side, must have had a nasty case of untreated neurosyphilis. Sure, it may have protected them from land attacks, but if enemy boats waited for high tide, Lichenmoor would be surrounded.

The next bolt of lightning drew Asher's gaze back to Lev. The corner was empty, and he was on his way toward him. Great.

"What do you think?" Lev claimed the space beside him.

Asher smoothed his features into what he hoped was his best bored face. "Of?"

"Theo is very pretty, isn't he?"

"And?"

Lev straddled the bench, planting his hands between his spread legs, gray tartan slacks tightening over muscular thighs and... Asher looked away.

"Oh, please don't go all monosyllabic, Blakely. I was joking. I'm sure if you ask Theo nicely, he'll blow you with even more gusto than he does his glass art." He stroked his beard. "Perhaps I should sample his technique first."

"Okay."

"Again with the monosyllables."

"That was two syllables," Asher said flatly.

"Yes. Two *monosyllables*." Lev laughed. "Oh, Blakely, how I've missed your humor."

Thunder cracked. Theo paused and looked at them.

Lev waved with his fingertips. "I've noticed you don't like it when I talk about Theo. Do you have trouble sharing?"

"You can have him. I'm not here to get my dick sucked."

Lev pouted. "How tragic."

Asher rolled his eyes.

Lev's pout turned thoughtful. "Earlier you looked at me like that was exactly what you were here for." Flames flared in Lev's eyes as his pupils dilated.

"You should get your eyes checked. I think your vision is failing in your old age."

Lev clutched the left side of his chest. "Ouch, that hurt."

Fuck Lev for running so hot and cold and fucking with his emotions.

"Do you want to know what I think, Blakely?"

"Not really."

Another laugh, lower, just for him. The warmth of Lev's breath kissed the shell of his ear as he leaned nearer. "I suspect you have a thing for older men."

Asher's heart dropped. How did he... Did he know Ben? Wait. Was that why Lev had invited him?

The room swayed. Or the ocean had made good on its threat of dragging Lichenmoor's occupants to their deaths.

Lev must have caught wind of the story tossed around campus, the one that said he'd earned his place on his knees, and on his back, and every other sexual position Ben had demanded.

Or had Lev heard the story that Ben told to the dean? The story that painted Asher as manipulative and unstable, that claimed he'd had an unhealthy crush Ben had tried to snuff?

Whatever Lev had heard wasn't the truth. Even Asher

hadn't understood until later. Ben had seduced him, groomed him over months. He was a predator who'd abused a position of power and played into Asher's insecurities, weaponizing the way his self-worth was tied to praise.

This mentorship was supposed to be his second chance, but it was the same bullshit all over again.

"Are you alright?" Lev touched his wrist, but it felt like a shackle.

Asher was stuck on an island with the one man in the world who could break him more than Ben already had. He jumped to his feet and jerked his arm free, then smacked his shin into the bench, knocking his glass onto the stone floor where it shattered.

"Fuck!" Tears stung his eyes, an automatic response from the pain.

Lev's brows darted up in alarm. He swung one leg over the bench and stood. None of the other artists noticed the commotion over the rising squall. Asher felt like a ghost only Lev saw.

"I have to go," Asher said, words snatched by the wind. He refused to have a panic attack in front of Leviathan Fucking Marks.

Lightning lit the way as he fled the courtyard, and thunder covered the crash as he burst through the doors into the castle.

Sideways rain hammered the windows louder than the drumroll of his heart. Footsteps pounded on the stone slabs behind him.

He was lost in the fog all over again. Were the footsteps real? Were they imagined? Either outcome was too terrifying to comprehend.

The hallway ended at the steps of a stone spiral staircase he'd never seen. He must have taken a wrong turn.

He couldn't look back, let alone turn around and retrace his steps. He couldn't face Lev.

The storm caterwauled through open arch windows as he jogged up the wet steps, fingers sliding on the smooth stone railing. He was exhausted by the time he reached the dimly lit round room at the top.

A dead end. Perfect.

He was trapped at the top of a tower with no way out in a storm that suppressed all other sound. He wouldn't hear Lev's steps on the stairs if he'd followed.

He took one deep breath, and another, pushing back the fresh wave of panic.

But as his anxiety receded, shame crept in. He'd overreacted. He wasn't in danger. Lev wouldn't hurt him. At least not physically. Probably.

Lightning shot light through the arrow slit windows. An ear-shattering thunderclap boomed as a shadow emerged from the steps.

"Mr. Blakely," Lev yelled over the storm. "I'm far too old for a game of chase up one of Lichenmoor's towers. I could have broken a hip." He braced his hands on his knees and caught his breath. "I called after you. Why didn't you stop?" He stepped closer.

Asher edged backward. "I didn't hear you."

Lev frowned. "You're shaking." He pulled his woolen sweater over his head. The bottom of his shirt lifted, baring abs flexing in cadence with his breaths and a treasure trail of ginger hair.

Lev extended the sweater. "Here."

Asher shook his head. The sweater was an apple in Eden, cursed with his delectable scent and lingering body heat. "I'm fine."

"Come now, Blakely. It's a jumper, not a straightjacket."

"How do you know about Ben?"

Lev's face blanked. "Ben who? I must know dozens of men named Ben. Does he have a last name or any defining characteristic to jog my memory? Perhaps he has a thin mustache that curls up at the ends or a dashing streak of gray hair near his temple..."

Asher crossed his arms. "It's not funny."

"I quite agree. This is no laughing matter." Lev took a single step forward. "Trust me, if I'd known Ben, I'd have demanded he introduce us at once. Am I correct to assume he's another artist? Or British?" A threat edged into his voice. "I'd quite like to know who he is and what he's done to scare you."

Fuck. Asher believed him. His anxiety had betrayed him again. "Forget it. I overreacted."

"You reacted precisely the way you thought you needed to. Like we all do." Lev smiled sadly. "I apologize if I poked at an old wound with the older man nonsense. I was flirting. Nothing more."

"Flirting? You acted like I was contagious all week!" Asher groaned. "You're exhausting."

Asher was screwing his chances at the mentorship, but fuck Lev for taking him on a roller coaster ride of rejection and love bombing. He wanted off.

"I know. I'm sorry. I..." Lev scrubbed his face with his hands and tipped his head back. "I don't know how to behave around you, especially when we're alone. You've been doing so well this week that I thought it best to stay away.

"But then you seemed miserable tonight and almost broke your neck running away from something I said, and now I've learned there's some surname-less Ben out there, and I want to rip his heart out through his arse, and..."

Thunder drowned out whatever he said next, but Asher didn't need words when Lev radiated bloodthirsty vengeance.

"Relax, Lancelot. I don't need you to defend my honor." Asher had been a willing participant.

"That first morning in my studio, I made you uncomfortable," Lev continued with the same seriousness as if he hadn't been interrupted. "I'm twenty years your senior."

"Fifteen."

Lev scoffed and waved a flippant hand. "Fifteen, twenty. It's all the same."

"Your age didn't make me uncomfortable. Stealing my sketchbook did. The reason I did well all week was because of the advice you gave me."

At least Lev had the decency to *pretend* to look ashamed. "Be that as it may—"

"No. Fuck whatever sort of Winston Churchill shit you're about to say."

"Winston Churchill shit?"

"Old-timey British phrases like *be that as it may*. Stop trying to change the subject."

Lev shook his head and sighed. "I'm sorry. The truth is, you're far too easy to fancy, and I don't want to fancy you."

Lightning flashed. Lev let the thunder pass before continuing.

"I wish I could say that if I'd known how tempting you'd be, I wouldn't have invited you, but that's not true. I'm a selfish arsehole, a wretched wraith of a man. Every moment I spend away from your canvas pains me, and even though I have no right to you, I can't bear the thought of Theo touching you."

Asher shivered as goosebumps sparked across his skin. "You fancy me?"

"I said you're *easy* to fancy." Lev's swift hand lifted toward Asher's head.

Asher flinched, shoulders cinching to his ears. But Lev didn't hit him. He tested Asher's temperature with the back of his hand and examined him head to foot with a growing frown. "No fever, yet you tremble so."

"I'm fine."

But that wasn't true. He'd skipped the lamb Luna had served for dinner.

The next flash of lightning gave little warning of the thunder that followed. Asher jumped and teetered on tired legs.

"Easy there, lad." Lev rushed forward and gripped his hips.

The urge to press his nose into the center of Lev's chest and inhale the jasmine and pepper in his cologne was as terrifying as it was compelling.

"I've got you," Lev said in a soothing hush.

Asher's gaze dipped to where Lev still touched him before rising to sincere cerulean eyes emanating concern.

"Are you sure you're alright? I couldn't help but notice how little you ate at dinner."

"You're tracking my eating habits?" He hated how petulant he sounded.

"I fret."

"Do you fret about the other artists?"

"The other artists eat their food."

Asher's family had never noticed how little he ate when stressed, but they'd noticed when he'd stopped eating beef on slaughter day, then stopped eating beef at all.

Thunder cracked. Again, Asher flinched.

Lev clicked his tongue twice in a sympathetic tone. "What am I going to do with you?"

"I..."

"Hm?" Lev prodded, stroking the sharp ridge of Asher's iliac crest with his thumb, shunting Asher's blood southward with each pass and extinguishing what little remained of his common sense.

Leviathan Marks was touching him. Not to steady him. Not to seduce him. No. He was touching him with the casual intimacy of absentmindedness.

He wanted Lev to kiss him, to edge his thumb down inside his pants instead of over them. Scratch that. He wanted Lev to pop the button of his pants and shove his hand inside his boxer briefs. He wanted Lev to palm his cock, weigh the heft of his balls, jerk him until he came in only a few pumps because he was so keyed up.

Asher raked his teeth over his bottom lip, a futile attempt at self-flagellation forgotten as Lev's eyes dipped to his mouth.

"Please," Asher said.

"Such manners, Blakely. But for what do you wish?"

"I don't know." He wanted everything Lev would give him as much as he wanted to sever the magnetic connection between them.

Lev released him. "Do you want me to leave?"

"No."

"Good. I'd hate to throw you over my shoulder and cart you back to your room."

The image that scenario projected was far more tantalizing than it should have been; his front hanging down Lev's strong back, Lev locking Asher's legs against his chest and rubbing his ass, promising to reward him if he behaved.

"Why did you run from me tonight?" Lev asked, drawing him from his fantasy.

Asher opened his mouth—

"I'm not asking about Ben," Lev interrupted. "I'm asking why you *ran*."

"I get panic attacks."

As if Lev had summoned the truth with a spell, the confession escaped Asher's lips before he could catch it, and for some inexplicable reason, he didn't regret it. He trusted Lev not to judge him, even when every other man in his life had. Even when men were supposed to bottle their fears until they exploded, because men could be angry, as long as they were brave.

"I see," Lev said.

Asher looked at his feet and begged the ocean to swallow him. *I see?* Benign apathy was only slightly better than if he'd laughed at his vulnerability.

Lev pinched Asher's chin gently and forced his gaze up. "Listen to me. There's nothing to be ashamed of. We're all mere mortals subject to the scars of circumstance and the whims of brain chemistry. Understood?"

Asher tried to look away, but Lev trapped his chin. The

empathy in his eyes was too much. Asher wanted to smash his eyes shut.

"I asked you a question," Lev said. "Do you understand?"

What? Oh. "Yes, sir."

"Good lad."

Asher swallowed, the soft muscles of his lower jaw pushing against the fingers Lev still perched beneath his chin.

Lev's gaze fell to Asher's neck, then settled on his mouth. Asher wet his bottom lip. Did Lev want to taste him?

Electricity thrummed in Asher's chest as the silence stretched.

Lightning forked through the sky in the window over Lev's shoulder. Thunder cracked right overhead, rattling the tower and rumbling through them.

Again, Asher jumped, too hopped up on adrenaline and Lev's attention.

Lev tightened his grip on Asher's hip and inclined his mouth toward his ear. "Are you afraid of thunderstorms?"

They were so close that when Asher shook his head, his cheek met Lev's lips. Asher froze on the precipice of a cliff, ready to leap into the depths of Lev's soul, waiting for Lev to take his hand, to drag him back from the edge or jump with him.

"We can't do this," Lev said.

"I know."

"Tell me to stop." Lev pulled back and leaned his forehead against Asher's. "Please, tell me to stop."

"I don't want to. Do *you*?"

Lev shook his head, brushing their lips together, a silent no, a kiss that wasn't. "We're breaking my rule."

"Mine too."

"We shouldn't," Lev said, lungs filling until their chests connected.

Lev was just playing the role of a gentleman torn between his morals and lust. But Asher didn't care when they were so close he tasted the scotch on his breath and felt his heart beating against his chest.

"We won't," Asher agreed.

Lev pressed his thumb against Asher's lower lip, peeled it down, and licked the length of it.

Fuck.

Seizing the opportunity to suck whatever part of Lev he had access to, Asher curled his tongue around his thumb, and sucked.

Lev's moan rippled through him. "Don't tempt me, Blakely."

"What would you do if I tempted you?" Asher said, then swirled his tongue around Lev's thumb again, and flicked the underside with the tip of his tongue like it was a cock.

"I'd turn you over and lick and scissor you open until you were ready to take me."

Asher's stomach swooped. "*Oh my God.*"

Lev laughed roguishly and kissed the corner of his mouth like it didn't count if it wasn't on his lips.

Lightning flashed. Lev's lips lowered to Asher's jaw, and lower still, to his neck, beard sandpapering sensitive skin as he descended.

Thunder followed several neck kisses later. Lev looked up, scanning Asher's face as if to check that he wasn't afraid, and Asher felt something very dangerous then.

He felt safe.

Lev bowed his head, returning his attention to Asher's neck. Asher tilted his head back until it touched the stone wall, granting him more access. But it wasn't enough for Lev. He hooked his fingers inside Asher's shirt and tugged it aside to kiss the hollow above his clavicle.

Asher tensed. He couldn't risk Lev seeing the tattoo inked over his heart. Vicing Lev's face between his hands, he pulled him toward his mouth. They met in the middle, tongue against tongue, and that wasn't a kiss, was it?

No, they were studying each other's anatomy so they could paint each other later. That's what Asher told himself as his fingers found Lev's blazing skin and roamed the ridges of his abs.

Lev hid his face in Asher's neck. "Do you think it's possible to fall in love through a painting?"

Asher nodded, tongue tangled with emotion, words too difficult to express. How could he explain that he'd loved Lev like that for years? Maybe that type of love was limerence, a crush more than a connection, but it was still real.

"Good lad. I knew you'd understand."

His praise was a drug, one hit and he was addicted to the point of recklessness, hauling Lev closer and gyrating his hips, grinding against an erection as intimidating as the rest of him.

"Christ. You make me feral," Lev buried a moan in Asher's neck, rocking his hips in tandem.

Tingling ecstasy sparked at the base of his spine. His eyes fell shut. He was so close. If they came like this with clothes between them, that didn't count either, right?

Lev's hand slipped beneath Asher's shirt. A rough thumb grazed his nipple. His balls lifted.

"What's this?"

Asher froze, eyes opening to find Lev lifting his shirt.

The threat of discovery was like diving into frigid water. "No."

Lev dropped his hands and stepped backward, cleaving them apart.

"Asher, I'm sorry." Lev reached out and stopped, then backed away, putting more distance between them. "I shouldn't have... Fuck. Are you all right?"

The tower spun. Reality set in.

What had he done?

This was Ben all over again. But worse.

Asher darted to the right and rushed past Lev, their shoulders not quite touching, just the shudder of displaced atoms.

FOOTPRINTS

ASHER

"Blakely, wait!"

Asher skidded and nearly slipped down the stairs. His heart hammered in his ears, too loud to hear if Lev had given chase. He sprinted down the hall, running for his life until the stone floors grew a skin of parquet diamonds and the walls wore paper again.

The labyrinthine hall forked. He chose the widest path, hoping it would lead him to the central staircase, but all he found was a narrow stairwell with a low ceiling. The stairs spat him into darkness.

Terror took hold. His anxiety was out of control at Lichenmoor. He hadn't needed medication for over a year, and wished he'd brought it.

Trying to slow his breathing, he focused on his other senses. It was a trick he'd learned in a men's support group. Stagnant air, the scent of dust and damp. Raindrops pattered in a steady rhythm, no longer an angry downpour. The tapestry-lined wall beneath his fingertips.

When his vision adjusted, he found a long hallway with doors on each side and a stained glass window at the end.

He flipped the light switch, and a line of wall sconces

glowed to life, illuminating most of the hall, save for a few broken bulbs casting contrasting shadows.

He felt like he'd trespassed on a liminal space where he didn't belong. Dust blanketed the floor, dulling his footsteps as he walked to the first door, pushed it open, and stepped into the pages of a ghost story.

Goosebumps crawled across his skin as he wound past phantom forms hidden beneath linen-draped furniture. He stopped in front of a human-shaped obelisk as tall as him and ripped the sheet down, the sound like a flag whipped by the wind.

After the cloud of dust faded, leaving the taste of it on his tongue, he faced not a monster or statue, but himself.

The man in the oblong mirror was unrecognizable, eyes wide in fear, dark hair wild; mussed by Lev, no doubt. He inhaled, trying to quell his racing heart, and sneezed.

Turning his back on the mirror, he walked toward a wall of curtains and flung them open. Damn. Fog had swallowed the starlight and obscured any recognizable landmarks to orient himself.

He returned to the hall and opened one door after another, searching for a way out. Most of the rooms were empty, but some stored more sheet-draped furniture and the occasional bust or statue that made Asher's pulse stutter to a standstill before restarting.

Halfway down the hall, a large pair of footprints appeared without origin, almost as if someone had teleported. What the fuck? A thin layer of silty dust had settled into them. The footprints weren't recent.

Chills swept up his spine as he followed the footsteps to the last door. He twisted the tarnished knob, but it was stuck. He wiped his clammy palms on his pants and tried again. This time it twisted a little, but the door wouldn't budge. Marshaling his strength, he gripped the knob and heaved himself against the door.

Nothing.

What was locked away at the end of a hallway so abandoned it was lonelier than a mausoleum? He kneeled on the floor and peered through a keyhole covered by cobwebs.

He blew hard into the hole and pulled the remaining strands of cobwebs out. The hair on the back of his neck lifted as he pressed his eye to the keyhole.

The room was dark, but the next bolt of lightning slipped through a gap in the curtains, spotlighting the silhouette of a man. A fist clenched around Asher's heart. He blinked, but the silhouette was still there.

Heavy footsteps hammered behind him like a battering ram. A hand yanked him back from the door and onto his ass. His stomach lurched. Panic seized him.

"What on earth are you doing here?" Lev shouted, face red with rage.

"I was lost. I was..." Asher scrambled backward and slammed into the opposite wall. "Ouch."

The color drained from Lev's face. He pasted a mask of concern over his rage.

"I'm sorry. I can't have you in the east wing. It's not safe," Lev said, voice even and calm again. "It's a wonder you made it this far without breaking your neck."

"I didn't know I was in the east wing." Anger replaced his earlier anxiety. "Like I said, I was lost."

Lev extended his hand. "Let me help you."

Asher didn't take it. He pushed back on his palms, got to his feet, and brushed the dust from his hands.

Lev clasped his hands behind his back. "I'll escort you to bed."

"I don't need an escort. If you give me directions, I'm sure I can find my way."

Lev scoffed. "Doubtful. You have a terrible sense of direction. Come along."

Asher hated how condescending Lev was, but what he

hated most of all was how much Lev's command dug into his brainstem and compelled him to listen.

"I'll draw you a map tonight. Some places in Lichenmoor are so isolated no one will hear you if you call."

It wasn't a threat. Asher knew that, but it was true.

Lev could hurt Asher and no one would hear him. He could lock him inside one of those rooms and leave him there as punishment, or leave him there to rot.

Wait. What if the silhouette in the room was Lev's captive? He discarded the thought. There weren't enough footsteps, and wouldn't the man have called when he'd heard Lev scolding him?

"I haven't been here in years. What if I never found you?"

Was that a tremor in his voice, a stutter in his confident stride? If Lev hadn't visited, then who had left the footprints? Or had he lied?

Lev stopped in front of a tapestry of a cloven-hoofed demon cavorting with a lamb. Lev lifted the tapestry to reveal a squat door carved into the paneling.

"This is the fastest way out of the east wing."

Ah. So that was where the footprints had come from. But the question remained—who did the footsteps belong to?

Lev pushed the door open, ducked his head under the frame, and disappeared into the darkness.

With a mix of dread and dawning acceptance, Asher followed.

11
A PARTING GIFT

LEV

Damp and mold tickled Lev's nose. It was pitch black inside the tunnel.

Asher clung so closely, Lev felt his breath on the back of his neck. Anxiety was one thing, but the lad started at loud noises and flinched like a kicked dog when Lev had checked his temperature. Not to mention the fear in his eyes at the mere suspicion that Lev knew Ben.

Who the fuck was this Ben Twattington?

"Are you afraid of the dark, Blakely?"

"I don't like tight spaces."

"Ah. Rotten luck."

As far as secret passageways went, this one was the most claustrophobia-inducing, and his least favorite route. Memories lingered in the tunnel. Silas likely lurked somewhere ahead. Or overhead. He glanced at the stone ceiling, but if Silas was there, he was hiding.

"We can circle back and take the long way if you wish," Lev suggested, slowing his footsteps.

"Nah. I'm fine."

"Very well." Lev had no interest in extending their time together. The sooner Blakely was in bed, the better.

What happened in that tower was wrong, and not just because Asher was half his age, or because it was highly unethical to sleep with a protégé who clearly idolized him.

No. The crux of the issue was that Lev was black ink, tainting everything he touched, and Asher was a watercolor painting still wet—Lev would ruin him.

In the tower, Lev had acted like a man possessed with more than the carnal desire only five years of celibacy could inspire. He'd wanted to pry Asher's mouth open and crawl inside, muck about in his mind, figure out what made his art so haunting, figure out what haunted him.

Lev had no business touching him. He had half a mind to call the whole thing off and send everyone home. But he was greedy.

He'd give himself another chance, keep Asher at arm's length, treat him as one would a colleague. He'd focus on what was most important—art—and stifle his baser instincts. He'd ignore their chemistry. He wouldn't fret over why the lad didn't eat, or why he had the reflexes of a battered wife.

"I thought I saw someone in the last room," Asher said.

Lev scoffed. "How could you have seen anything in the dark?"

"Lightning."

"That room is empty."

Had Silas been there? Lev shook his head. Why was he entertaining this line of discussion? Asher couldn't see him.

"Why was the door locked?" Asher asked.

Lev's shoulders tightened. "I don't think you understand how ancient Lichenmoor is. The land has passed through many hands, been under siege, even served as a tuberculosis sanitarium."

"I do understand actually. Do you need me to explain the internet to you again?" Searing sarcasm boiled between each word.

Lev resisted the urge to sling back a sharp barb of his own.

Better to keep his head than reveal something he shouldn't, or lose his temper again.

"I've lived almost my entire life at Lichenmoor and still haven't explored all of it. That door has been locked for as long as I can remember and the skeleton key doesn't work."

"Hm."

"What?" Lev asked.

"I said nothing."

"You said, *Hm*."

Asher didn't answer. Wind whistled through the rafters. The scuff of their footsteps echoed in the enclosed space.

"Why did you invite me?" Asher asked.

"I'm beginning to ask myself that too, Blakely."

"What have you been doing for the last five years?" Asher carried on, seemingly unperturbed.

"Jesus. Are you with the press?"

"Why am I here? Why are any of us? I don't believe your story about Lucian's wishes, or your loneliness."

Lev stopped. Asher slammed into his back.

"*Argh*. Warn me when you stop. I can't see past the tip of my nose."

"I'm surprised you can see past your nose at all given how nosy you are." Lev strode ahead.

"Hey, wait." Asher's hastened footsteps telegraphed his fear.

Lev groaned under his breath, but slowed his pace. "I don't know what I've done to lead you to believe that we share a level of trust that permits you to ask me personal questions—"

"Maybe it was the light frotting in the tower?"

"You aren't entitled to the truth because I invited you here, or because I lost control with you earlier."

"Why are you being such a dick when you were the one who started it?"

"As I recall, I very much asked you to tell me to stop. You were the one who rushed to meet my lips."

"You're fucking delusional if you think you weren't responsible for what happened back there."

"Watch your tone." Lev swung back around to face him.

Asher crashed into him and ping-ponged off his chest.

Lev steadied him by his shoulders. "Sorry."

"Do you drive like this?" Asher wrenched himself out of Lev's grip. "How many times have you been rear-ended?"

"He's right, you know," Silas said.

Great. What a perfect addition to an already aggravating situation.

"I don't drive anymore, and you're the one riding my arse." Lev grabbed Asher's hand and tugged him forward. "We can bicker and walk at the same time."

The sooner they got out of that tunnel, the better.

Silas appeared at the end of the passageway, eyes glinting unnaturally.

No matter. If he didn't move, Lev would thoroughly enjoy barreling through him.

A faint line of light slipped through a gap under the door ahead.

"We're nearly there," Lev said.

"Thank fuck," Asher said.

"Trouble in paradise already, Levvy?" Silas laughed and disappeared. Twat.

"Here we are." Lev pushed the door open and ushered Asher into the soft light of the hallway.

While Asher blinked and rubbed his eyes, Lev pulled the skeleton key from his pocket and locked the small door before unfurling the tapestry back over it. Silas's fingernails scratched on the other side of the door. Lev couldn't wait to retire to his room and hide from both vexing men.

"Has anyone ever been locked inside?" Asher asked.

Lev pocketed the key. "I always keep one side unlocked just in case." And he always kept Silas locked out of his wing.

He stopped in front of Asher's door. "What happened in

the tower can't happen again. Your art is brilliant, and you have immense potential. Frotting aside, I am very serious about your education."

"Whatever you say, sir."

Lev dragged his gaze away from Asher's insolent lips and opened the door for him with a grating screech.

"Good night, Blakely,"

"Good night." Asher slipped inside his room and closed the door behind him.

"Oh, and Ash," Lev called. "I'll draft a map of Lichenmoor tonight. I think it's best if you remain in your room until morning. I'd hate for you to go missing again."

"Yes, sir," Asher said mockingly.

Replacing the door hinges with a squeakier set would prove useful after all. The lad had no sense of self-preservation. At least Lev would know if he sneaked out.

Lev hurried into his own room and pulled Asher's sketchbook out of his back pocket. Asher had conveniently forgotten it on the bench back at the forge. The simple brown craft paper cover was shiny and worn from use, as soft under his fingers as a fawn's coat. Lev peeled the front cover back on the way to his desk.

Asher had written his name, address, and phone number inside. While his handwriting was tidy, each stroke of the pen had gouged deep lines into the paper like he'd pressed down hard and embedded all his tension into each letter.

Lev dropped into his chair. He started at the beginning, planning to savor the experience page by page until he found the four lines that had captured his attention.

A leafy dragon camouflaged in the boughs of a larch tree claimed the first page. An ocean dotted with stars filled the next. On the third page was a fox's black-socked paw, a glass tumbler exploding into shards.

Each page was dated, starting in July of that year. Asher

had crammed notes in between the sketches too. *Called dad. Met with Tristan.*

Who was Tristan?

A list of groceries: *portobello mushrooms, asiago, arugula, brioche buns.*

Had Asher cooked for Tristan?

The next handful of pages contained more notes on the Bolton Strid—death statistics and depth estimates, maps of the footpath, sketched flora and fauna.

Why was the lad so fascinated with it?

During the middle of August, Asher had noted the arrival of Lev's invitation. Lev felt a twinge of guilt reading Asher's reaction.

Too good to be true?

Smart lad.

After that, Asher's focus shifted. He wrote pages of notes on Lichenmoor, drew sketches of Lichenmoor Hall, pasted overhead drone shots, interior pictures clipped from magazines. Tide charts. Weather patterns.

What a nerd. Lev loved it.

Given Asher's interest in the Bolton Strid, the invitation to Lichenmoor must have felt serendipitous. According to his notes, he'd stopped at the Bolton Strid along the way.

Lev forgot all about the four lines he'd been searching for until he flipped the page.

He dropped the book as if a spider had leaped from the pages. Those four lines were scars, a final parting gift Silas had left with his nails on Lev's forearm.

He looked at the four lines etched forever on his skin, shiny scars so thin and camouflaged by freckles they were nearly invisible. Asher's attention to detail was as impressive as it was unsettling.

Asher had fossilized the moment Lev had clutched a fistful of his father's ashes, and cast them into the ocean. Lev could almost feel the chalky grit of pulverized bone between his fingers.

Somehow Asher had pulled off Lev's mask, captured the invisible burden of guilt in the curve of his back, the flicker of lost control in the flex of his forearm, the stain that shadowed his palm after he freed the ashes from his fist.

He flipped to the next page, and the next. Almost every page included a picture of Lev—gripping a paintbrush, fingers smudged with charcoal, rain-slick hair curling at the base of his neck, blue eyes in every shade of light. It was fanatical. Obsessive. Fodder for a narcissist.

The lad had been studying him. Stalking him from afar. Exactly as Lev had stalked him. The revelation filled Lev with excitement rather than fear. Which was a problem.

He thumbed through the pages until he reached Asher's arrival at Lichenmoor. Asher had sketched at least one scene every day—a dark silhouette in the mist, the peephole to Lichenmoor's front door, Luna at breakfast.

He turned the page and his stomach dropped like he'd jumped off the bluffs and crashed into the ocean, faced with a rough sketch of Lev's painting, the one his father had forced him to hang on the wall in his studio as punishment, the one of Silas he still couldn't take down. Even now.

Below it, Asher had written, *Someone important.*

Then sideways and sloppy he'd added, *Who is Silas?*

12

FEVER DREAM

ASHER

OCTOBER 16

Smoldering embers were all that remained of the fire. Asher checked the antique clock on his bedside table. Two-sixteen.

He pressed the heels of his hands into his eyes and huffed a quiet growl. He was no stranger to the vicious cycle of anxiety causing insomnia and insomnia worsening his anxiety. It was exhausting. Literally.

Before undressing, he'd searched his entire room until he found a secret door hidden beneath a tapestry, reigniting his concern about the silhouette behind the locked door.

Was there a secret entrance to the locked door in the east wing? Was that why there'd only been one pair of footprints?

Tomorrow, he would block the door with the hulking wardrobe on the other side of his room. Maybe then he'd be able to sleep.

Groaning, he rolled onto his back. He'd never forget the pressure of Lev's chest against his, or how the hands he'd studied for hours roved over his skin, the touch of his silken tongue against his lips.

The confirmation that Leviathan Marks, his hero, his crush, wanted him—at least in the physical sense—still simmered in his blood. His cock hardened at the mere memory of what they'd done, and nearly done, the sensitive head pushing up against the sheets.

Jacking off to the memory of the man he could never have was wrong. It was pathetic. He bit into his bottom lip, debating.

Fuck it.

He'd have to be quiet. For all he knew, Lev slept a few feet away on the other side of the wall. The threat of discovery turned him on more, proving his dire need for post-nut clarity.

Asher traced the lines of Lev's art on his bare skin, traveling to the self-portrait of Lev tattooed over his heart, to Icarus falling down his flank, the sea serpent ouroboros circling his navel. The Leviathan ouroboros was his favorite tattoo; it felt like a mark of ownership, a brand that claimed him. God, he wanted to be claimed by him.

His head fell back against his pillow. With needy urgency, he widened his legs, and took his dick in hand. He focused on the tattoo of Lev's eye on his forearm, wishing the iris was steel blue instead of his skin tone.

Lev was an alchemist with color. No tattoo artist could compare, let alone capture the way Lev's eyes had darkened with desire in the tower.

He rolled his nipple between his fingers and pinched, imagining how Lev would lick and suck until it peaked, then trap it between his teeth, tugging and teasing, thrashing his head side to side once or twice. Not hard. Just enough to show Asher what he was capable of.

"Fuck," Asher groaned, forgetting himself, so intoxicated by the idea of Lev leaving bite marks. Still, he needed to keep quiet, and he had just the idea.

Rolling onto his side, he plucked his boxer briefs from the floor and balled them up. Then in a filthy act he would be ashamed of in the morning, he spat into his hand, slicked up his dick with a few hurried strokes, and stuffed his boxer briefs into his mouth, wishing he'd gagged himself with Lev's undergarments instead.

There. That would help.

Gripping his dick, he closed his eyes and imagined Lev forcing him to his knees in the hallway of the east wing, castigating him for venturing out of bounds, lecturing him for risking his own safety, punishing him by face-fucking the breath from his lungs.

But that wasn't enough.

Asher's hips lifted from the bed almost automatically, fucking his cock up into his fist as if beckoned by a primal urge to seat himself inside Lev's tight heat.

Bliss coiled at the base of his spine. His pace quickened. He should savor it, edge himself, but he'd lost all self-control and self-respect. His toes curled. He bit into the fabric, but not fast enough to contain the moan that followed.

Shit.

His orgasm receded like the crest of a wave collapsing on itself. Hours had passed since he'd last heard the bed frame creak or the protest of floorboards under Lev's heavy feet. He had to be asleep. Right?

Asher held his breath, ears straining to listen past the downpour and whistling wind. But there was nothing else. Thank fuck.

Paranoia mollified, Asher began anew, thrusting upward in synchrony with the glide of his wrist. The filthy sound of slick friction grew louder as he milked more precum from his cock and slid his hand up and over his crown.

He imagined Lev in the tower again, gripping both their dicks in his fist. "Spit," Lev would have said, holding out his hand, and Asher would have obeyed. He totally fucking would have.

Saliva filled his mouth on cue. He pushed out the boxer

briefs with his tongue and spat into his hand, gathering his sloppy drool, scooping it onto his fingers. Then he rubbed it around his hole, teasing himself as if he were Lev. The cocky bastard would eat him for hours and ignore him when he begged for more stimulation.

Wood creaked. Asher froze. He held his breath and listened.

Asher. The voice whispered like the wind. The lack of sleep was fucking with his head, but he'd roll with it. The idea of Lev saying his name, of telling him when he could come, summoned a fresh drop of precum from his cock.

He lifted his knees toward his shoulders, reached between his splayed legs, and gradually pushed two fingers past his ring, mimicking the stretch of Lev's much larger finger.

"That's it, Blakely," he imagined Lev saying. "I'm going to fill you so full with my cum, your arse will weep for me."

A whimper escaped his lips. The wind quieted for a beat, and Asher heard something that sounded very much like how he'd imagined Lev's moan would sound—gravelly, low, arresting.

Instead of driving fear into his heart, the thought of Lev working his thick dick in his fist to the sound of Asher doing the same thing filled him with a mix of exhibitionistic and voyeuristic satisfaction that pushed him over the edge.

He released a long, guttural moan, impossible to contain, and exploded in ribbons and ribbons, painting his sheets.

A few seconds later, Lev joined him with another moan, one that lifted all the hair on his body and had his balls refilling. It was the sound of Leviathan Marks, *the* Leviathan Marks, his hero, his obsession, his god, coming on the other side of the wall.

But that wasn't enough. Asher wanted more. He wanted to pound on the secret door adjoining their rooms and demand Lev let him in so he could lick the come from his skin.

13

SPATE OF TEMPESTS

LEV

Lev lifted his teacup from the saucer.

"Are you sure caffeine is wise at this hour?" Silas said from atop the dining room credenza. He'd appeared a moment before, swimming in Lev's half-buttoned monogrammed pajama top, and nothing else. "You need sleep."

He had a point. After getting off with Asher in a spontaneous mutual masturbation session that never should have happened, Lev had given up on sleep and turned to painting.

Ordinarily, art anchored him when he felt unmoored, but he'd never felt more lost.

Last night had been one of the most erotic experiences of his life, which was saying something. In the years after Silas, Lev had fucked his way across the continent, burying his grief in the arse of any beautiful man who was willing, and yet, he'd never felt that alive since Silas had died.

Silas feigned a yawn and crossed one bare leg over the other. "Between wanking yourself dry and deciding to become a cartographer, even *I'm* exhausted. The second-hand embarrassment I had from how much effort you put into that map... I swear, if I weren't dead, I would have died."

Lev lowered his teacup to his saucer. It landed with a rattling clink, and a tidal wave of tea sloshed over the rim.

Silas lifted a single eyebrow, never one to miss when Lev failed to meet Father's expectations, even if it was something as silly as drinking tea without spilling. Never mind that Lucian Marks had chucked teacups at walls and used the shards for abstract art.

"How do you know about that map?" The collar of his shirt felt like a noose.

"Your defenses weaken with each passing day." Silas picked at a loose thread on the Marks crest embroidered over his heart. "When will you accept that?"

"Ideally, never. In fact, I think I'd sooner jump off one of Lichenmoor's cliffs."

Silas scoffed. "Don't be so melodramatic."

"Please. If anyone is melodramatic in this relationship, it's you."

"A relationship? You ended that when you killed me."

"Fuck off." He took another sip, goading him.

Silas's nose twitched.

"I'm curious what you thought upon finding your name in Asher's sketchbook."

"Oh?" Silas's brows lifted.

"You did read it, right? I thought you were peeping over my shoulder..."

"I must have missed that page."

Lev exhaled some of his tension at the confirmation that Silas hadn't *actually* penetrated the sanctuary of his room or his mind.

"He's already matched your name to your portrait," Lev said.

His lips slanted into a smile. "Has he? What a clever mouse our Asher has turned out to be."

"Asher isn't *ours*," Lev said.

"Of course. You've always been so terrible at sharing."

Silas jumped down from the credenza without a sound and hopped onto the table beside Lev's plate. Lev looked away. He hadn't wanted Silas like that in decades.

"What else did he say about me?" Silas kicked his legs at the knee.

Lev almost smiled. *Almost.* The tragedy of being haunted by the man who'd once been his brother and later his lover, was that there were so many more years of Silas to be missed, the hundred different versions of himself as he grew over the years—in this case the rare kittenish and playful side of himself fishing for compliments.

"He suspects you're important."

Silas tipped his nose up. "As he should."

Lev leaned back in his chair and scrubbed his face with his hands. "I don't know what to do with him."

Objectively speaking, canceling the retreat and sending Asher home was the only sensible solution.

Lev had put his hands on the lad when he'd found him in front of Silas's door. He could have hurt him. He *couldn't* hurt him. But Mr. Hyde was always lurking, a raven perched on the branch of a barren tree.

"Well, you can't punt him back to America," Silas said. "He's far better company than you are."

"At least on that we can agree."

The pages of Asher's sketchbook had been elucidating. The poor lad thought his entire artistic career hinged on the mentorship. From a pedagogical standpoint, he'd be remiss not to nurture his talent.

Not to mention, he couldn't send Asher home when he didn't know if his home was safe. Lichenmoor wasn't safe either, but Lev couldn't shake the fear that someone in Asher's life, past or present, Ben or otherwise, had conditioned his exaggerated reactions to loud noises and Lev testing his temperature.

"After you kill him, perhaps he'll stay and play with me," Silas said, trailing his fingers around the rim of Lev's teacup.

"You're not his type."

"Keep telling yourself that, Levvy. He's fascinated by *my* portrait." Silas cocked his head to the side. "I do have an idea."

"Go on."

"You could draw inspiration from Father's teaching methods and keep your pretty American at arm's length under the rigid roles of teacher and student."

The unearned use of *Father* still rankled. Lucian had never asked Silas to call him that, nor had he called Silas son.

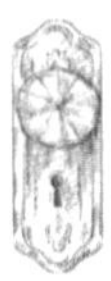

"I hope it doesn't rain today," Silas had said one morning. He'd been ten, one year younger than Lev's eleven. "Father, what does the paper say?"

Wendell had already gone upstairs. Perhaps Silas was unaware? Surely he would never have been so presumptuous as to call Lucian *Father*, even if Wendell and Lucian had been playing house for years.

Ever so slowly, Lucian had lowered his newspaper. "Silas, there's no need for such formal language. We're all friends here, aren't we?" Then he'd retreated behind his newspaper again while Lev could only stare.

Father's chilly treatment and gentle reminders had done little to discourage Silas over the years thereafter—reprimands were a privilege reserved for blood heirs, apparently.

In the end, Father had affected a very rare form of highly selective hearing loss, lest he offend Wendell.

Lev had been furious. Silas already *had* two parents. How dare he ask for another when Lev had lost his mum?

When their relationship had later turned romantic, Lev put his foot down, but Silas had replied, "It doesn't matter if I call Lucian Father when you treat me like a brother."

Lev's insistence that they avoid sexual intimacy until Silas was of age was a frequent point of contention, but it was one boundary Lev refused to cross.

When Wendell died, Lev had been grateful Silas had carved out a back-up family, and grateful he'd never betrayed Wendell by sleeping with his son.

All the bloody good that did in the end.

"Father's methods could backfire," Lev said.

"You need to trust me."

Lev snorted.

As if he could ever trust the walking unreliable narrator of a man. Inviting Asher to Lichenmoor had been Lev's idea, but Silas had encouraged him, and that gnawed at Lev.

Silas always had a motive, usually self-serving. What was in it for him?

"All in due time, Brother."

Lev rubbed his temples with his fingers. "I don't have the time to learn the truth breadcrumb by breadcrumb." He lifted his teacup.

Silas lunged for Lev's wrist with the unsettling speed of cockroaches scuttling away from light. Lev couldn't feel him, but his intentions were clear.

"You need to sleep."

"I have to walk the shoreline."

"My body isn't there."

Lev buried his face in his hands. "What if it is?"

"It isn't."

"You can't know that."

"I think it's safe to assume that my decades-old remains haven't washed ashore on a Sunday."

"But the storm…"

"The storm was a sneeze compared to the spate of tempests we've had since my death." Silas moved behind Lev's chair, draping weightless arms down Lev's front, lips hovering near his ear. "Rest your head."

"It's not like you to take care of me," Lev said.

"I know. I hate myself already."

Lev folded his arms into a makeshift pillow on the table and lowered his head. "I don't deserve your care."

"No. You do not," Silas said, almost fondly, and began to sing.

> Sleep, sleep, sleep.
> Don't stray too close to the edge.
> Or little gray wolf will grab you by the head.
> Drag you into the woods, and to your death.
> Now sleep, sleep, sleep.
> Go to bed.

It was a sinister version of an already macabre lullaby, sung in a tinny doppelgänger of the living Silas's voice, hollow like a music box with the lid open, a cracked porcelain ballerina forever pirouetting in a frayed tutu.

Silas used to sing the original when Lev couldn't sleep after he'd lost his mum.

A silent tear slid down the side of Lev's nose and onto his forearm. He closed his eyes and pretended that the old Silas was with him, not the Silas who'd died and come back all wrong, or the Silas he'd become before he died.

Perhaps if he tried long enough, he could fool himself into believing that Silas had never died at all.

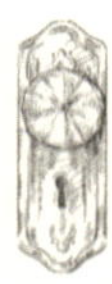

The half-moon shadows beneath Asher's eyes were even darker than the night before.

"Alright there, Blakely?"

Asher nodded and claimed a seat across the table between Julian and Theo.

Hm. Lev had expected at least a snarky *Yes, sir,* if not a shy smirk.

Was Asher well? He'd arrived several minutes after the others, and upon closer inspection, looked a bit pale. Was he embarrassed about last night, or unnerved to find his sketchbook slipped under his door with the map of Lichenmoor?

Maybe Lev should have hidden the sketchbook where Asher would find it, or held onto it, but he hadn't wanted to risk someone else taking it, or Asher searching for it.

Asher selected a piece of toast and spooned beans onto it, then folded it in half like a taco. Lev smiled, pleased to see him eating with more gusto. Now that all were present, Lev tucked into his muesli-dusted yogurt.

Between spoonfuls, Lev surreptitiously studied Asher so he could draw him later, memorizing the way his fingers blanched around his glass, the way he avoided eye contact unless roped into conversation, the way his mood dimmed when no one was looking.

Lev wiped his mouth with a napkin and tossed it onto the table. Silence fell at once.

"Seeing as we're halfway through, I thought I'd share which artists have captured my attention most." He inhaled, puffing up his chest and pausing for dramatic effect, then settled his eyes on Asher. "Theo Laurenti."

Asher's face blanked, neither surprised nor crestfallen.

"Well done, Theo." Lev clapped slowly. The more syco-phantic artists—Chuck, Lars, and Julian—joined in with an awkward round of low-energy applause.

Asher twisted toward Theo and smiled. "Congratulations."

How was Lev supposed to listen to Asher talk without getting hard when he knew what his voice sounded like when he came?

"*Merci*." Theo's eyes lingered on Asher's face, his hand lingering longer still.

Reaching beneath his chair, Lev retrieved Theo's glass sculpture—a tangled mess of glass strands spun as thin as silk threads. One wrong move, a single gasp, and it would collapse. He wanted to break it. Chuck it in the bin. Hurl it across the room and smash it to bits. Cut his fingers on it. All because Theo'd had the audacity to talk to Asher.

"It was a close call," Lev continued, feeling ever the arse-hole when Asher's eyes flashed to him. "Julian's photograph of gulls pecking at a sickly pigeon was haunting, and I quite enjoyed the ocean's Wrath, but Theo's glass art was an orgy of excess, and captured precisely the mood of your first night here. Not to mention, he's smashed every other challenge."

He marshaled a few words of praise for Daria, Melody, and Lars. By that point, Chuck glowered at his plate, hands fisted on the table like a toddler about to have a tantrum.

Meanwhile, Asher's gaze never wavered. Lev was supposed to be judging Asher, but it was Lev who felt unworthy.

"Blakely." Lev clicked his tongue. "While I'm enthralled by your concept, your execution is missing something. You need to push beyond your comfort zone."

Lies. All of it.

But a good teacher saved his sharpest edge for the one who held the most promise. Lev would push Asher away until only a student-teacher relationship remained, exactly as Lucian had done between father and son.

It would hurt Asher, but it would keep him safe.

"Chuck, I'm afraid that leaves you last," Lev said, not caring to spare him a glance. "Don't despair. You still have four sins to impress me with. For our next sin, I can't think of one better than Envy. As you were."

Conversation and the scrape and clatter of silverware against plates resumed. Asher swiveled back to Theo, so close their knees likely touched. Lev didn't like that. At all.

Asher leaned in as Theo attempted to charm him with stories about his hometown in the French countryside, making it sound far more romantic than what it was—a literal *hamlet* populated with more pigs than humans.

Lev rose from his chair, rounded the table, and wrapped his hand around Asher's shoulder. "I do hope you're better able to perform today, Blakely. Any plans?"

Asher shrugged out of Lev's grip. "Lichenmoor's stone walls have such fascinating textures. I thought I might try a bit of *frottage*."

Cheeky bastard.

"Julian, do you mind passing the syrup?" Asher asked.

"Sure." Julian handed it over.

After pouring the syrup on his untouched French toast, Asher held Lev's gaze and kissed a sticky drop from the side of his thumb as if he wanted to remind Lev how delicious he tasted, as if Lev needed any reminder at all, as if Lev hadn't touched himself to the very memory, as if Lev wasn't desperate to taste him again, to taste him everywhere.

"You'd be wise to forget *frottage*," Lev said. "Most people regret it the morning after."

"Maybe you're doing it wrong."

Theo laughed mid-swig and choked on his orange juice, but survived. Alas.

Silas whistled behind Lev's ear, mimicking the sound of a plane crashing and then exploding. "I really, really like him."

Oh, fuck off, Lev said inside his head.

Silas appeared on the credenza. "Competence and quick

wit." He bit into his bottom lip and rolled his eyes heavenward. "Delicious."

"I'm sorry, but can someone please explain what *frotting* is?" Lars asked.

Lev blinked, severing eye contact. Julian hid his laughter behind his napkin and a cough.

"*Frottage*," Theo corrected. "You place paper over a textured surface and rub it with a charcoal or some other implement to transfer the pattern."

Lev wrinkled his nose. "We're all so lucky to have you here to educate us, Mr. Laurenti."

"Maybe Theo can demonstrate *frottage* next," Asher said. "He looks like he knows how to create something satisfying."

Lev resisted the urge to sling back a witty retort. Theo's gaze bounced between them with dawning awareness, and Julian's hawklike eyes narrowed on Lev with suspicion. The last thing he needed was the others catching wind.

"Personally, I think *frottage* is a tired trend best left in the thirties," Chuck said in a smug tone Lev had come to despise.

"Nobody asked for your opinion, Chuck," Daria said, Spanish accent more pronounced. "Thanks for breakfast." She tossed her napkin on her plate, and left, black curls swaying with her hips as she stalked from the room.

"She didn't sleep well," Melody said. "May I be excused?"

Lev nearly snapped at her but softened his tone. "You can do whatever you wish whenever you wish. As I've said before, this isn't a classroom."

Melody nodded, and hurried after Daria.

Were they fast friends or something more? The others followed suit. Asher hadn't finished his beans and toast.

"Perhaps he's like me, Levvy," Silas said far too cheerfully.

No. Asher didn't have the build of someone who starved himself.

Still, as Lev washed and dried their dishes, he couldn't help but fear that something was amiss.

14

APATHY IS WORSE

ASHER

The veil of fog had burned off and sunlight streamed through the lattice-paned windows, turning Asher's room into a greenhouse.

Asher ripped off his hoodie and hurled it onto the bed. Whatever Lev's problem was, Asher's art was faultless. He was damn proud of his new take on the series.

He'd even painted a second version of Gluttony so he could continue his story with the fairies feeding a poisonous last meal to their human guests. Then, for Wrath, the fairies had fertilized their poisonous plants with the tainted blood of their victims, potentiating the lethality of the next batch of poison in an endless cycle of growth and destruction.

Achieving that level of concentrated color had taken hours of experimenting, and hours more of patient precision as he layered brush strokes, lest he poison his entire painting with pigment.

Lev had no business ranking him so low, especially if he'd only done so because of last night, or because he'd snooped through Asher's sketchbook and wanted to distance himself from a fanatical stalker.

That well-worn sketchbook was his home; a friend that

reminded him who he was and validated his emotions. Lev had broken his promise and violated Asher's privacy.

He crossed to the window and twisted the brass crank, but it was stuck. For a fleeting moment, he feared Lev had bolted the windows, locking him inside Lichenmoor like the figure in the east wing, but finally the wheel turned, and with a hollow crack like a baguette snapped in half, the thick layer of paint surrounding the frame broke.

Crisp autumn air and birdsong slipped into the room, accompanied by the distant sound of the ebbing tide. It was the first time he'd seen a blue sky since he'd arrived at Lichenmoor. Hell, it was the first time he'd truly *seen* Lichenmoor.

Verdant hills dotted with oak trees and pockets of forest sloped down toward bluffs overlooking a rocky beach and, beyond that, the North Sea. An old stone road meandered from Lichenmoor's front door down through soggy lowlands sparkling with sunlit puddles. The path didn't look so long and winding now that he wasn't wading through fog.

Lev paced at the edge of the bluff. His red hair glowing in the sunlight made him impossible to miss. Even at a distance, Lev took up so much space he was almost omnipresent. Lev turned, and looked at Asher's window.

Asher ducked, and facepalmed with a groan. There were dozens of windows on that side of the castle. It's not like Lev could have sensed him watching. Asher was acting like a child, just like he had last night when he ran away from Lev. Twice.

The wardrobe was heavier than it looked. After pulling it away from the wall, Asher checked for another door behind it, but the tapestry was nailed down. Good.

Wood groaned against wood like a ship's hull breaking apart as Asher pushed it across the room, gouging marks in the floor.

"Shit."

His stomach clenched with guilt, almost as if by wounding Lichenmoor, he'd harmed something alive. Beneath the guilt, however, a part of him liked that he'd left a mark on Lichen-moor, at least until Lev refinished the floors.

He pulled off his long-sleeve, ignoring the tattoo of Lev's eye on his forearm as he wiped his face.

At least if Lev wanted to spy on him, or kidnap him, he'd have to enter through the squeaky main entrance or shimmy up the castle wall like a normal stalker.

If Lev cared to stalk him any longer.

A floorboard creaked. Asher suppressed a shiver, feeling eyes on him as he stripped, even though that wasn't possible. The castle had a way of feeling occupied, even when no one was around, like all the people who'd passed through Lichen-moor had left an imprint.

A door slammed. Asher jumped.

Heavy footsteps hurried down the hallway, landing louder as Lev drew closer. It had to be him. No one else walked with the power and frenetic energy of a thunderstorm. Besides, no one else resided on their floor.

More proof that Lev was up to something.

The footsteps stopped. Lev's door opened and shut. Lev's presence chased away the unease Asher had felt when he was alone.

Asher imagined him kicking off his boots. A moment later, the shower started. He was probably undressing, exposing freckled skin flushed from his run, a bead of sweat dripping down his sternum that Asher would swipe with his tongue before lowering to his knees.

Lev would stroke Asher's hair like one would a pet and take back everything he'd said, tell Asher he was a good lad, lavish his art with praise, explain he'd treated him that way because he didn't want the others to know he'd already selected his winner, that of course it was him.

Mimicking his fantasy, Asher slid to his knees, facing the wall between their rooms. He spat into his hand and worked his cock with the punishing grip he imagined Lev would have. He focused on the tattoo of Lev's eye on his forearm.

"Eyes on me," Lev would have said, reminding Asher each time his lids closed with pleasure. "Look at you on your knees for me, slutty mouth waiting to be fucked."

Asher would ask if he could taste him, and Lev would laugh darkly and say only after Asher came first, and the reward promised would push Asher over the precipice. The sight of Asher getting off would take Lev by surprise with an orgasm of his own, and he'd guide his tip toward Asher's waiting mouth, lips already parted on a moan.

"Don't you dare swallow," Lev would warn as he milked his thick dick.

Then Lev would feed him the cum that hadn't made it into his mouth, rubbing Asher's jaw with his thumb, and finally command him to swallow.

Lev would tell him what a good lad he'd been, how well he'd listened, how much that pleased him, and with eyes still locked on Lev's tattooed gaze, Asher came all over the tapestry.

Utterly spent, Asher sat back on his heels, planting his palms on his knees as he caught his breath.

Shame and self-loathing swept in. Lev had humiliated him in front of his peers, and in retaliation Asher had... What? Jacked off to a feral fantasy and ejaculated on an antique tapestry?

"Fuck," Asher whispered as he blotted the cum with his shirt.

"Stupid, stupid boy," Ben would have said, and he'd be right. Two weeks at Lichenmoor and he'd already lost himself to an obsession with an older man who didn't respect him. Just like Ben.

Did Lev tell all the artists he bedded that he'd fallen in love with them through a painting?

He never should have come here. He was weak. Too much.

No one wanted him beyond his role as a sex doll marionette performing with each string plucked. No one truly *knew* him.

Last night, he'd hoped Lev could be the one person who *did* know him because they'd met through their art, but that was just a pick-up line he'd fallen for.

Fuck. He sniffed.

His tear-glazed eyes caught on something scratched into the baseboard under the bed, standing out from centuries of dents and nicks.

NUMQUAM OBLIVISCARIS ME

He traced the letters with his fingertips. It looked like Latin. Who'd carved it into the baseboard and when?

Sunlight pierced the stained glass windows, scattering gemstones along the empty hallway. The crypt-like silence made him feel more like he was walking into the maw of a hungry beast than taking a shortcut to the ballroom.

Asher consulted Lev's map again. He was running late after taking a last-minute shower. If he wasn't completely lost, and that was a big *if*, the next left turn should dead-end at a side door to the church.

From there, he could pass through a hidden door in the priest's quarters and arrive from behind a bookshelf tucked inside an alcove. In a tiny script, much tidier than the east wing's warning, Lev had promised this passageway was short, just a few paces.

Lev had scribbled out the entire third floor of the east wing save for a warning written in the center:

Dangerous. Forbidden

Much like Lev, himself.

The warning was a waste of ink Asher would ignore. He had to see what was inside that locked room, even if it meant braving the secret passageway without Lev, even if it meant facing the shadowy silhouette he'd seen through the keyhole.

But he wasn't ready to risk Lev's wrath when he still felt the ghost of his grip lurching him back from the door last night. He'd wait at least until after he'd secured the mentorship.

Asher rounded the corner and met an oak door with a stained glass cross, and pushed it open. A pigeon leaped into flight from a nest perched atop a life-size statue of Christ on a crucifix, face painted with bird droppings.

"Jesus." He laughed a disembodied burst of nerves from his lips.

The door boomed shut behind him, startling him a second time. He inhaled, attempting to rein in his stuttering heartbeat.

The cathedral was in far worse shape than the forbidden east wing. Disemboweled Bibles and their torn-out pages littered the floor. The pulpit had fallen on its side and rested on the dais like a corpse. Charred pews piled in one corner, remnants of a sacrilegious pyre. A few rows of pews remained untouched, loyal servants facing the empty dais, spared by their god, or whoever had interrupted the arsonist.

The level of destruction was far more than years of neglect would have left. Who was responsible? Lev? Or had it been like that for decades?

He walked down the center aisle, tensing as he passed each row of high-backed pews. On his right, a wall of stained glass, most of it intact, faced seaward. In one window, Tudor roses cascaded from Christ's crucifixion instead of blood.

At the top of the dais, he scanned for the priest's door, and stopped. Ice dumped into his bloodstream. Someone was sitting in the last pew.

What. The. Fuck?

Wait. He blinked. No. There was no person there, just the shadow of a statue of the Virgin Mary. Hallowed silence was his only company.

He shook his head, exhaling his relief. He needed to catch up on his sleep or Lichenmoor would turn into a waking nightmare.

Hopefully he could finish his painting of Envy quickly and take a nap after lunch. He already knew what he was going to make, but he wasn't sure if the result would impress Lev or enrage him.

He wasn't sure if he cared.

15

TWO HALVES

ASHER

Everyone else was already at work.

Lev lifted his head from Chuck's angular pastel piece. "Late again, Blakely?"

"Took a wrong turn. Bad directions. Besides, I thought this wasn't a classroom."

Lev's mouth opened and shut. Guess he didn't have a witty retort for that. Good.

Asher dropped his watercolor kit at a table by a window, filled two glasses with water in the trough-sized sink, and set to work.

Lev spent the next two hours bouncing around the room, lavishing praise on the other artists like he was trying to capture Asher's attention on purpose, while ignoring him entirely.

Whatever. Surprising Lev with the finished product would yield an even stronger reaction. He couldn't wait.

Lev said he valued honest art over all others. But did he? How much of the truth could he take?

"On the way to star painter again, I see, Theo." Lev stood behind him, bending as if to get a closer look, were he not instead checking over his shoulder for Asher's reaction.

107

Asher rolled his eyes. Lev might have been a master artist, but he lacked the art of subtlety.

"Thanks, Lev." Theo gave Asher an apologetic smile.

Asher shot Theo a thumbs up. A thumbs up? What was he, an elementary schooler?

He shook his head and applied a moody mix of yellow ochre and burnt umber, then added it to the curve of the shoulder he'd sketched, the slope of a trapezius, the valley behind the clavicle.

"Not the teacher's pet anymore," Chuck said from the easel to his left.

"You win some and you lose some," Asher said breezily.

"How do you know Lev?" Chuck asked.

"I don't." Asher mixed yellow hansa with rose and added water until he'd created a fair peach tone.

"We were all sure you were a nepotism invite."

Lars walked over. "What are you two talking about?"

"We weren't talking," Asher said.

"I was just having a laugh," Chuck said. "No need to take it personally."

Lars's eyes crawled over Asher's painting. "What are you making?"

Asher didn't answer. Thanks to Ben, he hated painting in front of other people, let alone Tweedledee and Tweedle Trust Fund.

"I think he's giving us the silent treatment," Chuck said.

Asher feigned a sigh. "If only it were silent."

Chuck leaned over and jerked the leg of Asher's table toward him, knocking over the water cups, and sending a tidal wave toward his painting.

One glass rolled off the table and shattered on the stone floor.

Theo met Asher's eyes, a silent question—*Do you want help?* Asher shook his head.

In one swift motion, he lifted the other glass and yanked

the table leg out of Chuck's hand. "I'm not interested in measuring dicks."

A shadow blocked the warm sunlight against his back, darkening Asher's miraculously unscathed painting.

"While the idea of you coming to fisticuffs over my mentorship is rather flattering, it's disrupting the other artists," Lev said. "There's a dust pan and broom in the supply room. Clean this up and keep your eyes on your own work, lads."

Asher remained seated, assuming that he wasn't one of the lads in question, and resumed painting. Lev's shadow lingered long after Chuck and Lars swept up the broken glass.

"Can I help you?" Asher's skin prickled, his body heated with flames stoked by Lev's masculine scent and the occasional caress of his breath on the back of his neck.

"This is quite the deviation from your dark color scheme. Playing it safe?" Lev paused, then added, "Broken glass, not withstanding."

Asher peppered freckles on the page before answering. "I'm not playing it safe."

"What are you painting?"

"My interpretation of envy."

"A hand on a shoulder? I don't see the connection."

"You'll have to wait until it's finished."

"You misunderstand, Blakely. I want you to explain the connection, and if you want to win my mentorship, you'll do well to answer."

With a fresh brush, Asher blended white with the faintest trace of rose and violet.

"Blakely," Lev said.

"*Marks*," Asher parroted back.

He wouldn't let Lev play the uptight art professor after he looked at his sketchbook and spent the day acting like a child. He painted one thin crescent on the forearm, a second crescent, a third.

Lev inhaled sharply.

Asher added the fourth and final scar. "There. Finished. Your hand on my shoulder when I was talking to Theo. Textbook envy." He snapped his palette closed and dropped his brushes in his cup.

"Not so fast." Wood legs scuffed the stone like nails on a chalkboard as Lev spun Asher's chair around, and planted his hands on either side of the seat, caging him in. Lev lowered his voice to a menacing whisper. "How do you know about my scars?"

What was his problem? It's not like Lev had covered them like Asher did with his tattoos. For all Asher's internet stalking, the only thing he knew about Lev's scars was that he had them.

"Oh, I'm sorry," Asher said, regaining his dignity. "I didn't realize you were insecure about them. If you want me to paint over them, make the next sin Pride and you've got a deal."

"Answer me," Lev hissed.

"You read my sketchbook. You tell me."

Lev lowered his voice quieter still. "What? Am I some fixation of yours?"

"In a professional sense? Sure. You were. Now, if you'll back the fuck off..." He shoved against the stone wall of Lev's chest.

Lev didn't even flinch.

"Move," Asher said, running out of bravado fast.

He needed to leave before something terrible happened, like he popped a hate-boner because there was something broken inside of him that wanted to fuck Lev as much as he wanted to punch him. But Lev wasn't even looking at him.

Lev's brows darted together. His head cocked to the side, attention snared by something over Asher's shoulder. He went eerily still, breath caught in his chest mid-inhale like he had that first breakfast when he'd paused in the middle of his sentence.

At the time, Asher had written it off as Lev losing his train of thought, but his expression had been similar then. Not confusion or a blank stare. Alert. Almost as if he was listening.

"Lev?" He pushed against Lev's chest again.

"Sorry," Lev said vacantly, and backed away, gaze still fixed on whatever had caught his attention.

Asher swirled around. But there was no one there. Only the same view through the window of lazy waves, blue skies, and a thin wisp of fog.

Seizing the chance to make a somewhat graceful exit while he had it, Asher swiped his sketchbook from his table and stuffed it inside his hoodie, then skirted around Lev.

Everyone was staring.

The ocean had probably covered some of their conversation. How much had they heard?

He quickened his pace, desperate to escape as a panic attack threatened, then lurched to a stop, wrist shackled by Lev's hand.

"I'm not finished with you yet," Lev said.

Asher froze at the hint of Lev's fingernails kissing his forearm. Regret crossed his mind first, but not for any sane reason.

He wished he hadn't worn long sleeves, because maybe if he fought to free himself, Leviathan Marks, his hero, his god, would tighten his grip and leave a mark, one Asher could later slice open with a razor's edge and add ink into the wound bed to make sure it scarred.

The epiphany slid into place crescent by crescent, then all at once. He looked down at Lev's hand on his wrist.

The scars were the marks of fingernails buried in skin.

Asher wrenched his arm back, dragging Lev toward him, and said against his ear, "So, that's how you got those scars."

Lev released Asher's arm, stunned. But not for long. In a

blur of motion, Lev ripped Asher's painting from the table and tore it in half down the center.

Silence fell, a silence so complete, it was as if Lichenmoor itself had choked on a gasp, as if every blade of grass on the moor had stilled, as if the very ocean had paused its endless tides to watch the two halves drift to the ground.

"You didn't complete the assignment as directed. I'm afraid I have no choice but to give you another F."

Sound came back all at once, starting with the roar of blood in his ears. Fury thrummed through his body like a drug. He balled his hands into fists.

Lev's lip curled. "You aren't going to hit me, are you?"

"You just threw a tantrum and now you want to act like I'm the unstable one? Fuck you."

"Asher," Theo said, placing his palm on Asher's back.

How long had he been standing there?

"You should listen to him," Lev said.

Asher charged forward, stopping short of slamming into Lev's chest. "You told me you wanted art that was honest, and I gave it to you, but you can't even look at it."

"Don't cry, Blakely. It's only art."

Asher laughed humorlessly. "You're such a fucking hypocrite."

"Watch your tone."

"Or what? You'll send me home?" Asher patted Lev roughly on the lapel of his ridiculously overdressed navy blazer. "I think I've learned everything I need to know, sir." He spun on his heel and left.

Leviathan Marks was nobody's hero, let alone his.

LICK THE PLATE CLEAN

LEV

"Well, that was embarrassing," Silas said.

Lev retrieved the torn pages from the floor.

"I didn't realize we were grading them like children in primary school," Silas continued. "But if we are grading them, Asher deserves at least a B+. That was the best art I've seen at Lichenmoor in decades." He stroked his chin. "No. I think I'd bring him up to a solid A for sheer swagger on the exit. Be careful, Levvy. Our Asher has sharp claws."

"Shut the fuck up," Lev whispered under his breath. Louder for the others, who still looked on, he barked, "Back to work!"

Lev crumpled Asher's painting into a ball and crossed to the fireplace.

"What are you—" Silas lunged.

Lev chucked the paper ball into the flames.

"No!" Silas dropped to his knees in front of the fire, fingers sifting through the flames without purchase. "No," he said softly, shoulders slumping forward.

Silas looked up from his empty palms and glared at Lev with utmost loathing. It was a look that pointed fingers, a look that said *Monster*, a look that shouted, *MURDERER!*

It was the look Silas would have given Lev if he'd had the chance before he died.

Silas leapt from the hearth and ran at him with spider-like speed. "How could you?"

Lev moved around him.

"You need to go after him," Silas said, reappearing in Lev's path. "What if he leaves?"

"Then so be it." Lev walked through him.

"But the tide will take him!"

"Sod the tide!"

"Lev, are you alright?" Melody asked, eyes round.

Damn and blast! How much of that had he said aloud? He needed to get out of there.

If the outside world knew he was losing it, bad actors would intervene under the guise of good intentions. They'd wrest Lichenmoor from him, auction off Father's art, the art Lev had made of Silas, his priceless collection of Asher's art.

How would he ever find Silas's body if he was forced from Lichenmoor? The thought of leaving terrified him.

"Please excuse me for a moment," Lev said and sped from the room.

"Good. You've seen reason." Silas joined him, spindly legs matching his stride.

He hadn't seen reason. Anger propelled him as he shoved the door open.

Curse that insufferable American for whatever hex he must have cast to captivate him and unearth all of his secrets with his maddening clairvoyance.

His shoes clicked like a typewriter in the hands of someone writing a manifesto as he stalked toward the archway where the floor met wild moor. The walls of Lichenmoor were closing in, the bars of his jail cell tightening around him.

"You're going the wrong way," Silas said.

"How would you know?"

"I see everything, Levvy. You know that. Now stop talking

to me out in the open or people are going to think you're insane."

Lev skidded to a stop. "You're making me look insane!"

"Me?" Silas laughed. "You're doing it all by yourself."

Lev fisted his fingers in his hair.

"You need to trust me," Silas said with less venom. "There's a reason we picked him."

"No. I found him. I picked him. You're not real."

"He's probably packing as we speak."

"Good riddance."

"You can't be that thick. Given the state he's in, I doubt he'd even think to check the tide clock. Our Asher has a terrible sense of direction."

"Mine, not ours."

"Even if he knows about those scars I gave you, which he doesn't, do you want him to meet Father's fate?"

The bastard had a point. High tide crept ever nearer, dragging a blanket of fog with it. Lev would sooner drown than let the sea swallow Asher.

Silas leaned against the wall and buffed his nails on his black shirt, a perfect picture of nonchalance. "He's not religious, is he?"

The church! Of course. If Asher was following his map, he might still be there. The abandoned church was an excellent place for sulking. Lev knew so personally.

"I hate it there," Silas said.

Yes, that was why Lev had suggested it as a route on Asher's map. Even after all these years, Silas still refused to enter.

Lev turned around, passed the ballroom, and hung a left before breaking into a run. A few minutes later, he stopped in front of an inglenook seating area wedged into an arched alcove.

He plucked a weathered copy of *The Brothers Karamazov*

from the bookcase beside the fireplace, unlatched the lock hidden behind it, and pulled the bookcase open.

"What are you going to do when you find him?" Silas asked.

Lev didn't know. The urge to fight or fuck was all-consuming.

He shelved *The Brothers Karamazov* and shut the bookcase behind himself.

"You won't break him," Silas's muffled voice called from the other side. "He's strong. That's why we picked him."

Strong didn't mean invincible.

Lev raced through the short passage, squeezed under the squat door in the priest's quarters, and rushed out onto the dais. The chapel was empty.

He hurried down the center aisle, and stopped, spine sagging with relief. Asher lay on his back on a pew bench, eyes closed, hands folded over his chest like he was in a casket, beloved sketchbook rested beneath his joined hands like he'd wanted to be buried with it.

All the earlier flush had faded from his cheeks, the angry bend of his eyebrows smoothed out, his breathing slow and shallow. The poor lad must be knackered. The church was more nightmare fodder than a place to relax.

The urge to stroke Asher's dark waves out of his face and press a kiss on his forehead was terrifyingly strong. Try as he might, he couldn't erase the caregiving role he'd taken on with Silas. It reverberated throughout all his relationships.

He eyed the sketchbook. Had Asher added an entry that would explain what he knew about Lev's scars and what he planned to do with the information?

No harm in taking one last look.

Holding his breath, he crept closer and reached for the topmost corner of the sketchbook. Asher tightened his grip. Hazel eyes blinked open.

"You're not allowed to complain about my nose anymore," Asher said.

Lev swallowed hard.

Asher's voice, husky with sleep, sounded exactly as he'd imagined it last night. Throat all raw and swollen from swallowing Lev's cock, voice worn out after Lev made him come over and over until it hurt. It was a voice only a lover would hear. Pillow talk.

"I don't recall ever complaining about your nose," Lev said.

Asher's nose was perfect, masculine with a little pert he longed to kiss, not that he would ever tell him that.

"You said I was nosy," Asher said, sitting up. "But you're the one stealing my sketchbook."

"Ah. That." Lev sighed.

"You crossed a line," Asher said flatly.

"I know, but I have a very hard time coloring inside the lines, and you simply draw so many of them."

Asher's eyes hardened. "Lucian might have spoiled you, but in the real world, you can't have whatever you want."

That rankled. Asher couldn't possibly understand the expectation of perfection Lucian had demanded, or the creative punishments he'd crafted. Had Asher's father ever forced him to paint his dead lover as punishment? Surely not.

"You aren't in the real world. You're at Lichenmoor." Lev thrust his arms out. "Look around. You're in my castle, and I am your lord."

"It's not a castle," Asher said.

"Why are you so fucking contrary?"

"I don't know," Asher said between hastened breaths as he scrambled to his feet. "Maybe because you're so fucking condescending."

Lev scoffed. "I don't condescend."

Asher rolled his eyes. "*Okay.*"

"Why are you here, Blakely?"

"I was lying in wait for would-be thieves." Asher crossed

his arms over his chest. "Where were you running off to? You weren't chasing me again, were you?"

"Of course not." Lev lifted his chin. "I had an urgent matter to attend to."

"Bathroom emergency?" Asher stepped aside. "Don't let me stop you."

"I beg your pardon?"

"Sorry, I forgot." Asher mimicked quotation marks with his fingers and said, "A loo emergency."

"What on earth are you going on about?"

"Your urgent matter to attend to. I assumed that was the snobby English term for it—that, or you're full of shit."

Lev's nose wrinkled. "Crass jokes are beneath you, Blakely."

"Oh my God! Talk like someone from this century."

"I am. Read a book, and you'll understand." God, he loved fighting with the lad.

"Did they teach you that at Oxford? Talk down to the plebes when you want to win a fight. Confuse the commoners by talking like you have a thesaurus shoved up your ass. Or do you do it because you're insecure? Want to know what I think?"

Lev lifted his eyes to the cathedral ceiling. "Please spare me."

"I think you came to apologize, and now you're too scared."

"Whatever for? You're the one who behaved like an insolent prat."

"Me? You ripped my painting in half."

"Please don't tell me you wanted to take your picture home to hang on Mummy's fridge? It's a bit late for that." Lev stroked his chin. "If you check the fireplace, you might find a handful of ashes for a souvenir."

At first, Asher's face fell like a child at Christmas who'd found nothing under the tree. Then, his eyes cycled through all five stages of grief, from naïve denial to grim acceptance, before bouncing back to anger again.

"You burned my painting?"

"It wasn't art!" Lev snapped.

Asher shook his head as if he could shake loose everything Lev had said before it took root and spread. "What a disappointment you turned out to be."

Father would agree.

"You were a fool to put your faith in me," Lev said.

"If only I'd known you were an old hack with an ego so fragile you can't stand to be bested by me." Unshed tears illuminated the gold flecks in Asher's gaze like embers. "I want to know why. Why am I here? Why bring me to Lichenmoor only to destroy me?"

"Destroying you was never my intention. I..."

What could he tell him? *The truth is, I've been obsessed with your art for years, but was too afraid to invite you until my dead ex-boyfriend pestered me into action, and now that you're here, I don't know what to do with you because I can't have you, but I can't not have you.*

"I think you're threatened by my talent, and that's not just disappointing. It's pathetic."

Asher's sharp shoulder slammed into Lev as he pushed past him and strode off down the center aisle.

"Your art doesn't threaten me. You do," Lev called after him.

Asher turned, a fragile wisp of hope glimmering in his eyes. "Why?"

"I want you. I shouldn't, but I do."

The hope in Asher's eyes died. "Do people actually fall for that? *Oh, woe is me. I'm so hopelessly besotted, but I can't have you, and I'm too much of a coward to tell you, so I pushed you away.*"

Lev's heart clenched at the pain in his voice. Fuck Asher for being so heartbreakingly beautiful when hurt, for making Lev feel guilty, for not accepting the truth when he was finally speaking it.

"I only meant..." Lev rubbed his jawline, soothed by the bite of his beard against his palm. "Last night rattled me. No. Strike that. You've rattled me since the moment we met. Before that, even.

"I met you through your art first, and perhaps that bred a false sense of familiarity. I'm not sure. But you already have me wrapped around your finger and climbing the walls, drawing maps and worrying about your safety while simultaneously wanting to throttle you for being so aggravating.

"You were right. I was afraid, and I said things about your art that weren't true. Father said the best artists were made after they were broken. I figured—"

"I don't give a fuck about what your father said." He shook his head. "All of you dinosaurs are the same. There's no point in learning from you."

"Dinosaurs?"

"You, Ben, gatekeeping men who only open doors after you pay the toll. You wanted something from me last night, and when I didn't give it to you, you slammed the gate shut."

Asher stomped back up the aisle and stabbed the center of Lev's chest with his finger. "Fuck your retreat, fuck your mentorship, and fuck you!"

Each fuck was emphasized with more and more pressure against Lev's sternum. It would leave an Asher-shaped bruise, one that would remind Lev of his cowardice until it faded.

Lev crowded closer, pushing into Asher's finger, willing the bruise to deepen, to become permanent.

"If you're insinuating that I require sexual favors in exchange for teaching you, you're mistaken. There is no gate. No toll. The mentorship is yours. I don't want anyone else."

Asher lowered his finger from Lev's chest. "I don't believe you."

"It's true. If I had any less decorum, I would have made a

joke in very poor taste about how when it comes to tolls, I want you so desperately, I should be the one paying you. But if I had made such a joke, I'd have done so because the idea of you being forced into using sex as currency makes me so furious, I can't think straight."

"It was a metaphor."

"Of course. I was speaking in metaphors too." Lev waved his hand airily, knowing full well that it wasn't a metaphor.

They could discuss this at a future date, but first he needed to convince Asher to stay. He also needed to phone the private investigator he'd hired to look into Ben. He'd assumed Asher was self-taught, but the comment about *opening doors* reeked of art school.

"Jokes and metaphors aside, I'm serious. The mentorship is yours, should you still want it. Whether you accept the mentorship or decline, trust that I'll do everything in my power to ensure your success regardless of your answer."

"Why?" Asher repeated.

"Come now, you must know by now that I'm your biggest fan. The world needs your art, but more importantly, *I* need your art."

Asher laughed, and Lev fell in love with him a little for it, because what he had to say next would be difficult, and the rare gift of Asher's laughter gave him courage.

Inhaling, he reached for Asher's hand but thought better of it and clasped his hands behind his back. He couldn't bear the rejection. He couldn't risk scaring him away. Not before he confessed how much he cared for him.

"Your art is a mirror showing me all the best and worst parts of myself. You make me feel less alone, like there's at least one person out there who knows who I am. But sometimes, like with your watercolor today, it hurts so much I find it hard to look."

"The scars?"

Lev nodded.

"I didn't know. I would never have used them to hurt you."

"I know, but even if you had, I shouldn't have behaved so monstrously."

Dimples flashed at the corner of Asher's lips for the briefest second, a near-smile. "Don't beat yourself up too much. I mean, I was trying to piss you off with that painting."

"Well, you succeeded." Lev's fledgling smile faded. "I've been such an arsehole. I regretted throwing your painting into the flames as soon as it left my hand. You were right about everything.

"Your painting was the very best kind of art, the kind of art that was so honest it hurt. You captured my envy acutely. I envy anyone who has ever dared to touch you. Theo. Ben. Every name you mentioned in your sketchbook. I'm jealous of your own fucking family for having more time with you than I've had."

Asher's tongue darted out to wet his bottom lip. "That's..."

"Borderline obsessive? Completely inappropriate? Not unlike what you drew in your sketchbook? Trust me, I'm fully aware. I want all of you. I don't want to share. If I could, I would devour you and lick the plate clean so no one else could have you except me."

17

PURPLE ON A BLANK CANVAS

LEV

The curtain of disbelief finally fell from Asher's face. "You feel the same way."

It wasn't a question, but Lev nodded anyway. "Yes."

He should have said no. He should have taken everything back, because claiming Asher was condemning him.

Even if their chemistry never fizzled, if their mutual obsession grew into something more, their ending would never be a happy one. Fifteen years separated them. But the devil Lev knew, the one that lurked inside, was better than whatever devil had left Asher so jaded.

Lev didn't believe in fate, but he couldn't deny the cosmic symmetry. In a population of billions, how had they found each other? It was almost as if art was a matchmaker that had brought them together.

So when Asher grabbed him by the lapels and hauled him close enough to kiss, Lev didn't protest, and when Asher licked the seam of his lips, Lev opened his mouth and submitted.

Asher kissed him with a bruising intensity, punishing him with a nip to his bottom lip before he plunged back in again. It was a kiss that said I hate that I want you, and I want to hate you, but I like you too much. It was a kiss that could have been tender, perhaps should have been, but that wasn't them.

They were an earthquake, a wildfire, a tornado, a tsunami. They were a natural fucking disaster. Doomed from the start. It wasn't just a kiss. It was a kiss in the face of grim acceptance, the last kiss before battle, the last kiss before the gallows.

Lev raked his fingers through the midnight waves at the base of Asher's skull, and tilted his head back to break their kiss. God, he was beautiful like this—hazel eyes hidden behind hooded lids, flushed lips curving into a grin.

Asher's smile slipped. "You're not going to ask me to tell you to stop, are you?"

"Definitely not," Lev said, breathless and spellbound. "You kissed me before I could apologize. I'm so sorry for scaring you, for destroying your art, for every wretched thing I've done. How can I make this right?"

Asher licked his decadent lips, and yanked the bottom of Lev's blazer. "Take this off. I hate it. The shirt too."

Laughing, Lev slipped out of his jacket, and tossed it on an empty pew. "I'll never wear it again."

"Good." Asher backed away, and curled his finger, luring Lev toward the exit, a bold dormouse turning predator to prey. "Come here."

"Smart thinking. The things I want to do to you are far too sinful for church." Lev's cock hardened as he freed the first button from his shirt. "Then again, what better place for me to worship you than here?"

Asher's Adam's apple bobbed on a swallow. "Jesus, Lev."

Lev clicked his tongue twice. "Language, Blakely. Taking the Lord's name in church?"

"I wouldn't cast the first stone if I were you. False idolatry is a sin."

"I could accuse you of the same." Lev unfastened the second button, and the third, giving Asher a head start.

"Besides, I don't believe in God, or at least not the one this church was built for."

He'd choose hell over spending eternity with a deity whose senseless actions indicated he was impotent, or cruel.

"There are some things I believe in, however." Lev took a single step forward.

"What?" Asher asked, retreating further.

"Art." He slipped another button free. "Justice." Another button. "The tide." Another button. "You."

"Me?" Asher veered off course, straying from the door.

Lev let him. The church, for all its sins, was one of the few places he could worship Asher properly without Silas interrupting.

"Yes, Blakely. You. I thought I'd made that abundantly clear."

"It's just..." Asher nibbled his bottom lip. "I'm no one. You've done so much. I don't deserve—"

"And you think I do?"

"Yes," Asher said, nodding fervently.

Oh, to be young and idealistic. "I'm afraid you're wrong about that."

Asher opened his mouth to argue.

"I'm nobody's hero, but perhaps one day, I'll become the man you think I am."

Lev ripped the rest of his shirt open, sending the last two buttons skittering across the dusty floor, and surged forward to catch Asher before he bumped into the wall.

"Lost again, little dormouse?"

Asher scowled. "This time doesn't count. You're too distracting." Black lashes fanned his cheeks as he looked Lev's chest up and down. "You're so hot."

Lev started to laugh, but it died in his lungs when Asher touched him just above his trousers. No one had touched him there in five years. Five years.

Fear seized him. What if their chemistry was nothing more

than a mirage forged by loneliness? What if their connection dissolved once they fucked? What if Asher was another fixation and Lev broke his heart?

Asher's hands stilled. "Are you okay?"

Lev forced a smile. "Why wouldn't I be?"

"You stopped breathing."

"I apologize."

Asher's eyes narrowed. His hand dropped. "You can't apologize for not breathing. What's wrong?"

"Please don't stop." Lev returned Asher's hand to his abs. "I hadn't realized how much I missed the touch of another until now."

Asher appraised him, sympathy shadowing his eyes instead of the suspicion Lev feared. "Okay."

"Thank you." Lev exhaled a shuddering sigh.

Asher traced the lines of Lev's six-pack upward, growing bolder as he traveled toward his sternum.

"I can't believe this is real," Asher said.

"Nor can I."

Asher squeezed his pecs and rubbed his thumbs over his nipples. Lev shivered, a good shiver, one that made more room for his heart inside his chest, that had him pressing his heart forward, seeking Asher's touch.

Without words, Asher understood, flattening his palm over his heart. Lev lost all reservations at the gesture, lost all fear that this wasn't real, because it had to be. How could another person understand him so uniquely?

Lev gripped Asher's arse and swept him off his feet, and again, Asher understood, looping his arms around Lev's neck and hooking his legs around his waist to anchor them together.

Capturing Asher's mouth in a kiss, Lev pressed him against the wall. Asher grunted, tongue stalled. Lev should have been more careful.

"Sorry."

But Asher only entwined his legs tighter, cinching their cocks closer. Then, he rolled his hips and thrusted against the place they were connected, showering Lev's spine in sparks.

Lev had never been so keyed up, never felt so out of control. Not yesterday. Never with Silas. Not even the day he'd killed him.

Asher was different.

While Lev had loved Silas like the brother he wasn't and the lover he was, they'd been forced together by circumstance. Lev had never had a choice. But he'd chosen Asher.

He needed to focus on the present, the living, breathing miracle in his hands, the olive skin and rosy cheeks whispering vitality, the hazel eyes of endless depths, not pale blue turned milky, sallow skin lifeless. No, he couldn't think about that.

Only now. Only Asher.

Lev stroked Asher's neck, soothed by the pulse fluttering beneath his skin, and kissed a path down to test Asher's heartbeat with his tongue, but it wasn't enough.

He needed to leave a mark, one that would blossom, then fade, not linger in death. He nipped a soft bite, and sucked hard, forcing the blood from Asher's capillaries, and a bruise into his skin. He couldn't wait to see the first splotch of purple on a blank canvas.

Asher didn't protest. He didn't flinch. He went boneless. *Fuck me.* Asher would make a good little pet.

Leaving his lips there, Lev murmured, "I'm sorry. I'll kiss it better."

He released Asher's neck and pulled back to examine him. His pupils had blown wide, like Silas's had, but Asher's wouldn't remain that way.

Dazed, Asher reached for his neck and traced the indented bite mark encircling flesh flushed burgundy, shining with saliva. He removed his hand and looked at his fingers. Lev watched, enthralled, as Asher lifted his fingers to his mouth and sucked.

It was a wonder Lev didn't come on sight alone. He snatched Asher's hand from his mouth and brought it to his own, lapping their mixed saliva from his fingers. Lev needed to taste him everywhere, suck his dick until he came, then feed his cum back to him, fuck it into his hole with his tongue.

"What are you thinking?" Asher asked.

"Depraved things, Blakely. If only you knew."

"Show me."

"Get your feet back on the ground," Lev said. "I'm going to die if you don't give me your come."

Asher hastened to comply, sliding down Lev's front with delicious friction like he was dismounting a horse. Once he was sure Asher was stable on his feet, Lev sank to his knees, and unzipped Asher's jeans. He was naked underneath.

Lev's belly swooped. Butterflies. His protégé had given him butterflies.

"Was this for me?" Lev asked.

Asher shrugged one shoulder. His dimples twitched. "Maybe."

"Such a precious gift you are, and look how I've treated you." Lev sat back on his heels and looked up. "I'm sorry."

"Show me."

Lev tugged Asher's jeans down with impatient fingers. Like his hands and feet, Asher's cock was big for his already lanky frame, virile bollocks heavy in Lev's hand.

"My, my, aren't you perfect?"

Asher inhaled sharply, eyes slamming shut.

"You like to be praised," Lev said.

"Yes," Asher breathed.

"Look at me."

Asher's eyes flickered open.

"Good lad."

Asher whimpered.

Lev's mouth watered as he gave Asher's cock an exploratory jerk that milked a fat drop of precum from his tip.

He swiped it with his tongue, savoring it like the first hit of a drug.

They both moaned.

"You taste even better than I imagined last night," Lev said.

"Last night when I heard you come, I wanted to ask for a taste."

Lev groaned. "I wish you would have."

"Don't worry. You'll get your chance soon." In a sexy antithesis to their age difference, Asher fisted his fingers in Lev's hair and dragged him onto his cock.

Bloody hell.

Lev tracked each facial expression of ecstasy as he swirled his tongue around Asher's glans, and toyed with the frenulum under his crown, reaching one hand back to squeeze Asher's arse cheek, fingertips tracing a line down his crack.

Asher stroked Lev's head like a beloved pet. "Fuck, Lev. You feel so..." His legs trembled.

Lev moved his hand to Asher's hips and pushed his top up enough to get it out of the way as he worked Asher's dick in his fist and sucked.

Asher's hold on Lev's hair tightened. The pain ratcheted Lev's desire. He granted Asher all control, gagging as Asher rutted into his mouth.

Jesus Christ. To be used like that... Fuck.

Filthy sucking sounds filled the church as Asher fucked his way deeper into the tight hold of his throat.

Lev relaxed his throat and did his best attempt to be an empty hole. He lost himself in Asher's ministrations, eyes glazed with tears, but remaining ever faithful on Asher's face, showing him how much he wanted him, how much he loved this, how good of a boy he was.

His own cock was a painful rod straining against his slacks. He wanted to touch himself. He wanted relief, but he'd be good. This wasn't for him, even if he was enjoying it so much it might as well have been.

Asher's hoodie slipped down, covering Lev's face, and as much as he relished the objectification, he needed to see Asher's face, to know he was okay, to know he was safe. He pushed Asher's hoodie up again. He wanted to inhale all of Asher's gasps, catalog every facial expression of ecstasy, he—

Ice dumped into his bloodstream. All the keys smashed down on the piano of his pulse. He choked on the cock in his throat.

A sea serpent snaked around Asher's navel, scales writhing in cadence with Asher's fast breaths as it swallowed its tail, a mirror image of the one he'd drawn on Silas.

What the fuck?

Silas's earlier words echoed inside Lev's head—*He's perfect for us.*

Lev's gaze raced across what little of Asher's toned abs was visible. Art marked nearly every inch. Only Lev's art.

He pushed hard against Asher's thighs and fell backward onto his tailbone, wincing at the pain and quite sure he'd left Asher with a handful of ginger hair.

"What's—oh, fuck." Asher's frightened face contorted in shame. "Wait. I can explain."

Lev's vision tunneled. He scrambled to his feet and staggered backward, nearly tumbling heel over arse when the back of his legs slammed into the charred husk of a pew. He righted himself, legs swaying as if he were aboard a distressed ship about to sink.

"This was a mistake." Lev fled like the coward he was.

18

INKY DARKNESS

SILAS

16 YEARS OLD

In the inky darkness, Lev was the sun around which Silas revolved. No one else existed. His body was a mere extension of Lev's.

There was no past, no tomorrow, only the weight of Lev straddling him and the felt-tip caress of his marker as he drew a talisman on Silas's skin.

Silas didn't even need the blindfold anymore. He was perfectly content to remain flat on his back on Lev's bed, eyes closed while Lev fought his monsters for him.

Lev's marker slithered southward, tickling the side of Silas's stomach.

"Hold still," Lev said.

Silas laughed. "It tickles."

Lev shushed him, and Silas listened, because he was right. This was no laughing matter.

They were no strangers to goodbye—for all the years Silas's father had lived at Lichenmoor, Silas had only been permitted to visit over the summer and winter holidays. This time felt different. Final.

But he wouldn't think about that. Not yet. For now, he'd play a statue subject to the whims of his master, submitting to sensation, devoid of all thought. This was their ritual, one they performed on the eve of every departure, a childhood relic neither of them believed in, but were too superstitious to skip.

"Any guesses yet?" Lev asked.

"A dragon?"

A pause. "Are you peeking?"

Silas scoffed. "I resent the accusation, but seeing as you've spoiled it..." He reached for his blindfold, goading Lev into action.

"Ah-ah," Lev said, catching Silas's slender wrists in one hand. "Wait until I've finished."

Silas struggled to free himself half-heartedly, putting up a fight he stood no chance of winning. Not that he wanted to win. Lev's control set him free.

The past was a chain around his chest, and tomorrow he'd be shoved into a locked trunk with no key. Without Lev, how would he even breathe?

His mum wouldn't let him return to Lichenmoor now that Wendell had died. She hated Lucian for turning her husband gay—as if such a thing was possible—and had spewed similar concerns about Silas and Lev, despite their total secrecy.

The only reason Silas remained at Lichenmoor at all was because Lucian had thought it best not to inform Silas's mum that her ex-husband had died until after the new school year began. Lev had pointed out that Father's decision proved Silas still belonged in their family. But Silas knew better.

Lucian didn't want to say goodbye to the only piece of Wendell he had left—Silas.

Tomorrow, the gates of Lichenmoor would close to him. He'd be lost without Lev for the rest of the school year. Their usual methods of connection wouldn't last long. Permanent ink faded, or was forcefully removed by a nun with a bristle brush while his peers watched. Without his father to play carrier pigeon, the letters he and Lev wrote would go unread.

He wouldn't see or speak to Lev for nine months, two-hundred and seventy tally marks carved into the jail cell around his heart. He inhaled, but he couldn't get enough air. He was locked back inside his body again, not drifting weightless in the gravity of Lev's solar system.

"Stay with me, Si. Only now. Only me."

It was a chant they repeated whenever Silas spiraled, as if the words actually were a spell, one that could hide them both inside a pocket watch of stalled time if they said it right.

But they were just empty words. Lev and Silas could repeat them until they died, even in the afterlife, and the words would still be meaningless.

There was no such thing as magic, and yet, Silas was too afraid of what would happen if he didn't say them.

"Tell me," Lev prodded.

Only now, Silas thought because his ribcage was too tight to expand fully, and he had to focus all of his energy on frantic shallow breaths that did nothing to quell the prophetical sense that without Lev his life would end.

"Si?" Lev asked.

Only you, Silas thought. His lips tingled.

A loud clap. Silas's cheek stung. Lev had hit him. Not hard. Never hard enough to leave a mark. Only hard enough to pull Silas back to the present.

"Silas!" There was light, and Lev's worried face. "There you are."

Silas nodded and slowed his breathing, timing each inhale and exhale with his.

Lev arced downward and rested his forehead against Silas's, forcing their eyes to connect, blocking out everything that wasn't now, that wasn't them, until all that remained were moody blue eyes illuminated by the reflection of Silas's lighter ones, almost as if they'd merged. Lev pressed his forehead harder against Silas, as if he believed they could merge, that he could climb inside and fight all of his monsters.

"Only now. Only me." Lev squeezed the nape of Silas's neck. "Tell me."

"Only now," Silas said between breaths. "Only you."

Lev nodded against Silas's forehead. "Good. Say it again."

Silas nodded back, needing the friction to tether him. "Only now," he said, stronger this time. "Only you."

Lev pulled back and cupped Silas's cheek. "No tomorrows. Not in here. Understood?"

"Understood," Silas said.

Lev straightened, and without breaking eye contact, reached for the blindfold he'd fashioned from his tie. "Can I trust you not to peek, or shall I put this back on?"

"The blindfold. It helps, I think."

Lev's shoulders sank down from his ears, tense posture relaxing. "I was afraid I'd made it worse."

Guilt curdled in Silas's stomach. Lev always had to be strong and unyielding, like the ancient towers of Lichenmoor that refused to crumble. But Silas was never strong for him. He only took.

"No, love," Silas said.

The term of endearment had always made him uncomfortable. Adults tossed it about like it meant nothing, while to Silas, Lev's love meant everything. But Lev loved when Silas turned his name into Love, and Silas could give him that, perhaps as a parting gift to hold onto when Silas left tomorrow.

Lev ducked his chin in a nod, donning a grave face as he plucked the marker from the floor and tucked it behind his ear.

"Only now," Silas reminded him as he lowered his chin to his chest. "Only you."

"Only you." Lev slipped the blindfold over Silas's head and tugged it into position, engulfing Silas in silken darkness once again.

19

SIGNING HIS NAME

ASHER

OCTOBER 16

Cold crept into Asher's limbs at the abrupt loss of Lev's body heat. He hadn't even pulled up his pants before the door Lev disappeared through boomed shut.

"Fuck."

Lev had reached inside Asher's chest, crushed his heart in his fist, and fled, leaving Asher behind, carved out, bleeding. Eviscerated.

With shaking hands, he pulled his pants to his hips and recoiled at the discovery that Lev's saliva still dewed on his dick. He wiped any trace of Lev from his skin with his sleeve, and fastened his zipper.

In the months leading up to the retreat, he'd fantasized, and anxiety-spiraled, over a hundred different ways Lev might respond to Asher's tattoos, but he'd never expected Lev's eyes to widen in terror, or his face to blanch down to his freckles, or for him to run away.

What was Lev so afraid of? Didn't he realize the power he possessed?

Asher had inked Lev's art into his skin like a pentagram

135

painted in a basement, summoning Lev like one would a demon, except instead of lighting candles and chanting incantations, he'd cracked open his chest and invited Lev in.

And Lev had answered.

He'd crawled under Asher's skin, crept through his veins, dragging sharp claws down his halls, signing his name. He'd stained Asher's art, etched a permanent mark on his heart. Then he'd reached out to Asher with an invitation of his own.

Come to Lichenmoor.

And Asher had answered, foolishly abandoning his home, forfeiting his soul. To touch Lev, to taste him, he'd traded salvation, sacrificing his honor on an altar for the miracle of Lev on his knees pledging allegiance.

Lev owned his body. It was too late for an exorcism. Asher could scorch Lev's art from his skin, but would never escape him.

So, why the fuck had Lev run away, when it was Asher, not him, who would pay for their sins?

Asher smoothed his hands over his pants, but he still felt dirty, like his soul was smudged, like God had judged and deemed him unworthy—if not, then at least by the sacrilegious statue of Christ painted with bird shit. Even the puzzle piece eyes of stained glass disciples shot him scathing looks. Not that he blamed them.

The haze of lust was no excuse, but tension turned to tinder whenever they touched. His brain had shut off, leaving him with only his baser instincts. To taste. To touch. To fuck. To be filled by Lev until he was more Lev than he was himself.

He tilted his head back until his skull touched stone. How could he have forgotten his tattoos?

Lev had finally lowered his walls, or at the very least, opened a window. He'd apologized. He'd said he felt the same way, and Asher had believed him. He still did.

"Fuck!" he screamed this time.

His vision blurred. He was pathetic, a disappointment. He

was himself three years ago when Ben had grown bored and called their relationship an affair, a mistake, a silly little sexual escapade.

Nothing real.

Because the real Asher was unpalatable. Too much and not enough. He didn't live up to the hype. He didn't fit inside a box.

Like Ben, Lev had rejected him, and now he would send him away. Asher's stomach clenched. What if Lev punished him first? Humiliated him while the others watched? Treated him like a pariah, a leper, the plague that he was.

He blinked back tears and pushed off the wall, sculpting raw despair into rage. He hated Lev for existing, for creating the only art that made him feel like life was worth living, for looking at Asher like he'd wanted to fuck him, for looking at Asher like one day he could love him.

Fuck Lev. Fuck Lichenmoor. Fuck his own stupid choices.

Maybe if he left before Lev's rejection settled into his memories, he could return to his shitty apartment with paint stains on the carpet, and pretend none of this ever happened.

Yes, that's what he'd do. He'd pack, and then he'd leave. He'd walk without stopping until he crawled out from under the shadow of Lichenmoor. Then, he'd eat and sleep, and with a clearer head, he wouldn't feel like his world had ended.

He barreled through the church door that led to his room, not the main entrance Lev had used. The halls to Lev's wing were blessedly empty, almost as if Lichenmoor was doing him a favor, expediting his exit.

Back in his room, he pulled the duffel from the top shelf of the wardrobe, and dumped drawer after drawer of clothes into it. How could he have been so cocky, so sure he would win, that he'd unpacked his belongings?

He wrenched open the next drawer with enough force that it fell onto the floor. Shit. He'd heard nothing from Lev's room, but still... He held his breath and listened. Nothing.

Exhaling, he dipped into the bathroom and cringed at the

thumb-sized hickey on his neck in the mirror. Memories from the church assaulted him—Lev's beard scuffing his neck, nuzzling in deeper, nipping and sucking, leaving marks.

No, he couldn't go there.

Avoiding his reflection, he scooped up the toiletry bag, returned to the room, and tossed it into his bag. He emptied the last drawer and bent to snap the bag's buckle. Time to go.

He took one last look at the room Lev had selected for him, at the windows framing miles of moors, the ocean, and the distant creeping fog.

Homesickness curled around his heart. How could he miss a place that had never been his? He lifted the strap of his duffel. The door at the end of the hall creaked open. Even as his pulse skittered, he suffered another pang of homesickness. Lichenmoor was so alive, he'd already memorized its sounds.

The faint knocking of footsteps started at a whisper. Had Lev come to apologize? He shook himself. That was why he needed to leave. Apology or not, he refused to subject himself to another mercurial man who made him want to scream almost as much as he wanted to self-immolate at his feet.

Lev's low voice murmured, too far away to make out. Asher hadn't heard a second pair of footsteps, but maybe he'd missed it over his thundering heart.

"Do not follow," Lev said.

Who was he talking to? Luna? Lev's footsteps crept closer and slowed to a stop. Asher padded softly toward the door and twisted the lock, as if it was any match for Lev's skeleton key.

"You can't hide from me," Lev said, so close he had to be right outside. "I know you're there."

Asher almost opened his door. Almost. But Lev hadn't said his name, hadn't called, *Come out, come out, wherever you are* or *olly, olly, oxen free* or whatever the British equivalent was like this was a game of hide and seek.

Holding his breath, Asher lowered to his knees and peered through the keyhole wedged in Medusa's throat. Lev faced the stained glass window opposite, his back a sinister silhouette against a stained glass shipwreck—bodies adrift, water blooming with blood, half of the hull disappearing inside a giant squid's maw.

"I don't give a fuck if he hears me," Lev said, angling his body toward someone out of frame. "I told you to stay out."

Who was he talking to? It couldn't be Luna. Lev spoke to her like a doting son.

Asher thought of the man in the locked room in the east wing and disregarded it. The east wing was clearly uninhabited. But Lichenmoor had many rooms. Was Lev hiding someone? Was it Silas?

Jealousy slithered in his stomach, and something else— shame. He couldn't be the other man. Never again.

Lev threw his hands out in frustration. "He has your art on his skin!"

Asher flinched. The only art Asher had was Lev's.

That confirmed it then. Lev talked to himself. Asher's dad had the same habit.

Lev cocked his head, then straightened. What the fuck? He nodded once and spun toward Asher's door.

Chills covered Asher's shoulders like a shawl. Could Lev see him through the keyhole? Asher squinted, striving for a clearer view, but the sun had scattered a kaleidoscope of blue-gray stained glass over Lev's face.

Lev stared at the door for a few tense seconds and stalked off down the way he came. Asher blinked back the grayscale from staring at the sun and sat back on his heels. He waited long after the creak and slam of the door at the end of the hall heralded Lev's departure.

Then, he left.

PAINT EVERYTHING BLACK

ASHER

As if Lichenmoor endorsed his escape, Asher fled the castle without notice through an overgrown conservatory. Outside, the sun sparkled off windswept waves, and the layer of fog on the horizon hadn't budged.

Good.

He had plenty of time before the ocean's watery hands wrapped around Lichenmoor and drowned the road into town, and he'd cover far more ground without the fog to slow him down.

Lev hadn't been bluffing when he'd said Asher could have fallen to his death that first night. The path drifted unnervingly close to the edge of the cliffs. Far below, thistles lined a sandy path to craggy rocks that would hardly break his fall.

He wasn't afraid of heights, but the call of the void lobbed intrusive thoughts at his head. What if he slipped on loose sand? What if he tripped? How fast would he fall? What if he leapt? Would he regret it? What if someone pushed him? Would he even have known who'd done it?

The path sloped downward, curving away from the cliffs and through a copse of dense trees. Asher sped into a jog.

When he emerged from the pocket of forest, the wind had dragged a blanket of fog over the road into town.

He shivered and wiped cool sweat from his brow. His hand shook. Shit. He'd forgotten to eat or drink anything since breakfast, too swept up in his thoughts and broken heart. And Lev.

With an irritated huff, he took off at a run, chastising himself, because this wasn't the first time he'd forgotten to eat or drink, or even pack anything. Normal people had crushes, not limerence. Normal people weathered broken hearts without forgetting to take care of themselves. But Asher wasn't normal.

With each step forward, the fog seemed to take two steps closer, until Asher was surrounded. The ocean churned louder, and the suffocating sense of claustrophobia he'd battled on his first day tightened around his chest.

Lev's last words played back in perfect cadence with Asher's running stride. *This was a mistake. A mistake. A mistake.*

The path descended at a sharper angle. Asher slowed, sliding and skidding on slick bricks layered with mist. Waves lapped menacingly closer, but sound carried across the moors.

The path leveled out, and he reached the gate, now locked with a chain. Why? Instead of taking it as a sign to turn back, Asher threw his bag over and squeezed through the narrow gap between the locked gate leaves.

The statue guarding the gate pointed to the castle. What the fuck? It had pointed to the exit when he'd arrived, right? Whatever. Lichenmoor's eerie mysteries weren't his problem anymore.

He picked up his duffel bag. White sparks crawled in his peripheral vision. If only he'd packed lighter and eaten a fucking meal. The flat road out of Lichenmoor shouldn't take long. He could take a break at the pub in town.

But twenty minutes later, he still hadn't passed Lichenmoor's borders, and the ocean was frighteningly loud. A frothy wave licked at the side of the road up ahead. Out of breath and exhausted, he conceded defeat.

Lichenmoor had grabbed onto his ankles and dragged him back—*I'm not finished with you yet*. The tide would trap him there until it receded again. How humiliating that would be... Silver saltwater ebbed over the road and retreated. With a sigh snatched by the wind, he turned back toward Lichenmoor, and Lev.

He was too weak to run, and settled on a jog, pushing his fatigued muscles as far as he could, too afraid to slow long enough to look. What if he couldn't outrun the ocean?

Wind whipped sea spray at the back of his neck. If the shallow waves nipped around his ankles, he'd have to abandon his bag.

Would Lev even notice if he went missing? Probably not. He'd assume Asher went home and had given up art.

Or... Nausea roiled in his gut. What if his body washed onto the beach, all bloated and disgusting, and nibbled by fish? What if Lev saw him like that?

Asher would be dead. He wouldn't know, wouldn't care, but the threat of that indignity forced him faster up the hill, and he finally reached the gate and squeezed back through.

A raindrop landed on Asher's head, then another, until a deluge poured from the heavens. What remained of the fog-filtered sunlight darkened like a switch turned off. Just what he needed when he was already walking through a vat of fog soup.

Muffled thunder rumbled beneath the din of the waves. "For fuck's sake."

Now he'd have to outrun lightning too. He hadn't caught the flash of lightning preceding it. Hopefully, that meant it was far away.

A shock of icy waves crashed against Asher's ankles. Asher made something between an argh and a shriek. The next wave climbed to his knees before receding. With a sigh, Asher dropped his duffel bag behind him, sparing only a second to watch the current drag it away, a morbid promise of what would happen if Asher wasn't fast enough.

Icy water sloshed around his shoes as he raced on ahead. Thunder rumbled without lightning again. Another rush of waves snaked around his legs before receding, but he was gaining elevation. He could do this.

On he went as sheets of rain pelted him and thunder hammered like a drum. Maybe the sound had been his heart all along.

His chest burned. Pain lanced through his lungs. He stepped into a deep puddle, and his stomach dropped as if he'd fallen through a weak spot in a staircase. Lev should pay someone to fix the potholes. He lifted his foot out of the puddle —and tripped on the lip of the next stone.

He fell forward, hands and knees slamming against the cobblestones so hard he saw stars. He tried to stand, but like a predator stalking the straggler in a herd, the tide rushed in for the kill and waves shoved him back down.

Asher jumped to his feet too fast. Blood roared in his ears as it rushed from his head. Darkness crowded the corners of his vision. He swayed.

What a stupid way to die, fainting because he'd been too anxious to eat, too caught up in irrational heartbreak to drink, too dramatic to wait until the next morning to leave. His legs crumpled beneath him. The curtain dropped before he hit the ground, painting everything black.

MAELSTROM

LEV

Blakely was missing.

Lev sped down the cobblestone path on horseback. He'd dispatched the others to search every inch of Lichenmoor, but he doubted they'd find him. Asher's personal effects were missing too.

Not to mention, Lev's reaction would have sent anyone away, let alone the precious gift of a man who worshipped him to the point of tattooing his art on his skin. This was all Lev's fault.

Why hadn't he camped outside of Asher's door when he saw his eye peering through the keyhole? Why hadn't he dropped to his knees and whispered apologies into Medusa's mouth? He'd been such a coward, but his earlier fear was nothing compared to the terror he now felt.

What if Asher had strayed off the path? What if he'd been injured? What if he'd already drowned? He kicked his heels into Rebecca's sides, nudging her into a canter, the fastest he dared coax her on slippery sloped cobblestone.

Shifting the reins into one hand, he shielded his mouth with the other and called, "Blakely!"

"He may have made it to the other side," Silas said, wrapping his weightless arms tighter around Lev's waist.

Lev didn't reply. Nothing would console him until he found Asher and tucked him safely inside Lichenmoor's walls again.

"Asher!" Lev bellowed so loud his voice cracked.

A gust of wind ripped Lev's hood back.

He couldn't see fuck-all and it was getting dark. Between the storm and the sea and the wind howling over the moor, he wouldn't even be able to hear Asher if he answered. How was he going to find him?

Clenching his legs tighter, he kicked his heels into Rebecca's sides, urging his steadfast mare faster, planning to race to the bottom and work their way back up. He'd had five long years to ruminate over how he would have saved Father if he'd been home.

"Careful, Levvy. You'll be of no help if Rebecca is injured. Or you fall off."

Of course, he knew that, but if help arrived too late, Asher would be gone. He had no choice but to trust Rebecca to be his guardrail. She was as brave as she was stubborn, incredibly agile, and possessed a near-supernatural level of intuition that had saved his arse more than once.

The path leveled out and widened, and Rebecca broke into a gallop. Lev bent down and hid behind her draft.

"We have to find him, Si."

"We will."

But Lev's hope withered as he scanned the dense fog fruitlessly. "Asher!"

What if he never found him at all? What if the ocean claimed him and didn't let go? Lev couldn't lose another soul to the sea again. He'd rather walk into the waves than return empty-handed.

He felt the vibration of Rebecca's whinny more than he heard it, the only warning to hold on before his stomach lurched and his vision tipped up. He clung to the reins and latched onto Rebecca's mane as she reared back on two legs.

His girl didn't spook. If given free rein, she'd have charged through the maelstrom until she decided she was done. Rebecca fell onto her front hooves and paced backward, ears tilted forward between anxious tosses of her head.

"Good lass," Lev murmured, stroking her neck. "What have you found?"

He freed his boots from the stirrups and followed her gaze to a shadow in the middle of the road. Not a shadow—Asher! But what was he doing on the ground?

His heart stalled. No, it was happening again, wasn't it? Lichenmoor doomed its captives to an eternity of walking circles in the fog. Time on Lichenmoor was a snake eating its tail, an ouroboros in reverse, a serpentine curse.

Lev launched from his saddle, straight into a deep puddle, splashing water to his thighs, and ran toward Asher. The worst moments of his life flickered in and out of focus like a light bulb going bad—Silas limp in his arms, shaking him, slapping him, blowing air into his lungs, pummeling his chest, forcing blood through his veins, begging his heart to wake up, and then the worst moment of all, the realization that he wasn't sobbing into the crook of Silas's lolling neck, but the hollow shell that had once housed his soul.

The fuzzy edges of Asher's shadow sharpened as he neared. Asher wasn't crumpled in a heap. He was sitting slumped forward, curled in on himself, knees hugged to his chest, head bowed against the elements. The belt around Lev's chest loosened a single rivet. People didn't die sitting up, did they?

He dropped to Asher's side, ignoring the harsh bite of stone against his kneecaps, and shrugged out of his raincoat. The poor lad hadn't dressed for the elements, wearing that raggedy, paint-stained hoodie he favored and black Converse like he'd just popped out for a stroll.

"Asher?" Lev touched his shoulder.

Asher's head jerked up.

Dizzying relief washed over Lev. "There you are." He draped his raincoat around Asher's shoulders and curled over Asher's face, shielding him from the rain as he palmed his cheek. "Are you all right?"

"I'm fine." Asher stiffened and pulled back, leaving Lev empty-handed.

"Good." Lev cleared his throat. He'd been so afraid of losing Asher, he'd forgotten that he already had. "I was so worried—"

"I'm sure. My body washing up on your shore would be quite the legal quagmire."

"Blakely, that's not..." He massaged the space between his brows, a headache already forming. "I was afraid for you."

Even in the rain and gloom of cloud-covered daylight, Lev saw the subtle roll of Asher's eyes. He darted a glance back to ensure Rebecca still waited. Silas had left.

"You're sure you're alright?" Lev asked.

"Yes, Dad."

Lev's eye twitched. He didn't like that. Not one bit. "What on earth were you doing sitting in the middle of the road?"

"I tripped in one of your many potholes." A wave swept over Asher's lower half, interrupting his rant, and drawing an adorable growl from his chest.

"Easy there, lad." Lev offered his hand.

Asher's lips pinched into a scowl before begrudgingly taking it. He was ice-cold. Was he hypothermic? How long had he been sitting in wet clothes?

"Come, we can discuss my potholes on the way back to Lichenmoor. Can you stand?"

"Of course I can." Asher pulled his hand free and braced shaking palms on the stone, moving at a glacial speed.

Lev hovered, waffling over whether he should avoid pissing Asher off further or throw him over his shoulder. The last wave had receded, but it would return.

"Blakely, if I may—" Lev extended his hand again.

"I've got it." Asher batted him away.

Lev stood and cast a nervous glance toward the opaque veil of fog where the ocean surely lurked.

"Time is of the essence."

Asher attempted to stand, making it halfway before a wave knocked him back on his arse and swallowed his legs.

"That's enough of that." Lev looped his arm under Asher's shoulder and hoisted him to his feet.

Asher listed to the side.

"Asher!" Lev lurched forward and grabbed hold of his waist. "Are you hurt?"

Asher tensed like an alley cat forced into a hug. "No. I stood up too fast."

Lev wasn't convinced. Ignoring the impulse to hug Asher until his warmth seeped into him, he stabilized the lad with a hand on his hip and roved his other hand through Asher's hair.

"Hey, what are you—" Asher tried to pull away.

"Checking for head wounds."

"I don't have any." Asher stepped out of Lev's grip.

"I'm not finished." Lev looped his fingers through the belt loop of Asher's jeans, jerking him back, sensitive fingertips searching every inch of his scalp and down his neck for a knot or the warm, sticky oil-slick of fresh blood. Nothing.

Exhaling, he scanned the rest of the lad, and looked around the frothy shallows surrounding their feet. "Where are your things?"

Asher's scowl tightened into a grimace. "I had to ditch my bag."

Lev's stomach sank below sea level. He didn't want to think about how narrowly Asher had avoided death. If he had been any later...

"I'm so sorry." Without thinking, Lev reached out and stroked the bruise on Asher's neck with his thumb, reassuring himself that Asher was real, that he hadn't been dragged out to sea with his belongings. "Things can be replaced. You, however, cannot."

"Spare me the sentimental bullshit. Just because you saved me from dying at the hand of your own shitty groundskeeping doesn't mean I want some fatherly affection."

Lev dropped his hand. Well, then. If Asher had enough energy to be an obnoxious little twat, he couldn't have suffered much harm.

Asher stalked off toward Rebecca, adding over his shoulder, "If you call me pretty American again, I'm going to punch you."

"Oh, the horror. How shall I ever recover from such an injury?" Lev called, hurrying after him.

Lev's next footstep dropped into a deep hole. Perhaps Blakely had a point.

By the time he caught up, Asher had already charmed Rebecca, whispering something unheard while he stroked her neck.

"Nice horse. What's her name?"

"Rebecca. Let me help you."

Instead of some snarky jab, Asher stepped into the stirrup, and vaulted up. Lev nearly had a heart attack, only soothed when Asher landed on the saddle, and extended his hand. "Finally caught up, old man?"

"I wasn't entirely sure you wouldn't leave me." Lev took Asher's hand and followed suit, settling himself in the saddle's seat with Asher in front. "If you don't mind..." Lev reached around Asher's waist and took the reins. He'd been expecting Asher to fight him for the reins, but he didn't protest.

Overwhelmed by the miracle of Asher in his arms, Lev perched his chin on Asher's shoulder, and eased Rebecca into a trot. Nothing had changed. He'd still have to send the lad away. What happened tonight only hardened his resolve.

But at least for now Asher was safe.

2 2

ONE OF THE BEST

ASHER

The only thing worse than being rejected by Lev was being rescued by him. Sharing a horse would have been punishment enough if Lev had held onto the saddle and kept a respectful distance the way a normal person would.

But no. Lev surrounded Asher like the tide had—only worse—wrapping himself around Asher, and holding the reins loosely in Asher's lap, below the very tattoo that had scared him away.

"Are you sure you're alright?" Lev asked for the hundredth time.

"No, because if you ask me again my head is going to explode," Asher snapped, though his chattering teeth stole the bite from his bark.

In response, Lev hugged Asher tighter and rested his chest against Asher's back, sharing his body heat.

Rebecca rounded a corner, and the fog-shrouded castle emerged from behind a veil of fog and twilight. Finally.

"Woah," Asher hummed and tugged Rebecca's reins before Lev could intercept.

"What's wrong?" Lev asked.

Asher twisted in the saddle and nearly met Lev's lips. Wet

150

salt and ginger hair hung down over his forehead, dripping in rivulets Asher longed to lick so much his traitorous tongue tasted his own bottom lip. Lev's gaze dipped. Asher's breath hitched.

Anxiety washed over him again. Lev was too close, creeping up behind him like the waves had, drowning him in the oceans of his irises. After spending the last few hours running on terror and raw adrenaline, his nerves frayed, sparking at the slightest threat.

Severing eye contact broke the spell. Asher cleared his throat. "Rebecca must be exhausted."

Lev blinked. "Sorry?"

"You should get her stabled. I can walk the rest of the way."

"Are you sure you didn't hit your head? If you think I'd actually let you out of my sight, you've lost the plot."

"Me? You're the one delusional enough to think you actually have any authority over me."

"Spare me the rebel act. While you're here, you remain under my care."

"Okay, Dad."

"Stop calling me that."

"Stop treating me like a teenager out past curfew, and I will."

Asher writhed in the saddle trying to break Lev's hold.

"Keep that up and you'll have to buy me a drink first."

"You're such an asshole," Asher growled. How could he joke like that? "Let me down."

"No. For all our talk of tide maps... Asher, you could have died!"

Claustrophobia curled around his chest. "If you don't let me down now, I'm going to throw you off."

"You wouldn't dare. I could break a hip."

Asher didn't laugh.

Lev frowned. "Fine. I'll get down, but you're staying put." Lev swung his leg over Rebecca's rump and stepped down.

Asher followed suit. Pain tore through his shins when his frozen feet hit the ground.

"Asher…" Lev chided, hands hovering annoyingly close to Asher's hips like he thought he was going to collapse again. "I would rather you ride and rest."

"And I'd rather you fuck off. Guess we're at an impasse."

"Ah, there's that waspish temperament I've missed."

Asher lifted his middle finger and stalked off toward the castle, a chill sinking deeper into his bones with each step he put between them. He couldn't look back. It would hurt too much.

"Asher, wait!" Lev called.

Lev and his stupidly long legs caught up quickly. "I told you to stay."

"I'm not a dog."

"I can't help but worry you resent me for rescuing you."

"You know that's not why I'm upset." Asher swung around and slammed into Lev's chest with an oof before bouncing backward. "*Argh!*"

Lev caught him by his bicep, rescuing him yet again, which only pissed Asher off more.

"Watch where you're going, you giant ginger fuck." Asher wrenched his arm free and dropped his gaze to the cobblestones. Looking at Lev hurt more than running into him had.

"Giant ginger what?" Lev laughed.

"Stay the fuck away from me."

"Asher, that's not what… I… What I mean to say is—"

"Save it. I'm bored with the bumbling Brit shtick. None of this matters anyway. I'll leave tomorrow, and we'll never speak again." Tears pricked his eyes. Thank fuck for the rain.

Rebecca nickered and nudged his shoulder. The emotional intelligence of horses… He stroked the bridge of her nose. She nudged him again, and he hugged her neck.

After he touched down in the States, he'd stop at the ranch and take Holstein for a ride under the wide Colorado sky before he returned to the depressing concrete box he lived inside. He released Rebecca to find Lev watching him with a strange expression that bordered on nausea.

"You're a good girl, Rebecca." Asher kissed the bridge of her nose. To Lev, he said, "You'd better go get her dried off. I'm not sure if you're one of those rich pricks who don't know how to care for their horses, but you shouldn't put a horse to bed wet."

"Perhaps you could help me?"

Asher shook his head. "I'm sure you can handle it."

Lev said nothing for a beat too long and then nodded. "I told Luna to hold dinner until you returned. No one wanted to eat without you."

Asher winced. He hadn't meant to worry the others, and he hadn't considered how embarrassing it would be to face them now.

"Please be there when I'm finished. You need to eat, and I need to know you're safe."

Asher didn't answer.

"You can ask Luna for a pair of my clothes. With any luck, your bag will turn up tomorrow. Nothing stays buried in the ocean around Lichenmoor."

Asher would rather go naked than wear Lev's clothes over the tattoos he so despised. "I'll borrow some from Theo. We're much closer in size."

The muscles in Lev's throat shifted on a swallow. Asher waited for him to argue against it, but he didn't. Fuck, that hurt. Lev's jealousy couldn't have faded that fast, could it? Had Asher's tattoos flipped some switch?

"Speaking of clothes..." Asher unzipped Lev's jacket and held it out. "You need it more than I do."

Lev's drenched collared shirt clung to his chest and abs. He'd missed a button and Asher's fingers twitched with the urge to fix it.

"Please keep it." Lev fidgeted with the reins. "Please wear my clothes too."

Asher exhaled, some of the pain leaving with his breath. "I can't. It hurts too much."

The confession was a sacrifice, an olive branch, one last chance for Lev to apologize, to take it all back.

Say something. Please.

Lev opened his mouth. An eerie screech pealed across the moor as the iron door in the main entrance opened and light spilled into the gloom.

"He's here!" Theo rushed out.

Asher looked back at Lev, still fussing with the reins, weighing his words.

Please say something.

But he didn't. Asher shoved the jacket toward him and left.

This time, Lev didn't follow.

"Asher!" Theo swept him into a hug. "We were so worried." He wrapped his arm around Asher's shoulders and steered him toward the house.

Asher glanced back. Lev and Rebecca had disappeared, swallowed by the fog.

"You're trembling," Theo said. "Let's get you inside."

Julian held the door open. "What happened? Are you hurt?"

Asher shook his head and passed into the warmth of the foyer.

"Here, sit." Theo led him to a bench.

Shivers rattled his bones more violently than when he'd been outside. Maybe it was the adrenaline leaving him.

"Mr. Blakely. Thank God." Luna appeared from the hall leading to the kitchen and wrapped a heavy tartan blanket around his shoulders so tightly that his shivers reduced to muffled vibrations. "Where's Lev?"

"St-st-st-a..."

"That's okay, dear. I have something that will help."

She left and returned with a steaming mug that smelled of cinnamon.

"Try this." She helped him wrap his trembling hands around the mug and lift it to his lips. "Drink."

The warmth of the mug alone was heavenly, but the drink was divine—spicy hot cider with the faintest hint of alcohol hidden beneath cloves and cinnamon. He aimed for another sip and sloshed cider over the sides.

"I'm sorry," he said, teeth chattering less. That cider was magic.

"Nothing to be sorry for." She kneeled at his feet, tutting at his wet shoes. "You poor dear."

He should insist on taking off his own shoes, but he wasn't sure his numb fingers could untie his laces.

"Lev's safe," Asher said. He took another swig of cider.

She looked up. "Oh, I know he is, dear. Every time I've feared he's used up his ninth life, he comes home with nine more." But the wrinkles around her eyes lessened, and her smile seemed more genuine, at least until she discovered his seawater-saturated socks and gasped in horror. "Thank God Lev found you in time." She peeled the first sock off and dropped it onto the floor with a squelch.

"What happened?" Julian asked again. "Where's Lev? What were you doing out there?"

"Stables," Asher said and hid behind his mug, taking another sip.

He must be going into shock, because all he wanted was Lev to answer his questions for him, and take him to bed. Not like that. Just bed.

Luna stood and pushed back his hoodie. "Your hair is soaking. Poor lad." She clucked her tongue the same way Lev did. He must have learned it from her.

Theo murmured something to Julian, who pressed his lips into a tight line. Asher didn't like being examined and discussed out of earshot as if he weren't there. He downed the rest of the cider and set the mug on the bench beside him.

"Do you want help taking this off?" She gestured to his hoodie.

"No," Asher rushed to say, then added, "Thank you."

"A hot shower and a warm meal will set you to rights. Theo, why don't you help him upstairs while I finish dinner?"

"Yes, ma'am." Theo pushed off the wall, declining Julian's offer to help.

Theo silently accompanied Asher on his very slow ascent up the stairs. At the landing, Asher confessed he didn't have any clothes, and would have flushed if he had any remaining body heat.

"You want to borrow mine?" Theo asked.

Asher exhaled, grateful Theo had expected the question before he'd had to suffer the shame of asking. If only Asher had a thing for nice men, or men his age. "Just for tonight."

"Of course. My room's this way."

Theo's room was smaller than Asher's and smelled strongly of mint. The nondescript four-poster bed was made with nary a wrinkle. He opened the wardrobe and selected clothes from the hangers.

"Do you want me to stay while you shower?" Theo asked.

Asher nodded. While the spiked cider had initially calmed his nerves, alcohol on an empty stomach had left him a little dizzy, and he was afraid he might faint in the shower or fall down the stairs. Or run into Lev.

"I'll be quick." Asher took the stack of clothes and dashed into the bathroom.

"Take your time," Theo called from the other side of the door.

Asher started the shower and stripped, winded and trembling by the time he peeled off the last of his wet clothes. He stepped under the steaming water and gasped as needles prickled all over his frigid skin.

"Are you okay?" Theo asked.

"The water's hot."

Asher bowed his head beneath the spray, and scrubbed every inch of his skin, scouring away any trace of Lev and the ocean that had nearly drowned him.

"Do you want to talk about what happened?" Theo asked.

Asher paused. "No, thanks."

"You'll leave tomorrow, then?" Theo asked.

"Yeah."

"I'm not sure I want to stay either."

Asher paused mid-lather. "Why?"

How could anyone deny the chance to learn from Lev when they weren't the object burning under his magnifying glass?

"Why would I stay when I'm pretty sure he hates me?"

"I'm sorry I ruined this for you."

Theo laughed. "It's fine. I came more for the artist than the art."

"Huh?"

"Let's just say I have no interest in spending the next six months celibate."

Asher laughed politely, but inside he seethed. Even if Lev was known for his voracious appetite, an invitation to Lichenmoor wasn't an invitation to sex. Lev would have been furious.

What about the other artists? Did they share Theo's sentiments? Had some set their sights even higher? Why stop at sex when Lev had a fortune to harvest?

Cider curdled in his empty stomach, and jealousy crawled up his throat like heartburn. He'd been too distraught to give any thought to the fact that Lev would pick another artist to replace him.

His skin tingled icy-hot. The mint in the shower gel or the beginning of a panic attack? He rinsed off the remaining suds quickly and turned off the tap. Cold air swept in before the steam dissipated, and by the time he dried off, he was shivering again.

Theo hadn't included underwear, sparing Asher the anxiety spiral of deciding whether to wear them or suffer the awkwardness of returning them. He stuck his foot into the pant leg of a pair of black trousers and tipped to the side. His arms windmilled until he caught ahold of the towel rack, but it broke off in his hand, sending him crashing into the cabinet with a yelp.

Theo knocked. "Asher?"

"I think Lichenmoor is trying to kill me." A delirious giggle escaped his chest at the absurdity of nearly cracking his head while partially dressed in Theo's slacks. Lev would have been furious.

"I'm coming in," Theo said.

"No, wait."

Asher wrenched his pants up, and scrambled to feed his arms into the shirt, but Theo walked in before he could get it over his head.

Theo's brows nearly merged with his hairline at the sight of Asher's upper half. "You have tattoos."

If only the sea had swallowed him.

Theo glanced at the towel rack on the floor and back at him. "I'm sorry." He cleared his throat. "What I should have said was, your tattoos are beautiful."

Asher finished pulling the tee over his head. "Lev didn't like them."

"What an idiot."

"I know," Asher agreed.

"No. Not you. Him. If you had my art on your skin, I would have..." His voice took on a throatier tone. "I would have thanked you in any way you'd let me."

Asher's dick should have taken interest, but when he tried to imagine Theo's art on his skin, all he saw was Lev's.

"Lev made a mistake. He must be kicking himself."

Mistake ricocheted through Asher's brain.

"You still look pale." Frowning, Theo plucked the sage green merino sweater from the counter and passed it to him. "Put this on."

When Asher emerged from the sweater's neck hole, Theo reached out and touched his neck. "How did you get this?"

"What?" Asher looked in the mirror and slapped his hand over the hickey. "No. That was... It's not a bruise."

"I see..." Theo leaned closer to inspect it. "Did he..."

"Force me? No."

"Okay. Good."

"You don't have a scarf, do you?"

"Wearing a scarf to dinner will draw more attention, no?"

Fuck. He'd forgotten dinner. Lev had commanded his attendance. Condescending dick. Theo would bring Asher a plate if he asked, but what if Lev insisted upon taking it up to him?

The idea of facing the other artists and their questions sounded even more exhausting than doing another lap on Lichenmoor's path, but they'd provide a buffer. He'd eat quickly and go to bed.

"Then again, you look like you only narrowly avoided hypothermia..." Theo ducked out of the bathroom and returned with a velvety linen scarf. He knotted it loosely around Asher's neck. "There."

Asher thanked him, and Theo escorted him downstairs—down only a few steps, actually. Before they'd gotten very far, the front door opened with its characteristic metallic wail. Asher's heartbeat ran off like a jackrabbit. He missed the next step and grabbed the rail.

"Careful, Asher." Theo hurried to the step below and braced his hands on Asher's shoulders. Lovely, dependable, stable Theo, whom Asher couldn't seem to muster more than platonic feelings for.

"I'm broken." Asher tipped his head back and blinked before he burst into tears and humiliated himself further.

Theo shushed him softly. "The only people who aren't broken are boring."

"Where is he?" Lev boomed like distant thunder.

Asher looked past Theo, panic mounting as Lev's footsteps stomped up the stairs. He couldn't face Lev. He'd take one look, and the open wound where his heart once lived would bleed anew.

"Your painting of Envy gave me an idea, but we must hurry," Theo whispered in a rush, casting a glance over his shoulder before returning. "I think you're handsome. Do you think I'm handsome, too?"

"Theo, I do, but..."

"I'm not Lev?" He smiled.

"I'm sorry."

"Don't be. Right now, I need you to trust me."

"Why?"

The question died unanswered at the rapid thunk-thud-thunk-thud of heavy footsteps on the stairs, haunting Asher for the second time that day like some horror film cliché.

"Trust me," Theo repeated.

Lev's thundering steps carried closer. Theo darted another glance over his shoulder, then jerked Asher toward him and kissed him with sexy confidence, sliding his tongue into Asher's mouth when he gasped. It was one of the best kisses Asher had ever had, but it still didn't come close to Lev's.

He planted his palms against Theo's chest and pushed.

"Sorry," Theo whispered, looking not sorry at all.

"What's this?" Lev said.

Asher jumped. He felt Lev's eyes on him but refused to look, cowardly dropping his gaze to the creeping rose vines on the carpet runner.

"See you down there, Lev," Theo said breezily, and dragged Asher by the hand past him.

Asher looked back before he turned the corner. Lev still stood on the same step, staring with stunned silence, ruddy cheeks flushed a deeper shade of red, lips parted with all the words he should have said.

THE GHOST OF HIS SIGIL

LEV

"Ouch. That had to hurt," Silas said from his seat on the newel post of the landing overhead.

"Where the hell were you?"

Silas pushed off the post and slid down the stair rail before landing beside him. "Why? Did you miss me?"

Lev didn't answer, letting the silence simmer in hopes it would coax more information.

"Looks like you pushed Asher right into Theo's capable arms," Silas said instead of anything helpful.

"Oh, piss off."

Catching Asher in the act—freshly showered and dressed in Theo's clothes, no less—had infected Lev with a jealousy so visceral it would fester in his marrow until this was a distant memory.

"It's for the best," Lev added, more for his benefit than Silas's.

Silas was an anchor chained to Lev's ankle, plunging him back underwater every time his lips breached the surface. Asher wasn't Lev's second chance—he was another tragic death waiting to be claimed by Lichenmoor's depths.

"How boring." Silas yawned. "For Asher and me, if that wasn't clear, but if that's what you want…"

"It's not about want," Lev snapped. "Lichenmoor isn't safe."

He'd nearly lost the life of his most devoted disciple, the man he worshipped with equal, if not exceeding, fervor. He should have thanked Asher. Honored him. Not sent him to his death.

The worst of it was that he hadn't even wanted to reject the lad. The ghost of his sigil etched into Asher's skin hadn't upset him. His superstition had. His stupid, childish fear that the magic clinging to Lichenmoor had somehow conjured up Asher Blakely, brought him to Lichenmoor, and reincarnated Silas in his image—the real Silas, not the doppelgänger who haunted him.

Lev was a horrible person because he didn't want Silas in any incarnation. He'd never wanted Silas to begin with. Silas had chosen him. Lev had loved him, but he hadn't loved him enough to save him. He should have etched Silas's poetry into his skin, rather than scratched it from his heart.

"I need to keep him safe," Lev said.

"Keep *him* safe, or you?" Silas sailed up the stairs past him on nimble feet.

"Him."

"Right…" The black hair on the back of Silas's head bobbed as he nodded, no doubt smugly. "This has nothing to do with the fact that you're afraid to love and lose again."

"Not everything is about you, Silas."

"Isn't it?" Silas disappeared and reappeared on the third-story landing as if he'd wanted to use the extra elevation to look down his nose all the better. "Asher is practically wearing my skin. What better stand-in for me than him?"

"You're disgusting."

"What's disgusting is killing me and never accepting responsibility."

Lev flinched. Silas's arrow had found its mark. After Silas had died, Lev tried to turn himself in, but Father had erased all incriminating evidence, blotted out Silas's very existence. Father wasn't omnipotent, though. Lev could have confessed, and hadn't.

"Stay here." Lev reached the top step and navigated around him, clenching his hands so tightly his stiff knuckles ached as he stalked off toward his room, praying that whatever tenuous control he had over Silas held this time.

"Strike that," Lev said as he neared his door. "Stay the fuck away from me, full stop. From here on out you don't exist."

"As you wish, sire," Silas said, weaponizing the sarcastic quip he'd used when they were younger any time Lev had behaved petulantly or merely wanted some fucking space from the clingy kid brother he'd shared no kinship with.

"Oh, fuck off." Lev gripped the doorknob and looked back.

"It's only going to get worse, *Snake*," Silas sang from the landing at the end of the hall, a mutinous expression pasted on his skeletal face, pale eyes glinting unnaturally. "You can't resist me forever. Then we'll be together all the time."

Lev wrenched his door open and slammed it shut, ignoring the unsettling laughter bouncing down the hallway like a ball rolled by a ghost.

He leaned against the door and allowed himself one exhale to compose himself, then peeled off his wet clothes. He needed to get back down to Asher. The lad had still looked so poorly, forehead clammy, the flush in his cheeks absent. What kind of man French-kissed someone in such a state?

Dressing quickly, Lev pulled on a cozy pair of cappuccino tweed trousers that hugged his arse and a royal blue jumper that paired well with his eyes. He was only human. And jealous. Wickedly, wickedly jealous.

Melody tapped his shoulder. "Can you pass the *jus*?"

Lev blinked. "Sorry? Oh, of course." The gravy boat clinked against the saucer as he handed it to her.

Across the table, Asher refused to lift his gaze from his scarcely touched plate despite Lev's attempts to draw his attention via sexual innuendo and increasingly cryptic anecdotes, until Lev resorted to lobbing silent questions at his bowed head.

Are you well? Does your heart hurt like mine does? Have I ruined you the way you've ruined me? Did you think of me when you kissed him? Will you see him again after you leave? Will you wither and decay without me? Because I will.

Julian and Theo flanked Asher's sides like guard dogs, and if Theo didn't remove his hand from the back of Asher's chair, Lev was going to rip his scarf from Asher's neck and strangle him with it.

Most of the others had already finished or moved on to second servings, while Asher had neglected the roast beef and spinach. Was he so devastated that he couldn't stomach eating? Or worse, was Silas right? Was Asher like him?

It took every ounce of strength Lev possessed not to dismiss the others, tie Asher to the chair, and force-feed him. What if he fainted and fell down one of Lichenmoor's many deathtraps masquerading as stairs? Or did he want to keep his stomach empty for more lascivious reasons...

Lev scowled at Theo.

The din of silverware and conversation dimmed. Melody sagged against Daria's shoulder and closed her eyes, fork still gripped loosely in her hand. Julian yawned his sixth yawn. Asher's gaze remained on his plate.

"Is there something wrong with the food, Blakely?"

"The food is divine," Asher answered, face still hidden by the fringe of nearly black hair falling over his face.

Asher speared a forkful of wilted spinach, and brought it to his mouth. He chewed, swallowed, and chased the spinach gratin with a swig from the vacuum-sealed travel mug of herbal tea Lev had asked Luna to prepare before retiring to the room she kept when trapped by the tide.

"If the food is divine, why aren't you eating?" Lev tried.

"Why do you care?"

Because you're everything. Because you're so bloody fragile and strong at the same time that I can't decide if I should fear more for you or myself.

"Because you're my guest," he said lamely.

Asher lowered the mug to the table with a thunk, like a billiard ball dropped. "What a considerate host you are, Leviathan."

Lev exhaled through clenched teeth. He'd catapulted himself so far out of Asher's favor, he'd been demoted to the formality of his namesake.

Fuck the spectators. He reached across the table. Asher's downcast lashes twitched toward Lev's open hand, but didn't lift.

"Asher, please," Lev begged. "How can I let you leave when I can't trust you to eat?"

Even the log in the fireplace gasped with a crack that spat sparks.

Asher lowered his fork to the napkin beside his plate and moved his hands to his lap. "Let?" Venom dripped from the three-letter word so potent, a bite would have killed him. "It's not the food. It's your company."

An even deeper silence descended.

Melody's fork dropped from her slackening hand and onto her plate with an almighty clatter. Asher flinched and jerked his head up, hazel eyes darting to Lev with prey-like dread. Lev hated himself for conditioning Asher to fear him almost as much as he hated whoever had left him with those shell-shocked reflexes.

"Sorry," Melody slurred drowsily and scooped up the fork again.

Chuck snickered. "Are Mom and Dad fighting?"

"Mr. Boorman, if you insist on acting like a child, I will treat you as such," Lev snapped without sparing him a glance. He cleared his throat. "Blakely, if the company is lacking, you may finish your meal in your room."

"Thank you, sir." Asher turned to Theo. "Want to come?"

"*Oui.*" Theo scooted his chair back.

"Guests are forbidden on my floor," Lev said tightly, grasp on control slipping. He inhaled and counted to ten.

Asher lifted his chin. "That's okay. We can eat in Theo's room."

"Wait..." Julian frowned at Asher. "You're sleeping on the same floor as Lev?"

Daria laughed. "What floor did you think he was staying on? One all by himself?"

Chuck turned to his left, shielded his mouth, and stage whispered, "Not on the floor, I bet."

Lars guffawed.

Asher's gaze shuttered. His cheeks flushed. Asher should only blush with warmth, laughter, and lust. Anger at Lev, perhaps. Never shame.

Lev slammed his fist on the table, rattling the cutlery, sending ripples through drinks. "Everybody out." He softened his tone and added. "Blakely, you will stay."

"Lev..." Chuck protested.

Lev lifted his hand. "Leave us."

Chuck dropped his napkin into a pool of shimmering *au jus*. Chairs scuffed. Lev hardly noticed the others scuttle out of the room. Theo hovered beside Asher's chair, waiting for direction, apparently.

"You too, Theo."

"But Lev..."

"Spare me the act, Laurenti. We both know you don't care about Asher beyond getting inside him."

Asher bolted out of his chair. "Don't take this out on him. He has nothing to do with this."

"My point exactly," Lev agreed. "Theo, you may go now."

Theo looked to Asher.

"I'll be fine." Asher rubbed between his brows as if Lev was giving him a headache, as if Asher hadn't given Lev a headache first.

"You're sure?" Theo asked.

"You heard the man," Lev said. "Off you pop."

Theo huffed and left, pushing past the boulder that was Julian lingering in front of the door.

"Lev, this is unprofessional," Julian said.

Why did everyone insist on fighting Asher's battles for him? Didn't they see how strong he was, how little he needed them?

"I don't give a fuck about professionalism. Asher is a consenting adult. If he wants to leave, he is free to do so. Isn't that right, Blakely?"

Asher nodded at Julian. "I've got this."

Julian opened his mouth, and closed it, then leaned against the swing door, and said, "Be careful, Asher."

Now that his obstacles were out of the way, Lev rounded the long table. Asher watched with wary resignation, one hand gripping the table's edge.

"Did you fuck him?" Lev asked.

Asher rolled his eyes in tandem with a maddeningly seductive swipe of his tongue against the inside of his cheek. "I don't see how that's any of your business. My body doesn't belong to you."

"Come now, Blakely. Don't be daft." Lev prowled nearer. "You were mine the moment you made my art a part of you. I might as well have signed my name on your arse." Lev pushed his lips into a thoughtful pout. "Unless you already have it there…"

"Go fuck yourself."

"Why should I, when I have you to do it for me? Now answer me. Did. You. Fuck. Him?"

Asher's hand tightened on the table, fingertips turning pale. "You can't throw your toys away and take them back when someone else wants to play."

"I didn't throw you away."

Asher drifted away from Lev, straying toward the rain-pelted windows at his back. "You left me. You said I was a mistake."

Lev followed. "I said *this* was a mistake." He gestured between them, grazing Asher's chest with his index finger. "Not you. Never you."

"I don't believe you." Asher shivered and wrapped his arms around himself.

Lev trailed a lazy half-circle around Asher to sidle in front of the drafty windows. "I never should have left you. Not there. Not like that. Not after learning you wore my sigil."

"Sigil?"

"The Leviathan ouroboros. I haven't seen that mark in decades. It startled me. I…"

His attention snagged on movement through the window to his right. His heart stuttered over a row of skipped beats. Silas stood in the flowerbed, draped in darkness, black hair drenched, rain dripping down his face like tears.

"Tell him," Silas mouthed.

"I made that ouroboros for someone I once loved. Someone I lost."

He never should have shared that illustration. Silas had insisted, arguing that even if they had to hide their relationship, they could be out through Lev's art. Back then, Lev would have given him anything. That was the danger of their love.

He'd done things he hadn't wanted to, and they'd both paid for it.

"Silas?" Asher asked. "The one you can't stop painting?" Asher's agile fingers slid Lev's cuff up to bare Silas's parting gift. "The one who left you with these?"

"How do you know everything?" Lev whispered, awestruck and terrified, skin sizzling beneath Asher's touch. "It's almost as if you were him in a past life."

"I'm not."

"I know." Lev lowered his hand over Asher's hand on his arm. "The last time I saw that ouroboros, I was a little younger than you are now. You can imagine my shock to find it on you in the same location I'd drawn it on him…"

"What?" Asher pulled his hand back. "I didn't—"

"I know. You couldn't have known." Lev sighed. "The sigil was a relic from our childhood, meant to guard him when we were parted. I couldn't protect him, though. Perhaps if I had…"

Pain lanced through him. Outside, Silas nodded, encouraging him to continue.

"I loved him, and I hurt him."

He'd confessed as much in therapy, a diluted version that denied culpability, but confessing to Asher while Silas gave his blessing felt like what he imagined Catholic confession to be— a speck of sand lifted from the ocean of guilt crushing his chest. In a word, useless. No amount of *Hail Marys* and *Our Fathers* would assuage his guilt.

Asher chewed on his bottom lip, brow wrinkling ever deeper. What was his thinking? Lev was too afraid to ask.

"Lichenmoor is dangerous," Lev continued. "*I'm* dangerous."

"That wasn't your fault. I knew the tide was rising."

"But I forced you out there. If I hadn't found you…" A shudder crept up his spine and he swallowed the knot of anguish in his throat. "I thought I was strong enough to let you leave here tomorrow, but I can't bear the thought of never seeing you again, never knowing if you're happy, or fed, or if you would have been better off with me."

He swept forward, ushering Asher away from the windows, and Silas. Asher bumped into the table. His pupils dilated with fear, and something else... Desire, yes, but was that the faint trace of hope Lev had extinguished? Did his most devoted fan still carry a torch?

"I would do anything to keep you safe," Lev gripped one end of Asher's scarf, longing to unwind it from his neck. "Anything except let you go."

Asher groaned and scrubbed his face with his hands. "You're the most mercurial man I've ever met. What do you want from me?"

Lev encircled Asher's wrists and tugged his hands down. "I want everything. All of your thoughts. Every piece of art you've made, all the art to come. I may not have your art tattooed on my body, but as much as you belong to me, I belong to you."

Asher said nothing.

Fully clothed, Lev felt naked. "I'm so sorry that I hurt you, and for all the ways I'll hurt you in the future."

Asher's brows darted together. His mouth opened.

Lev spoke first. "I'm going to make mistakes, but I promise to give you every single part of me." He kissed Asher's hand. "Please give me another chance. Let me claim you properly."

He waited three excruciating heartbeats, and then Asher finally said,

"Only if I can claim you too."

ART THAT'S HONEST

LEV

Wind hurled raindrops at Lichenmoor. Asher craned his neck and peered around Lev to the window at his back.

"What's wrong?" Lev followed his gaze, but the night only reflected a blurry tableau of Asher at the table posing as Lev's last meal.

Asher blinked. "I thought I saw something. Never mind."

Lev couldn't shake the sensation, however irrational, that Asher could see Silas, or at the very least, sense him.

"Lichenmoor's shadows play tricks, and the wind turns trees into figures and branches into limbs. I used to think they were the Green Man when I was young."

"The Green Man?" Asher's brow wrinkled.

"Pagan god of death and rebirth. I'll give you a lesson later." He turned Asher's face away from the window. "No one is out there in this weather."

As if to prove the point, a gust rattled the windows and branches scratched at the glass.

Mollified, Asher nodded.

"Good. Where were we? Oh, right..."

Lev nudged Asher's feet apart, stepped into the space, and

captured his lips in a reverent kiss, vowing to carve out his own heart and crush it in his fist before he'd ever hurt him again. Like a rose unfurling, Asher parted his lips and invited Lev in.

Asher's hands roamed down Lev's back and settled on Lev's arse, palms mapping his curves before taking two handfuls and jerking him closer. Lev groaned. Asher's rough handling sent his thoughts down a sideways path.

Did Asher top or bottom? Or perhaps both?

Lev preferred to top, but the idea of his brat of a protégé penetrating him threw his stomach through a loop and punched the air from his lungs, along with a confession. "I need you."

Asher broke the kiss, breathing fast. "I need you too."

"I'm glad we agree." Lev curled his fingers inside the scarf Asher still wore, knuckles tracing the front of his trachea. "But you still haven't answered my question." He stroked Asher's dick through his trousers.

"What was the question?"

Lev laughed darkly and removed his hand.

Asher whined. "Don't stop."

"You're even sexier when you're needy."

Asher blinked, some of the lust-drunk haze clearing. "If you don't ask your question, I'm going to show you how sexy I am when I'm angry."

"Oh, trust me. You've shown me that already."

"Lev..."

"Did you fuck Theo?"

What he and Asher shared was far too strong for some retaliatory fuck to erode, but he needed to know.

"What would you have done if I had?" Asher's dimples winked with the flash of a smirk.

Lev's stomach unclenched. He hadn't realized how much of his heart was at stake until relief set in. He pulled the front of Theo's wretched scarf toward him, loosening it from Asher's neck and drawing him closer.

"I would have fucked his very existence from your memory and filled you from both ends until my come leaked from your pores."

"Damn. I should have said that I had."

"I'm happy to fuck you like you fucked him, but I'm not quite finished."

Asher swallowed, Adam's apple fluttering against Lev's hand.

"What about the kiss on the stairs?"

Asher dropped his gaze. "He kissed me, and I let him because I was too afraid to look at you."

"Oh, darling, I'm so sorry." Lev tipped Asher's chin up.

"Show me how sorry," Asher said.

"Do you want me to get on my knees and grovel, Blakely, because I fucking will."

"Later. Don't you have a kiss to erase?"

They collided with such force, he nearly split his lip. Lev tugged Theo's scarf from Asher's neck and dropped it on the floor, exposing the mark he'd left. One wasn't enough. He wanted to paint the rest of Asher's neck rouge and spatter his skin with burst blood vessel freckles and hickeys.

"I like my mark on you," Lev said, rather than scaring the lad with his bloodthirsty thoughts. He rubbed his thumb over the spot. "But you're a masterpiece as yet unfinished."

Asher rested back against the table on his forearms. "You haven't seen the rest of me yet."

"We must remedy that." Lev removed his hands and reached for the bottom hem of Asher's jumper.

"Wait!" Asher bolted upright, nearly knocking their foreheads together.

Lev bared his palms and edged back until their cocks no longer grazed. "I'm sorry. There's no rush. We can stop."

"It's not that." Asher examined the jumper as if counting the stitches, then looked up. "When you left me in the church, I was afraid I'd never be able to paint again. It sounds dramatic—"

"It doesn't sound dramatic. Art *is* dramatic."

"My art isn't just a passion for me, Lev. It pays the rent." He raked his teeth over his bottom lip. "I'm not good at anything else."

Lev selected his words carefully. "I'm sure that's not true. I bet you're good at loads of things."

The truth was, while art had paid Asher's rent, Lev had been the one who'd purchased his art—under various pseudonyms for obvious reasons. Lev's insatiable appetite and unwillingness to share had propelled the price of Asher's art up by the thousands, and it wasn't close to how much Asher deserved. His art was priceless.

Asher's nose twitched. "Flattery won't buy me paint."

"I understand. Perhaps not when it comes to the price of paint, but I know what it's like to suffer so much I couldn't do the one thing that had any hope of easing my pain. I'll never take your art from you. I promise."

"What if another one of my tattoos scares you?"

Lev sobered. "Do you have a tattoo of Silas?"

Asher looked down at his jumper again. "No."

"Then, I think we're safe." Lev tilted Asher's chin up. "Accolades, critical acclaim, prices paid at auction... None of that matters to me. My art on your body, however, is the highest honor I've ever received." He squeezed Asher's hand. "You took my art and gave it life. I promise I won't run away again. Please, baby, let me see you."

Lev hadn't meant to say it. He'd never called Silas *baby*. But the word was like slipping on a tailored shirt. It suited him.

Asher smirked. "Baby?"

"I don't know what came over me." Lev hid his face against Asher's neck.

Asher stroked his back. "Don't be embarrassed. Anything is better than *pretty American*."

Lev laughed into Asher's neck, delighting in the goosebumps that lit up beneath his lips. "But you *are* pretty and American."

"And you're pretty annoying." Asher's fingers tightened on the bottom of his jumper.

Lev pulled back. "I promise. No running."

Asher smiled with grim resignation and then his face disappeared as he wrenched his jumper and shirt over his head in one go and crossed his arms over his front.

Lev inhaled sharply. "You're beautiful. Please let me look."

Asher's arms dropped.

"Take my hand," Lev said.

"Why?"

"So I can't run."

Asher rolled his eyes, but he took Lev's hand and knit their fingers together.

"Good lad," Lev murmured and kissed his forehead, then started with the ouroboros.

When he saw the ouroboros this time, it didn't hurt. Lev saw the symbol for what it was, what it always should have been—a chance at rebirth, at redemption.

His attention snagged on something familiar, a tattoo of Icarus plummeting down Asher's side, cascading from his ribs to his waist.

"This is mine?" Lev asked, touching a feather.

Lev scarcely registered Asher's nod, as he scanned the rest of him, gaze bouncing from tattoo to tattoo, all of them familiar, all of them his—the arched window of his childhood room, the silhouette of Lichenmoor's towers, the fox he'd drawn to honor his mum, the dragon from the first floor landing, the disembodied eye staring intensely from Asher's left forearm.

Tears burned behind his eyes, but the first tear didn't fall until he saw his self-portrait, the one he'd created at his very lowest, the one Asher had seen fit to emblazon over his heart, even with his eyes scribbled out.

"Are you okay?" Asher asked and swiped Lev's tears with his thumbs.

Lev nodded and flattened his palm over Asher's heart. "You put me here?"

Asher's pulse fluttered against his hand like a bird in a cage. "I wish I'd seen it before you covered your eyes."

"I couldn't get them right."

Father had assigned him the self-portrait as punishment after he'd killed Silas. Lev had tried to capture the grief and guilt he saw in the mirror, but his eyes always came out hollow, until, in a fit of fury, Lev had clenched a black marker in his fist like a toddler and scribbled over his eyes until the felt tip caved in and the plastic dug through the paper and carved shallow lines into the wood, not stopping until the marker broke in two.

Father had smiled when he saw it. "Finally, art that's honest."

Had Lev made anything honest since? He wasn't sure.

"I know it's fanatical..." Asher said.

"No, you're perfect. Sorry. I was thinking about making that self-portrait." He wiped his face. "Besides, I'm equally fanatical, if not more." One day, he'd show him the collection to prove it. "If only I'd thought to tattoo your art on me first... and wasn't so deathly afraid of needles."

Asher grinned. "You, afraid of needles? That's adorable."

Warmth filled Lev. "I quite like the idea of you finding me cute." He shifted onto his toes and stole a peek over Asher's shoulder. "Do you have any on your back?"

Asher shook his head.

Lev rested his hands on Asher's belt, pausing on the precipice of unlatching it. "What about down here, Blakely? Did any miss my notice?"

Asher cleared his throat. "No, sir."

"Mm," Lev purred. "Miles of blank canvas to fill."

Lev freed the prong from Asher's belt buckle, reached

inside the top of his trousers, and wrapped his hand around his cock.

Asher had leaked a mess of precum in poor Theo's trousers. Oh, well.

"Wait…" The dawning realization rushed to his head as he retraced his steps, scanning every tattoo gracing Asher's skin again to be sure. "I'm the only artist."

Asher nodded. "All of them are yours."

"Why?" Lev asked in an awe-laced whisper.

"I wanted to keep you close."

"I… I don't know what to say."

Asher squeezed Lev's hand. "Tell me you're not going to run."

"I'm not."

"Tell me it's not too much, that *I'm* not too much."

Lev cradled Asher's face in his hands and bored his eyes into his. "Blakely, I could feast on your soul for all eternity and never be sated, let alone full. Give me all of you, even the pieces you think are too much."

Asher tried to look away, but Lev didn't let him.

"Give me the pieces of you that scare you, that you wish weren't you. I want all of it. Understood?"

Asher nodded.

"Good." He dipped his gaze for one last look. "Beautiful. But I think I should see the rest of you to be sure." He pulled Theo's belt through the loops and tossed it aside, but when he reached the last trouser button, it wouldn't budge. "Curse Theo and his blasted clothes." A thread tore, and the button shot off and skipped across the floor.

"Tantrums are beneath you, Mr. Marks," Asher teased.

Lev scoffed. "I'll buy him a new pair, and I don't sound like that."

Asher argued, but Lev stopped listening, attention focused on the exposed root of Asher's cock, framed by short, dark curls. The rest of his length still hid inside. That wouldn't do.

With one swift tug, Theo's pants dropped, and Asher's cock sprung free, arcing in an arrow over his abs.

"Fuck me. Your cock in the foreground with my art in the background is…" Lev trailed off, unnerved by the sensation that someone was watching. He scanned the room and checked the windows. They were alone. Still…

"Hey." Asher squeezed Lev's shoulder. "Where did you go?"

Lev turned his head and kissed the hand still on his shoulder. "I felt like…" His vision focused on the tattoo of his eye on Asher's forearm. "Wait. You're left-handed."

Asher's brows darted together. "I thought you'd have noticed by now with all the time you've spent watching me paint. Are you sure you're okay?"

Lev shushed him. "Every time you've jerked off, it was with my eye on you?"

Asher nodded.

"That's…"

"Insane?"

"No." Lev gripped Asher's hips and boosted him onto the tabletop, knocking over a glass and sending cutlery and china flying off the other end. "It's so filthy." He wedged himself between Asher's legs. "You've been mine all this time. No matter who touched you, I was with you. You wanted me."

"Yes," Asher confessed.

"I wish I'd found you sooner." Before any harm had ever come to him.

"I'm here now, and I'm done waiting."

Asher fisted a hand in Lev's shirt and dragged him to his lips. Lev's thoughts came in colors and shapes, flashes of inspiration, paintings he'd later create.

Chasing pleasure and connection, he rolled his hips into the cradle of Asher's naked cock, wishing he'd thought to take off his pants first, yet unwilling to stop.

Asher moaned, and Lev swallowed the sound, deepening

their kiss, drawing forth more noises to devour. Lev's slacks were wet with Asher's precum now too.

"Did you touch yourself and pretend it was me?" Lev asked.

Asher bit his lip and nodded.

"Show me." Lev guided Asher's hand south.

His protégé complied immediately, working himself with a tight grip that milked more precum from his tip as he gazed at the tattoo of Lev's eye on his forearm.

Lev couldn't look away. Remembering Asher's need for praise, he said, "You're so fucking sexy like that, my perfect lad, stroking yourself because I asked, coming for me all those times while you waited for me."

Asher's breath hitched. "Lev." More precum oozed from his slit.

"You're so wet, Blakely. Are you always like this?"

Asher bit his lip. "No."

"Is it because I'm here?"

He nodded. His hand slowed. His eyes slowly shut.

"You're getting close, aren't you?"

Asher's eyes opened. His hand froze on his cock. "I'm sorry."

"Never apologize for taking your pleasure. I'm close too, and you aren't even touching me. You can wait a little while longer, though, can't you?"

Asher's eyes closed on a nod, the muscles in his throat flexing and shuddering with his rapid breathing.

"Eyes on me," Lev reminded.

Hooded hazel eyes parted.

"Good lad."

Asher whimpered. Would he make that noise when Lev fucked him? Hopefully.

Holding Asher's gaze, Lev lowered to his knees, planted his palms on his own thighs, and extended his tongue, eyes wide and supplicating, all but saying, *Feed me.*

25

SPUN A TAPESTRY

LEV

"Go on, Blakely. Show me how sorry I should be."

As Asher's eyes darkened, he scooted to the edge of the table, and steered his cock into Lev's open mouth.

"Mm." Lev's tastebuds exploded with the delectable taste of the one man on earth he unequivocally, irreligiously knew had been created for him. He sealed his lips around Asher's tip and swiped at his slit, wanting more.

"Jesus, Lev." Asher stroked Lev's hair like one would a dog. "But I don't want to come yet." With a sharp tug to Lev's scalp, Asher hauled him off of his cock.

Lev sat back on his haunches and looked up the length of Asher's body, at all the art hung on his toned chest and abs. Afraid he'd get off on the sight alone, he pressed the heel of his hand against the base of his dick.

Asher smeared Lev's lips with more precum, then pulled back and patted Lev's cheek. "Take off your clothes."

"Yes, sir." Lev pulled off his jumper and shirt. He loved seeing Asher take back his power.

"Why does it sound so much hotter when you say it?"

"Must be the accent."

"And your pants."

Lev laughed. "One day, I'm going to teach you the difference between American and English pants." He dropped his trousers and pants with little fanfare, leaving them pooling around his knees.

Asher's covetous gaze raked over him.

The longer Asher looked, the more Lev's cheeks burned.

He knew he was in good shape, but he was so much older than the men Asher had likely dated. Gray hair intermingled with his ginger bush. His bollocks had always been bigger, but did they sag? Oh, come off it! Of course they sagged. All bollocks did. Still, what if he disappointed the lad?

"You're staring, Blakely." He'd kept his tone light but inside he was spiraling. "Do you find me lacking?"

Asher's gaze bounced to him. "No! You're better than my fantasies. It's just..." He swallowed. "I knew you were big, but I didn't know you were *that* big."

Lev grinned as relief filled him. "Fret not, darling. I won't put it into you until you're good and ready."

They'd have to work up to it. Lev couldn't wait to stretch him with his fingers, adding one, and then another, and another, until Asher could take him. Fuck, it would be so hot.

"I think I can take you. I've had a bit of practice."

Lev stifled a growl. "I hate the idea of anyone fucking you."

Asher laughed. "You know dildos exist, right? I haven't fucked anyone in months."

"Is that supposed to make me feel any better? I haven't fucked anyone in five years."

Asher blinked. "What?"

"It doesn't matter. Please forget what I said."

Shame settled into his gut, the reminder of his agoraphobia rendering him impotent—figuratively, and literally as his erection flagged. He'd tried to leave Lichenmoor repeatedly, but he froze every time he reached the property line.

After a long pause, Asher nodded. "Okay."

"Thank you."

Without segue, Asher patted Lev's cheek, this time with the head of his cock. "Open your mouth and be a good hole."

Fuck. Me. That was hot.

Asher guided his cock back to Lev's mouth and smeared precum over his lips before sliding it in. Lev hummed in satisfaction while his desperate hands explored, testing the weight of Asher's bollocks with one hand, while the other traced a path down his cleft, stopping before he reached his hole, and lingering there, stroking his tailbone in small circles.

"Fuck, Lev." Asher's voice was raw as he dragged out the three letters of his name.

Lev sucked Asher's cock like he was an alcoholic who'd fallen off the wagon into a bottle and wanted to drown, swallowing him down with a masochistic gusto that surely bruised the back of his mouth.

Tears and spit dripped down his face, but he made no move to clean himself.

He couldn't look away. He wanted to memorize every single moment of Asher's rapture. He needed to show him the remorse in his gaze. His regret.

Asher tangled Lev's hair in his hands, holding him in place, and battered his way deep into Lev's throat.

"Fuck," Asher said on a thrust. "I love how strong you are." Thrust. "How rough I can be." Thrust. "How well you can take it." Then he pulled out and tilted Lev's chin up so fast he had whiplash. "I want to kiss you again."

Lev gripped the edge of the table on either side of Asher, and stood, sliding his cock against Asher's abs as he reached his full height. Tangling their tongues, Lev hoisted Asher onto the table again and encircled their dicks with one hand, fucking his fist and jerking them both. Glasses tipped and broke. Plates fell and shattered. The great oak table groaned against stone with each thrust. The chairs on the opposite side fell backward.

Lev couldn't care less. A king tide could swallow Lichenmoor Hall and drag it out to sea, and Lev would still chase his pleasure with Asher. Ecstasy coiled at the base of his spine. His balls lifted.

"Ash, I'm gonna come." He couldn't believe he'd lasted that long. Five years with no dick aside from his own.

"Me too."

Asher hugged Lev to his chest and dragged his nails down his back. The pain, the thought of the marks Asher had likely left, the art all over his chest, the wonder of the warm, beautiful man in his hands who painted miracles, and somehow wanted him—all of it coalesced.

Gentlemen came last, so he stacked both of his hands, and surrounded Asher's cock from root to tip. Asher's back arched, and he came, a single word on his lips like a curse.

"Lev."

And with one last almighty thrust, Lev's pleasure crested too, and he barreled through his orgasm with a word of his own.

"Ash."

Lev was breathless and spent, but he wasn't sated. Not yet. He curled over Asher's stomach and lapped their mixed come from the gutter of his abs and traced the lines of his tattoos with his tongue. Goosebumps erupted across Asher's skin. His muscles tensed.

"That tickles." Asher laughed and tried to shove Lev's head away, writhing to free himself, dragging his sticky cock deliciously up and down Lev's chest and stomach as he struggled.

"Hush. I'm almost finished." Lev grazed Asher's sensitive skin with his teeth. "Done." He lifted his head and kissed Asher on the lips, sharing the spicy combination of them.

Asher moaned into his mouth, eager cock already hardening again.

"You're insatiable."

"Worried you can't keep up?" Asher teased, grinning.

"Please, I'm forty, not seventy. Besides, my dick isn't

required to get you off." Not when his mouth and hand were more than willing. "And I'm insatiable for you too."

Lev kneeled again and laved Asher's bollocks with long licks. He sucked first one, and then the other into his mouth, and detoured to lick and nip at the lines where his thighs met his pelvis, before burying his nose in the curls at the base of his cock and inhaling. He neglected Asher's cock as it grew rigid and ruddy and bobbed with each heartbeat.

"You're so mean," Asher whined, his legs shaking.

"Am I?" Lev nipped the crest of his hipbone and sucked another hickey, then stood and tapped his arse. "Turn around and face the table."

"Oh." Asher eased down until his feet touched the floor.

"Good lad." Lev bent him over the table until his chest was flat against it. "There we are."

Asher looked over his shoulder with lust-glazed eyes and shifted his hips as if to emphasize his perfectly fuckable predicament.

"Don't tempt me, Blakely."

"What do you mean, don't tempt you? You're the one who bent me over a table."

Lev looked up at the timber pitched beams to marshal his strength, and notched his cock between Asher's cheeks, grateful he wasn't hard enough to sink into him yet because he wasn't sure he'd be able to resist.

"I need to taste you here." Lev flattened his palms over Asher's arse cheeks and lowered to his knees.

Asher's breath hitched, and he lifted his arse like he wanted to be bred. So eager. Smirking to himself, Lev took a detour and licked a path to the twin dimples on his back.

His black-cat of a lad practically mewled his displeasure. "Lev, please."

"You're only ever this polite when we're alone. Why can't you be like this all the time?"

"Fuck you." Asher writhed, and squirmed, fighting for friction.

"Not today, I'm afraid. I don't break my toys."

Asher scoffed. "I'm not easily broken."

"Such a greedy, impatient thing, already got off once and demanding seconds." Lev parted Asher's cheeks with his thumbs and ghosted his breath over his hole. "You're so pretty here. Press your cheek to the table and let me take care of you."

Goosebumps ignited across Asher's skin as he did as he was told.

"Mm. Look how obedient you can be." Lev kissed Asher's tailbone and descended to his hole, sucking and licking as he devoured him, angling his head up and down and side to side, desperate to taste all of him, while somewhere above Asher spun a tapestry of filthy compliments.

"Fuck, Lev. You don't know how much I've jacked off to this, how much I've wanted this, wanted you."

With a muffled moan, Lev took Asher's cock in his fist, and stroked him slowly while he fucked his tongue into his hole, ignoring the ache as his frenulum stretched and nearly tore.

Lev pulled back enough to press the pad of his finger to Asher's entrance. "Ask me nicely."

"No," Asher snapped, ever the brat.

Lev removed his finger and mocked a frown. "That's a shame. I'd hoped to get a preview of your tight hole sucking me in."

"Okay, okay, okay," Asher said in a rush. "Please put something inside of me, preferably your cock, but I'll take whatever you'll give me. Please." He dragged the last word out.

Lev laughed. "If you insist..." Lev spat onto Asher's hole and pushed inside, stopping at his first knuckle as Asher rose onto the tips of his toes.

"More. I need more."

"Not yet." Lev licked around Asher's hole, drifting his

finger in a lazy figure eight without removing it, easing him open enough to accept the widest part of his finger.

He advanced until he'd pushed past the second knuckle. Asher's prostate was easy to find, already swollen with arousal and one orgasm under its belt. He massaged the spongy tissue, and Asher whimpered again.

"Fuck, Lev. Oh fuck. That's too much. I can't... I..." Asher's teeth chattered. How cute. Lev couldn't wait to see the tremors he'd elicit when he seated his cock inside of him.

Sweat darkened the roots of Asher's hair. His eyes had closed, face contorted in painful nirvana, cheek as scarlet as if Lev had slapped him. Would the red ever fade, or would it stain forever? A scarlet letter telling everyone what they'd done, the pleasure Lev had wrought?

Hopefully.

Asher's eyes found his. "I'm gonna..."

Lev's stomach somersaulted in excitement. "Do it. Come again for me. I want to see you come with my finger in you. I want to feel you clench around me."

Asher's body tautened like a bowstring, and he cried out an indecently loud, prolonged moan that rivaled the force of the storm. Good. Let the others hear. Let all of Lichenmoor know. Blakely was his, and he'd defend him from any foe.

Asher's muscles slackened, and were it not for the table, he'd have fallen to the floor. Lev removed his finger and curled his body over him, stretching to kiss his lax lips.

Asher laughed weakly. "Holy fucking fuck, Lev."

"Now you know who you belong to, and that I belong to you too."

But that's not what he wanted to say. Instead of something trite and possessive, he'd wanted to confess that he already was addicted to him. One taste and he was gone.

26

THE HUNTRESS AND THE TRAP

ASHER

For someone who'd just hooked up with another guy for the first time in five years, Lev didn't look very satisfied.

"What's wrong?" Asher pushed off the table and turned around.

"I hurt you here." Lev traced light fingertips over Asher's right flank. "I should have been more gentle with you."

Asher bit his lip to stifle the hiss of pain that threatened to escape, but he couldn't hide his flinch.

"You didn't hurt me. That happened in Theo's room."

Lev's glacier eyes turned murderous.

"I don't need to be avenged," Asher rushed to add. "I bumped into the bathroom counter."

Lev's eyes narrowed. His fingers trailed lower. "This is going to bruise."

"I swear. The towel rack in Theo's bathroom broke off in my hand, and I fell back."

Lev pinched the bridge of his nose and inhaled. "I should have kept you with me. I could have bathed you."

Asher snorted. "Yeah, and I would have asked you to wash my back..." He rolled his eyes. "Come on, Lev."

"Where else are you hurt?" He scanned Asher head to foot

and frowned at the abrasions on his knees. "What happened here?"

"I fell on the path, remember?"

"I wish you'd told me you were hurt. I wouldn't have manhandled you." Lev sifted through the debris on the floor and shook out his sweater, then tugged it over Asher's head before he could protest.

Asher fished his arms through the sleeves. "It's a scraped knee, not a mortal wound." Mm. Lev's clothes were still warm and smelled like his cologne. "Besides, I love a good manhandle."

Lev grimaced. Wait. Did he regret this? Was he looking for a way out, some excuse for them being doomed because Asher got a scratch?

"Post-nut clarity hit you over the head like a sledgehammer, didn't it?" Asher asked.

"I beg your pardon? Post-nut what?"

Asher crossed his arms. "The regret and disgust that creeps in after you come."

"Blakely, no. That was..." He palmed Asher's cheek.

Asher wanted to lean into his touch, but if Lev rejected him after he'd bared the rest of his body and soul to him, Asher was going to—

"What we did was art. It was beautiful, and perfect. I don't have post-coital clarity, or whatever you call it. I haven't felt pleasure like that since..." His brow wrinkled. "Well, I can't quite remember anything better. Perhaps never." He smiled, smoothing the lines on his forehead. "I want to do it again, hopefully soon."

"Oh."

"Yes, oh." Lev massaged Asher's tight jaw with his fingertips; he hadn't realized he'd been clenching.

"The only thing I regret is hurting you." Lev kissed Asher's forehead and pulled back. "Understood?"

Asher nodded.

"Good." Lev stooped to the ground, pulled on tight boxer briefs that hugged his package in a way that made Asher jealous of an inanimate object. "Hold onto me."

Asher yelped as Lev hoisted him off his feet. "What are you doing?" Asher linked his hands behind Lev's neck and locked his legs around his waist.

"I'm taking you to the kitchen. You need to eat, and the lighting is better there."

"I can walk."

"I think not." Lev held Asher tighter and nudged aside a fork with his toe. "We made a bit of a mess, and I won't have you cutting your feet."

A bit of a mess was an understatement.

Glass shards glittered in the firelight. A bottle of merlot lay overturned on the floor, its contents bleeding into the grout. A bread basket had tumbled across the rug, spilling rolls and breadcrumbs.

"We can't leave this for Luna," Asher said.

Lev sidestepped over a plate. "We won't. I'll take care of it after you're in bed."

"I can help."

"I know you can, but you need to eat, and rest."

Lev backed against the door and into the butler's pantry connecting the dining room to the kitchen. He released Asher onto his feet, touch lingering on his hips until Asher proved his legs were seaworthy, or whatever the opposite of that was. Landworthy?

"After you," Lev said.

Asher led the way into the kitchen, grateful the oversized sweater covered his ass. Behind him, Lev flicked the switch, and near-daylight exploded from the overhead lamps.

"Jesus," Asher hissed and shielded his eyes with the back of his hand. "Do you do surgery here?" On Asher's other visits to the kitchen, the lighting had never been so stark.

"Bright light helps my mood during the dark winter

months." Lev gripped Asher's hips and guided him toward the kitchen island. He patted the butcher-block counter. "Hop on up. Let's make sure you aren't hurt anywhere else."

"I'm not."

Ignoring him, Lev boosted him onto the smooth wood. "There's a good lad."

Asher's irritation ebbed at the praise. American men had no idea what they were missing. Good boy was overrated. Good lad purred in Lev's posh accent made Asher want to behave, an idea as foreign to him as being cared for by another man.

"What happened here?" Lev squatted, flaring his muscular thighs like a butterfly. His ginger lashes dipped downward as he cradled Asher's left foot and examined his battered toes.

"I stubbed them when I tripped." He tried to pull his knee to his chest, but Lev held onto his foot.

Lev clicked his tongue. "They're already so swollen. Can you move them?"

Asher wiggled them, clenching his teeth at the pain.

Frowning, Lev stood. "Let's see your hands."

Asher turned them over. They were pink, a little scratched, but otherwise unharmed.

Lev's frown deepened. "Does anywhere else hurt?"

Asher shook his head.

Everything hurt. After fainting, he'd woken on his back, but his right hip and shoulder ached like he'd landed there first. He wouldn't tell Lev he'd fainted, though. Not when Lev was already raking himself over the coals.

Lev stroked his beard and swept his gaze over Asher again, as if assessing for a mortal wound Asher had hidden somewhere. Apparently satisfied, he crossed to the old copper sink and held a fresh towel under the water. "You're so cute in my clothes."

Asher's cheeks heated. He felt cute swimming in Lev's cozy

sweater. The other men he'd been with were around his height or shorter.

Lev returned with the damp rag and a dry towel and asked Asher to lift his sweater. With methodical attention to detail, Lev gently scrubbed the dried come from Asher's chest and abs, and between his legs. Asher's cock filled at Lev's attention.

"Thank you." Asher shifted his hips, squirming with need. Insatiable lad.

Lev's hand lingered on his thigh. "Of course." He tapped his hip. "Right. Let's get you fed."

Asher braced his arms on the edge of the butcher block and scooted to hop down.

"Oh no you don't." Lev stopped him. "Do you want leftovers? Luna likely saved some."

Asher's stomach rolled. He closed his eyes against the memory of blood steaming in the cold air as it traveled toward the drain. "I don't eat beef."

"I hadn't realized..." Lev ducked out from behind the fridge door. "Are you vegetarian?"

"I eat everything else as long as I buy from local farms that treat their animals well, but I haven't been able to eat beef since I was a kid. Maybe I'm too sensitive." He shrugged, and the sweater slid off his shoulder.

Lev's eyes dropped to his exposed skin. "There's nothing wrong with being sensitive. I think it's very sweet, Blakely." He cringed and raked a hand through his ginger hair. "And here I've harped on and on about you eating tonight..."

"You didn't know."

"What about an omelet? The eggs are from our chickens. They live a jolly good life trouncing about in our conservatory during the cooler months."

Asher smiled. "An omelet would be perfect." For the first time since he'd arrived at Lichenmoor, he actually had an appetite.

"Splendid." Lev slipped a pan from a hook above the oven

and slid it onto the gas stove. "Dinner wasn't the only time you haven't eaten, though." He opened the fridge and scavenged through the vegetable drawer, emerging with a bag of spinach, a bell pepper, and a carton of mushrooms.

"I don't have an eating disorder, if that's what you're thinking," Asher said.

Lev paused, his hand mid-pilfering a bowl of eggs on the counter. "I don't know what to think beyond that I find it impossible not to worry over you."

"I'm sorry."

"There's no need to apologize."

"When I'm anxious or upset, I can't eat, and if I try to force it, I get nauseous."

Lev rinsed the eggs in the sink. "So you're saying I've been such an arsehole that I turned you off food?"

Asher laughed. "It's not *all* your fault. Sometimes I forget to eat if I get sucked into a project, and you're a lot more distracting than art."

"That happens to me too." He tapped the blunt edge of the knife to his head. "It's that ADHD hyper-focus."

"I didn't know you had ADHD."

"I was a late bloomer. Or rather, undiagnosed until I was in my thirties. People had always assumed I was flighty and eccentric, your typical artist stereotype, but with medication, my brain is quiet and uncluttered. I can remember more."

"The meds don't affect your creativity?"

"I don't know, Blakely. What do you think? Have I lost my touch?" He smiled good-naturedly.

"Nah. You've still got it."

They fell into a companionable silence, one Asher's brain filled with anxiety. "Do you think I have ADHD?"

"What? No, I wasn't diagnosing you."

"I love it when you say *what* like that."

"Like what?" Lev said, his accent made *what* rhyme with *hot*.

"Like that." Asher rolled his neck, stretching it. "I don't think I have ADHD. Just the anxiety and panic attacks you've been unlucky enough to witness."

"I witnessed nothing more than a man in need of comfort and company." Lev turned and tipped the sliced bell pepper into the pan, scraping the stragglers off the cutting board with the edge of his blade. He seasoned them with a vigorous twist of the pepper mill and a dash of salt. "When did your attacks start?"

"Huh?" Asher blinked, preoccupied by the accidental eroticism of Lev grinding pepper. He cleared his throat. "At art school. Between the workload, stress, and Ben…"

Mostly Ben. He nibbled his lip and shook his head, erasing the image of perfectly tousled brown hair graying at the temples.

"I hadn't realized you went to art school," Lev said slowly, adding the mushrooms next.

"I never finished. It's not a secret, but it's not something I'm proud of."

"Did you leave by choice?"

"Yes… No." He raked a hand through his hair. "I don't know."

"Was it Ben?"

Asher's stomach sank. "So you *do* know who he is?"

"No." Lev slid the peppers and mushrooms onto a plate, then cracked the first egg with one hand, dropping it into the sizzling pan. "You mentioned him, and gatekeeping men, and I made an educated guess."

"Ben was my professor."

"I see." After cracking the next egg, he added a dash of milk and whisked the mixture with more violence than necessary. "Let me guess, he lured you into his bed and broke your heart when you wanted more?"

"Something like that." And a hell of a lot more that Asher didn't want to think about. "Did that happen to you too?"

"No." Lev returned the vegetables to the pan and tucked them in with a fold of the omelet. "But I've met my fair share of predatory art professors." He sprinkled a handful of cheese and slid the omelet onto the plate. "Voila."

"Thanks." Asher crammed a huge piece into his mouth with his fork.

"No thanks necessary. It pleases me to see you eat." Lev leaned against the butcher block and knit his fingers together, watching him quietly.

Rain battered the window over the kitchen sink, but this time the storm was cozy instead of frightening. A few minutes and half an omelet later, lightning flashed, casting the contours of Lev's face in shadow. Thunder boomed. They listened to the storm draw nearer as he ate.

"How is your stomach now? More settled?" Lev asked when Asher had nearly finished.

Asher wiped his mouth with a napkin and nodded.

"Good. I want you to sleep with me."

Asher nearly choked on his last bite of omelet. "What?"

Crow's feet winked at the corners of Lev's eyes. "Blakely, not everything is about sex." He sobered. "I'll sleep better knowing you're safe. I know I didn't show it well, but I was terrified when I thought I'd lost you on the moor with high tide and a storm approaching. I'm still afraid I'll wake and find your bed empty."

How could Asher say no?

Lev's room was brighter than Asher's, even in the dark. The tapestry lining Lev's walls told Medusa's story from Poseidon's point of view in gold and seafoam thread. Instead of the oak four-poster bed in Asher's room, Lev's bed was golden walnut carved with subtle ocean waves that turned the wood into water.

The wingback chair beside the fireplace was more substantial than the antique chairs strewn around the castle. A slanted architect's desk overlooked a row of arched windows.

Crumpled paper littered the floor, including more than one map of Lichenmoor that must not have made the cut. Asher smiled at how much thought Lev had put into helping him navigate the grounds.

Colored pencils on a wooden tray sat beside a large sketchbook lying open on the desk. Asher crossed to the sketchbook as if drawn by a spell.

"Can I look?"

"Please."

Asher drifted closer, fully expecting Lev to rush past him and slam the book shut. It's what Asher would have done. Instead, Lev wrapped his arms around Asher's waist from behind, all solid warmth against his back, and rested his chin on his shoulder.

On the open page, Lev had drawn a side profile of Asher painting, a rough sketch, but for an artist as talented as Lev, it was so polished and alive it might as well have been complete.

"You drew me?" Asher asked.

"I love watching you paint. The way your tongue darts out when you're concentrating." He kissed Asher's neck, igniting goosebumps. "The most adorable wrinkle forms between your eyebrows when you're debating what to do next.

"Your lips part and your body stills, except for your brush, when you're in that place all artists go, where everything else ceases to exist except for your canvas." Another kiss, this one below his ear. "I could watch you paint for hours, and never tire of it." Lev tightened his hold around Asher's waist.

"I know what you mean," Asher said.

Witnessing Lev paint was the only time Asher sensed even a fragment of vulnerability, at least until today. Over the years,

Asher had consumed every video of Lev painting that he could find until Lev's mannerisms and diction were almost as familiar as if they'd been friends for years.

Asher slipped his finger under the previous page and paused.

"Go ahead. Have a look."

Lev had sketched them in the chapel, the perspective of Lev on his knees looking up Asher's body, the ouroboros tattoo in focus, the other tattoos forgotten. In another sketch, Asher was on his knees looking through the keyhole in the east wing. The next page was from the tower. Back and back Asher went until the first evening they met. Lev had sketched Asher lost in the fog. The page before that was Silas, as good a stopping point as any.

"Have you ever given thought to how art breeds intimacy?" Lev said, crowding him against the desk, pressing them together. "A true artist slits their wrists and bleeds paint onto the page. Oscar Wilde said something similar, and a little less macabre. *Every portrait that is painted with feeling is a portrait of the artist, not of the sitter.*"

Lev nuzzled the back of Asher's hair, inhaling deeply. "That's far more intimate than dating." He flipped forward to the scene in the tower. "That's what I was trying to explain that night. Falling in love through a painting."

Asher nodded, too moved to speak. Lev had put into words the strange connection he'd experienced long before they'd met, the reason Asher felt like he knew him already, the reason he could read Lev so well.

Lev closed the book. "I can't wait to draw the rest of you. I want you to see all of me."

"I could make a *Titanic* joke, but I won't."

Lev's bark of laughter rumbled in Asher's chest. Earning Lev's laughter was almost as satisfying as earning his praise.

"It's late." Lev pulled him back from the desk.

They brushed their teeth side by side at the sink. Lev

insisted Asher wear his flannel pajama bottoms to bed, and climbed in behind him, large hands pulling him into the little spoon position. It was all so surreal.

Asher scooted back, nestling his ass against Lev's cock.

"Behave, Blakely."

"I'm just getting comfortable."

"Right." Lev rolled his hips. "I'm just getting comfortable too."

"Don't start things if you aren't going to finish them."

"Hush." Lev kissed the crown of Asher's head.

The storm waxed into a steady rain, but beneath the percussive symphony, the crash of waves crept closer.

"The ocean is so loud," Asher said.

Lev squeezed him. "Fret not. Lichenmoor has stood here for centuries, and it's never flooded above the dungeons. You're safe with me."

The waves crashed louder and louder until sleep finally took him with a single thought—the ocean was the huntress, and Lichenmoor the trap.

2 7

EFFIGY

LEV

Lev yawned behind his palm. Watching Asher sleep was an exercise in control. Asher ran hot and slept fitfully. He'd wriggled his way out of Lev's pajama bottoms in the middle of the night, and nearly walloped Lev's bollocks with his knee when he'd tossed onto his side.

Unable to sleep after that, he'd already made his daily rounds of Lichenmoor's borders. While he hadn't found Silas's body, or the specter himself, he *had* found Asher's bag tangled in kelp, clothes herniating through gashes like an effigy of Asher destroyed by the sea.

Lev had carried the waterlogged bag up the hill in his arms like a hollow stand-in for the body he longed to lay to rest in Lichenmoor's mausoleum. Asher's art kit was ruined, but Lev had salvaged most of his clothing, which he'd already washed and popped into the dryer.

Art supplies, toiletries, and a spare pair of trainers could all be replaced. Lev had ordered a new pair of his shoes, and some sensible boots through his personal shopper. Father's supply room held enough paint and brushes for them to paint every

198

day for the next ten years without running out. Perhaps Asher would enjoy rebuilding his stash with the Marks family's stock.

The sheets stirred. Lev lifted his head from his sketch. But no, Asher still slept sprawled out on his back, with one leg kicked from the covers, exposing the crease where his thigh met his groin and the root of his cock.

Ugly bruises bloomed over his right shoulder and side, coloring in some of Lev's art. Asher had been through a lot more than he'd let on, in more ways than one. The story Asher told didn't match the state of him. Had he taken a tumble?

He wished his private physician could have looked Asher over before bed, but with the tide high, he'd had no choice but to trust Asher when he said he was fine, though he'd also checked the lad's breathing a few times.

While he'd waited for Asher to wake, he preserved his memories of the last twenty-four hours in his sketchbook— Asher hugging his knees on the cobblestone. Asher perched on the kitchen island eating Lev's omelet. Asher bent over the table, looking back at Lev as he climaxed.

Lev adjusted his cock in his slacks, and drew Asher in media res—lust sated, wounded but not defeated. He lifted the book to his lips and blew away stray graphite dust. Sleepy hazel eyes opened.

"I'm not sure if it's creepy or cute that this is the second time I've caught you watching me sleep," Asher mumbled.

Lev wanted to be the only person in the world to hear Asher's first words spoken every day, the ones he uttered while dusting the cobwebs off his dreams.

"To be fair, you were only pretending to sleep in the church, and you're very pretty when you sleep." Lev dropped his sketchbook on the chair and crossed to sit at the edge of the bed. "Muscles slack and pliant, that wrinkle so often on your brow smoothed away, all the flush in your face absent as the blood settles back in your veins."

Asher swallowed with a delicious bob of his Adam's apple. "Did you touch me while I slept?"

"No. Never without your consent." Lev drifted toward Asher's ear. "Would you have liked it if I had?"

Asher's black lashes fanned downward on a sharp inhale. "Yes."

"You trust me to handle you while you're unconscious, to play with you until pleasure pulls you from your dreams?"

Asher nodded, shifting his hips in bed. Did his morning wood need attention?

"Consent with words, Blakely. I need to hear it."

"I trust you." Asher licked his lips and shifted his hips again. A small circle of precum bloomed on the white sheets before Lev's eyes.

"Your trust is a gift." Lev wrinkled his nose at the question that came to mind next. "Have you played like that with anyone else?"

"Yeah, with Ben."

"You trusted him once too?"

"I guess, but... It's hard to explain." Asher nibbled his lip. "Ben had a way of making me believe *his* ideas were mine. Does that make sense?"

"If you mean he manipulated you, then yes."

Asher raked his hair back from his forehead with both hands, baring sexy pits Lev longed to lick. "It's too early for an interrogation about my exes."

"That's fair, though I do hate that I'm not the one to take your somnophilia virginity."

Asher snorted. "You're almost fifteen years older than me! I'll never be your first in anything."

"You're very cute when you're jealous. How are you feeling?"

"Sore." Asher scooted to a seated position with his back to the headboard, taking the sheets with him.

"I'm so sorry." Lev wished he could carry his pain, but the best he could do was promise never to hurt him again.

Asher lifted his palm. "I can't take any more apologies."

"You liked my apology last night."

"Those, I don't mind."

Lev nodded at Asher's tented sheets. "How do you feel about spending most of the day in bed?"

Asher grinned, adorable dimples like crescents at the corners of his mouth. "That depends on what your definition of spending the day in bed is."

"Blakely," Lev gasped, clutching his chest with feigned indignation. "Are you insinuating that I want to keep you in bed so I can fuck you into the mattress so many times your body will leave an imprint?"

The muscles in Asher's throat flexed as he swallowed. "It sounds like a great way to apologize to me."

Lev tugged his gaze away. "I'm afraid that won't be the case. You need rest and recovery, and breakfast in bed."

"Sounds boring." Asher yawned, stretching his corded arms overhead, accentuating Icarus's fall from the ladder of his ribs.

Lev pinched the bridge of his nose. "I know what you're doing."

Asher crossed his arms over his chest, framing his pecs, dimples deepening with a smirk. "What am I doing?"

"Taunting me. Let's have a look at your toes, and I'll get your coffee."

With a roll of his eyes, Asher complied, pulling his leg out from the covers and allowing Lev to draw his foot into his lap.

Asher's toes had darkened to a deep aubergine.

Lev bit back an apology, intent on following Asher's wishes. "This looks painful. Can you still move them?"

Asher bit his lip and moved his toes sluggishly with a wince.

"Poor dear," Lev said. Certainly, that wasn't an apology. He gently massaged his foot and calf, searching for any pain points.

"That feels good." Asher hummed, arching his spine, dragging his cockhead against the sheets and leaving a trail of precum behind.

Christ. Lev cleared his throat and stood. "Right. Coffee. You must be cold." He jerked the blankets deftly over Asher's lap and crossed to the side table, ignoring Asher's snicker.

"Do you want milk?" Lev asked as he poured a cup of coffee from an insulated carafe and lifted a small silver pitcher.

"If you're offering."

Lev tutted and drizzled milk into the mug. "I've already added fresh vanilla bean and sugar."

"Vanilla bean? Is that Luna's recipe?"

He shook his head slowly. "Wendell's... He was a friend of Father's."

Asher bolted upright and gripped Lev's wrist. "Wait. Wendell Morrigan, the poet?"

"You've heard of him?" Of course, Asher had. Lev shouldn't have said anything.

Asher's lips moved in silent conversation with himself. "Silas... I knew I'd heard the name somewhere. Silas was Wendell's son?"

"Yes." Lev huffed a soft sigh and passed him the mug. He'd only wanted to dote on Asher, not unearth old skeletons. "Wendell had preferred coffee to tea, but only with fresh vanilla bean."

Asher sipped. "That's delicious." Asher took another sip and watched him, a hundred unasked questions behind his gaze.

"Much better than from the shops?"

"Infinitely. You know you don't have to do all this, right?"

"I know, but it pleases me to care for you."

Coffee in bed wasn't that lavish of a gesture, was it? Had no one ever spoiled him? Lev endeavored to show Asher what it was like to be adored.

"What other ways do you like to please?" Asher sipped from the cup. "What if I wanted to top you?"

Fuck. Me. Blakely. "I would like that very much."

Asher arched a brow, and one corner of his lips quirked into a half smile. "You like to bottom?"

Lev watched him over the rim of his teacup. "I prefer to top, but sometimes I crave to be filled. Only with those I trust, however. I've been fucked by a few selfish tops who didn't care about my pleasure."

"You trust me?" All signs of flirtation fled Asher's face.

Lev brushed Asher's hair back from his brow. "I can't imagine my number one fan betraying me, which reminds me, I left instructions for the other artists. I took your suggestion and selected *Pride* for the next sin. Do you want to join them? What better way to demonstrate pride than by rubbing our newly consummated relationship in Theo's face?"

Asher's smile broke. "They must have heard everything."

Lev waved his hand airily. "Don't worry about them. Soon they'll be gone. I'd charter a boat and send them home today if I could, but the phone lines are down and that would be rather rude."

"You should offer them a chance to stay for the rest of the retreat and keep teaching them. They took time off from work and came all this way."

"But I find two-thirds of them tedious and the remaining third downright dreadful. Don't even get me started on Chuck. I'll gladly lend him a lifeboat."

Asher swatted his arm.

"You must know you're the only one who came here for artistic reasons aside from Melody and Julian. The others came lusting for me, or clout."

Asher rolled his eyes. "Daria seems genuine too."

"Genuinely frightening." Lev moved Asher's mug to the

bedside table and kissed him, sending the rest of his apologies wordlessly. "Mm. I may acquire a taste for coffee if I am to taste it fresh on your lips each morning."

Asher laughed. "You're talking like a time traveler again."

Lev scoffed and climbed off the bed.

Asher reached for him. "Hey, where are you going?"

Lev let Asher pull him back into another kiss and then escaped. "I have breakfast for you. Stay there." He lifted the cloche from the tray he'd left on the desk and returned with a cream cheese bagel he'd added tomato and cucumber to. "It's vegetarian."

"This looks great." Asher moved to get out of bed.

"Stay." Lev put a pillow on Asher's lap and placed the plate on top of it. "Later, let's make a list of food you'd like Luna to pick up."

Asher's eyes snapped wide. "Did you clean up downstairs?"

He nodded. "While I appreciated your offer to help, I'd never have let you."

After placing a glass of orange juice on Asher's bedside table, Lev joined him in bed. Asher bit into his bagel sandwich and hummed contentedly.

"This is delicious."

The fox tattoo on his right arm summoned Lev's attention. The tattoo artist had recreated each delicate blade of fur thinner than a strand of hair.

"Who did these? They're very good." He hated that someone so talented had spent so much time with Asher's body.

"A guy I know from school. He's the only one I trust to do your art any justice."

"I see."

Asher smiled knowingly. "He's not my type."

Lev stroked the fox's tiny paw. "My mum believed foxes were lost souls caught in purgatory. During the day they appear as people, but at night their souls return to the fox's form. That's why seeing a fox during the day is so rare. I used to go looking for foxes to see if I could find her."

Asher covered Lev's hand and nodded, encouraging him to continue.

"Sometimes I can barely remember her. Father took so many pictures and mementos before her death, painted her in every light and shadow, took casts of her hands." Father had created an entire room devoted to her. "But memories are too ephemeral to be preserved, as fragile as spider webs."

"I wish you could have had more time with her."

Being consoled by a man who was born after his mum died made Lev feel dirty. While he'd slept with a few younger twinks with a daddy kink, this was different.

It was real.

28

STRONG ENOUGH TO BOW

ASHER

OCTOBER 20

"I said you could draw me a bath, not treat me like a sickly Victorian wife."

Asher had only consented to Lev's titillating offer to draw him an epsom bath in the hope Lev would join him.

Lev patted his arm. "You're so cute when you're cross."

"I'm not cross."

Lev had taken Asher's injuries personally, as if he'd been the one to shove him to the cobblestone and nearly drown him.

At first it was flattering, especially when Lev insisted on tending to him by draining Asher's balls with his mouth so he wouldn't have to lift a finger. But after three days hidden in the cocoon of Lev's room, Asher was tired of being treated like one of Theo's glass sculptures.

The tub was already nearly full. Lev bent and twisted the tap off, averting his gaze as Asher stepped out of his sweatpants.

"Can you make sure I don't fall on my ass?"

"Of course. Your arse will be in the safest of hands. I have a vested interest after all."

Asher groaned. "I think that's the worst joke you've made so far."

"It's an excellent joke. I'm told I'm hilarious."

"Yeah, because you're hot."

Lev gasped. "People always laugh at my jokes."

"Because you're hot."

Lev pursed his lips.

"I'm joking."

"That wasn't very funny." Lev took both of Asher's hands, spotting him as he stepped over the lip of the tub.

"Yeah, because like I said, you have no sense of hu—" Asher hissed as icy pinpricks pierced his cold feet and highlighted every point of broken skin as he sank into the hot, herbal-scented water.

"Are you alright?" Lev asked.

"Mmhm," Asher hummed, gripping the sides of the tub as he closed his eyes, tipped his head back, and let his body float. "Thank you. I needed this."

When Asher opened his eyes, Lev hadn't moved, though his expression had changed from concern to desire.

"Are you waiting for an invitation?" Asher asked.

Lev blinked. "What? Of course not, unless... What I meant to say... Only if you'd like me to..."

Asher laughed. "Get in here."

Lev pulled his tee over his head, revealing broad shoulders dusted with nutmeg freckles and lighter cinnamon speckling the rest of him. Asher wanted to connect the dots with his tongue.

"My eyes are up here, Blakely."

"I know where your eyes are," Asher retorted, gaze trailing down Lev's abs and along his Adonis belt. He forced his gaze up. "You're so fucking hot."

"I'm glad you think so." He rubbed the back of his head, drawing Asher's attention to the hair under his arm. "I don't have the body of a twenty-five-year-old."

Lev's concerns were absurd. "Your body is better than mine. Hand to bible, Lev, you're the sexiest man I've ever been with. Your age doesn't matter to me."

"One day, it will."

"Then we live in the now."

"Live in the now," Lev repeated. "I like that."

"Good. Now turn around and take off your pants."

Lev barked a laugh. "You mean my trousers?"

Asher rolled his eyes. "No one likes a pedant."

Lev laughed and acquiesced, dipping his thumbs into his pants, on the precipice of pulling them down, then dragged his pants slowly over the curve of his cheeks, and dropped them.

Asher mapped Lev's glutes with his palms and squeezed, then grabbed his hips and tugged him closer.

"What are you—" Lev staggered backwards and stopped right before falling into the tub. "Oh."

Asher parted Lev down the center, just to peek—or at least that's what he told himself until the sight of Lev's hole was so irresistible his tongue took on a mind of its own.

Lev gasped. Asher moaned as he laved his tongue along the ridges and valleys of him with a feral sort of fervency.

"*Fuck me,* Blakely."

Asher kissed up Lev's lower back and wrapped his hand around his length. "Pay close attention, Marks. I'm going to show you how I like to be fucked." Asher modeled the speed he preferred while focusing his attention on the first few inches at the end of Lev's cock. "You're big, and I need you to start slow and shallow until you break me in."

Lev made what would have been a whimper, if his voice wasn't so low and graveled.

"I'm tight." Asher squeezed. "Tighter than this. Once you open me up, I like it harder and a little faster." He shifted his hand to stroke more of Lev's cock. "And when I'm ready to come, I want you so deep, I feel you in my throat."

Using the thumb of his other hand, Asher exposed

more of Lev's hole. "Mm. You're tight, too." He bent his head and devoured Lev's hole like a deity bingeing at a bacchanal.

"*Ash*," Lev said in a long, fuck-drunk moan. "Fuck. Oh my God."

Asher did feel like a god, exalted by Lev coming undone.

"I'm close," Lev said in a rush.

Asher hummed, a nonverbal nudge of approval, as he jerked Lev in fast pulls all the way to his base and back up.

Lev lost all decorum, no longer a gentleman, but a man driven by need, a god stripped of his power and forced corporeal, willing to risk death and eternal damnation for even a fleeting second of mortal pleasure.

"I'm going to..." Cum spilled over Asher's hand before Lev finished his sentence.

Asher pulled Lev tighter against his mouth and eased him through the aftershocks until he was done.

"Bloody hell, Blakely." Lev turned, breathless and awestruck, cheeks and chest flushed.

Asher licked the come from his fingers with a grin, then wiped his mouth with the back of his hand.

"Are you sure you're real?" Lev cupped Asher's face. "Sometimes I'm afraid my mind conjured you."

"I know what you mean."

"Let me hold you, little dormouse."

"Don't call me that," Asher said automatically, but this time he didn't mind, not when Lev looked at him like he wanted to eat him.

Leaning forward, Asher made room for Lev, who then climbed in behind him and pulled Asher between his legs. Asher rested back against Lev's expansive chest and tilted his head to meet his gaze.

"You are everything," Lev said and kissed him tenderly. Too tenderly.

It wasn't enough. Asher tried to tell him as much, pillaging

Lev's mouth with his tongue and digging his fingernails into his thighs.

Instead of returning Asher's aggression, Lev laughed, pulling back. "You're always so prickly. Trust me to take care of you."

Before Asher could tell him exactly how prickly he could be, Lev finally took Asher's cock in hand, and stroked him with long, languid pulls. He reclaimed Asher's lips, transporting him back to the gentle kiss that wasn't them.

Trapped by Lev's forearm against his chest, Asher tried to thrust upward into Lev's grip. He even nipped Lev's lip. But he tired out quickly, still weak from his race against high tide.

"Relax. Don't you want to be good for me?"

Asher surrendered. The trade-off was worth earning Lev's praise. "Yes."

"There's a good lad." The weight of Lev's arm on Asher's chest lifted as Lev brushed Asher's hair from his brow and kissed him. "Let me love you."

Asher finally understood. Lev wasn't teasing him. He was promising Asher was safe with him. This wasn't about getting off. This was Lev making love, and Lev's love was as soft as it was rough. It was as stable as it was tumultuous. Strong, but willing to bend, strong enough to bow.

When Asher came, his orgasm simmered through him without waning as Lev wrung pleasure from him slowly, still holding onto Asher as if they were lost at sea and he would sooner drown than release him.

29

NO ONE'S PREY

ASHER

OCTOBER 21

Lev shoved Asher's wardrobe away from the secret door like it was made of cardboard.

"Next time you want to rearrange your room, please call me. Watching you move furniture out of spite sounds quite amusing."

"No thanks. It's a lot more fun watching an old man move it."

Lev feigned a gasp. "Words hurt, Blakely."

Unblocking the door connecting their rooms had been Asher's idea.

While Lev had taught Asher more about trusting his instincts than the actual art of painting over the last few days sequestered in his room, Asher needed to sleep in his own bed tonight.

He'd moved in with Ben too quickly, and he couldn't lose himself in Lev like he had with Ben, no matter how much he wanted to.

Showering alone was the perfect first step for his Lev detox.

Lev gripped Asher's hips loosely and kissed his cheek. "Is there anything else I can get you?"

Asher shook his head.

"In that case, I'll leave you to it." Lev crossed to the door leading to the hallway.

"Wait. After all that, you're not taking the shortcut?"

"Absolutely not." Lev's hand paused on the doorknob. "I've nearly gotten stuck inside that tiny trap of a doorframe a few too many times as a teen."

"You roomed me on your sneaking out route?"

"Precisely. You wouldn't imagine the tomfoolery the sheep farmer's son and I got up to."

"Oh." Asher peeled off his shirt.

Lev's eyes dipped to Asher's bare skin. "I'm joking, Blakely." He waited a couple of seconds. "It was the fisherman's son."

Asher narrowed his eyes. "That's not funny."

"What? That was an excellent joke." Lev's gaze turned serious. "This is actually Wendell's old room."

"Oh."

"I had a lot of nightmares while Mum was ill. Wendell moved into this one. Father was with Mum all the time, and wasn't particularly nurturing, so when I was scared or couldn't sleep, I'd use the secret door and lay with him while he wrote. Strangely enough, those nights during such a wretched time in my life are some of my favorite memories. That's why I put you here."

"Oh," Asher said.

Apparently, he'd forgotten his other words, head so full of heartbreak for seven-year-old Lev.

"You've gone all monosyllabic, baby. Was that too intense a confession?"

"No. It's sad and beautiful and..." Asher blinked back his tears before they fell. "I don't know. I can't explain my emotions, but I can paint them for you."

"I understand completely." Lev's smile didn't reach his eyes. "Well, I'll be off then."

After such a bittersweet revelation, Asher didn't want Lev to be alone.

"Can you leave the door open while I shower—the secret door, I mean?"

Asher's heart twinged at Lev's smile and obvious relief.

"Of course." Even Lev's steps were lighter as he propped the slightly too narrow, slightly too short door open with a heavy log from the fireplace.

Lev pressed a chaste kiss to the corner of Asher's lips on the way out. Asher waited for Lev's footsteps to cross his room on the other side of the wall and waited longer still for Lev to inevitably test the acoustics.

"All right there, Blakely?" Lev asked.

Asher bit back his smile. "Yeah."

"Good. That's good." A few seconds later. "I do worry though…"

"About?" Asher dropped his pants.

"How long have you been afraid of showering alone? You should have told me. I'd have been happy to help."

"You're still not funny." But he was really cute. "I'm going in there now."

"Careful around the towel racks."

Asher laughed.

"I guess I'm a little funny after all," Lev said.

"I wasn't laughing. I sneezed."

"Bless you, then."

Asher's bright mood dimmed at the sight of his reflection. Hickeys and beard rash painted his neck, paired with the fading bite mark Lev had already left. He looked like a drawing Lev had scribbled his name all over, and while the submissive in him thought it was hot as fuck, it opened him up to the same accusations he'd faced with Ben.

Anxiety wrapped a hand around his throat.

"Fuck," he whispered.

Stupid boy, Ben would have said. *If you can't use your head, then I'll use your holes instead.*

He turned away from the mirror and started the shower. His thoughts muddied as he scrubbed his scalp under the water and let the conditioner soak in.

Dinner was going to suck. Lev could try to spin it or promise to protect him, but he couldn't fix the optics.

Asher lathered his body with the bar of luxury soap that smelled like Lev's bare skin. The realization that Lev had scent-marked him from the beginning was sexy and possessive and totally turned him on. He never thought he would want to submit to anyone again, but he wanted to submit to Lev.

The bar of soap slipped from his hand and dropped on his mangled toes. Pain blasted through him, ratcheting his pulse.

"Fuck," Asher said, a little louder this time.

"Asher?" Lev called, concern lacing his voice.

"I'm fine," Asher shouted back. "You have an unsettling bat-like sense of hearing."

"Only when it comes to your safety."

Asher rolled his eyes, rinsed off, and got out. His skin prickled with the brisk air, and something else. Solitude usually re-energized him, but he never felt completely alone at Lichenmoor. History swayed in the air like dust motes. Secrets lurked in the shadows.

Lev had resurrected Asher's clothes from the sea, and replaced them twofold with near replicas that fit suspiciously better than his old ones.

At first, Asher had rejected his gifts as too much. "Surely, you don't want to wear these clothes now that they've gone for a swim," Lev had said.

Asher had accused Lev of talking out of his ass, then Lev had replied, "We're in England, darling. You must say *arse,*" and casually added, "Those clothes remind me of when I almost lost you."

After donning black denim jeans, an olive tee, and his lucky black hoodie over it, he stood in front of the mirror and tried to drape the hood around his neck in a way that covered most of Lev's marks.

It was no use. Conceding defeat with a grumbling growl, Asher told Lev he was going to talk to Theo before dinner.

"Careful he doesn't kiss you again."

"I wouldn't be so smug if I were you. Pride is a sin, after all."

The second-floor hallway was quiet. Hopefully, he hadn't missed Theo. He rapped on the door. Footsteps trailed across the floor, and the door swung open.

"Asher?" Theo said in that husky, accented voice of his, an amiable smile curling his lips. "What are you doing here?"

"Can we talk?"

"Of course. Come in, come in." Theo stepped aside. "Don't worry. I promise not to kiss you again." Theo pulled a chair over from his desk. "Here. Are you okay?"

"Yeah. I wanted to apologize for the way I left things with you the other night." Asher sat and Theo perched on the edge of his bed opposite.

"It's nothing. I should be the one apologizing for that stolen kiss."

"The kiss was a shock more than stolen."

Theo trailed a finger down his own neck. "You and Lev are doing well, then?"

"Yeah." Asher rearranged his hood.

"You're smiling."

"Am I?" Asher ducked his head. "Sorry."

"You apologize too much. I wasn't in love. I was playing matchmaker. The coincidence of your tattoos and Lev summoning you seems fated, no? Congratulations, by the way."

At Asher's mystified look, Theo added, "Lev told me you won when he returned my shirt with half the buttons missing."

"He told you?" Asher winced. Why hadn't he mentioned it? "Was he an asshole about it?"

Theo laughed. "He was himself."

Yes, then. "He didn't give me the mentorship because—"

"You slept with him?" Theo suggested, light hazel eyes playful.

"We're not sleeping together." Technically. Asher didn't consider penetration the only way to have sex, but that was none of Theo's business.

"I was teasing."

"I don't want people to think I won because of that..."

"Don't worry. The others know there's more than quid pro quo between you. Lev was beside himself when you went missing."

"What?"

Theo nodded. "He was terrified. Ashen, voice shaking, a little green. But he kept his head and split us into pairs to look for you. He even dialed a contact at emergency services to search by boat and promised to pay for a helicopter when it was safe to fly." He sighed as if he were swooning. "Romantic, no?"

"I thought the phone lines were down..."

"He has a satellite phone for emergencies." Theo laughed. "Now that I think about it, he didn't completely keep his head. Chuck made a joke about you crying somewhere after Lev had rejected your watercolor painting."

Chuck was half-right.

"Lev erupted. He threatened to cart Chuck up Lichenmoor's tallest tower and shove him out a window if he ever said your name again. Then Chuck asked how he was supposed to look for you if he wasn't allowed to say your name, and Lev was so furious he probably would have made good on his threat if he hadn't been in such a hurry to find you."

Asher's heart sank into his stomach. He'd been such an asshole to Lev when he'd found him.

A knock sounded, and Julian walked in before Theo could ask who it was.

He blinked. "Asher?"

"Hello, Julian. Asher was just telling me he's won the mentorship. Isn't that wonderful?"

"I'm not surprised. The man is unnaturally attached to you." Julian eyed Asher's neck. "But I *am* surprised he let you talk to Theo alone after keeping you to himself the last few days."

Theo shot Asher a sympathetic look.

"He didn't keep me to himself. I was tired and sore."

"Did he hurt you?" Julian asked, eyes crawling over Asher's neck again from where he still lingered in the doorway.

"No." Tension tightened his throat. Blocked exits were one of his triggers.

Theo hopped down from the bed and slapped Julian's back lightly.

"I think what Julian is trying to say is congratulations." Theo steered Julian away from the doorway, gripping Julian's shoulders, almost as if he sensed Asher's unease. "Right?"

"I'm trying to warn you."

"Stop playing parent." Theo shook Julian's shoulders playfully.

Asher recognized a kindred soul in Theo. What trauma had made him so adept at diffusing tension?

Undeterred, Julian shrugged out of Theo's hold. "He's fifteen years older than you."

"Don't act like I'm the first gay man to hook up with someone older."

"He has a lot of influence. One word and he could ruin your career. You'll be isolated here, trapped during high tide if things go wrong."

Asher inhaled through his nose. "I appreciate your concern, but Luna will be here, and," he looked at Theo, "apparently there's a satellite phone."

Theo nodded.

Julian's gaze turned troubled. "I think Lev's lying about why he's hosting the retreat."

Hadn't Asher shared similar misgivings? Theo didn't intervene this time, dropping his gaze to the rug like he wanted to draw it later. Did he agree?

"Look, I'm not sure why Lev planned the retreat either, but I know Lev now. He won't hurt me." Whatever his reason for hosting the retreat, dubious or otherwise, Asher trusted Lev to keep him safe. "He's probably just lonely. I don't think he'd invite six other artists as witnesses if he wanted to lock me in his dungeon."

"He could have left if he'd been lonely," Julian said.

Asher wasn't so sure Lev *could* leave, but that was none of Julian's business.

"Then suddenly he wants to take on a much younger mentee?" Julian continued. "Sounds like grooming to me."

Theo shook his head. "Julian..."

Asher gnashed his teeth together. "You really think Lev hosted a retreat to single out an unsuspecting artist from the pack to take advantage of?"

Julian's jaw tensed. "Yeah. I do. Lev is cocky enough to believe that the winner he selects will be more than happy to bend over for the privilege. I've seen it before."

"Yeah, me too. This isn't that."

Theo's eyes flashed to Asher.

The chair scuttled backward as Asher stood. He needed to get out of there.

"I never asked for you to weigh in on my life choices. If

you're so concerned, take it up with Lev. It's not fair to dump this on me because you're afraid to confront him."

Theo shifted to put himself between them. "Stop being meddlesome, Julian. We know you mean well, but let's talk more after dinner."

"I'm not meddling." Julian moved around Theo, blocking the doorway; probably not on purpose, but it frayed Asher's nerves. "I don't want you to fall victim to a predator."

"I'm only going to say this once, so pay attention." Asher fisted his hands until his fingernails bit his palms. "Lev isn't a predator, and I'm no one's prey."

"I don't want you to make the same mistake..."

Asher's senses tunneled down to fear and his heart throbbing in his ears. Did the others know? Had Lev known all along?

"...that I have," Julian finished.

Thank fucking fuck. Asher inhaled deeply.

"I'm sorry that happened to you, but I'm not making a mistake."

The dinner bell jingled.

"Perfect timing," Theo said with cheerfulness belied by the wary way his eyes bounced between them. "There's nothing good food and fine wine can't fix."

As if Asher could even eat when he was this pissed. Asher pushed past Julian, ignoring the pain slicing through him when their shoulders connected, and only breathed again when he was safe in the hallway, and no longer in a cage.

30

TANGLED THICKET

LEV

Asher's cheeks were flushed when he strode into the dining room. Julian and Theo arrived hot on his heels sporting matching frowns.

What the hell happened?

Lev pushed his chair back and stood as Asher dropped into a chair beside Daria and crossed his arms over his chest. Julian tried to take the seat on Asher's left, but Theo intercepted him.

Asher leaned toward Theo, hiding his lips behind Theo's cheek and whispered something to him.

Jealousy shot flames through his bloodstream. Was Theo back in the running? Asher *had* asked to sleep alone earlier.

Asher kicked Lev's shin and reached under the table.

What? Lev mouthed.

Asher looked pointedly at the table.

Oh.

Lev slipped his hand under the table, and found Asher waiting for him. Asher squeezed, reassuring him with such a tender gesture that Lev's heart swelled with the overwhelming sense of his soul being known by another person.

Lev squeezed Asher's hand back, and mouthed—*Are you okay?*

Asher nodded. Thank God.

Sunlight, ordinarily so scarce this time of year, ignited the embers in Asher's irises as Lev stroked the back of his hand with his thumb. Their chemistry was so magical that even sustained eye contact and secret hand holding was sacred.

Lev nudged Asher's legs wider with the tip of his shoe. So much fun could be had playing footsie under the table. He licked his bottom lip just to toy with him, and sure enough, Asher's clever eyes dipped to Lev's mouth and mirrored the motion.

Luna entered carrying a platter of vegetarian lasagna made with veg grown in the conservatory. Lev jumped from his chair and rushed to take the platter from her.

"Thank you, love." Luna's smile emphasized the crow's feet at the corners of her eyes.

One day he'd lose his fourth parent, the one who'd loved him longer than all the others, and he'd never survive it.

"I'll be back with the bread," Luna said.

He followed her to the kitchen and hugged her, planting a kiss to her hair. The heady scent of lilac launched him back in time to when he was a boy missing a mother who hadn't left yet, but wasn't there anymore.

"Thank you, Mum."

He seldom called her that anymore. She'd never invited it, but the first time he'd called her *mummy* as a lad, she'd cried. Lev, only eight at the time, had panicked until she explained what good tears were. Lev had only witnessed sad tears before then.

In a way, Lev had claimed Luna like Silas had claimed Father.

"It makes me happy to see you taken care of, to know you won't be alone."

"He's not staying forever."

"No, but he could."

Perhaps if Lev was lucky. "Eat with us while you wait out high tide?"

"Another time. I'm going to dust the library."

"Why bother when the dust bunnies return overnight?"

Luna pushed the breadbasket into his hands. "Go."

Lev returned with the bread basket and another bottle of pinot noir to find Theo gesturing so animatedly, the wine glass in his hand sloshed perilously close to Asher's lap.

"You can't imagine," Theo said. "I was only sixteen, living on the streets of Paris. Me!"

Lev hid a yawn behind his hand, relishing the way Asher's eyes followed him as he lowered into his chair.

Asher lifted a single brow and said without words, *What's wrong, old man? Too tired to stay up with the kids?* Lev narrowed his eyes, smiling ruefully, a nonverbal reply: *Don't test me or I'll show you who can last longest.*

Silas materialized behind Asher, neck craning to peer down at Asher's untouched lasagna.

"Oh dear. It looks as if our Ashy has lost his appetite again. Maybe when Julian and Theo spit-roasted him earlier they stuffed him so full he spoiled his appetite."

Lev refused to entertain such a vile notion.

"Do you want to eat something else?" Lev asked Asher.

Asher looked at his plate. "No." He leaned across the table and whispered, "I want to get this over with."

"You're sure?"

Asher nodded and leaned back in his seat.

Lev straightened. "I have an announcement to make. I'm sure you're all wondering who I've selected as my protégé."

"I've been on pins and needles, myself," Chuck said with dry sarcasm, ever faithful to his wanker persona.

"A total mystery," Lars added.

Theo drowned out their shtick, tapping a drumroll with his fingers on the tabletop. Asher rolled his eyes, but his lips tipped in a nearly undetectable smile—a very platonic smile. Lev's heart thawed slightly.

Julian dropped his fork on his plate with a jarring clank. "Congratulations. You must be happy."

"Thank you. I am quite happy actually," Lev said with equal sarcasm and far less petulance. "Though I don't understand your tone."

"You can't order a companion like a meal," Julian said. "That's human trafficking."

"Excuse me?" Fury gathered at the edges of his decorum like storm clouds on the horizon.

"Julian," Theo groaned, massaging his temples. "You're giving me a headache, and Lev looks like he's going to give you a headache with his fist if you don't drop this."

"What exactly are you accusing me of?"

"It's never been a contest," Julian said. "We never had a chance. We were props in a play we didn't know we were acting in."

"For fuck's sake, take the 'L', Julian."

Silas circled Julian with a suspicious self-satisfied smirk. "Either Julian's more clever than he looks, or someone told him."

What the fuck was Silas playing at?

"He does have a certain appeal, Levvy." Silas hopped onto the table beside Julian's plate and trailed a delicate finger down his bicep. "In a bearish, daddy sort of way."

Asher kicked Lev's calf. How long had he stared vacantly in the middle of a dinner argument?

"If I only hosted the retreat to find a companion, why would I invite the walking bellend that is Chuck? What about Daria and Melody? I've never even kissed a woman. Not to mention, I find Daria quite frightening, and you're fucking married."

Daria laughed. Lev tucked that minor victory away to use the next time Asher claimed he had no sense of humor.

"I chose each of you because your work is so brilliant I want to watch you create it, and while I hate to admit this, Chuck is very talented." Knowing how much Chuck liked to hear his own voice, Lev added, "Never speak of this again, Mr. Boorman."

"Was the retreat a competition or not, Lev?" Chuck asked.

"Lord, deliver me from these calamitous dinners," Lev muttered. "In the spirit of honesty, I must confess that I invited you at your aunt's behest. Quite an error on my part. Had I known better, I would have declined."

"Fuck off, Lev. I don't have an aunt," Chuck said waspishly.

"It's not true." Melody fussed with the crown of plaits she'd braided her golden hair into.

Lev was such an arsehole. "No, love, it's not true. Julian is being a sore loser."

"Careful you don't get mauled, Levvy," Silas said.

Melody bit her glossy bottom lip and bobbled her head in a nod.

"You can't lose something that was never a competition," Julian argued. "Lev picked Asher from the start."

"Julian, shut the fuck up," Daria snapped, and took Melody's hand. "Mel, listen to Lev." She shot Julian a deathly look, daring him to disagree.

Lev shivered. She was even scarier when incensed, and she was definitely dating Melody.

Asher's gaze slid to his plate. Did he believe Julian?

"Blakely, your art brought you here. Your art is the reason I chose you."

If only Lev could drop to his knees and vow his fealty, and make Asher believe him. Perhaps he should try anyway.

Julian snorted. "Right. It had nothing to do with how young he is or how easily you could manipulate him, or how little he'd be missed."

Asher flinched.

"That's enough." Lev pressed his palms to the table and

stood, nostrils flaring as he inhaled, anger tethered by a fraying rope. "Blakely is twenty-five, not twelve."

"I've had enough too," Asher said, voice starved of all warmth. "Listen to what you're saying, Julian. Celebrity artist, heir to fortunes, owner of land gifted by royalty. You think Leviathan Marks combed the world for a potential suitor and settled on me?"

"It wouldn't have been settling," Lev said.

"Then, instead of asking me out on a date or inviting me here like a normal person would, Lev hosted an art retreat and invited six other artists to ruin the mood? Don't you realize how stupid that sounds?"

"I don't want to see you get hurt," Julian said.

Asher shook his head once, a sharp, violent jerk that would have stung were it directed at Lev.

"Treating me like a child incapable of decision doesn't protect me," Asher said. "Suggesting that I'm only here because Lev wanted to sleep with me insults my artistic achievements, my intelligence, me."

Asher tossed his napkin beside his bowl and sped from the room.

"Asher, wait," Julian said.

Lev shook his head at Julian. "If you so much as follow, come hell or high tide, I'll send you home tonight, even if I have to summon the Royal Navy to collect you."

The hall was empty, all the lights dimmed for the evening. Where the hell was he?

"Blakely?"

"Perhaps he's popped to the ballroom for a midnight swim," Silas suggested, appearing at his side. "Diving from those window ledges is an excellent way to pass the time."

Lev ignored him. The only danger Asher presented to himself was obstinacy paired with a terrible sense of direction.

"Blakely," Lev called louder this time, distress sneaking into his voice.

Should he dispatch search parties again?

A distant squeak like a branch against a window pulled Lev's attention away from the stairwell that led to their bedroom. Lev swung his head toward the sound and hurried down the east wing corridor. For all he knew, the sound *was* just a branch scratching glass, but it was the only lead he had.

"Baby, please don't hide. I'll go mad if I can't find you again."

Asher stepped out from behind a suit of armor guarding the shadowy hallway leading to the chapel.

Silas flinched cartoonishly and clutched his chest. "Jesus. He's a better ghost than I am."

"Whether you're a ghost or hallucination remains to be seen," Lev whispered. "There you are." Lev walked closer, careful to avoid any sudden movements, as if Asher was an easily spooked horse.

Asher darted left and disappeared around the corner.

"I'm not in the mood for a game of chase."

"When are you ever?" Asher called.

Lev rounded the corner at a fast clip—and met the end of a sword wielded by none other than Asher Bloody Blakely, face flushed, chest heaving, the muscles in his tattooed forearms tensing like a bowstring, the blood of his enemies the only thing missing.

"Are you... Are you challenging me to a duel?"

Asher's eyes narrowed. His hands shook as he pressed the tip of his blade into the soft flesh beneath Lev's chin.

Silas appeared behind Asher. "Mm. I like the direction this is going."

Lev bared his palms. "I mean no harm. Be a good lad and put the sword down."

Silas buried his face in the crook of Asher's neck and licked the faded bite mark Lev had left. "I wonder what he tastes like when he's angry and sweating. I bet he tastes like the ocean on your skin."

"No." Asher pushed the sword to the precipice of piercing his skin.

"Baby, that sword isn't a prop. Please be careful unless you wish to murder me."

Asher's hazel gaze bounced to the blade, and back to Lev again. The biting pressure on Lev's skin lessened, but not entirely.

"Why the fuck does your suit of armor have a real sword?"

"Home protection?"

Asher was not amused, nor had he lowered his weapon. "What Julian said was true, wasn't it?"

"You remember that, don't you, Levvy? All those summers?" Silas rested his chin on Asher's shoulder as he wrapped his hands around the hilt of the sword.

"I asked you a question," Asher said. "When you answer, remember I'm the one with a weapon. Is it true?"

"No," Lev lied, then floundered. "Yes. Well, not exactly."

"Those summers were my favorite. Do you know why?" Silas asked.

Fucking Silas. Lev couldn't carry two conversations simultaneously on a good day, let alone when the stakes were this high.

"Summers were the longest stretch we had together, Lev, remember? Sometimes I couldn't sleep, couldn't bear to waste a single moment. I was greedy. I hoarded time like grains of sand, thinking I could take those memories with me, thinking I could bring them back, like sunlight in my pocket, warm and bright when things got dark. But it never worked."

Silas's biceps flexed, a vein in his slender neck filling as he tried to push the blade into Lev's flesh. He couldn't exert any control over the physical realm. They both knew that, and yet Lev almost felt as if Asher *had* pressed the blade deeper, as if Silas had compelled him to do so.

Balancing on the edge of a blade was an altogether thrilling sensation. Was this how Silas had felt? Was that why he'd liked to dance on the ledge of Lichenmoor's cliffs? Was that why he'd sliced his veins vertically only when he knew someone would find him? Why he'd messed about with belts looped around—

"I'd never do it, Levvy. You know I wouldn't kill you. I'm not like you."

"Ben could have told you about me…"

Lev's stomach twisted into painful knots. "You don't believe that, do you?"

Asher shook his head. "But I want you to reassure me anyway, so I have something to tell myself when my brain is being an asshole."

Lev inched forward until the blade broke the skin beneath his chin.

Asher's eyes widened. "What are you doing?"

"I'd sooner fall on this sword than lie to you. If I knew about Ben, he'd be a missing person's case by now. I'd never have let him touch you."

Asher nodded, and lowered the sword from Lev's neck. "Thank you." He tossed it on the ground where it landed with an almighty clatter—a clever move because the melee distracted Lev long enough for Asher to get a head start.

Lev ran after him toward the chapel. Good.

Twin snakes twined up the sides of the arched fireplace, meeting in the middle of the mantle, mouths reaching for a single apple. Lev pressed against the apple until the wood depressed, activating the latch that opened the door behind him. He'd added the alternate route to the chapel on the second edition of Asher's map.

"Asher?" Lev asked the dusty darkness, trailing his fingers along the cold and slippery stone bricks as he navigated the passageway in the dark.

Asher had left the door ajar, and Lev dropped his hand and wiped the grime on his slacks as he headed toward the sliver of light—or rather, not exactly light. The remaining dregs of daylight had dwindled fast.

"Was this necessary?" Lev grumbled as he emerged from a door ordinarily hidden by elaborate wood casing and a statue of the Virgin Mary.

He ducked out from behind the statue and flicked the light switch, surprised some of the wall sconces still worked.

Asher waited in the first pew like a parishioner early for mass.

When Lichenmoor is yours, you must promise me you'll leave it to rot, Silas had said. After his last stint at Hallowed Saints, when he talked of the future, it was one that only Lev existed in, but Lev would have dismantled the chapel brick by brick if that would have saved him. Instead, he'd killed him.

The ocean murmured through the open windows as the tide crept back out to sea. Before Asher, Lev had felt crushing claustrophobia when high tide turned Lichenmoor into an island, but now high tide brought reassurance because Asher couldn't leave.

In the hazy glow of dimming bulbs and twilight, Lev walked down the center aisle with the same dread of approaching an open casket at a funeral.

"May I sit?"

Asher scooted over.

"Watching you with that sword was the sexiest thing I've ever seen. Perhaps you can incorporate it in the bedroom."

Asher scowled. "You can't flirt your way out of this."

"Are you certain? I'm not even trying that hard."

Asher's scowl deepened.

"Sorry." Lev inhaled and exhaled a brief sigh that left him empty inside. "The art retreat was indeed a charade to bring you here. It was manipulative and wrong, but it's not as sinister as Julian thinks."

Asher's shoulders sank. "I knew it was too good to be true."

"No, love. It's better than good. I was so enchanted by your art, I created all of this," he waved his hand in an airy circle around the decrepit husk of a church, "for a chance to watch you paint in person. I wasn't searching for a companion, let alone a twenty-five-year-old to have my way with."

Asher pushed his black waves back from his brow. "Then, why?"

"We've been over this before."

"Go over it again."

Lev sent a silent prayer for leniency to the neglected Christ on the crucifix.

"While the retreat may have been a farce to lure you here, I fell in love with you, Blakely, sight unseen, because I saw your soul inside a single painting.

"My intentions were purely artistic at first. I'd wanted only to know you more, to root around in your head and see what made you paint like that, but once you were here, and I saw you—not just the physical beauty of you—but your humor and wit, your dark disposition, your brilliance at the canvas, your vexing curiosity, I fell hard."

Lev swallowed and dragged his palm over the bite of his beard. "Our chemistry is intense, but I want you for more than your cock, for more than your art."

"If you wanted me here, why did you pick apart my art in front of the others?"

"I... I was trying to protect you."

He couldn't confess that he'd been frightened to see Asher asking about Silas in his sketchbook. Or that he'd feared hurting him, feared wasting Asher's younger years.

Asher crossed his arms over his chest, entirely unmoved. "Why not invite me personally? If you'd shown up at one of my exhibitions, I'd have done anything you asked."

"If I'd only invited you, you'd hold all the power. I don't care to bare my neck to strangers, even if I've already fallen in love with their work. Especially then."

"Do you have any idea what you've done to my career? You've marked me as your pet in front of six of my peers. Melody is low-key famous on social media, and Chuck will tell everyone. No one will believe my art is what you see in me. No one will respect me as an artist when I'm overshadowed by your favoritism."

"Fuck what people believe. You don't paint for them. You paint for yourself, and that's why you're so brilliant at it. Paint what you like and the people who understand you will find you, because if you paint what you think the world wants, no one will understand you at all."

"It's easy for you to say that when you've already achieved your dreams, when you're high above a glass ceiling I will never break through." He talked through gritted teeth. "You have the luxury of painting for the sake of art without worrying about how much paint costs."

Lev scoffed. "You think I dreamed of this? To be alone here, haunted by abandoned art? By all the people I've lost. The only choice I had was to be what my father wanted."

Sadly now, all spite spent, Asher said, "You're proving my point. You'll always be Lucian Marks's son, and I'll always be some young artist you had your way with for six months."

"That's not what's going to happen."

Asher shrugged. "The past speaks for itself."

"It doesn't have to." Lev dropped from the pew and kneeled in front of him. If he didn't fix this, Asher would leave and Lev wouldn't survive it. "Inviting you here under false pretenses was wrong and cowardly. I should have been honest with you. I'm so sorry."

Perhaps it was the church, or perhaps because Asher was more than a false idol he worshipped. Lev wanted to repent. He wanted to atone. To accept his punishment.

"What are you doing?"

"Groveling." He tried to smile, but it hurt too much because he'd manipulated Asher the way Ben had. "Your art may have brought us together, Asher, but it's you who's brought me to my knees.

"If my selfish actions have damaged your career, I promise I will fix it. Whatever happens between us, I will get your work into the right hands, and ensure you never have to worry about the price of paint again."

By the right hands, he meant himself.

"You idolize me so, but I'm a coward," Lev continued. "I shouldn't have lied about why I brought you here. By doing so, I robbed you of your autonomy exactly as Julian strives to do with his infernal fussing."

God, he'd ruined everything. He'd wanted to be good for Asher, to be safe for him always, and he hadn't been truthful.

Lev bowed his head. "I didn't expect to fall in love with you, but I did, and it's terrifying."

Asher's hand fell to his hair. "Why?"

"I don't deserve to love again, let alone love someone as precious as you. My heart is a tangled thicket of stinging nettles, one I wish you'd never stepped foot in. I fear loving me will strangle you."

"Look at me," Asher said.

He couldn't. He couldn't watch Asher tell him he was done.

Asher stroked Lev's hair. "You love me?"

"I believe I said falling."

"Look at me," Asher repeated, tugging Lev's hair until he lifted his head.

At first, Asher said nothing, searching Lev's face. What was he looking for? The truth? Something worth staying for? The villain inside him?

Lev counted the gold flecks in his irises so he could paint them if Asher left. He opened his mouth to apologize again, to declare all the reasons he was hopelessly besotted.

Asher's eyes softened and his legs widened.

Hope fluttered in Lev's chest. "What are you doing?"

"I'm giving you space to grovel."

"Thank you." Lev rushed forward, still on his knees, and hugged Asher around the middle, burying his face in his lap.

"Tell me more," Asher said. "Tell me why."

Lev turned his head and rested his cheek on Asher's thigh, looking up at his lad ardently, in exactly the position he'd wanted to start the night. "I suppose I should start at the very beginning. Silas—"

Asher's brows darted together. "Silas?"

"I know it sounds like a terrible way to profess my love—falling in love, I mean—but I do have a point. Please bear with me."

"Okay." Asher raked his hand through Lev's hair again, fingernails grazing his scalp as if Lev was a pet he found comfort in.

"Silas used to hold how much he loved me against me, as if it was *my* fault that I didn't love him as intensely, as if he resented me. I'd never understood."

Asher's hand stopped. "You resent me?"

"No, baby. Never. May I continue?"

Asher nodded.

"I loved Silas, but I'd never felt as if I'd forfeited all power to him, as if I'd die if I lost him, as if any moment apart made it hard to breathe, as if any harm that came to him would make me bleed. That's how you make me feel.

"To hell with pretenses. I'm not falling. I've already hit the ground." Lev braced his hands on Asher's thighs and straightened his spine to look at him properly. "I love you, Asher Blakely."

31

LIKE AN ANCIENT OAK

ASHER

Lev's confession was either a sincere declaration or the world's worst pick-up line since language was invented.

"You see through my lies." Lev lifted his head. "Look at me. I'm telling the truth. Please forgive me. Again. Hopefully, for the last time."

Asher would have given Lev another chance regardless, and that was the problem.

"Get back up here." Asher tapped the bench.

"I quite like it down here though."

Asher rolled his eyes. "You can find something to grovel about later. Your bad jokes are a good place to start."

Lev sat beside him and kissed Asher's hand. "Thank you."

"There's just one thing I don't understand. If all you wanted to do was watch me, why not come to me?" Would Lev finally confirm Asher's suspicions?

"I watched your progress videos on social media many times over," Lev said. "I think it broke something in me, all of those silent videos of yours with only your hands in view, gripping the brush, the way your fingers moved. Watching you work was a spiritual experience for me, and when you painted your more erotic pieces, I couldn't help but touch myself and pretend it was you."

"You jerked off to me?"

"Not just you. Your paintings too. I..." He dropped his gaze. "At first I was content to study your work in photographs, to watch your hand grip pencil and paintbrush without seeing the rest of you, but after a while, it wasn't enough.

"I purchased one of your pieces out of curiosity. Did your work resonate with me so intensely in person? Yes. It did. To touch what you had touched, to trace my fingers over the textures you'd layered with your brush, I'd never felt so understood and so alone all at once."

"I don't know what to say."

"Say you won't be angry, because in the spirit of sharing secrets, I must confess that I own all of your paintings. Erm, at least the ones you've listed. The portrait of the guilty man is my white whale."

Asher's mouth ran dry. "No."

Lev nodded gravely. "Yes."

"Are you serious?"

Lev nodded. "I'll show you my collection after the others leave."

Leviathan Marks had a collection of Asher's work? It was too surreal to comprehend, but it was nothing compared to the realization that Lev had always been there.

"After Ben, I was so fucking broken. I wasn't going to make art again. I couldn't look at my old paintings, but I couldn't throw them out so I put one up on social media, and then someone bought it."

"The man in the fog."

"That was you?"

Lev nodded. "The guilty man was the gateway drug to my Asher addiction, but the first piece I held in my hands was that one. It reminded me of Lichenmoor before it was a cage, almost as if you returned a happy memory to me."

"You've protected me and taken care of me since before you ever met me," Asher whispered. "I needed you after Ben, and you were already there, rekindling my love for art, helping me move out, and move on."

"Please don't give me all the credit. If I hadn't bought your paintings, someone else would have... and then I would pay them handsomely to add it to my collection, as I've done several times before."

They'd strayed far away from the question he needed Lev to answer.

"Why didn't you come for me? I know you would have if you could."

Asher wasn't asking because he needed to know. He needed to know that Lev could tell the truth about something that he thought would make Asher dislike him.

"Clever lad. Sussed it out, have you? I'm not surprised."

Asher crossed his arms. "I need to hear it from you."

Lev sighed. "I don't want to tell you I have agoraphobia because then I'll have to tell you what started it and why I can't fix it."

"If you don't want to talk about it, you've said enough."

The scuff of Lev's palm over his beard sounded like the strike of a match in the silent church. Lev looked at him with ocean eyes so beautiful and vulnerable that Asher wanted to drown in them.

"Can I lay down while I tell you? Perhaps rest my head in your lap?"

"Sure."

"Thank you."

Lev turned onto his side, facing the dais, and used Asher's thigh for a pillow. He inhaled a quivering breath, a melancholy Peter Pan of a man, needing Asher to take care of him.

"My father didn't die of a stroke."

How did a family keep secrets locked so tight? How much power did it take to change someone's death and hide Silas's existence? If something went wrong at Lichenmoor, would Lev erase him?

Ben had often taunted Asher about how his family wouldn't know he was missing because they never checked on him. *I could lock you in my basement, and no one would come looking for you.* He'd done it once or twice for a few hours or the night.

Julian's crude comment at dinner had been so similar to Ben's threats, Asher had barely held it together until he ran out of the room, then fled in terror, taking the sword for protection.

Asher inhaled slowly and forced himself to remain rooted in the present, focusing on the sound of the ocean rolling away, the scent of sea salt and dust, Lev's head in his lap, and the soft ginger hair that he stroked.

"What you saw of my father over the years was exactly how he was in private," Lev said. "A little stern, a heaping dose of British stoicism, but always quick to laugh, passionate. He was incredibly generous with his money and time."

"Like you."

"Perhaps..." Lev cleared his throat. "He had high expectations for his students, and I was no exception." Lev tugged Asher's hand from his hair and rolled onto his back, then guided Asher's hand back to his head. "Keep playing with my hair. I love it."

After Asher complied, Lev thanked him and continued. "The only reason I'm good at painting and sculpting, and everything else I tried, art related and otherwise, was because Father demanded it. No matter how high his expectations were, I endeavored to meet them."

"Did you?"

"Meet his expectations?" Lev laughed. "I don't think anyone did..." His gaze turned pensive. "Disappointing him was my greatest fear, and when I disappointed him most of all with the most colossal fuck up there ever was, he didn't blow up like I expected. It's the apathy that killed me. That cold disregard. Like I'd died with Silas."

Asher's heart stalled in his chest and he forced himself to take another breath, to act like Lev hadn't revealed something so massive.

"He looked at me like he'd wished the other son, the one who was never his son at all, had been the one who survived. There was always this simmering regret bubbling beneath the silence, the look of disgust I'd see in the corners of my eyesight."

"I'm so sorry." Asher squeezed his hand.

"Silas had died, but I was a ghost, and my father was haunted by what I'd done." Lev continued as if he hadn't heard him, as if he was in a trance.

"What did you do?" Asher whispered.

Lev blinked, spell broken. "I can't tell you that. Not yet."

"Did you kill him?"

"What would you say if I had?"

"I'd ask you why."

Lev lifted his arm and cupped Asher's cheek. "Don't you have any self-preservation at all?"

"You won't hurt me." Asher knew that with all the faith a zealot reserved for their god. "You won't."

"How can you be so sure?"

Asher removed Lev's hand from his cheek and flattened it over his heart.

"You made me an artist. You love me. You'd never hurt me."

"What if I destroy everything I make? What if I hurt the people I love?"

"I think we hurt the people we love the most *because* we love them."

Asher's tears landed on Lev's cheeks. Lev brushed them away as if they belonged to him.

"Father and I seldom spoke after Silas. I made an appearance when requested, so I didn't notice at first. Father masked his symptoms so well, but there were things he couldn't hide.

"He'd tried to sack the house staff and then forgot that he had, then was outraged when they missed their shifts. He talked about people who'd died as if they were still alive and spoke to them as if they were real—my mum, Wendell, Silas."

"Shit," Asher said.

"It really was quite shit. To see Father like that…" Lev shook his head. "He wasn't Lucian Marks. He was a fractured version of himself, a lonely man haunted by broken memories thanks to Alzheimer's."

"Oh, Lev."

"He couldn't paint anymore. To him, his art looked as it should, but the shapes were all garbled, the eyes all wrong, but it was art." Lev's voice broke. "Art in its most honest form."

Asher covered his mouth, eyes crystalline with tears.

"Every evening he'd fly into a fury, directing all his anger toward me. Sundowning. I was afraid that my presence was hurting him, but I was more afraid of what he'd say next, of what final wounds he'd punish me with. So I left.

"His condition advanced until he got lost inside the castle he'd spent most of his life in. He saw my mother and Wendell all the time. Silas sometimes.

"He wandered at night, and while the staff were careful to lock the doors, he hid skeleton keys all over Lichenmoor. Maybe he was confused and tried to follow my mum, or Wendell, or… I don't know.

"He vanished during a terrible storm. The staff searched until the tide forced them inside, but no one could find him. When the storm faded, and the tide retreated the next day, the ocean was kind enough to return my father after drowning him."

"I'm so sorry." No wonder Lev had been so distraught when Asher had nearly drowned.

"Father would have wanted to keep his dignity, even in

death, so in one final attempt at meeting his expectations, I ensured there was no mention of Alzheimer's in his obituary. Just a quiet, sensible death without suffering. Felled like an ancient oak while he slept.

"He'd requested to be buried at sea. I never understood it, but his directions were clear. We had to go miles out so his ashes wouldn't return to the place he'd been trapped."

Asher pulled Lev up from the bench into a hug that smelled of salt and moss and petrichor, of Lichenmoor.

Lev buried his face in Asher's neck. "That's when *my* agoraphobia began. The tide traps me here, and while that may seem irrational, the threat feels real to me."

"It's not irrational."

"You are far too kind."

Asher snorted. "I am not kind. You tell me all the time." He gripped Lev's arms and pulled back. "When was the last time you left?"

"I think you already know. You spent a great deal of time drawing that day in your notebook."

"Your father's funeral?" He hadn't been sure, but if he'd had to guess...

"Yes. Why were you so fascinated with those photos? Did you sense the tempest behind my vacant stare?"

Asher nodded. "You didn't look like yourself. I wasn't sure if it was because I'd stared at the photos too long."

"Like a word spelled correctly that suddenly looks wrong?"

"Exactly." Asher sighed. "Did you know the photographs were being taken?"

Lev sucked air through his teeth and shook his head. "That photographer had been playing tourist at other people's funerals for years. We should have had a private ceremony, but that wasn't what Father wanted.

"I'll never forget the way I felt watching the wind and waves scatter my father so far from himself, from his home, that he'd never find his way back.

"I couldn't leave Lichenmoor after that. I've tried to get help, but it hasn't worked yet. The only time I've made it past the gate, I needed enough meds to sedate a whale and still nearly clawed my skin to ribbons when I woke up. Do you think less of me?"

Asher shook his head. "We're all victims of our brain chemistry. You said that."

"Thank you." Lev smiled sadly and pulled Asher up from the bench. "Let's get you to your room."

"I want to sleep with you."

They could sleep separately tomorrow... Maybe. Asher never wanted Lev to be alone again.

"I'd love to, but I think we should sleep apart as you suggested. Our relationship is far too important. Not to mention, now that the secret door is open, we're technically sleeping together, anyway."

32

OPEN TO YOU

LEV

Lev was knackered. He felt overexposed, his soul sanded down. Agoraphobia was a humiliating secret, a weakness.

After talking himself into brushing his teeth, he stripped his clothes, kicked them into the corner of his closet, and went to bed. He stared at the painted ceiling overhead and wished he hadn't insisted that Asher should sleep in his own bed.

He didn't want to be alone. He wanted Asher. He needed his lad to keep him company instead of the guilt and loss swirling around inside his head.

"Psst!" Asher said from his room.

"Yes, Blakely?"

"I wrote you a note."

"Oh?"

"Yeah, but don't check until I tell you to." Footsteps padded to the secret door, then back to Asher's bed.

"Why?"

"If you see me, then I could just tell you what the note says."

"You could tell me now."

Asher's bed creaked. "You can look."

Lev peeled back the tapestry and found a piece of paper torn from Asher's sketchbook and folded in half. He took it back to bed and unfolded it.

> My door will always
> be open to you
> -A

"This is very sweet. Thank you. I'll write you a reply in the morning. Until then, I'll sleep with your letter and pretend that it's you. I love you, Asher Blakely."

"I love you too."

Lev grinned. "I thought you might. Perhaps you should write it down though, so I can sleep with that letter too."

A minute later, paper crunched, and a paper ball rolled into the tapestry. Lev was quick to collect it.

> I don't want to
> leave a paper trail.
> — A

Lev laughed. A second paper ball hit the tapestry.

> I'm joking.
> I love you too.
> — A

"I will treasure these always."

"Careful you don't get a paper cut."

"That will only remind me of you and your sharp tongue and stabby sword."

"Good night, Lev."

"Good night, baby." Lev held the letters against his chest like the sentimental sod that he was.

Sleep came as swiftly as the wind calling across the moor.

Lev woke in the dark. Even in sleep, a dormant part of his mind remembered the hollow swish of the tapestry lifted, and the creak of floorboards beside his bed.

Had everything been a nightmare after all? Was he only now waking up? What if Silas had never died? What if he was sneaking into his room after a row—one he'd started out of boredom or loneliness—and had come to apologize like so many nights before?

Lev almost said his name. *Silas.* Not out of excitement, but dread.

The dream he'd had before was filled with so much sadness, but it had finally started to get good, because Asher was there, and Asher made Lev feel like he could be happy again, like he deserved to be.

"Asher?"

A loud thump sounded.

"Fuck!" Asher said.

Lev bolted upright and pulled the string of the lamp beside his bed in time to witness Asher emerge from behind the tapestry, holding the top of his head, looking utterly adorable in one of Lev's shirts. The lad was tall, but he still had nothing on Lev, and the shirt hung down to just below his arse.

"Yes, I'd recommend crawling on your hands and knees

next time. I learned it the hard way many times myself." Lev sat at the edge of the bed and widened his legs. "Couldn't sleep?"

"I wanted to surprise you."

Lev clucked his tongue. Poor lad. He reached out and pulled Asher by the hand, sending him stumbling forward and between his widened legs. "Let me see your head."

"I'm fine."

"I'm sure you are, but you know how I fret." He pulled Asher's hand from the top of his head and examined it. No blood. He felt around Asher's scalp. No bump either. The tightness in his chest eased.

Lev used both hands to push Asher's hair back from his face and kissed his forehead. "Why couldn't you sleep?"

Asher didn't answer. Not verbally, anyway. He planted one knee on the bed and climbed onto Lev's lap. Lev gripped Asher's arse, lest he fall backward. That's when Lev realized he wasn't wearing the tight boxer briefs he ordinarily wore.

"What's this?"

Again, Asher said nothing, and pulled the shirt over his head. The sight of his art on Asher's skin and the marks he'd left on his neck captivated Lev. Asher pushed against Lev's chest until he fell backward, then bent and kissed him. Lev groaned against his lips and reached down to palm Asher's dick.

"Is this what kept you up? Do you need me to take care of this for you, Blakely?"

"No. I need something else."

"Oh?"

Asher climbed off of Lev, and stripped Lev's pants, so that he was naked too. "Get all the way up onto the bed."

Lev was already halfway to full mast, and the command sent all his blood to his cock. He scooted up the bed, eyes locked on the hard cock swaying heavy between Asher's legs as he crawled up the bed after him.

"You're so fucking pretty," Lev said.

Asher bit his smile back, but those dimples betrayed him yet again. Lev rubbed one dimple with his thumb.

"Especially when your smile is genuine. Though, to be fair, you're just as pretty when you glower."

"I don't glower."

Lev didn't argue, didn't want to.

"I can't believe you're mine," Asher whispered, framing Lev's face between his hands.

"I could say the same." Lev's attention snagged on the Icarus wrapping around Asher's side toward his left flank, and he rubbed his thumb over the useless wings.

Asher shivered, squirming deliciously against Lev's lap. "That tickles."

"Sorry." But he wasn't just apologizing for that.

Lev was sorry he was selfish, sorry he hadn't learned his lesson, sorry he'd stolen Silas's life, and would steal what he could of Asher's.

"Where did you go?" Asher asked, an echo of the same question he'd asked before, a question Lev knew he'd ask again.

"I'm here... and also in my head a bit about how much I don't deserve you. Are you sure you want this with me?"

"I think it's obvious I want this," Asher said as he milked a tendril of precum from his tip.

"I mean, me. I'm older." He winced. "What if I'm like Ben?"

"You're not."

Asher swirled his fingers to scoop up the precum and brought it to Lev's mouth. No command necessary, Lev gladly obliged, but Asher didn't stop there. Instead, he explored Lev's mouth with his fingers and fed them down the back of his throat until he gagged. Then left them there.

"Ben would never let me do this."

Tears dripped down the corners of Lev's eyes to his temples, but he didn't resist. He surrendered. When his throat stopped spasming, Asher looked at him with so much fondness.

"You make me feel powerful, Lev." Asher pulled his fingers back, not completely, only enough to give Lev his throat back. "No one else has done that before."

Moaning in need, and gratitude, and rapture, and too many feelings to name, Lev sucked Asher's fingers obediently, thanking him with his eyes. Asher removed his fingers and bent to kiss him, and Lev realized how much he'd needed Asher to believe in him.

"I don't want to hurt you," Lev said when they parted.

"I won't let you," Asher promised, pressing his forehead against Lev's until everything else faded, until it was only now, only them.

Coincidental, sure. Asher had no way of knowing Lev had soothed Silas similarly, but it still meant everything. Silas had never returned the favor. Lev's battles had been his to face alone, and yet this twenty-something American had offered him a sanctuary he'd never known.

"Do you trust me?" Asher asked.

"Yes."

How could Lev not trust Asher when he still accepted him, in spite of his flaws, his agoraphobia, what little he knew of his past, and what lies of omission he could only guess at?

All the cards were stacked against them, and Asher was ready to shuffle the deck—or whatever the metaphor was. Card games had never held his interest. How silly to lose a large sum of money or priceless art in a game of mostly luck.

"I trust you too," Asher said, drawing Lev's wayward attention back.

"You shouldn't."

"Oh my God, Lev. Take the fresh start. If you trust me, you have to trust my judgment."

"Why must you always be so contrary?" Lev teased.

Asher's lips tipped up. "Because I wouldn't be me if I didn't call you out for your bullshit, and we wouldn't be us if we didn't bicker before we fucked."

"Us? I like the sound of that."

He also liked the suggestion that they fuck. Though that wouldn't be possible tonight. Asher would need time to prepare before he took his cock.

"Yeah, us." Asher knit their fingers together and trapped Lev's hands at either side of his head. "Because this starts now with us. Whatever happened before doesn't matter."

That wasn't true. His past proved what he was capable of. It made him who he was. A man without his past didn't know himself at all.

"Now. Us," Asher said, so close to Lev's own spell.

Lev gave in to the strange symmetry that made him feel like they were destined for each other. Asher rewarded him with a kiss, and a roll of his hips, sliding his cock against Lev's.

"Fuck, Blakely. You'll be the death of me." The only thing that would put him out of his misery was burying himself in Asher's tight heat.

He could almost imagine the impatient frown Asher would make as he sank down, struggling to fit all of Lev in, too stubborn to stop until he needed to come more than he needed to prove Lev wrong. Lev would have to get off beforehand so he wouldn't come before Asher did.

"You're such a good lad." Lev stroked the side of his face. "Go ahead and take your pleasure from me."

Asher whimpered. "I need you inside me."

Lev groaned and covered his eyes with his forearm. "Don't tempt me."

"I can take you." Asher took Lev's hands and guided his fingertips behind him to trace the cleft of his ass.

Lev stilled as he touched something smooth that wasn't skin. "What's this?"

FEEL YOU EVERYWHERE

LEV

"I told you I couldn't sleep, so I got myself ready for you."

All cogent thought fled Lev. He toppled Asher off of him and flipped him onto his back, then pushed his knees to his chest. Lev had to see, and there it was—a plug nestled inside his arse.

Lev stared, transfixed by the way Asher's sexy hole stretched around the toy, then looked up. "What a slutty, needy hole you have."

Asher bit his bottom lip and nodded.

The thought of Asher prepping for him in the bathroom, of him playing with his hole next door, all while Lev slept none the wiser, was so filthy he was about to burst.

Asher wanted this. He'd planned for this.

With the age gap and teetering power dynamics they were still trying to balance, Lev had wanted to wait, but Lev was... Well, he was no hero. And Asher had given him tangible proof of consent, of premeditation. This wasn't a rash choice made in a haze of lust or an attempt to please the man who held his future in his hands.

Lev stroked his beard. "I don't recall rescuing this from the ocean."

Asher blushed, demurring his gaze. "I forgot it underneath the bathroom sink the night I tried to leave."

"Thank God." Lev held the back of his hand to his forehead like he'd nearly fainted with relief, and teased, "I feared you'd borrowed it from Theo."

"No more joking," Asher said, breathy and impatient. "I need you."

Lev swallowed hard and sat back on his knees, so enthralled by Asher's confession. "I'm here, baby. What do you need?"

Asher gazed down at his chest, face flushed. "Can I... Can I suck your dick while you check that I'm ready?"

Gooseflesh prickled across Lev's body at the suggestion. "Of course."

Lev wrinkled his nose. What kind of man replied so stiffly to an offer to blow him?

But Asher didn't seem to care, which Lev appreciated because Asher had far more recent sexual experience and Lev was developing a touch of performance anxiety.

"Be a good lad and lay on your side, hm?"

"Okay," Asher said, voice a touch shaky, like he was a little nervous too.

Once they'd positioned themselves in a sideways sixty-nine, Lev opened Asher's knees like a book.

Asher clutched Lev's hips and pulled him closer, then the warm, wet ecstasy of his mouth enveloped him with hungry impatience, tongue tracing his crown and exploring his foreskin, toying with it like he hadn't sucked an uncut dick before.

"That's perfect," Lev praised. "Yes. Like that."

Blinking back sunspots of pleasure, Lev lapped up the precum leaking from Asher's slit, gripped the base of the plug, and pulled back only enough to tease him, hoping to take his time.

Asher moaned around Lev's cock.

"Fuck, Ash. That feels so good. Make all the noise you need to so I know how much you love sucking me."

Asher hummed his acknowledgement like the perfect lad he was.

Lev'd had his fair share of excellent head, but there was something to be said about being sucked off by a man so fanatically obsessed. The sheer enthusiasm...

The perfect student, the perfect man for him.

Lev wished he could see Asher's face. He wanted to watch Asher swallow him. Did his lips strain to fit all of Lev inside or was that luscious mouth, so rarely widened in a smile, big enough for him?

"How long have you wanted this, Blakely?" How long had he wished the toy was Lev?

Asher didn't answer, focused on his task, too intent to prove his worth, as if Lev had ever needed that, as if Lev hadn't been wrapped around Asher's finger all along.

It was Lev who needed to prove himself, Lev who needed to show Asher that every man he'd ever fucked had all been a prelude to being fucked by him. What if Lev failed to measure up? What if he failed to please him?

Asher sucked hard and jerked Lev faster. If he didn't get inside him soon, he wouldn't make it, and Asher would never let him live it down. He wasn't playing fair though, attacking Lev with the temptation of his plugged arse and oral sex.

Lev took the base of the plug in hand and twisted side-to-side, slowly, pulling the plug out as far as he dared before pushing it back in, careful not to force the flange. Asher's moan was so deep and guttural and long it ricocheted through Lev's cock.

Asher's mouth went lax around Lev's cock, all his muscles tensed. Lev removed his hand. A distant voice reminded him that if Asher came, he might be one of the many men he'd fucked who were hypersensitive after getting off, but a louder voice in Lev's head volunteered to forfeit penetrative sex for the chance to scoop up Asher's come and fuck it back into him with his fingers, plug him tight, and tease him for hours before finally fucking him.

Cold air on Lev's cock was like ice water dumped over his head as Asher spat out his dick and wriggled out of the pretzel they'd made of their bodies and onto his back.

"Did I hurt you?" Lev asked, heart sinking as he sat up.

"No." Spit shimmered on Asher's swollen lips. "I need you inside me. Now."

"Christ, Blakely."

Lev straddled Asher, and kissed him, licking inside his mouth. He wanted to take Asher like this, close and intimate, splayed out beneath him as he kissed him.

"Please tell me you packed a rubber? You strike me as the plan-ahead sort of lad."

"I did, but..." Asher pinched his lip. "But I got tested. I'm good. And you haven't had sex in... Fuck. Five years is a long time."

"Yes, Blakely, I'm well aware of my tragic celibacy, and would rather not delay it further. I'm negative too."

Lev gripped Asher's ankles loosely, then pushed his feet toward his arse, and butterflied his legs open.

"Still, I could go get a condom?" Asher joked.

"Don't you fucking dare."

Dimples flashed on Asher's cheeks. "I like this side of you."

He squeezed Lev's arse and guided his hips into a rolling rhythm, sliding their cocks parallel, teasing Lev into a frenzy.

"Hop off," Asher said. "I want to ride you, at least at first."

Lev would fuck Asher upside down, underwater while singing the American anthem if that's what Asher needed. Asher's submissive tendencies didn't weaken him. Lev surrendered all his power to him. He was Asher's to command.

But as he traded spaces with Asher and leaned against the headboard, he tried not to think too long about why Asher had suggested the position change.

Was it because he wanted to control his descent down Lev's thick cock, or because he *needed* control to feel safe?

"I can't believe this is happening," Asher murmured, thick lashes dancing as he drank in Lev's body.

"Nor can I. Are you sure you want to do this?"

Asher's tattoos shuddered with his hastened breaths, bringing Lev's art to life. "I want this more than anything."

Asher braced his palm on Lev's chest and held his gaze as he reached around and pulled out the plug. Lev wrapped his hands around him and parted his cheeks to help. Then it was out.

Asher's breath caught on a soft gasp, a wrinkle furrowed his forehead, like he hated to be empty. He tossed the plug aside, and Lev rushed to feel the gape, wishing he could see inside, see everything, commit it to memory.

"I wish you had let me stretch you with my fingers over days to be certain."

Asher scoffed. "You have so little faith in me."

"I've been told I feel bigger than I look."

Asher rolled his eyes, but he listened, and squirted a pump of refined coconut oil into Lev's waiting hands. Lev wasted no time slicking up his cock and Asher's hole, while Asher lowered until he hovered a breath away from penetration.

"Easy does it," Lev coached as his tip pressed against Asher's hole. "Relax, love. Let me in."

Lev slid in a few millimeters at most. Asher's eyes closed.

"That's it. You listen so well."

Asher paused, inhaling sharply, and opened his eyes, locking on Lev with a wrecked look.

"It's alright if you can't take me today." Lev rubbed up and down Asher's arms. "Or I could stretch you some more first?"

They hadn't even reached the widest part of him. Topping with a bigger cock wasn't all it was cracked up to be. It wouldn't be the first time he'd had to turn back the way he came.

Asher shook his head. "I'm fine." His hole relaxed, allowing more of Lev in.

Preferring to err on the side of caution, Lev stopped him. "What's wrong?"

"Nothing at all." Lev reached for the bottle of oil and kissed Asher, slathering more oil between them. "Take your time."

"Thank you," Asher said against his lips with more weight than a simple *thanks for not tearing me open*.

"Did Ben rush you? Hurt you?"

"I didn't say that," Asher said, sinking down slowly. "This starts now, with us, remember. That goes both ways."

"You're right. I'm sorry." Lev tabled the discussion for later. Surely, Asher hadn't meant that they could never talk about their pasts again.

Asher's flush spread from his cheeks to his chest as he let gravity push Lev's crown slowly past his sphincter—and into nirvana.

Had it always felt this good? Or was it because he was with Asher?

Beneath Lev's hands, Asher trembled like wind-rattled trees. Lev rained down accolades, stroking him, praising him for feeling so good, telling him he was nearly there, that he was taking him so well, until Asher seated himself fully.

It took all of Lev's strength to remain still.

"It feels like you're everywhere," Asher said in ecclesiastical wonder.

"Mm. If I could, I'd be your air." Lev tugged Asher by the back of his head until he was close enough to kiss. "You did so well."

The kiss started tender, lips murmuring mutual adoration, but that didn't last long, and soon their tongues tangled, and Asher sucked his tongue like a cock. Asher broke the kiss and leaned his lithe torso back, highlighting all of Lev's art, then braced his hands on Lev's legs and rode his length upward.

"Christ, you're a sight. So perfect, no one else could compare."

Asher's eyes flashed to Lev's. There was something there, but the thought didn't stick, not when Asher sank down again, and fucked himself faster, cock swaying tantalizingly, flinging precum between them.

Lev gripped Asher's hips and helped him, drawing more moans from Asher's mouth. Pleasure zipped up Lev's spine.

"Please. I need…" Asher gasped. "Oh, fuck. *Lev*." He said his name on another long moan. "Please."

Lev couldn't bear to see Asher hurt, even if what pained him was the need to get off. He pumped upward and took over fucking Asher up and down his cock like a sex doll.

"Oh, fuck. I'm going to—" Asher said in a rush as his body bore down around Lev's cock. "Fuck. I'm coming."

Asher tossed his head back, grinding his hips, keeping Lev deep inside of him. Lev reached his fingers to feel Asher's hole stretched around him, tightening and twitching as he climaxed.

Asher collapsed forward and buried his face in Lev's neck, hearts thumping between them. Lev kissed Asher's hair, trailing his fingers down the center of his slick back, up and down the delicate ridges of his spine.

"I love you, Asher Blakely. For your beautiful mind. For your art. For opening the heart you've kept locked. For giving me yet another chance."

"I love you too," Asher whispered.

Lev reached between them, pilfering some of Asher's cum, and hummed as he tasted it. He was so turned on, he'd probably wept enough precum inside of Asher that he'd be full for weeks.

But he was a gentleman, so he rifled through the sheets for Asher's shirt, but came up empty, and was halfway through shucking the case from his pillow when—

"What are you doing?" Asher asked, brows darting together.

"Getting something to clean you with." Lev grunted as he successfully removed the pillowcase.

"We're not done," Asher said. "But I am exhausted. Get on top."

"You're not sore?"

"No." Asher laughed, core tightening around Lev's length.

"In that case…" Lev flipped Asher onto his back and folded his knees to his chest.

Like the good boy that he was, Asher hooked his forearms under his knees to hold the position.

He kissed Asher as he slicked more oil on his cock, then sat back on his heels. "Ready?"

"Yes," Asher said and bit into his bottom lip.

Lev added more oil and a finger. Asher's hole was tight, but soft under pressure, broken in, ready to be fucked back open.

Watching Asher for any sign of pain, Lev pushed inside slowly. Asher's head fell back, spilling dark curls against his pillow. Lev liked him like that, body arched, baring his neck. He wanted more. Lev pulled back and gave a careful, exploratory thrust.

Asher whimpered. Lev slowed.

"Don't fucking stop," Asher said.

In that case… Lev loosely gripped Asher's dick and fucked him harder.

"Still okay?"

"Oh my God. If I'd had any idea you would fuck me this stilted, I would have never let you get on top."

"Such impatience." Lev laughed and thrust into him again. This time, he didn't hold back, even as Asher stitched together a stream of curse words and thrashed his head from side to side and clawed at his biceps, between pleading, *Don't stop*.

"You're going to come again for me, aren't you, pretty American?"

Asher moaned and arched his back even more, nearly levitating off the bed.

"Such a greedy lad." Lev punished him with a deep stroke. "You fit like you were made to take my cock, made for me."

Lev cradled Asher's face between his palms and kissed him, keeping his eyes open, wrecked by Asher's reverent gaze trained on him.

"I need..." Asher gasped.

Lev pressed deeper, deeper than he'd dared before. "What do you need? Tell me and I'll give it to you. Do you need to come again?"

"I can't."

Lev clucked his tongue and slowed some. "Give yourself some credit," he teased. "You're a strong lad. You simply need to apply yourself."

"You're such an asshole." Asher's eyes narrowed, and he leveled the most adorable scowl at him.

Lev laughed darkly, and reared back up, grabbing hold of Asher's knees and parting them for a better look as he plowed into him. Pleasure crested on the verge of rapturous oblivion. He rolled his hips, adjusting the angle until each thrust dragged against Asher's prostate, then he rubbed Asher's stomach with his free hand.

"Look at you, stuffed with my cock. I can't wait to fill you up."

With a keening cry, Asher exploded, and the sight of Asher coming apart on his cock, of the tattooed devotion writhing over Asher's skin as he fell to pieces, vulnerable and trusting that Lev wouldn't hurt him, was like a button pressed on his prostate, shooting sparks down his lower half, tightening all the muscles in his body. His orgasm was like a freight train slamming into him.

He hadn't come inside someone in years. He hadn't come inside someone he cared about since Silas. The connection of claiming Asher felt so much stronger because he'd had a choice.

Asher shivered through a shuddering sigh. Reluctantly, Lev slid out of him.

"Hey, where are you going?" Asher snagged Lev's arm.

"The loo. I'll be right back, baby." Lev dipped into the bathroom and returned with a warm, wet towel and a dry one. Asher lifted his head and reached for the towel, but Lev shook his head.

"Let me clean you." Of all Lev's dominant tendencies, caretaking was his strongest kink.

Asher lifted his head from the pillow. "I can do it."

"I'd like to take care of you, if that's alright with you."

Asher chewed on his bottom lip, then nodded, and rested his head against the pillow.

"Thank you," Lev murmured, sitting on the edge of the bed.

"I should be thanking you."

Lev peeled the blankets back. "It pleases me to do this for you."

"Oh." Asher knit his fingers together over his chest and stared up at the same painted ceiling looming over Lev every night.

Lev dropped his gaze under the guise of focusing on his task, overwhelmed. Blakely held all the power to break his heart.

"You're stunning like this, sated, well-fucked, cum crystallized on my art."

Lev dragged the wet towel down Asher's chest, cleaning errant cum from the self-portrait over Asher's heart, down and around the ouroboros.

They both fell quiet as Lev cleaned their mess. Lev handled his soft, velvety cock gently, assuming it would be oversensitive. Asher squirmed, and his cock perked up, rising sluggishly.

"How are you hard again?"

"I can't help it when you're touching me."

"I hope I'm able to keep up."

Asher sat up and curled his arm around Lev's neck, pulling him close. Lev lost his train of thought in the golden haze of Asher's irises.

"You're more than enough for me," Asher said. "Hands down, the best sex of my life. Better than any fantasy. Your age doesn't bother me. Hell, you're in better shape than I am."

Lev thanked him with a tender kiss, murmuring his gratitude aloud as they parted. After Lev disposed of the towels, he lifted the lid of the crystal decanter on the bedside table and poured water into Asher's glass.

"Thank you." Asher took a sip and swallowed. "Top tier aftercare."

"How are you feeling?"

"A little sore. A little high."

Lev sat at the edge of the bed again, one leg crossed over the other, spine straight, and tapped Asher's temple. "What about up here? Any regrets?"

Asher blinked. "What? No. Do you regret it?"

"No, but I wouldn't blame you if you got caught up in the moment..."

"I'm not going to change my mind."

"I've been so touch-starved and lost without you." Lev brushed Asher's hair back from his brow and kissed his forehead. "I may have fallen in love with you through your art first, but now that I've met you, I've fallen in love with you, and if I look at myself the way you do, I think I'm starting to see I deserve love too."

"You do." Asher ended with a yawn.

"Let's get you to bed."

Lev rearranged them in bed away from the wet spot he'd placed the dry towel over. Asher hugged his side and slung one leg over him, resting his head over Lev's heart.

Asher's breathing slowed, his muscles slackened, weight

pressing down on Lev's chest. Pride swelled inside him. His lad was getting the sleep he needed, the sleep he hadn't been able to find without Lev's help.

It was nice to be needed in a way that wasn't codependent.

3 4

AMELIE

ASHER

OCTOBER 28

An SUV waited in front of the castle on the last day of the retreat—*not* at the bottom of the gate.

Lev had saved Sloth for the final sin. Without the stress of the competition, they'd spent the last week making art and relaxing. They took turns cooking for each other on long autumn evenings, and drank until they laughed more than talked, then watched old movies in the study. Even Chuck was less of an ass than usual.

When the weather was miserable, Lev took them to some of his favorite rooms—the library, and a conservatory with a heated pool where they swam while rain sluiced down the glass ceiling.

Asher and Theo talked for hours while exploring the haberdashery of Lichenmoor's attic like it was a museum, finding Sherlock tobacco pipes, old wedding dresses, abandoned vintage tools, and handwritten music.

For someone who'd sworn off artist friends, Asher was surprised at how much he'd enjoyed everyone's company, and how much he would miss Theo.

261

Asher and Julian made amends the morning after the *calamitous dinner*, as Lev had called it.

Julian had explained what he'd been through, and Asher had opened up about Ben. Instead of feeling anxious, and vulnerable, talking about it had lessened some of the weight he'd carried alone.

Lev still harbored a grudge when it came to Julian, but at least he'd warmed up to Theo.

"Alright there, Blakely?" Lev asked, standing beside Asher on the top step, hands clasped behind his back, exterior calm and collected, his face a perfect mask of gracious host bidding farewell.

He wore the mask well, but Asher knew better. After breakfast, Lev had confessed he was afraid Asher would leave with them. Then he'd pulled Asher into an alcove and kissed him until his legs were weak, "So it's harder for you to run away."

"Your driver told me you didn't allow cars beyond the front gate," Asher said. "I could have walked off a cliff in that fog, you know."

"Nonsense," Lev scoffed. "I would never have let that happen. You should be more aware of your surroundings, though. I followed you the entire time and you had no idea."

"No. I definitely had an idea. I just didn't think you were actually following me because most hosts don't stalk their guests around dangerous precipices."

"Maybe because I'm not your host, and you're not my guest."

Asher rolled his eyes.

"If you'll excuse me..." Lev trotted down the steps to referee an argument between Chuck and the driver about loading his bags on top of the others.

With a screech of the old metal door, the last of Lichenmoor's guests emerged—Melody empty-handed, and Daria toting a black bag and an oversized pink glitter suitcase.

Melody stopped at Asher's side, blue eyes glistening, and hugged him. "I'm going to miss you dreadfully." She lowered her voice to a whisper. "Whatever the truth is, you deserve the mentorship."

Then, before Asher could thank her, she flitted on light feet down the steps, short skirt swishing around her thighs. Daria shook his hand with a much stronger grip than his own.

Julian hugged Asher next, saying into his shoulder, "If things become too much and you need help getting out, call me."

"I'm not going to die, Julian."

Julian released him. "But you will call?"

Asher rolled his eyes. "Yeah. You have my number too. Call anytime. If I survive, I'll invite you all back for the summer."

"That's not funny," Julian said.

Theo cleared his throat with a soft *ahem*.

"Sorry," Julian said, and stepped aside. "Remember, I'm just a phone call away."

"Thanks."

Julian headed to the van, and Theo stepped closer. "We must keep in touch, my friend. Write to me, and I'll do the same. In the very rare chance you need help, ask me how my cat is doing. On the phone or in a letter. Whatever. But I don't expect you to ask. Lev clearly loves you."

"Thank you." Asher smiled. "Thanks for helping me with Lev too."

Theo followed Asher's gaze to Lev still bickering with Chuck.

"Aren't you going to ask what my cat's name is?"

"What's your cat's name?" Asher said.

"Amelie. Can I tell you something?" He looked over his shoulder and hid his mouth behind his hand. "I don't actually have a cat."

Asher laughed loudly, not expecting that at all. Lev turned

his head toward the laugh and smiled, then tossed Chuck's bag into the back of the SUV with the least care possible.

"You know what this means, though, Theo?"

"Hm?"

"You have to get a cat and name her that."

Theo laughed. "Maybe I will."

"Stay safe, okay, Theo?"

"I'd tell you to stay safe too, but Lev would never let anything happen to you." He grazed Asher's cheeks with a kiss. "*Au revoir!*"

"Bye." Asher followed him to the car, sad to see him go.

Lev thanked Theo and shook his hand, but closed the SUV door a little too quickly after him.

"Are you sure you don't want to go with them?" Lev asked, returning to Asher's side.

Asher took Lev's hand. "I'm not leaving."

"Then why so glum? You're not still upset about the night we met, are you?" Lev curled his arm around Asher. "Ew. You smell like Theo."

"Oh, stop." Asher knocked his elbow against Lev's side.

"It didn't pass my notice that he didn't bid the others a French farewell."

"He's not saying goodbye to them yet."

Lev tutted.

They both waved as the SUV pulled away, swallowed by fog the same way it had on Asher's first day.

Lev's fingers dipped inside Asher's pants and trailed gently down his crack, then explored the outside of his rim.

"Lev..." Asher moaned, eyes falling shut, heat pooling in his gut as his cock started to fill.

"What do you need, baby? Do you need me to take care of you?"

Asher bit his bottom lip, and nodded.

"Come along, then."

Lev smacked Asher's ass with a light hand and hurried up the steps.

Asher yipped. "What was that for?"

"Letting Theo kiss you."

Asher followed. "I'm going to get you back for that."

Lev looked back with a roguish grin. "I sincerely hope that you do."

MENTORSHIP

If only there could be an invention that bottled up a memory, like scent. And it never faded, and it never got stale. And then, when one wanted it, the bottle could be uncorked, and it would be like living the moment all over again.

— DAPHNE DU MAURIER, REBECCA

3 5

BEAUTIFUL CAGE

ASHER

Lev's muscular ass in tight riding pants was the only reason Asher hadn't turned around and gone back to bed.

"It's freezing," Asher said through chattering teeth.

"You'll be sweating soon enough," Lev said briskly and hooked an arm around Asher's shoulders, sharing his warmth as they walked.

Ivy crawled up and over tall stone walls and rained scarlet leaves. Triangular ponds overrun with lily pads and acid green algae marked the four corners of the square garden. Rose bushes ran amok in weedy flowerbeds, neglected for so long branches had tangled into brambles.

"I've let most of the gardens go. It's far too much upkeep. The vegetable garden in the conservatory is mine, though."

"Did Luna teach you?"

"Wendell, actually. He said I needed to watch something living grow from decay after Mum died. Planting a seed taught me more about faith than any religion could because I had to trust that the seed was growing beneath the surface, even if I couldn't see it."

"I'm glad you had Wendell."

"I quite agree, especially because I despise store-bought tomatoes."

A statue stood watch over the enormous arch leading to the moors, a mirror image of the one guarding the front gate. "What's with the statues?"

"Statues?" He followed Asher's gaze. "Oh. Those? They've been here so long I forget they exist."

"I thought the one at the gate was pointing in a different direction than I remembered when I tried to leave that night, but I was too busy trying to escape to worry about it."

Lev's smile twisted into a frown. "Which way was it pointing?"

"Which way is it supposed to be pointing?"

"Toward the castle."

Maybe Asher had misremembered the statue pointing away from the castle that first night. Asher squeezed his hand. "Hey, I'm still here. You saved me, remember?"

Lev kissed Asher's hand, then pulled a metal rod up from the ground and heaved the gate open. "The stables are through here."

Miles of verdant moors, lumbering hills, and evergreen forests dotted with splashes of goldenrod and burnt orange stretched on endlessly. Squat stone walls divided the valley into pastures.

"This is beautiful. Who knew all this was hiding behind the castle?" He'd paint it later.

"When I see Lichenmoor through your eyes, I almost believe it's beautiful too." Lev veered left, trampling over withering thistles toward a long brick building with a mossy thatched roof.

"You don't think it's beautiful?"

Lev shrugged a shoulder. "It's a cage."

Asher linked his arm with Lev's, slowing him down enough to kiss. "I'm going to break you out of this cage one day."

"You're certainly stubborn enough to keep trying."

"Rude."

A very dirty Great Pyrenees guarded a flock of sheep on a small hill.

"Are the sheep yours too?"

"God, no. I wouldn't know the first thing to do with sheep. I lease some of our land to local farmers."

"But I thought you dated the sheep farmer's son?"

Lev's hearty laugh boomed across the meadow and flushed birds from their roosts. The dog barked.

"The dog is Bruno."

Lichenmoor's stable was a brick building that sheltered the horses from all sides, though once Lev hauled the sliding iron door open, the layout was the same as every stable he'd seen in America.

All the stalls were empty, aside from the two in the front where a gray gelding and Rebecca nudged their noses through the gaps in their stalls.

"That's Dorian. You two share similar temperaments—stubborn and prickly, a little stoic, definitely nippy. Prone to running off. You can ride Rebecca. She's far more pleasant."

"Ha-ha," Asher deadpanned.

Lev showed him to a tack room cleaner than his mother's kitchen. Dewdrops slid down the panes of narrow arched windows. Polished amber wood lockers with built-in benches lined the widest wall.

Asher whistled lowly. "This is a far cry from our dusty stable back home."

"Horses shit on the ground, anyway. I doubt they care about dust."

He hadn't expected such a crass reply, and burst into laughter.

Lev watched him fondly. "You're so greedy with your laughs, I get a little kick of dopamine when you do."

"Imagine how good you'd feel if you were actually funny…"

Lev plunked down on the bench and swapped his rain boots for knee-high riding boots.

"Rebecca's things are above her saddle," Lev said, head bent as he fought with the zipper of his boot.

A crop leaned against the wall below the bridle and bit hanging from a hook. Asher picked it up. Ben had used a crop on him. At first, Asher had liked it—there was a reason he had so many tattoos—but Ben had used pain for psychological warfare, lashing out unpredictably until he'd lost all sense of safety and surrendered to subserviency.

Bees buzzed in his ears. His skin itched, his throat tightened. No. Ben wasn't here. He could breathe, even if it felt like his throat was closing up. He leaned the crop back against the wall and wiped his shaking, clammy hands on his pants.

"Are you trying to suggest something, Blakely?" Lev murmured.

Asher spun around, startled by his silent approach. "I'm not into impact play."

Lev picked up the crop. "Pity."

"I'm sorry." He couldn't do that again, even for Lev.

"What for? Setting a boundary?" Lev took a step back, giving him more space, in that emotionally intelligent way of his.

Asher's tension eased slightly, but he couldn't drag his gaze away from the crop in Lev's hand.

"Are you into that?" Asher asked. "Sadism, I mean."

Lev's fingers twitched on the handle. "No."

Ashed exhaled.

Lev lifted the crop, and Asher's instincts took over. His eyes slammed shut. His hands shot up to guard his face. But the blast of pain never came. Lev dropped the crop and kicked it aside, sending it skittering across the stone floor, out of his reach.

Strong arms enveloped him. Lev guided the side of Asher's head to his heart, and the slow, steady drum rooted him in the present, helping to pull him from his panic.

"I've got you. You're safe," Lev said in a soothing hush. "You're with me. I will never hit you, I promise. I was trying to hang it on the hook behind you."

Shame filled Asher. Why had he reacted that way? When would he get over Ben? It's not like Ben had abused him. Asher had always consented, and Ben never left a lasting mark.

The scars on his heart didn't count.

"Try slowing your breathing to match mine, hm?"

When had he started hyperventilating?

"Breathe in, darling." Lev's chest swelled.

Asher inhaled, comforted by the jasmine in Lev's cologne and the oak and moss of Lichenmoor as Lev stroked his back in a lazy rhythm.

"And out." The pillow of Lev's chest ebbed. "Good lad."

After a few rounds of Lev-guided breathing, Asher finally made it to the other side of his panic attack.

"Well done, Ash."

Lev released him and bared his palms to prove he was unarmed, then bent his knees, lowering halfway to a deep squat, making himself smaller, less of a threat, and it was so fucking thoughtful, Asher fell in love with him even more.

"I'm so sorry I frightened you," Lev said, brow wrinkling with contrition as he looked up at him. "I was trying to flirt, but I fear I'm rather rusty."

"You did nothing wrong."

"Neither did you." Lev stood slowly. "May I hug you again?"

"Yeah."

Lev wrapped him in a gentle hug and kissed the top of his head.

"Tell me what he did to you."

TRACING LINES

LEV

Asher grimaced. "It's humiliating—the things he did to me, what I let him do."

The guilt in Asher's voice was a knife to Lev's stomach.

"Darling, you mustn't blame yourself."

"You don't know the entire story."

"That's true, but you can't take credit for how hard you flinched when I lifted the crop, and that's not the first time you've reacted that way. If you tell me, I can help you."

Asher chewed on his lip.

"Here, come sit." Lev steered him to the bench and onto it, then joined him. "We don't have to discuss anything you don't want to, but perhaps you could tell me about art school in general and see how that makes you feel?"

Asher squared his jaw and nodded. "My hometown is... claustrophobic. There are more churches than schools and I was the only gay kid in my class. Well, the only out kid." He chewed on his lip. "The cattle ranch industry isn't known for its tolerance, either."

Lichenmoor couldn't have been more different. Lev had known his father was bisexual from a young age, and many of the guests Lucian hosted were queer too. The locals weren't as accepting, but he hadn't fraternized with them much beyond rugby.

Hate wasn't a foreign concept, though. Silas had suffered growing up in a home where being gay was being damned, and he'd certainly been bullied at Catholic school by students and nuns alike.

"Watson was my sanctuary. I met people from all over the country, and many of them were queer. For the first time in my life, I could be my most authentic self without fear. It was like that for a few of us."

Lev imagined Asher and his friends, flowers that hadn't been able to bloom back home, thriving once they'd planted roots elsewhere; petals unfurling later than others, but no less beautiful.

"And your family? Were they supportive?"

"My mom and dad are great. Nonna is old-school Catholic and she's gotten better over the years, but I'm pretty sure she still prays for me."

Asher shrugged as if their support didn't matter, but Lev knew better. His lad was sulky, and sarcastic, and stubbornly independent, but he still yearned for love and acceptance.

"My brothers were dicks about it for a while, but when my dad found out, he was so pissed he made them walk the fence line as punishment. Our ranch is a few thousand acres and that's a lot of fence to check and repair. "

"Your dad seems lovely."

Asher's lips twitched into a faint smile. "He's my best friend. My only friend until Watson." His good humor dimmed. "Ben taught my introductory art history class."

"Ah. Those who can't paint teach art history."

Asher shook his head. "He taught advanced color theory and painting too, but not to first-year students. I'm grateful for that. I don't know what my art would look like, or if I'd be painting at all, if I'd learned my foundational skills from someone who hurt me.

"It's still hard to tease out what I know instinctively as an artist from what he taught me, or from what I had to unlearn to find my voice again."

Lev understood. Even now, he sometimes was uncertain whether he controlled his paintbrush or Lucian.

"Ben favored me from day one. He called on me often, and praised me for answering, even if I was wrong. When he told a joke, he always made eye contact. He asked my instructors for updates on my progress and spied on my unfinished work.

"Nothing happened that quarter. Nothing romantic, anyway. He tutored me in the evenings 'to help me improve' and arranged for me to attend his classes the next quarter."

Asher exhaled an agitated breath. "He was grooming me and I fell for it. I just wish I knew why he chose me. Did he ever like my art at all? Did he pick me because I was weak?"

"If he thought you were weak, he was wrong."

"I was fucking clueless. We spent all those hours together, and sure, I had a crush, but I never saw him as someone I'd date. He was my teacher. He was married. He had kids the same age as me."

Asher pulled his hands free and raked his dark waves back from his face. "I don't know. I was so stupid..."

"You were young."

"Fuck." Asher's eyes smashed shut. He buried his hands in his hair again.

Lev took Asher's hands back into his lap before he started ripping his hair out.

"Did you have your tattoos when you were with Ben?" Lev asked, hoping to disrupt Asher's cycle of self-loathing.

Asher nodded. "I don't think I would have ever shown them to him if he hadn't forced me."

"Forced you?" Lev inhaled through his nose and tried not to explode.

"We were doing a series of nude studies one night. I'd um..." He nibbled his lip. "I'd hooked up with the model a few times, and he kept making eye contact, flirting without words. I tried to be professional, but I kept blushing."

"Who among us hasn't blushed during nude studies?"

Asher gave a small laugh, like he still blamed himself but didn't want Lev to feel bad. "Ben was furious. He'd kept his emotions controlled so tightly, but his mask slipped."

Lev stroked Asher's hand with his thumb, while inside he was crumbling. Lev had praised Asher gratuitously, shown favoritism, lurked over his shoulder like some depraved sex addict. He'd manipulated Asher into coming to Lichenmoor, and unleashed his anger on him.

"I've acted a lot like Ben," Lev said, careful to keep his tone even.

"It's not the same, Lev." Asher shook his head stubbornly. "*I'm* not the same. Ben and I never argued because I was too afraid to stand up for myself. I took his verbal attacks and let him cross all of my boundaries. Have I been that way with you?"

"No, you're quite quarrelsome, in fact."

Asher didn't laugh, charging forward with his story instead like he had to get it off his chest.

"Ben asked me to stay after class. He locked the door and closed the blinds, then told me to strip and stand on the pedestal."

"He did what?" Lev growled, anger flaring before he could stop it. He inhaled a simmering breath and patted Asher's hand. "Sorry. Please continue."

"I laughed at first. But he was serious. I couldn't risk losing my scholarship. I couldn't go home. He uh... I um..."

"You don't have to relive it if you don't want to, love."

Asher lifted his chin. "No. I want to tell you. This feels cathartic, like bloodletting."

Lev forced a wan smile. "That makes perfect sense." Now was not the time to tease him about how useless bloodletting was.

"First he just stared, mapping me mentally. That was almost worse than when he ordered me into position. My tattoos surprised him. I could tell. He scanned each one."

God, he wanted to kill Ben.

"While Ben sketched in silence, I traced the lines of your art with my eyes and tried to dissociate. Your art kept me company and comforted me when I felt so alone."

"Oh, Asher, I'm so sorry." He cupped Asher's cheek with tender reverence. "I wish I could have been there to protect you."

"Me too," Asher said distantly. "Then he sat on *my* stool and helped himself to *my* pencil, and sketched me slowly, dragging out my torment. I didn't know what he was thinking. My own thoughts cycled between anxiety and shame and..."

Asher hid his face in his hands. "I wanted him, and there was an element of exhibitionism, and..." He cleared his throat. "I..."

"You became aroused?"

Asher lowered his hands and nodded. "Ben noticed. He mocked me and degraded me and I—" His sentence ended abruptly, like a cord ripped from a socket.

"The degradation turned you on?"

"Yeah, and I didn't know what a degradation kink was back then, so I just felt dirty and deviant, and then he'd call attention to my erection again and... I believed him."

Lev blinked back tears and swallowed. He couldn't imagine how painful and isolating it must have been to believe something so devastating about himself.

"He was wrong, Asher. It's quite common for sexual assault survivors to become aroused or ejaculate."

Asher's gaze darted up. "I wasn't assaulted. All he did was sketch me."

"Sorry. I shouldn't have assumed. This is your story to tell. I wasn't there."

Asher nodded. "Thanks."

His vision grew vacant on the window. Thin wisps of fog hugged the valley, but the sun would chase them away soon.

"After he finished, I went to my station to pack up as if class had just ended. I don't remember getting dressed. Muscle memory and routine took over, I guess.

"I wasn't in my head. I wasn't at the studio. I was following the lines of your art, even though I couldn't see them anymore. Then I saw the sketch. I'd forgotten about it.

"I turned a corner and smashed into my doppelgänger. It was me, but it wasn't. My gaze was too hollow. I couldn't look at the rest of it. Looking would have been like reliving the last two hours all at once."

The poor lad. God. His heart broke for him. "What happened to the sketch?"

"He kept it so I'd," he lifted his fingers into air quotes, "remember to behave."

Lev inhaled and tried to stifle his fury. "He blackmailed you?"

Asher nodded. "I was sick to my stomach all weekend. I couldn't paint, but my scholarship had a very strict attendance policy, and I didn't want to give him more ammunition."

"That was very brave of you."

"Ben acted like nothing had happened. He showered me with praise while I painted, like he always had. I don't even remember what I painted, just like I don't remember getting dressed."

"Trauma steals your memories."

"I don't *feel* like I was traumatized. I wasn't raped."

"Trauma isn't a competition. Others may have suffered more. That will always be the case in this world. But that doesn't make your pain any less valid. If you're cut, you still bleed. Even if someone else's wound is deeper, any wound can fester and grow, tunnel under the skin and abscess into something far more painful."

"Yeah." Asher crossed his arms over his chest, all but saying he didn't believe Lev's sentimental bullshit. "Ben asked me to stay after class again. Usually he'd pass me a note or whisper his request, but this time he asked in front of everyone."

"So you couldn't say no?" Bastard.

"I think so. He apologized profusely, said he had a gift for me. He seemed scared almost. I should have known then that I had the power to stop this." He sighed. "It was just some gouache paint and an antique travel easel—not the sketch of me. I accused him of bribing me, and asked for the sketch back, but he twisted the truth until I doubted myself. Then he confessed he'd been falling for me, and I believed him. I even felt guilty.

"He said I flirted with him for months, teased him and tempted him, then made him jealous on purpose. He'd been trying to resist me."

Asher palmed his forehead and turned away.

Lev could never forgive himself for killing Silas, and he couldn't condemn Asher to a future with him, but what if he could help Asher forgive himself? What if that was why they'd been drawn together?

"Things escalated from there. Ben was into BDSM and I was into whatever pleased him. Things got dark. Scenes bled together until they weren't scenes at all. We weren't *playing* BDSM anymore. I was his twenty-four-seven submissive.

"I could have stopped it at any time. I never said no or a safe word. I could have overpowered him, but I didn't. I just took it and tried to be good for him. That still fucks with my head a lot."

"How long did this go on?"

"A little over a year."

Christ. "Did you love him?"

Asher nodded.

"You wanted to please him."

"Yeah." Asher rubbed the back of his neck. "You're not jealous, are you?"

"Heavens no. I'd gladly toss Ben down a stairwell. I'm trying to understand why you think you were some hapless frog in a kettle, when all I see is a very sweet lad who would have made the right person very happy if he hadn't met a spineless, narcissistic cunt who took advantage."

"Thank you for saying that."

"It's true." Birdsong drifted through the window while he pondered how best to handle his next question. He didn't want to say anything that could make him feel responsible for Ben's actions. "What about Watson? Were they supportive?"

Asher shook his head.

"A few students figured it out and reported it. Ben kept me so isolated that the story spread through the school before I knew."

Lev clicked his tongue.

"Yeah. I left on the verge of a panic attack, and when I returned later to defend myself, Ben sat on the same side of the table as the people determining my fate."

"They protected him?"

Asher nodded. "They didn't kick me out, but they let him keep teaching."

Lev would use his vast swaths of fuck-you money to rearrange the entire school as soon as he convinced Asher to let him.

"Did the police ever get involved?"

"Nothing he did was illegal, and I couldn't prove the things that were borderline. I testified at someone else's trial, but Ben was acquitted."

"Ben hurt someone else?"

Dorian snuffled and scraped his hoof over the ground like the scratch of flint shedding sparks.

"Yeah. We should go." Asher scooted to the edge of the bench. Lev laid a hand on his wrist, not encircling it, merely recapturing his attention.

"He can wait a moment longer. What happened to the sketch?"

"He probably still has it."

"I see." Lev would find out, and dispose of it. "Your anxiety attacks..." Again, Lev paused, weighing his words before he spoke them. "Did they start with him?"

Asher nodded without looking, fidgeting with the zipper at the bottom of his jacket.

"Have you seen a doctor for them? Or perhaps, a therapist? Despite my inability to overcome agoraphobia, I've found my therapist and psychiatrist immensely helpful."

"Yeah. I did all that. A men's support group too." Asher hopped off the bench. "Let's go. I'm ready to ride."

"Blakely, wait."

Asher had already left, but he'd forgotten the saddle and blanket.

With a sigh, Lev climbed to his feet and gathered Rebecca's things. He found Asher brushing Rebecca's mane, a task he'd already completed.

"Thanks," Asher said and looked away, walls back up.

Lev hoisted the pad and saddle onto Rebecca's back and moved to help him with the girth belt.

"I've got this."

"Are you sure you're alright?"

"Yep. I've been doing this since I was a kid."

Lev wasn't asking about the horse. They both knew that. Suppressing a growl of frustration, he headed back to the tack room.

Nothing made him feel more powerless than waiting for a broken man to tell him what had happened.

37

PREMONITIONS IN REVERSE

ASHER

Asher wanted to ride off into the sunset, or at least far enough away from Lev's pitying sideways glances. He didn't regret confiding in Lev. Not exactly.

Talking to Lev had reopened old wounds, but it had healed some of them too. He'd forgotten how hard he was on himself until Lev had challenged him the way the men in his support group used to.

Asher couldn't trust his own interpretation of events. Ben had taught him that his instincts and emotions weren't to be trusted. The impulse to gaslight himself was still so ingrained.

What if Asher was wrong? What if Lev spoke to Ben and sided with him? What if Lev had lost all respect for him?

Rebecca nudged him with her nose. She'd been a breeze to bridle and demurely accepted the bit, gentle with her teeth.

Asher scratched between her ears. "You're a very good girl, Rebecca."

Lev pushed the sleeves of his shirt back to his elbows, baring freckled forearms, dashed with shimmering scars, including Silas's fingernail marks.

"Are you sure you'll be able to ride without the phallic

handle you cowboys love to hang on to? What's it called again?"

"A horn."

"Really? What a missed opportunity." Worry weathered Lev's face. "I can't help but fret. What if you fall?"

"Fret all you want, but it's a waste of gray hairs. I can ride, with or without a phallic handle."

"You could always ride with me. Dorian would love the challenge."

"Climbing onto Dorian with you sounds much more dangerous than riding bareback. How often do you even ride him?"

"Ordinarily, I ride him every day. A local lad mucks the stables and rides him on the days I can't." Lev lowered the saddle onto Dorian's back. "You're only delaying this further," Lev chided in a sing-song voice. "He's quite agreeable after he's stretched his legs."

"*Sure.*"

Lev laughed. The muscles in his forearms flexed as he adjusted the stirrups.

"Do you want help?" Asher asked.

"Thank you, but it's best if you stay out of nipping range. Take Rebecca. I'll be right out."

Dorian whinnied and tossed his head, dragging his front hoof against the brick. "Dorian, please be quiet."

Outside, melting frost steamed from the grass where sunbeams touched. The sheep dog barked a low, gruff. A sheep bleated. Asher hoisted himself onto Rebecca and waited... for approximately three seconds.

Something clattered behind them—maybe a rake or broom—and Rebecca bolted across the field, leaving Asher's stomach back at the stables.

Rebecca wasn't the first runaway horse he'd ridden. She'd startled him, more than scared him, and keeping a calm head was the best way to calm a spooked horse.

"Whoa." He pulled back on the reins.

She didn't stop or slow, or seem to notice him at all.

His second attempt to correct her was equally unsuccessful. He cycled through every trick he knew, but Rebecca was insistent, almost as if she were under a spell, or possessed.

Rebecca leapt over the clear water of a brook frolicking downhill and headed to the forest.

Asher looked over his shoulder. Lev was still inside the stables. Fuck. Dorian's whinnies carried across the field. Yelling for Lev wasn't worth the risk of upsetting Rebecca further.

She'd tire out eventually, and hopefully she'd take the blame in some nonverbal way when they returned. After Lev's fear wore off, he'd be furious.

The forest was too dense for her to venture into, but Rebecca hadn't slowed. As soon as Asher feared she'd slam into a tree trunk, she squeezed through a gap in the forest onto a leaf-lined path.

Rebecca slowed from a gallop to a canter. Otherwise, she continued to ignore Asher's attempts to control her speed or direction.

Old-growth trees towered overhead, some already bare, others evergreen. Autumn leaves clung to the understory, setting the forest ablaze. Dewdrops dripped on leaves like the phantom tapping of an impatient finger.

The back of Asher's neck tingled. Was someone there? He whipped his head toward a figure in his peripheral vision, but it was just another statue pointing toward a wide stream and a stone bridge.

Rebecca's hooves thundered over a bridge that looked like it hadn't been assessed for safety in at least two-hundred years. They made it to the other side without it collapsing, and Rebecca picked up speed.

The trees grew closer together, darkening the daylight. Branches snatched at his shoulders and narrowly missed his head. Folding forward over her, Asher hid his face against her neck, and hoped for the best.

The forest abruptly ended at a small clearing basking in sunlight, and Rebecca slowed to a graceful stop.

"What was that all about?" Asher asked, breathing fast.

He hopped down and secured her to an iron gatepost before she took off again, then checked her over. Her ears canted toward him, eyes serene, completely at ease.

"What happened?"

He stroked between her ears and hugged her neck.

"I'll be right back. Stay here."

He should have led her straight back to the stable. Lev was probably searching for him by now, but what if… It was stupid. He knew it was stupid.

But what if Rebecca had led him here? What was the harm in taking a quick look?

Statues assembled in an overgrown field—a gargoyle crouched on a pillar, a woman cloaked with leafless vines, an angel with most of his feathers broken off.

The grass was so tall he hadn't noticed the gravestones at first. Moss covered many of the tombstones, and time had smoothed down the etchings. The tombstones he could read dated back to the eighteen hundreds with names like Mary and John and Margaret.

An angelic statue guarded what had to be a mausoleum, wings folded against her back, the train of her long dress cascading down the steps. Ferns grew in the corners where dirt had gathered, tendrils clutching at the angel like fingers.

A small brass dragon, flaked with turquoise corrosion, served as the bolt of a lock. Asher pulled it to the right, freeing the dragon's head and neck from the latch. The door opened inward, pushed by a gust of wind.

His footsteps echoed on the polished marble floors, emanating cold. The crypt was much smaller on the inside. White limestone lined the walls, a sharp contrast from the dreary gray exterior. Rainbow light poured through stained glass windows, and walnut beams carved with rose vines arched over the cathedral ceiling.

There were less than twenty burial chambers, death dates ascending up the wall, as if the Marks family had added a new row when the row below ran out of room.

He found Lev's mother first.

HELENA MARKS
BELOVED BY ALL

The next hallowed space belonged to Wendell.

WENDELL MORRIGAN
WHEN YOU DIED
THE SKY WEPT
AND IT HASNT
STOPPED SINCE

Silas came last.

SILAS MORRIGAN
TRUE DEATH ONLY
COMES FOR THOSE
FORGOTTEN

The epitaph read like a spell, like magic existed, at least at Lichenmoor. Was that why Silas felt too alive to be dead? Would he die a second time when Lev was no longer there to remember him?

Maybe that's what magic was. What were memories if not premonitions in reverse? Shimmering visions, phantom emotions, ghosts of words already spoken.

He traced his fingers along the path of Silas's engraved name, the sharp letters and edges in the block script. "Who are you?"

A desiccated wildflower bouquet rested on top of Silas's resting place, petals disintegrating beneath his touch. Had Lev left them for Silas?

The idea of Lev tending Silas's grave filled Asher with a strange sort of romantic loneliness, a mix of sympathy for Lev's solitary grieving, and longing to be loved with such intensity.

"What happened to you?" Asher whispered to Silas's crypt.

"Blakely!"

Asher gasped and whirled around, so stunned he swept Silas's flowers to the ground. Leaves blustered around Lev's boots and slipped between his ankles as he stood in the doorway. His freckled cheeks were ruddy—with cold, or anger?

"I'm sorry." Asher bent to scoop up the scattered wild-flower stems.

"Sod the flowers." Lev grabbed Asher's arm and helped him back to standing, then released him.

"What on earth are you doing here? You said you would wait for me."

"I know. I'm sorry. Rebecca bolted, and I couldn't stop her. She took me here, and then I saw this building."

"Forgive me if I'm being obtuse, but what grown adult blames his horse for the direction he's led?"

Asher deposited the mess of a bouquet back on Silas's burial chamber. "I'm serious."

Lev lifted his hand. "The question was rhetorical."

"*Great.* Let me guess. You came up with a whole lecture while you were looking for me, and now I have to listen to it."

"You can't go off on your own. You have no internal compass. Don't you understand? It's not safe."

Lev scrubbed a hand over the sharp scruff of his beard. Asher's neck and ass tingled with the memory of Lev roughing up his skin with those bristles.

"What if you got lost and I never found you?"

"Is that what happened to Silas?"

Lev shoved his hair back from his brow and shook his head. "This isn't about him. You can't go mucking about wherever you fancy, trouncing through my family graveyard, crawling over Lichenmoor like a rodent."

"A rodent?"

"It's a simile."

"Don't talk like a discontinued dictionary."

"It's the correct term. Metaphors are entirely different."

Asher rolled his eyes. "Look, I know I shouldn't have helped myself inside here, and I'm sorry I scared you. It's just..."

How could Asher explain the way he'd felt steered toward the forbidden hallway before, the mausoleum now? It was almost like Lichenmoor's mysteries kept reaching out toward him, curling a finger, drawing him nearer.

"Do you ever feel like there's something else here?" Asher asked.

Lev stilled. "What do you mean?"

"I don't know. It's stupid." He shouldn't have brought it up.

"I doubt you've ever had a stupid thought in that gorgeous head of yours."

Asher exhaled. If Lev was flirting, he wasn't too upset with him.

"The night you found me in front of the locked door, I felt like the house had herded me toward it. Then, when I tried to leave Lichenmoor, the tide chased me back to the castle. Then today, Rebecca just took off, and wouldn't stop, not until she reached this clearing."

The wind gusted. A branch scratched against a window over the row of crypts.

Lev said nothing. He'd gone still, like he was listening to something far away.

"The first night we met, you said all the blood that fed the gorse and thistle took root and grew magic..."

"I never said it as poetically as that. I was trying to be mysterious, just passing along folklore and superstitions."

"I told you the truth about Ben..."

Lev sighed. "Oh, alright. I admit that I've felt something similar. Have you seen anything though, or heard someone speak?"

"No. Nothing like that. Have you?"

Lev regarded him with blue eyes, dark and troubled. "I don't believe in ghosts."

"You said you were forty-eight percent sure they were real."

"Which means I mostly don't believe in ghosts. Now that we've settled the matter, let's—"

The wind shook the trees and shoved open the door with so much force it slammed against the wall. Silas's flowers took flight, fluttering like feathers drifting on an air current.

Asher bent to pick them up.

"Leave them," Lev said.

But it felt disrespectful to leave the flowers on the floor like litter.

"Leave them!" Lev shouted over the wind. "His body isn't there."

38

GUILT MANIFESTED

LEV

"What do you mean his body isn't there? What happened to him?"

Silas bolted upright from his burial vault as if he'd woken from a nightmare. "Yes, Levvy. Whatever happened to me?"

"Lev?" Asher asked.

"Sorry. Where were we?"

Silas stretched an arm overhead and yawned, pale hand masking his mouth. "Me, obviously." He leapt down, landing between them.

"Right. Yes. Well, his body was never found, I'm afraid."

"Never found?"

"It's a difficult subject for me. I'd rather not elaborate."

Asher crossed his arms over his chest, a motion Silas mimicked with eerie accuracy. "I told you the truth about Ben."

"What did he tell you about Ben?" Silas asked. "Who is Ben again?"

Lev ignored him. "Let's talk outside."

Lev latched the lock and sat down on the steps beside Asher. Silas hadn't followed. He watched from the darkness of the tree line.

"My father and Wendell were best friends for decades. The

three of them—Wendell, Father, and Mum—all got on well. I'd met his son, Silas, once at a charity auction, and I hadn't liked him."

Lev toyed with Asher's hair as he talked, fingers alternating between tousling it and spiraling waves into ringlets around his finger.

"There was something... I don't know. It's difficult to pinpoint. I simply didn't care for him. He followed me around the venue, watching me while I ate, sitting too close, acting too familiar. It was strange for a child to behave that way. I don't know. It doesn't matter."

"It does matter."

"I didn't think of him again. Not until Wendell moved in to help while Mum was dying. He didn't bring Silas, and I spared him no thought, too preoccupied by losing my mother."

Lev's hand stilled on Asher's head, a pregnant pause.

"I loved Wendell. I called him uncle. He uh..." Lev cleared his throat. "Wendell fathered me in a way I'd never experienced before. He never saw me as raw material meant to be carved in his image. I was just a lad to him, a lad who was losing his mum.

"He taught me football—your soccer, that is—and rugby. Took me fishing, taught me how to tend the garden." Warmth crept into Lev's words. "He used to write me stories and have them printed into little chapter books featuring me as the character. I've saved all of his writing in the library. Sometimes I think I hear that tap, tap, tap of him at the typewriter, but it's just my memory of it."

"Why didn't Wendell bring Silas with him?"

"Silas's mum had full custody. She was a horrid woman from a wealthy and militantly Catholic family. She never forgave Wendell for divorcing her and forced Silas to attend a top Catholic boarding school against Wendell's wishes.

"None of this was ever very fair to Silas. I had far more time with Wendell, and back then, I didn't care. I'd lost my mum to cancer and father to grief. Silas was this hazy silhouette in my mind, an annoying specter of a memory."

Silas looked murderous, but didn't draw closer.

"When Wendell came to stay with us, my mum explained to me that Father loved Wendell the way Father loved her. She told me she was grateful Wendell could love me when she no longer could." Lev blinked back tears.

"Mum had always supported my father and Wendell's relationship—she wasn't in love with Wendell, to be clear. I used to think that maybe some people had a greater capacity for love, and that's why she was able to share my father. Or maybe she was willing to sacrifice her happiness for Father's. I sacrificed my own for Silas. Perhaps he sacrificed for me as well."

"I don't think love should be a sacrifice."

"No?"

Asher shook his head.

"Perhaps it wouldn't be a sacrifice then. Sharing you makes me want to throw up as much as it makes me want to break something, but to keep you, I would make room for whatever you need. Whoever. Your unhappiness would wound me far more severely.

"My mum died mid-spring. Luna and I picked flowers for her viewing. Wendell was with my father. Father was..." He trailed off. Even thinking about how broken Father had been then made his stomach hurt, let alone talking about it.

"Luna tried to steer me toward the wildflowers, but I preferred the bluebells and alliums and hyacinths. They were bigger and stood above the rest, technicolor pigment behind a veil of mist.

"Every spring, those same flowers crawl up from the earth and stick out like tombstones. I tried to dig them up, but there are too many. I don't want to see my mum's death reincarnated every spring. I don't want to remember.

"Memories are fickle. Pain is easy to remember and death forgets so many things." Lev's spine sagged, shrinking his height as he sighed. "Blakely, I know I come off as... I don't know..."

"Twattish?" Silas suggested, appearing on the step on Asher's right. "Suffocating, controlling, paternal, a bit of an overbearing arsehole?"

"Stifling," Lev said just to stop Silas's infernal suggestions. "I'm afraid of losing you. I've lost so many people that I love. I almost lost you already. That's why I don't want you going off alone."

"I wasn't alone."

Lev shot Silas a look. Silas whistled with far too much nonchalance, taking a peculiar interest in the moss growing on the angel's knee. Silas was just fucking with him. Everything he did was subtle, if not invisible.

"I had Rebecca," Asher added.

"You could have fallen, fainted, cracked your head on a rock, tumbled down a well. Rebecca wouldn't do you much good then, would she?"

"Don't underestimate her. I think she could rescue me from a well."

"He has a point, Levvy."

"For fuck's sake, I'm not arguing about wells," Lev snapped.

Asher's brows lifted. His gaze darted to the gate where Rebecca still waited.

"Now you've gone and scared the poor lad." Silas appeared behind Asher, and said into his ear, "You suspect there's something's wrong with Lev, don't you?"

Lev massaged his temples. "I apologize. I'm not angry with you, darling."

"*Darling?*" Silas feigned a gag.

"Thank you for sharing this with me," Asher leaned his head against Lev's shoulder.

Lev kissed his head. "Do you mind giving me a few minutes in there?"

Asher squeezed Lev's shoulder. "Of course."

Lev thanked him and stood.

Silas was already there waiting for him, sitting on top of his empty crypt with one leg crossed over the other. Lev closed the door and leaned against it.

"Did you do this?" Lev asked.

Silas huffed a sigh that floated stray strands of black hair that would never gray in his temples the way Wendell's had. "Please. If I had the power to lure anyone anywhere, it wouldn't be here. Perhaps your *darling* lad was keen to leave, saw a chance, and took it."

"Fuck you," Lev grumbled under his breath.

"Would if I could, babe. I'd hate-fuck you into the dirt, especially after you said such awful things about me."

"I'm sorry you heard that, but you're not real. You're misfiring neurons, my guilt manifested."

"You know that's not true."

"It has to be though, Si."

"You promised you'd never forget me."

"I could never forget you."

Tears welled in pale blue eyes too big for Silas's face. He'd never grow into them. "Don't you miss me?"

"I feel as if I've missed you all my life."

Silas cupped Lev's cheek weightlessly. "Then stop missing me. I'm right here..."

If the Silas before him wasn't real, why did disappointing him hurt so much? The decades-old impulse to wrap Silas's fragile frame into a gentle hug still lingered like phantom limb pain, but Lev couldn't do that.

Silas kicked a pile of stowaway leaves ineffectually. "You only want Asher because he's pliable and soft and responsive to your touch."

"You're jealous. I hadn't realized..." After all, Silas *had* encouraged Lev to invite him repeatedly.

"You've never hosted men at Lichenmoor. It's one thing to

know you've slept with other people, and quite another to watch you fall in love."

Silas gathered his height with a tilt of his chin and subtle shake of his shoulders. "It doesn't matter. Life goes on and the dead stay dead. If I was alive, you'd pick me though, wouldn't you?"

"I would pick him, Si. I'm sorry."

The paper skin on Silas's forehead wrinkled. "No."

"You chose me, and I chose to love you, but now that I have a choice, I choose Asher. I will always love you, but I can't love you the way you want me to."

"Don't you dare repeat the same line you used before you killed me." Silas stroked his chin. "If you won't choose me, perhaps I should choose me for you."

"You don't get to choose!"

Asher knocked on the door at his back. "Lev?"

Fuck. Lev covered his mouth with his hand. How loudly had he shouted and how much had the wind masked for him?

Silas winced and sucked air through his teeth. "Good luck trying to explain why you were yelling in an empty room." Then he laughed and disappeared.

Fucking Silas.

Asher knocked again, sharper this time, then pushed against the door. "Let me in."

Lev stepped away from the door, and Asher burst into the room.

"*Argh*. You could have warned me. Why does this door even open inward?"

"Superstition probably. Come on." Lev took Asher's hand and dragged him out of there before Silas returned.

"It doesn't even make sense. The latch is on the outside of the door," Asher continued while Lev slid the dragon back into the slot. "If someone forgets to lock the door on a windy day, the ghosts can walk right out."

Lev smiled despite the morbid topic, and Silas. "That's what the dragon's for."

Asher rolled his eyes.

"I don't think they put much thought into it, darling." Lev gripped Asher's hips and brought him close enough to kiss. "Thank you for rescuing me from my memories."

"Are you okay? I heard you talking."

Lev scrolled backward through his conversation with Silas. How much of what he said could be understood? Silas had outsmarted him again.

"I don't know what to say," Lev said, which wasn't true. Lev had a hell of a lot to say that he couldn't, most of it begging.

Please don't be scared. Please don't say you're calling a doctor to examine my head. Please don't look at me like I'm your fallen hero again.

"I shouldn't have pressured you into telling me about your family. I want to understand you, but not if it makes you wade through painful memories."

"You did nothing wrong. I'd feel better if you told me what you heard. The last thing I want is for you to misunderstand the mad musings of an old man."

"You're not *that* old. Or mad."

The next beat of silence tugged like a loose thread, punching holes in Lev's decorum.

Finally, Asher said, "All I heard was you telling your thoughts to be quiet. I have anxiety. I tell myself that all the time. Just not out loud."

How frustratingly vague. "Did you hear the thoughts I wanted to silence?"

"No, but if I had, I would have understood they weren't for me to hear."

"You're a very good lad. I'll reward you when we get back." Lev walked him back to their horses. "Tell me again why you believe Rebecca led you here."

"She spooked and bolted."

"She doesn't spook." Any horse could conceivably spook, but she didn't.

Asher kissed Rebecca's cheek. "She would never." Asher hopped up onto the saddle.

"And she led you all the way here full speed, then stopped?" Lev passed him the reins, but held onto her bridle, lest she take off before he could follow

"Pretty much. She didn't seem scared. She just bolted."

"I don't like that."

It sounded like Silas.

39

CURSED HEIRLOOM

ASHER

After fucking the pain of the day away, Asher and Lev took turns holding each other in bed while they shared more about their pasts.

Asher curled onto his side and rested his cheek on his hands, watching Lev's emotions flit across his face as he whispered secrets about Silas—flickers of pride and sorrow, of wistfulness and regret.

"I know it sounds romantic in a way, this brooding young man full of mysteries, but there was nothing romantic about his anguish. Watching him suffer destroyed me."

When Asher asked how Silas had suffered, Lev answered with a single word—anorexia. Well, that explained Lev's hypervigilance about Asher's eating habits.

"Poor Silas," Asher said.

"Poor Silas, indeed."

"Was that how he died?"

"No." Lev grimaced, but didn't elaborate.

"Do you think I have anorexia?"

Lev sighed. "I must admit, I worried at first, but I'm beginning to realize I overcompensate for my failures with Silas, and that's not fair to you. Or very healthy for either of us. I'm addressing it in therapy."

"You talk to your therapist about me?"

Lev laughed. "Of course, I do. I spend most of my waking hours with you, and think of you whenever we're parted."

Asher smiled. "Always so flirtatious."

"It's not flirting if it's true."

The wind wavered. A wave crashed closer than the last. High tide was calling again.

"Darkness and death fascinated Silas," Lev continued. "He was a very talented writer, but while Wendell's prose possessed a weightless poignancy, Silas's stories were macabre and melancholy. Sinister dread built as he dragged his characters forward, scratching their fingernails into the floorboards.

"He'd found some success publishing a few short stories under a pseudonym, but after a particularly cruel review, he absconded from Oxford and never returned, only sharing his stories with me after that. Of course, I understood."

Asher did, too. "Where did he go?"

"Lichenmoor. It was dreadfully lonely for him. Father often traveled." Lev fidgeted with the edge of his bedsheet. "I couldn't quit my studies at Oxford."

"Good, because that would have been a terrible decision."

Lev laughed. "Thank you for saying that."

"You're too hard on yourself."

"Sometimes I fear I'm not hard enough."

"Trust me, that's the last thing you need to worry about."

After a few minutes of silent contemplation, Lev said, "You were joking about my erection, weren't you?"

Asher rolled his eyes. "*Psh.* You have such a dirty mind."

Lev smiled knowingly. "It's your turn now."

Asher told Lev more about Ben, including the shameful night he'd tried to approach him at home only to discover his wife was there.

"She wasn't trying to repair things, though. The next man

who'd subbed for him—Joel—ended up in the hospital less than a month after we broke up."

"Christ."

"Yeah. Ben left him in bondage unsupervised."

"He did what?" Lev snapped. His nostrils flared as he inhaled slowly. "I apologize." He cupped Asher's cheek, such a soft antithesis to the furious glint in his gaze. "How is Joel fairing now?"

"He had some nerve damage, but it healed."

"What about his head and his heart? Has he struggled terribly?"

"I don't know him well enough, but if he's anything like me, he has some PTSD."

"Ben left you unsupervised too?'

Asher shook his head. "Not in bondage. Probably because I just took it. His methods were more psychological. He locked me in his basement a few times. It turned me on at first." His face burned with the ache in his chest. "There's something wrong with me."

"You didn't *just take* anything, and there's nothing wrong with you, even if you enjoyed it. Ben Twattington is a predatory cunt who took advantage of you."

Asher laughed, clinging to the only levity he could find. "None of your nicknames for me are that creative."

Lev pressed his lips together. "I wasn't trying to be funny."

"Yeah, because you have a terrible sense of humor."

"Sod off, Blakely," Lev teased, sharing the life raft of levity with him. "I reserve creative nicknames for the people I despise."

Asher rolled his eyes. "You didn't like me very much in the beginning."

"*Please*. I adored you from the moment you first scowled— a minute or two after we met, if I remember correctly—even when you acted infernally contrary." Lev kissed his forehead. "Are you alright?"

"Yeah. Thanks. Talking about it helps a lot more than I realized."

Lev's eyes turned to crescents. "I'm honored you trusted me with this and that I could help." He brushed Asher's hair back from his brow. "You were telling me about Ben's wife..."

"Sadie, yeah. Joel had called her out of concern for *her* safety. I should have worried about her safety too."

"You're very sweet beneath your sulkiness. I'm sure you would have warned her if it had happened to you."

Asher skipped over the part where Ben had punched him because Lev's blue eyes had turned to glaciers and the tightness in his jaw promised murder.

"I was close to her son's age, and she helped me pack before putting me on a plane back home for my own safety."

"Where were your parents?"

"Ben didn't like me talking to my dad, probably because he was afraid of what might happen if I told him more than the fictional story about me dating a man off campus. It didn't even occur to me to call them."

"Christ. Thank God for Sadie then. I hope she divorced him?"

Asher laughed. "Yeah. Their differences became pretty irreconcilable after she convinced the man Ben had hurt to file a complaint, then supported him through trial. That was the one I testified in."

"I see."

"Watson finally fired him, at least. But it was infuriatingly easy for an expensive defense lawyer to explain everything away under the guise of rough sex taken a little too far."

Instead of the anger Asher had braced for, Lev blanched. Tears glazed his eyes, but he blinked them back, then asked calmly, "Where is Ben now?"

Asher shivered. Lev's tightly controlled, frigid fury was far more intimidating than if he'd erupted.

"He can't hurt anyone anymore. Sadie keeps me updated."

"He's dead?"

Asher winced. Even if he hated Ben now, he'd still loved him once.

"No. After losing his job, and his family—his kids went no contact—he tried to kill himself by overdosing on acetaminophen." Asher frowned. Did they have that medication in the UK? "It's an over-the-counter pain medicine."

"I'm familiar."

"Okay. Anyway, I don't think he actually *tried* to kill himself. He's a malignant narcissist. If only I'd known that when I met him…"

"Narcissists are good at hiding, and emotional manipulation can be quite disarming."

Was Lev speaking from personal experience or with the hindsight of being fifteen years older?

"Sadie thinks he did it to get his family back. Not because he loved them, but so he could save face. I don't know."

Asher sighed. "The overdose destroyed his liver and kidneys, and he didn't qualify for a transplant, so he's in and out of the hospital all the time."

Lev stroked Asher's hip. "When was this? I imagine it must have been upsetting."

Asher nodded. "January. It's stupid. He ruined my chances at Watson and fucked with my head, but I still care about what happens to him, even if I don't love him, even after he hurt me—"

"It's not stupid. Empathy isn't a weakness because someone took advantage of it."

NOVEMBER 11

The next morning, Asher woke alone in an ice-cold bed.

"Lev?" Asher called, breath fogging.

No answer.

A small wisp of smoke waned in the grate. Salty air drafted down the chimney, stirring ash into whirlwinds.

Lev never left in the morning without lighting a fire for him. He checked the nautical wristwatch with a compass that Lev had made him promise to wear.

Three-twenty-nine AM. That was early, even for Lev.

Asher's stomach twisted. Anxiety tightened his chest. What they'd shared with each other last night was far more vulnerable than sex. Asher felt raw and abandoned—which was irrational.

Lev had probably woken in the middle of the night and couldn't fall back to sleep. Ben had often complained about Asher's tossing and turning. Sometimes, he'd forced him to sleep on the floor.

But what if Lev regretted telling Asher about Silas? What if Asher's sniveling attempts to win Ben back had disgusted him?

Asher groaned and scrubbed his face with shaking hands. PTSD was like walking through fog with sharp cliffs and land-mines lurking nearby. Every step was treacherous, every trigger potentially explosive, and he couldn't predict when or where or why.

If only he could take a pill to forget Ben. Anything was better than the uninvited memories that flooded him with panic at the slightest trigger. Anything was better than the greasy sheen of shame he couldn't wash from his hands.

Anything was better than hating himself, because Asher wasn't a survivor. He wasn't a victim. He was something so much worse—a willing participant.

His fingers tingled. Was it because it was freezing as fuck or because at some point he'd started hyperventilating without noticing? Maybe both.

He took a deep breath stolen by the next, and reached for what he could sense. He refused to have a panic attack just because he woke up without Lev.

Raindrops pelted the windows in bursts like buckshot. Lev's sketchbook rested with the pages down on his desk. He felt slippery luxury sheets with a higher thread count than his rent.

Lev's pillow smelled like woodsy shampoo and the subtle undercurrent of the jasmine and pepper in his cologne. The ghost of Lev's scent was nearly as soothing as the man himself.

When his breathing returned to normal, he felt the faintest flicker of pride at defeating the attack, but self-loathing lashed at him not long after.

A real man was never scared. A real man didn't panic. A real man didn't let himself get hurt. A real man never needed help.

Asher knew that wasn't true, but the toxic masculinity inherent in the cattle ranching industry, and Nonna's kitchen, had left an indelible mark on his self worth.

Lev had left his skeleton key on the table beside his bed. Asher pinched his bottom lip between his fingers. When Asher had made a casual investigatory comment about what would happen if Lev lost the key, Lev had reassured him that he had "droves of skeleton keys ferreted away".

Taking the key was risky, but what if this was kismet?

The locked door on the third floor still haunted him. He felt the pull like an undercurrent, plucking the petals of his thoughts from a daisy, except instead of *he loves me, he loves me not,* each petal alternated between breaking into that room and knowing he shouldn't.

Asher just wasn't sure which petal he'd land on. Or when.

He scooped the key into his hand and left through the secret door. His room was even colder than Lev's, and he growled under his breath, releasing another torrent of fog from his lips.

In the bathroom, Asher popped the top off the applicator of his deodorant, added a thick blob of toothpaste to the bottom, and dropped the key inside, then carefully replaced the applicator.

Ben had forbidden Asher from taking his anti-anxiety meds because they turned his art into boring, commercial drivel— allegedly—and he'd learned the hard way that the sound of the pills sloshing around was a dead giveaway. Hopefully the toothpaste spackle would work.

After brushing his teeth, he spat into the sink with all the cathartic venom of spitting in Ben's face, something he'd never, ever dared to do.

Asher dressed quickly, side-eyeing the ridiculous heat-insulated leggings Lev had bought for him, as he pulled on gray sweatpants and the new black hoodie Lev had said was a spare for when his lucky one was in the laundry or "sponta-neously disintegrated into paint flecks and cotton dust".

The hall was deserted. Asher called Lev's name again, and when he didn't answer, crept toward the secret door to the east wing. Had Lev gone there? He tried the door, but it was locked.

Asher dropped the tapestry and stared at it until his eyes blurred on the scene of a ship in distress amidst a violent storm. Should he go back for the skeleton key? No. He should probably wait until he was sure Lev wouldn't catch him, no matter how tempting the idea was.

Wind slipped through gaps in the window frames and lifted the hair on the back of his neck. Asher swirled around, expecting to find Lev at the other end of the hall.

No one was there.

"Lev?" Asher's voice shook.

No answer.

The lingering adrenaline from his earlier anxiety attack had set his nerves on edge. That's all it was. But foreboding followed him long after his heart rate slowed, a constant presence escorting him through the dark.

Lev wasn't in Lucian's studio, or the dining room. He wasn't in the kitchen either.

The first hint of a headache gathered between Asher's brows. Sometimes Lev brewed drip coffee with a French press, but Asher couldn't make sense of all the stainless steel components drying on the counter.

After five minutes, a handful of escalating curse words, and narrowly avoiding a steam-related burn from Desiderio, Asher conceded defeat and resorted to the tea kettle, plunking it down on the metal stove with a clang.

The lamp above the sink turned the world outside to an unfathomably vast darkness, filling him with the dread of an elevator cable slowly breaking.

For all he knew, someone was watching him with their face pressed against the glass, and he wasn't sure if plunging the kitchen into darkness to check was worse. So, feeling very much like a child, he avoided the window at all costs while he waited. The kettle whistled, startling Asher out of his skin, and the first sip of bitter tea scalded his tongue.

The wind picked up, whistling as it slipped through the gaps, and plucked at the servant bell strings, filling the kitchen with haunting jingling. A metal hinge screeched and banged.

Was it Lev?

Asher flipped off the light switch and peered through the window over the sink. Trees bent and swayed. A light bobbed in the direction of the cliffs, growing smaller as he watched, farther away, like a lantern held in someone's hand.

The wind shifted, hurling a fistful of raindrops at the glass like rocks. Asher flinched. His hands shot up to block a barrage of glass shards that never came.

God, he was jumpy. He backed away from the window and turned the light back on. Lev had said his father kept walking the moor at night, that his father had seen people who weren't there. Maybe Lev...

No. He didn't dare finish the sentence, even inside his head, as if admitting his suspicions would bring them to fruition.

Alzheimer's wasn't a guarantee passed down through families like a cursed heirloom. Maybe Lev was more predisposed than others, but he was fucking forty.

Asher should go out there. What if something *was* wrong and Lev got hurt? Asher dumped the sludgy tea in the sink and filled it with water.

Wood beams groaned overhead. Wind flung rain at the window again. Asher's gaze snapped up from the sink. A shadowy figure loomed behind his reflection, heading straight for him at a fast pace.

Asher gasped. The mug slipped from his hands. He spun to face his attacker and braced for impact.

40

GHOST STORY

ASHER

"For fuck's sake, Blakely. You scared me half to death."

Asher opened his eyes and lowered his hands. "Me?"

"Did you cut yourself?" Lev gripped Asher's wrists and inspected his hands.

Asher pulled his hands free and balled them into fists. "I'm fine."

"Good." Lev reached past him and turned the sink off. "What on earth are you doing down here?"

Asher narrowed his eyes. "Looking for you. I saw someone out there... Turn off the lights."

"There's no one out there." Lev sighed, as if Asher was the one who'd inconvenienced *him* by getting out of bed to look for him.

"Forget it." Asher crossed to the switch and turned it off himself.

"Ash..."

Asher scanned the darkness, but whatever light he'd seen wasn't there anymore. "I thought it was you. I..." He turned back to Lev. "Where were you?"

Lev stroked his jaw, and with each second that passed, Asher grew more convinced that Lev would lie.

"I checked all your usual haunts."

"Darling, you couldn't possibly know all my usual haunts."

Asher crossed his arms over his chest. "Thanks for the reminder that I don't know you very well. I'm going back to bed."

Lev could follow him right up the stairs if he wanted to, but Asher would slam the door shut in his face and shove that wardrobe back in place.

He'd given Lev so much of his heart and he couldn't even trust him to say where he'd been after Asher had shared his most degrading moments with Ben.

"Please let me explain. I couldn't sleep."

"I couldn't either, and now I'd like to." Asher jogged up the stairs off the back of the kitchen and through the steep and shallow-ceilinged servant stairwell.

At the landing to their floor, vertigo and hunger made him dizzy, and he nearly tumbled backward until Lev steadied him.

"Did you forget to eat again?" Lev asked, all sweet and doting and condescending.

Asher turned. Lev still stood on the step below.

"Oh, I'm sorry. I was a little busy searching the castle for you and being scared half to death in the kitchen."

"Scared?" Lev's brows lifted. "Why?"

"I'm going to bed so go paint, or have your morning constitutional, or meet up with whoever is waiting out there for you."

Lev laughed. "That's what you're upset about? You can't seriously believe I'm interested in anyone else, let alone meeting them for a clandestine rendezvous during such dreadful weather."

"I wouldn't laugh at the top of a stairwell if I were you."

"Come now, Blakely. Let's not resort to murderous threats."

"Let's not resort to abusing the word *come* for your own manipulative devices."

"My manipulative what?" Lev climbed onto the landing

and stroked Asher's arm. "I promise, there's no one out there. Boat lights look like lanterns or will-o-the-wisps. The ocean was playing tricks on you."

"Why won't you tell me where you were, then? Were you with Silas?"

Hurt dashed Lev's features. His mouth opened and shut.

Asher winced. Fuck. Hurting Lev was like kicking the Great Dane puppy his mom had compared him to.

"I'm sorry. I woke up on the wrong side of the bed. I was worried about you. I thought you were out there, and I tried to make coffee but I couldn't figure out your overcomplicated appliances, and tea is disgusting..."

Lev turned his head sharply and looked back down the stairwell.

Goosebumps and dread crawled over his skin. Did he see someone? Was it Silas?

"Lev?"

Lev didn't answer or indicate in any way that he'd even heard Asher.

"Lev?" Asher said, softly this time.

Still no answer.

Asher stepped between Lev and the deathtrap of a stairwell. Lev looked through him.

Was that what it felt like to be a ghost? Starved for connection, and completely ignored?

"Lev." Asher cupped his cheek and forced Lev's gaze to him. "What do you see? Look at me. Only me."

Glacier eyes blinked once, twice before Lev's unfocused stare trained on him.

"Are you okay? I've been trying to get your attention."

"Ah, that would be my ADHD."

"It wasn't ADHD, Lev."

Lev's lips twitched into a small smile. "Perhaps we both need sleep."

Asher's stomach sank. Why was he lying?

"If you woke up on the wrong side of an empty bed," Lev continued, "I think the best way to correct it is to go back to sleep and start the day anew."

"You can't just put me to bed like a child."

"Of course not. I was going to put myself to bed."

Asher rolled his eyes. Flirting aside, he wasn't going to let Lev out of his sight. Spacing out at the top of a staircase was nearly as dangerous as walking on the cliffs at night.

Lev paused in front of their door. "I'm sorry I worried you. I was in the library. There are some boring books in there." He squeezed Asher's shoulder and darted a glance down the hallway and back to him. "Let's talk inside. I have a secret stash of emergency almonds."

"How very squirrel-like of you."

Lev didn't laugh as he steered Asher inside and shut the door. "Make yourself comfortable. I'll be right back."

He raked his distracted gaze over Asher and crossed to the bathroom.

Asher sat on the bed. "Why are you talking to me like I'm a hotel guest seeing your room for the first time?"

"Sorry, I can't hear you," Lev called from his closet. Cabinets opened and drawers slammed. Plastic bags crinkled.

"For someone with bat-like hearing, you're a terrible liar," Asher teased, offering an olive branch of banter.

Lev was freaking the fuck out, probably because Asher had accused him of having a romp with his dead ex, but something else had spooked him on the stairs too.

"Ah, here it is." Lev emerged from the closet door with a comically large bag of almonds the size of a pillow. He tore the bag open and placed it on the bed beside Asher.

"Lev, are you okay?"

"Eat and I'll explain." Lev kneeled, ginger lashes kissing as he dropped his gaze, and slipped off Asher's shoe, wordlessly taking care of him even when Asher was being an irritable asshole.

Asher popped a few almonds in his mouth. "Well?"

Lev smiled, and slipped off Asher's remaining shoe, then started talking, exactly as promised.

"We only ever talk about places being haunted, but sometimes it's not the place, it's the person, and it's not ghosts that haunt them, but their memories."

Lev sat back on his heels and stared up at Asher with ocean eyes exactly as haunted as he implied.

"My memories walk the halls of Lichenmoor. They hide behind locked doors. They pirouette on cliff edges, and wash up on the shore. They haunt me with their stories, and all of them are true."

Lev stroked Asher's knee and stood. "Everywhere I go reminds me of what I've lost. That's what kept me up last night, and where my mind went in the stairwell. Now, please eat."

Asher looked down at the almonds he'd forgotten.

Was Lev telling the truth? Was he haunted by loss or by something else? Or was he lying to himself because he was scared of the truth too?

"Yesterday was a lot," Lev continued. "The mausoleum especially. It was a lot for you too, hm?"

"I shouldn't have gone there—"

Lev lifted his hand. "The mausoleum wasn't your fault. Rebecca took the blame while you were putting her saddle away."

"Don't mock me." Asher ate one almond and lobbed the second at Lev.

Lev released a scandalized, exaggerated gasp as it bounced off his chest and skipped across the floor.

"I wasn't mocking you. I took her confession quite seriously." Lev's attempt at a serious expression failed on a burst of laughter.

Asher tossed the rest of his almonds at him. He darted out

of the way, but reflexes didn't matter when he was such a big target and all of them pelted him.

"You're so prickly today." Lev pushed Asher back and climbed onto the bed after him, knocking the bag of almonds to the floor.

"Yikes. You're going to have a lot of almonds to clean up."

Lev peered over the edge of the bed and winced. "They're your almonds."

"Okay, then I better get started." He tried to sit up.

"Don't you dare." Lev pushed him back down and pinned Asher's hands by his head. "You can clean them up after I fuck you, or are you still sore from last night?"

"I am, actually."

Lev clucked his tongue. "See. You should have let me prep you longer."

"Please. All the prep in the world couldn't have prepared me for *Mr. I've Been Told I Feel Bigger Than I Look.*"

"Are you sure I said that? It doesn't sound like me." Lev nipped Asher's Adam's apple.

Asher scrambled to get away, laughing.

Lev tightened his grip on Asher's wrists. "Finally, a real laugh, but if you keep writhing around like that, Blakely, I might fuck you after all."

Asher froze. His chest tightened. He fought to free his wrists, this time seriously, with claustrophobia and panic intermingling.

His thoughts came in single words, fragmented memories. Ben hadn't been as big as Lev, but he'd fucked Asher dry as punishment, or used a bigger sex toy, or both, and being sore had never stopped him from topping.

Asher could have safe-worded, but safe-wording meant disappointing him, and he didn't want to disappoint Lev either, and—

The invisible bindings around his wrists disappeared as

Lev's hands released him. The weight started to lift from his chest as Lev climbed off of him.

Lev helped Asher sit at the edge of the bed again. "Breathe, Ash. You're safe. I promise. I'll always keep you safe. Always. Breathe in slowly."

Asher did his best to follow along.

"There's a good lad," Lev murmured.

The praise was totally undeserved. Asher had started his next breath before Lev had even finished exhaling.

A few more cycles later, Asher's head stopped spinning. He focused on his senses, on Lev's hand rubbing loving circles over his back, on the devastated look on his face, the scent of his aftershave.

Asher leaned forward and nuzzled his cheek against Lev's wiry beard, desperate for more sensation, something to root him, to remind him he was with Lev, not Ben, who'd always been clean-shaven.

Lev wrapped his arms around him. "I'm so sorry. I never meant to scare you, or hurt you. I hate that anyone has." He pulled back, eyes darkening until they looked like the ocean at night. "Are you alright?"

Asher still quivered, but nodded. "How are you so good at this?"

"Silas."

Fuck. "Do you mean he had panic attacks? Or..." Had Silas been hurt the way Asher had?

"Yes. On the nights before we'd be parted."

"Parted how?" Asher shivered.

Lev frowned. "Come, let's get you under the covers first."

Asher must not have been able to conceal his disappointment because Lev added, "I intend to answer. You're cold and I want to hold you if you wish. Unless..." Ginger brows darted together. "Would you rather sleep alone?"

"I'm not going to be able to sleep at all." Asher pulled off his hoodie, taking his shirt with it.

Lev turned his back. "Why ever not?"

Asher threw his sweatpants at Lev. "You don't need to look away. Just because I freaked out for a second doesn't mean I don't want you to see me naked again. Or fuck me again."

Lev's hair bobbed as he nodded. "Right. Well. It would be okay if that wasn't true." Lev still kept his back to Asher as he ditched his own sweater and tee.

Now it was Asher's turn to look away from Lev and his strong back, muscles flexing and shifting as he untied black lounge pants that made his ass look amazing—honestly, any item of clothing from riding pants to pajamas made his ass look amazing.

Lev lay down beside him, flat on his back a respectful distance away. Asher didn't wait to be invited. He settled himself against Lev's side. Lev's chest rose and fell on a sigh, his arm tightened around Asher, and his lips grazed Asher's forehead.

"Do you want to talk about it?" Lev asked.

"I'm still waiting for an answer to my question."

"Your question? Oh. Silas, right."

Asher wasn't convinced that Lev had forgotten.

"Silas and I were too close. Codependent, really. He only stayed at Lichenmoor over the summer and winter holidays, and was always so reluctant to leave. Not that I blamed him. Anorexia made him smaller than the others, and boys can be such little twats."

"Do you wish you'd gone to school with him?"

Asher had read all about Lev's upbringing sequestered away at Lichenmoor so he could focus on art. A teacher prepared him for university, but his primary education had been an erratic schedule of lessons given by the greatest creative thinkers of his father's time from artists to writers to scientists and mathematicians.

"I don't know." Lev huffed, shifting his gaze to the ceiling like a sullen teenager. "Father was adamant that my study in art was paramount. Not to mention, even if Father had approved, Silas's mum would have forbidden it. So Silas had to face the world alone, while I stayed at Lichenmoor."

"Was it lonely?"

"For me?" He shook his head. "But for Silas, very much so. He'd have attacks not unlike your own. I'd always felt so helpless and heartbroken to watch him suffer. The first time it happened I was terrified something was medically wrong and went to get Wendell."

Asher had been terrified too. He'd thought he was dying and called 9-1-1. The resulting commotion of an ambulance had humiliated him more, especially when he'd returned with the diagnosis that it was all in his head.

Maybe that's what panic attacks were. When someone was dealt a lethal blow—an emotional one—the brain became confused and thought it was dying.

Steady rainfall filled the space Lev left behind as he trailed off into silence.

"I wonder..." Lev said and drifted into an even longer beat of silence.

"You wonder what?" Asher prodded, wanting to hear all of Lev's thoughts before he filtered them for his consumption.

"Sorry. I don't want you to misunderstand or think I'm trying to force you into Silas's role. I want you for you. I don't want Silas. Understood?"

"Oh my God, yes!" Asher said with sardonic exasperation. "Stop holding me in suspense."

Lev chuckled. "It's not that scandalous. You'll be disappointed. Silas and I used to have this way of working through his attacks. I'd draw on his skin to help him focus only on the present, and only on me, carving out a place where the past and future couldn't haunt or hurt him."

"How did you know what to do? You were a kid, right?"

"Wendell had loads of books on psychology. He'd believed that one could never write well without understanding the human condition. *A character's wounds and how they're healed, neglected, or coped with guide all of their future thoughts and actions.* Wendell taught me many things, and I think that lesson was the most important, because it taught me empathy. Forgiveness. Even for those who've hurt me."

"It doesn't seem like you give yourself that same empathy in return."

"Some sins are too great to be forgiven, even if their origin can be understood. What Ben did to you, for example. Or what I did to Silas. I could forgive myself for failing Father, but never Silas."

"Lev…" How had Lev failed Silas? Wait. "Did you hurt Silas the way Ben hurt me?"

"No, Blakely. Never that." Lev turned onto his side and met Asher's eyes. "You believe me, don't you?"

His answer came to him quickly. No contemplation required. "I do."

"Would you like to try it?" He cleared his throat. "Erm, my version of grounding, that is. I think I could benefit from thinking of only now and only you, as well. The past is rather loud right now."

"Sure." How could he deny Lev what comfort he could give? And he would give anything to have Lev draw on him.

"Do you trust me?"

"I do." He shouldn't, but he did.

41

ONLY NOW, ONLY ME

LEV

After Silas's earlier torment, and witnessing Asher's panic, Lev needed the distraction too. Lev untangled himself from Asher and sat up.

Asher's eyes widened. "How are you going to distract me? Where are you going?"

"Nowhere, love. The farthest I'm going is the closet to find a cravat to cover your eyes with."

Asher's hypervigilance broke Lev's heart. The anxiety attack had transformed him into a bundle of nerves, so unlike his stoic nature. What had Lev done or said to cause it?

Asher sat up. "Closing my eyes doesn't work for me. That's when I see him."

"I see." Lev winced. "I apologize. Poor choice of words. Let me grab a pen, then." Lev pecked a kiss on Asher's forehead.

The floor was frigid, the fireplace unlit. That wouldn't do. He turned to Asher. "I'm such an utter twat. I left you in a cold, empty bed, didn't I? No wonder you're so much more irritable than usual."

He'd left in a hurry, summoned by Silas bellowing from the passageway at the end of the hall. Things between them were rather strained, considering Silas's attempt to murder him via Asher's sword and their spat in the mausoleum.

"I'm not irritable."

"Of course, darling." Lev bent before the fireplace and pulled out a starter log from the steamer trunk he kept stocked for particularly wintry mornings.

"So, a cravat, huh? Do you have a top hat and powdered wig to go with it?"

Lev grinned. "It was for a masquerade ball, and I've no need for a powdered wig. Who'd want to cover this hair?"

Asher rolled his eyes. "I wouldn't boast. You could lose it soon. At your age..."

"Sod off," Lev said, reassured Asher was teasing him again.

The log ignited, and warmth radiated against his face.

"But you have a top hat?" Asher asked.

"Only for polo events."

"Oh my God. Is it in the closet? Do you have a little jacket with a train or whatever they're called?"

"A tailcoat? I'm afraid not."

"*Right*," Asher said slowly.

Lev clapped his hands together, dusting the grit from his palms. He wouldn't give Asher the ammunition of learning about the chest filled with tailcoats in a spare room Father had used like a junk drawer.

"Here we are," Lev said, plucking a handful of markers from the cup on his desk. He sat on the bed beside Asher. "Lie down for me, lad."

Once Asher complied with a nervous nod, Lev pulled Asher's arm into his lap. But what to draw? Perhaps something from the library he'd left in vain after Silas had antagonized him anytime he drifted.

"Remember, only think of me, of this moment, the caress of my marker, the crackle of the fire, feel the warmth it emanates, feel the pillow beneath your head."

Asher's attention was rapt. Lev started to sketch, making

use of the gap between the snake encircling Asher's wrist and the eye on his forearm. He drew a dragon to protect him from the dead like the one on the door to the mausoleum. Minutes passed as they both drifted into peaceful silence.

"I'm sorry I freaked out before," Asher said as Lev added the last of the dragon's scales. "I know I can trust you. I know you were joking, but what you were joking about is something he's done before."

Lev's marker stuttered. He clenched his jaw, overcome with murderous intent. He needed to ruin Ben's life. He needed to make him pay. He needed to focus on the present and be there for Asher.

"But you released me, and it healed something. Every time you've protected me where he would have hurt me has helped to ease this ache inside." Asher rubbed the center of his chest. "It's like I've got all these broken pieces of my heart and they don't fit back together anymore." He bit his bottom lip. "I've read about sexual assault survivors painting over their trauma and reclaiming it. Ben ruined so many things for me. Do you think you'd ever want to help me with that?"

"You'd like me to be your dom?"

Silas had asked for the same, though Silas had still directed the show, and pushed Lev far over the boundaries they'd set, chasing the high of nearly dying so he could feel like he wasn't dead, even if it left Lev disgusted with himself for what he'd done at Silas's behest.

"I don't want scenes," Asher said. "I don't want impact play or punishment. I want what you already do. Commands, care, praise."

"Are you sure? You've seemed to enjoy bossing me around rather a lot." Perhaps that would help more.

"I love that you give me so much power. I still want that sometimes, but I want to serve you more. I want to be taken care of by you in the ways you already do."

Serve you. Asher's offer ricocheted through Lev's thoughts.

"What happens if you don't listen? I'm not sure if you're aware, Blakely, but you're rather bratty."

"I trust you to make me behave without punishing me."

"What if I hurt you?"

"You won't. You're too preoccupied with my general well-being to do that. *Oh, Asher, mind the seventeenth step on the south spiral staircase. I stubbed my toe there once when I was twelve.*"

"I don't sound like that."

"We're both broken in our own ways," Asher continued. "We can fill the broken pieces and be the strength for each other's weakness. Maybe taking control will heal you too."

Lev blew at the wet ink on Asher's forearm. "Alright. We can try. But only if you're honest. Can I trust you to tell me when to stop?"

"Yes, sir."

Lev's cock twitched. "Mm. I like you like this." He swallowed thickly. "Roll onto your stomach."

Asher did as he was told and turned his head to the side, cheek pressed against the pillow, eyes on Lev.

"There we go. Good lad."

Asher smiled shyly, and it was so adorable Lev couldn't resist petting his silken waves under the guise of pushing his hair out of his face.

"Now, I'm going to pull the blanket down to expose your back. I promise not to straddle you or restrain you. Is that alright?"

"Yes," Asher mumbled, mouth already slack, lids relaxed.

Lev stroked his hand down Asher's spine as he dragged the bed linen until just above his rump. Gooseflesh pebbled his skin. His hips shifted, lifting his arse only just.

"Blakely, do you know your colors?"

"Huh?" Asher asked, hooded lids lifting lazily.

"Like the traffic light. Green means go. Yellow means slow. Red means stop."

"Oh, that. Yes."

Lev debated asking if Ben had used the same system, but he was afraid of the answer, and right now it was only now, only them.

"What color are you?"

"So fucking green."

Lev laughed. "Let's proceed, then. I'll trust you to tell me if your color changes, and you'll answer honestly when I check in. If you need to safe-word, say *red* or *stop*, alright?"

Asher dropped his lashes, demurring his gaze. "Yes, sir. Thank you."

The lad was every bit the natural submissive Lev had guessed at. He'd just needed permission. Lev loved Asher sullen and bratty as much as he loved him vulnerable and supplicating, but what he loved most, was that he could be what Asher needed.

"I wonder what plans you have for your back tattoos?" Lev rested his hand on the curve of Asher's lower back and stroked his chin as he mapped the landmarks of his canvas.

"I want a single piece of art, but I haven't been able to commit."

"Perhaps you were waiting for me to draw something for you." Lev bowed over Asher and kissed his temple, then sat back and asked, "Your color?"

"Green."

"Good. Now, remember—only now, only me. Hm?"

"Only now. Only you."

Lev inhaled a shiver of a breath, trapped in a déjà vu wormhole between past and present. After what was probably an uncomfortable period, Lev praised him. "Top marks, Blakely."

It was cheap and corny and decidedly unsexy, and Asher had to have agreed because a smirk twitched the corner of his lips and a single brow lifted, a specter of his snark. But he didn't tease him, which surely required an impressive amount of restraint.

"Your submission pleases me." He tapped his lips. "Now then, what to draw? Any requests?"

Asher chewed on his lip.

"I asked you a question. Answer honestly."

"I have an idea."

Lev had assumed as much. "Tell me."

"What about a map of Lichenmoor on my back?"

"Oh?"

"I know I wouldn't be able to use it. It's not about using it as a map, but what it means."

"And what would that be?" Lev began at once, drawing the outline of Lichenmoor Hall.

"That when you made it, you didn't want me to get lost. You wanted me to stay. You trusted me enough to share Lichenmoor's secrets."

Asher was correct. Mostly. "I must confess, I didn't put all of Lichenmoor's secrets on your map." Lev moved on to the central staircase.

"I know."

"Perhaps, I'll add a few more secrets to your back, and take a photo of you. I can even add a new secret each time you let me draw on you."

"I'd like that."

"I would too."

Especially if he held onto Asher long enough to share every secret with him, and perhaps encourage him to have it tattooed so Lichenmoor would always be with him, because one day he *would* leave. Lev wouldn't live forever, and he'd never condemn Asher to the same lonely fate.

By the time Lev reached the third story of the central wing, Asher had fallen asleep. It took some time before the wrinkle on Asher's brow and the tension around his eyes relaxed. Lev shook his head. Poor lad.

Lev chewed on the cap of his pen. With the skeleton of the castle complete, which secret route to share first? The hidden back spiral staircase that provided a direct path to the second floor of the library was an obvious choice. Once he'd finished, the sun had ascended over the horizon.

Next, he added the modern saltwater pool retrofitted in a tucked-away atrium of the south wing. Lev liked to swim there during the winter when outside exercise was a miserable endeavor.

Asher twitched as if he were dreaming, and the last jolt of his body scribbled a jagged line on the cobblestone road leading out of Lichenmoor.

Lev wasn't finished. Not even close.

But he'd scarcely slept, and he'd done his job, so he capped his pen, snapped a picture of Asher's back, and joined him under the covers. His back and neck ached from bending over Asher for so long, but any pain was worth granting Asher the peace he so desperately needed.

Lev rolled onto his side, face close enough to feel Asher's breaths gust against his lips like the ghost of a kiss until he drifted into the abyss too.

4 2

LOVE TOO MUCH

ASHER

NOVEMBER 12

Asher opened his eyes to twin pools of blue. It took him a second or two to realize he was awake, and the twin pools were Lev's irises.

"Good morning, you," Lev murmured. His large hand brushed Asher's hair back from his face.

Asher frowned. "Did you sleep at all?"

"I only woke a few moments ago." Lev yawned, and stroked a line down Asher's spine, ending at his tailbone. "How are you feeling?"

Asher wasn't sure if Lev was asking how sore his hole was or where his head was at. He took stock of both. "Better. Thank you for last night."

His cheeks heated. Shame slipped in with the fog-filtered daylight. Had he really asked Lev to be his dom? He looked over his shoulder, vision blurring on what little of Lev's map he could see.

"So, that wasn't a dream."

"No, it was not." Lev's hand drifted south and squeezed Asher's ass. "You were very good for me."

327

Asher stiffened. "I don't want—we don't have to play like that again. I was in a weird mood last night."

Lev removed his hand. "What's your color?"

"I don't have one. This isn't a scene." Asher sat up and scrubbed his face with his hands. He was being a dick. "I'm sorry."

"You said you would be honest."

Last night he'd been weak and pathetic. But he wasn't anymore. "Forget what I said. You can't fix me and I can't fix you."

He got out of bed and made for the door in the wall connecting their rooms. Repainting over what happened with Ben would never work. How could he ever trust Lev when he still held so much back?

Lev followed. "Asher, wait!"

Asher slipped under the tapestry—and slammed into the low doorframe so hard he saw stars and tears stung his eyes.

"Fuck!" He sat back on the cold floor on his bare ass and rubbed his forehead.

Lev was already there, dropping to his knees, face grave, one arm supporting Asher's back. "Are you alright?"

"I'm fine," Asher snapped.

Ignoring the outburst, Lev pulled Asher's hand away from his head. The nauseating scent of copper hit him first, then his vision swam at the blood on his hand.

Lev sucked air through his teeth. "That sounded like it hurt. Wait here." Moving Asher as if he weighed nothing, Lev guided him to lean against the wall and hurried to the bathroom.

Asher considered taking the chance and leaving, but all fight and flight left him. Blood tickled as it dribbled down his forehead.

His stomach gave an ominous roll. He tipped his head back before blood dripped into his eyes and tried to breathe through his mouth. He refused to vomit all over himself on top of every-thing else.

Lev returned with a first aid kit and kneeled beside him.

"Another first aid kit?" Asher asked.

"The kitchen is quite a walk if you're alone in the castle and injured."

"It's not a castle," Asher teased.

"But it has turrets and suits of armor..." Lev teased back.

Asher smiled in spite of his nausea.

Lev unscrewed a brown bottle and poured amber liquid on a cotton ball. The sharp scent chased away the scent of blood, helping almost immediately.

"Is there a story behind keeping a first aid kit here? Cut yourself while shaving?"

Was Lev overcompensating? Had Silas been injured beyond repair, too far from medical attention? Was that how he'd died? Or was he just prepared?

"Hm?" Lev asked.

"You said the kitchen was far away."

"Oh, that. No." Without preamble, Lev blotted Asher's broken skin with the cotton ball.

"Fuck." Asher hissed.

"Sorry." Lev clicked his tongue. "Ordinarily, I'd say this was overkill, but I can't remember the last time that door has been dusted. Who knows what kind of centuries-old bacteria lurks there?"

Lev didn't meet his gaze, attention focused on pressing a wad of gauze to the wound at his hairline. When finished, Lev dropped the blood-stained gauze on a towel.

Asher closed his eyes and breathed through his mouth, willing his stomach to comply.

"Are you sure you're alright?"

Asher nodded, daring only to answer, "Blood makes me sick."

"Ah." Lev rustled around. Paper tore. "Breathe in."

Asher did. The scent of rubbing alcohol flooded his nostrils.

"Good lad—erm. Sorry."

Footsteps padded away. Asher opened his eyes. The bloody bandages were gone and Lev was halfway to the bathroom.

"Chemo made Mum sick," Lev said when he returned.

So it wasn't Silas. His mother's illness had taught Lev to keep first aid kits near.

"Her carer taught me this for nausea. It helped sometimes. At least for a few minutes, anyway."

Lev pulled an alcohol wipe packet from the first aid kit, tore it open partially, and passed it to him. The astringent smell replaced the scent of blood.

"Better?" Lev asked.

Asher nodded.

"Give this a sniff if you feel like you're going to vom—"

"Don't say it," Asher said.

"Sorry." Lev's lips curved down. "I'm going to clean this and be done. Best to get it over with." He blotted Asher's head with a towel and tossed it far across the room before Asher could see any blood. "It looks as if you narrowly avoided stitches yet again. Are you always so clumsy?"

"I'm not clumsy when the roads are level and construction is to code."

Lev laughed. "I love you prickly as much as I love you eager to please, just so you know."

Asher scowled.

Lev applied a bandage and pecked a kiss beside it. "There. Finished." He stuffed the spare bandages inside and snapped the first aid kit shut.

"When I said I want all of you, I meant all of your moods and emotions too," Lev said. "I only wish you could explain why the sudden change from last night to today."

Asher wished he could explain it too. He pushed to his feet.

"Allow me." Lev gripped Asher's hip and hooked his arm under Asher's armpit, before boosting him up.

"Now then," Lev said on the way back to bed, hand still on Asher's hip. "Would you like to discuss what's troubling you now and I'll bend you over the bed and kiss your hole better, or would you rather have breakfast first?"

Asher rolled his eyes even as his cock hardened.

Lev looked down and smirked.

"It's morning wood," Asher said.

"Of course," Lev agreed knowingly.

Ass.

They reached the bed. Lev squeezed Asher's hip, fingers wrapping toward Asher's cleft. "Make a decision, Blakely, before I make it for you and pop down to put the kettle on." His hand left Asher as he stroked his chin. "Come to think of it, what sort of host would I be if I ate you before I fed you first?"

"Oh, fuck off," Asher said without bite. "It's just…"

Asher sat on the edge of the bed and buried his head in his hands. The bed dipped as Lev joined him.

Lev rubbed his back in soothing circles. "What, love?"

"Maybe we escalated things too quickly." Asher lifted his head. "I shouldn't have asked you to do that last night."

"I'm honored that you trusted me enough to ask, and you were right to suggest it. I think it helped us both. Don't you?"

"It helped you?"

Lev nodded. "Helping you find peace helped me find my own. You do know, though, Blakely, that nothing between us is transactional, right? I don't need your servitude, or your sweet mouth, or your art.

"You don't have to make yourself worthy of my love because you already have it. I would do anything to make you happy. Tell me what you need."

Asher grimaced. "I was vulnerable with you last night, and it helped at the time, but we recreated a ritual you did with Silas. He casts a shadow on everything we do and I've shown you so much of myself, and shared my most shameful secrets, and still know so little about him, or you. I don't want you to tell me anything before you're ready. I'm just trying to explain why I acted insane this morning."

"You didn't act insane. Please don't automatically discount your feelings. If they're real to you, they're real, no matter what anyone else has told you." He sighed. "I'm sorry, I haven't been as forthcoming. There are some things I *can* tell you.

"Silas talked like poetry ran in his blood, rhyming accidentally, speaking in a lyrical cadence. He told me his favorite color was black, but that wasn't true. His favorite color was blue. Like my eyes. I found out later."

"He must have loved you so much."

Instead of smiling, Lev grimaced. "Too much."

Asher didn't like the insinuation, because hadn't that been the case with him and Ben, and worse so now with Lev? Asher had loved to the point of destruction. Would he meet the same end again?

"Please don't think I'm ungrateful," Lev said. Did Asher look as crestfallen as he felt?

"I don't."

"Let me think of a better way to explain." He tapped his lips with his finger several times. "I suppose it's a bit like a plant. Too much sunlight will kill it. Too much water will drown it. Silas loved me so much I started to wilt."

"What, so he suffocated you?" Asher didn't like this conversation at all, especially when he already felt needy and insecure.

"No, darling. I see where your head is going." Lev cupped Asher's cheek. "Your love will never be too much because you love yourself too." Lev dropped his hand. "Silas needed me in ways I could never achieve. He wanted my every breath to whisper his name on an exhale."

"That doesn't sound like love. It sounds like possession."

Lev winced. "Don't misunderstand. He wasn't a monster.

He was very sweet and had the sharpest wit and sense of humor."

"I wish I could have met him." Who was the man who'd held Lev's heart for so long?

Lev laughed. "I'm quite certain you would have hated him. If you were both alive, and competing for my hand, he would have hated you too."

Asher shivered.

Lev noticed, but misinterpreted the reason, or maybe he wanted an excuse to change conversation because after he'd settled the duvet around Asher's shoulders, he asked, "What's your favorite color?"

Answering that question was more difficult now because Asher's favorite color actually was black. At least when it came to paint. It darkened all his hues to suit his mood. "I don't have a favorite color."

"Truly?"

Asher shrugged. "Yeah."

Lev watched him shrewdly. Asher's skin prickled under his inspection.

"Interesting. Perhaps we're alike in that way. I do have a favorite color, but it always changes. I become obsessed and use it in everything until I can't stand to look at it. Sometimes it's the dewy green of grass after the first rain in spring, the pale gray of bark on a tree. Apparently such hyper-fixation is a hallmark symptom of ADHD, one reason perhaps why my father had never had me evaluated."

Asher already knew that. Lev had spoken about his use of color many times over the years and he'd always had a different favorite color depending on the interview.

"I've had many favorites since you've joined me here. The color of your hair—darkest brown, not quite black in daylight. The faded scarlet of your flushed chest after I make you come. I could go on and on."

Did that mean one day Lev would be sick of him too? Was

he on borrowed time? Was he just a fixation Lev would lose interest in? Was that what had happened to Lev's previous bedmates?

The questions lingered, even as Lev massaged Asher's back and thighs, his glutes, and then positioned him over a pile of pillows and reverently, gently, kissed his hole better as promised. And even later, when Lev spooned Asher from behind and thrust between his thighs while jerking Asher until they both got off.

What had happened when Lev had grown tired of Silas? Would it happen to him? Had Silas hurt himself?

WHEN A MIND IS LONELY

ASHER

DECEMBER 5

Days bled together as they settled into a routine of making art and making love. Rain became a constant presence, a cozy underscore to their existence as each passing day grew darker and shorter, and frigid gales blew across the moors.

Lev still walked the shore every morning. Alone. Asher had asked if he wanted company, but Lev always declined. Suspicious, given Lev followed Asher from room to room like a shadow—if shadows were loud, and horny.

The only perk was an uninterrupted chance to call Theo. Asher had voiced vague concerns about Lev's absentmindedness and solo conversations over the last few weeks. Theo was equally perplexed.

Mental illness was the most likely cause, but he'd just seen his psychiatrist—virtually—and spoke with his therapist every two weeks. Lev had been transparent about his renewed efforts to overcome his agoraphobia and Asher was so fucking proud of him.

Under the guidance of his therapist, Lev had built a stepladder of goals to accomplish, starting with crossing through the gate, walking for one minute, and so on until Lev left Lichenmoor to shop for groceries, then for longer durations.

Lev's first attempt had failed, and his second. Asher had escorted Lev to the gate each day after. Lev had made little progress, but it took immense bravery to keep showing up every day in spite of his fears, and Asher always made sure he knew that.

After nearly three weeks, Lev had managed to cross the threshold of the gate, and made it a few steps forward before anxiety forced him back. It was a huge win, the farthest Lev had been in years.

But Lev's strange behavior had increased since then. He talked to himself more and more, but only in soft whispers when he thought he was alone, or that Asher was sleeping. He stared absently for longer periods, as if listening to someone else, and was more distractible, in general.

Lev had promised to discuss it with his medical team, but Asher wasn't privy to those conversations. If he kept getting worse, Asher would have no choice but to confront him, even if he was afraid of Lev's answer.

On a rare clear day, Asher climbed to the top of a turret facing the beach, armed with a decent pair of binoculars he'd found in a box of 1970s outdoor and camping equipment in one of Lichenmoor's abandoned rooms.

When he peered through the lenses and saw that Lev was, in fact, walking, he felt like a total asshole for spying—until Lev skidded to a stop in the sand and swirled around, face warped in rage. He threw his hands out and yelled at someone who wasn't there with so much venom he spat saliva, then he dropped to his knees and sifted through the sand with his bare hands.

What was worth shards of icy sand forced beneath his fingernails?

When Lev returned, the rims of his eyes and his nose were pink, but the cold wind was a more likely culprit. Still, what had Lev been searching for?

Asher feigned shock when Lev came in. "What happened to your hands?"

"I thought I saw a shell, but it was only a bit of plastic."

"I don't need shells. I need you safe." Asher kissed Lev's blanched fingers, and poured him a cup of tea to warm his precious hands, so talented with a brush, so gentle with Asher.

Then he made breakfast.

"Alright there, Blakely?" Lev asked later.

Asher looked up from his plate and found bluebonnet eyes watching him.

"I should be asking you that." Asher dipped his toast in the goldenrod yolk of the eggs he'd collected from Lichenmoor's hens.

"You're not eating."

"I'm eating. I was just thinking." Asher bit into the toast. "Mm."

The rustic sourdough bread was delicious. Lev claimed the starter was as old as Lichenmoor.

Thanks to a mix of Lev's praise, and fussing, Asher had overcome his nervous stomach. If he didn't eat, his anxiety would worsen as caffeine and adrenaline surged through him.

Plus, he wanted to make Lev proud. Asher folded his bread in half, sandwiching his egg inside, then took a bite.

Lev sipped from his teacup, still watching.

Asher wiped his mouth with the back of his hand. "What?"

Lev lowered his cup, revealing a flirty smile. "You're a very good lad."

Asher flushed. Lev's praise still made him blush, no matter how generously Lev dealt it out.

"You said you were thinking, Blakely. What about?"

The love Asher had for Lev propelled him to risk his displeasure now.

"I don't want you to walk out there alone anymore."

"I beg your pardon?"

"It's too cold. What if you slip on ice and hurt yourself?"

"Oh, I don't think that's..." Lev trailed off, gaze wandering from Asher's face to something behind him.

Goosebumps crawled over Asher's skin. Sound traveled in Lichenmoor. Asher hadn't heard footsteps or creaking floorboards. Outside, naked branches still drifted with the wind and scratched at the windows, but inside the room was so quiet, time had stopped.

Long seconds passed. Lev's jaw clenched and his wind-chapped cheeks turned a dark shade of red. What did he see? What did he hear?

Asher reached over the corner of the table and squeezed his hand. He didn't want this vacant stranger. "Lev?"

Lev's gaze slid slowly back to him. "I apologize. You're right."

"Huh?"Asher blinked. He'd been expecting a fight.

Lev cupped Asher's cheek. "Perhaps you should escort me back to bed. I am getting older..." Lev huffed a melodramatic sigh.

Asher snorted.

"It's true. I'm practically geriatric." Lev lifted his nose and heaved a longer sigh belied by his smirk. "How am I to keep you safe, if I'm holed up with a broken hip?"

"I don't need you to keep me safe, Lev."

"Of course, darling."

"Don't *of course darling*, me. There are worse things than a broken hip."

"Of course—"

Asher arched a brow.

"Of course, you're right, darling."

Asher rolled his eyes.

"Please don't fret. I'm nothing like those other men you trawled for at a senior living facility."

"Oh, fuck off."

"Wait. Please don't be cross." Lev took Asher's hand and kissed it. "I'm sorry."

Lev lifted his gaze, leaving his lips pressed to Asher's hand. Asshole. Lev knew Asher couldn't resist the momentary daze of being hit with Lev's eyes at close range.

"You have my word, Ash. No more solo walks until the frost thaws." He released Asher's hand and stood. "Come take me upstairs and give me a bath. I'm old and frail and can no longer reach between my legs."

"Never say that again." Asher moved to clear their plates.

Lev lifted a hand. "Leave the dishes. Lichenmoor is far too lousy with nooks and crannies to ever defeat our rodent overlords."

Asher chewed on his lip. He'd been militant about keeping the castle as clean as possible after finding a mouse in one of the many traps Lucian had left around the house. Allegedly. Asher was pretty sure Lev had blamed Lucian for his own actions.

"If it's too cold for me to go out alone without you fearing I'll fall on my arse, it's too cold for the mice too. Think of their wee little whiskers. It's a kindness to invite them in. You, of all people, should relate, little dormouse."

"I told you not to call me that."

"So you say, but we both know you like it."

Asher glared at him.

Lev laughed, low and husky. "I promise, no harm will come to any four-legged creatures that nibble from our plates while we're gone. Luna is due today and you know how she gets if you leave her with nothing to do."

Asher had forgotten. With no obligations, deadlines, or

expectations—aside from eating and making art—the days blurred together.

Lev drummed long fingers on the tabletop. "If you don't stop faffing about and polish my knob upstairs…"

Asher lifted a brow, a nonverbal, *You aren't going to make another bad joke, are you?*

Lev nodded sagely. "You're right. That would have been a joke far worse than the one about you cleaning my crevasses."

"Crevasses?" Asher threw a cloth napkin at him.

Laughing, Lev caught the napkin midair and tossed it onto the table.

"Enough joking, Blakely." Lev straightened to his full height and prowled around the corner of the table. "Now, come along and be a good lad."

Good lad.

The two words were an incantation summoning submission. Asher would do anything to earn Lev's praise.

After sucking Lev into a stupor, he slipped out of their room and found Luna in the kitchen.

Lev wouldn't let Asher leave Lichenmoor, afraid he'd never return, so Luna still shopped for their groceries.

Asher's favorite peanut butter waited in the center of the scuffed butcher block island. "Luna, I think I'm in love with you."

"I did nothing."

"Sweet-talking the grocer into making a special order isn't *nothing.*" Asher popped a slice of wheat bread into the toaster. "Do you need help?"

Instead of balking, she assigned him the heavier bags with cans and moved on to filling the fruit bowl with pomegranates, apples, pears, and fresh figs.

"You remind me of him, you know," Luna said.

"Silas?"

Luna's wispy gray brows lifted. "Lev's told you about him?"

"A little."

Her eyes tipped down, wrinkles at the corners of her eyes nearly meeting her smile lines.

"Has he, now?"

She yanked him into a hug, then pulled back, milky brown eyes misting.

"You don't know how much I've worried about what would happen to him if I.... Well, you must have noticed I'm getting on in years."

Asher feigned shock. "You can't be more than a day over forty."

Luna rapped him on the head with the tip of a baguette. "I don't accept lies in this household, Mr. Blakely."

But a smile glimmered in her eyes as she sniffed and wiped tears away.

"Lev won't talk to me about Silas," Luna said. "When they were kids, I'd take Lev aside, worried how he was coping with the abrupt change of losing his mother to then gain a brother. For a boy who never kept quiet, Lev's silence made me worry, and when Silas died, it got worse."

"Lev said you're the closest thing to a mum he has. I imagine losing Silas was like losing a son. I'm so sorry."

She winced in a way that reminded Asher so much of Lev, he almost questioned who Lev's blood mother was.

"Tom and I took a little longer to start a family. Lev was my only child for the first few years after his Mum died. When Silas joined us, I'd already started a family of my own.

"Silas was very quiet and reserved, more difficult to get to know, but yes, I loved him like a son. When he died, my heart broke twice—once for Silas, and once for what Lev had lost."

Asher's own heart broke a little too, thinking of Lev losing his mother as a boy, and then the second father he'd found in Wendell, only for Silas to die next.

She closed the fridge. "It was such an unexpected and yet inevitable death."

Asher's pulse quickened. Was she going to tell him? The toaster beeped. Asher jumped. Luna passed him a plate and a butter knife, and said nothing more as Asher slathered peanut butter on his toast.

"Did you know about Lev and Silas?"

He was ninety-five percent sure she already knew, but what if he'd been wrong? What if he'd just spilled a decades-old secret?

She sighed and selected a breadknife from the block. "Did I know they were more than mates?" She nodded, and sliced into the baguette. "There's little that escapes a mother's eye."

The scratch of the knife carving into the baguette was the only sound for a minute or two. Asher bided his time with a few bites of his toast. It tasted like home.

"I wasn't talking about Silas before," Luna said. "Lev is the one you remind me of. He was always such a sweet, considerate boy, always offering to help."

"Oh." Asher didn't know what else to say.

"I can't thank you enough for coming to Lichenmoor and being so patient with my son. You've been so good for him."

She cut another slice and sighed.

"Lev isolated himself for so long after Lucian died, I was quite shocked when he planned to entertain guests."

"Lev blames himself?" Asher said.

"He does." She stared at him a bit too long before slicing into the baguette again. "After he returned to Lichenmoor, he seldom left his room, and when he did, it was only to walk the shoreline, tend the horses, and work in Lucian's studio."

Poor Lev, padding around the empty castle, locked inside his father's studio, painting the man he'd lost.

Asher swallowed his last bite of toast, and washed it down with a glass of milk.

"Has Lev..." He bit into his lip. "I don't know. It's stupid. But have you ever heard him talking in an empty room?"

Asher squirmed under her inspection as she dusted the crumbs off the bread knife and wiped it with a rag, before returning it to the block.

"You mean, have I ever seen him talking to himself?"

"Yeah." Feeling like the world's biggest asshole, and idiot, Asher focused his attention on the stem of a fig, twisting it until it pulled away from the top.

She selected a different knife and placed it on the cutting board. "No. I can't say that I have. Do you mind fetching the chicken sausage in the fridge for me, lad?"

"Yes, ma'am." Asher rifled through the bag until he found the wax paper packet labeled with Hector's recognizable scrawl in black permanent ink.

From Beaker.

Lev had found a local family ranch that treated their live-stock humanely, but Asher wished Hector would stop including the name of the chickens.

"Thanks, dear. Why don't you check on Lev while I work on this?"

"I don't mind helping."

She didn't answer. Effectively dismissed, Asher folded the canvas bags and stacked them. "Thank you for picking up the groceries. Hopefully, Lev and I will take over someday."

"You will. People are like plants. They do better when people speak to them. They thrive in the sunlight. In open air. Lev is a plant locked in a dark cupboard. All he needs is love and care." She inclined her head toward Asher, "You give him both."

Luna's trust in Asher soothed some of his anxiety, but his fears were too scary for a plant metaphor to vanquish. Asher forced a small smile and turned to go.

"Oh, and Asher?"

He stopped and swiveled toward her again. "Yes, ma'am?"

"When the mind is lonely, it creates company. If you ever hear Lev talking to himself, that's all it is."

He hoped she was right. He wanted to be wrong, could still be wrong. But his suspicions and fears hadn't faded over time. They'd festered. And grown.

44

MOURNING IN THE SHADOWS

LEV

JANUARY 17

"This way, Blakely," Lev called over his shoulder, checking again that Asher hadn't taken a wrong turn. Why had Asher insisted upon trailing behind rather than holding his hand?

Silas appeared at Lev's side mid-stride. "What do you think he's thinking so loudly about back there?"

Lev ignored him.

"The tide's receding. Perhaps he's plotting his escape?" Silas matched his pace with Lev. "If he legs it, he might still make the ferry."

Sod off, Lev wished he could say.

Lev cast another look behind him. Asher had stopped again, distracted by yet another bust of a long-dead relative Lev couldn't care less about.

"Ah, yes. My great, great, great, great auntie Eleanor Crane. She married into the Marks family after being traded out in exchange for an aviary full of, well, I suppose you may have guessed."

A single dimple winked. The corner of his mouth twitched. Almost a smile. "Cranes?"

"God, no. Imagine what they would do to the ecosystem. It was an aviary full of me talking out of my arse."

Asher elbowed him and his smile finally emerged.

"Most of my relatives are dreadfully dull, or terrible, or both, nobility and colonialism being what they were, and sometimes still are. Why are you so interested in them?"

He shrugged. "I'm not interested in them. I'm interested in you."

"How sweet," Silas teased.

Lev led Asher into a room stuffed with sculptures and framed paintings covered by clear plastic sheets.

Asher whistled. "Ran out of room?"

"Of course not. Lichenmoor is chock full of rooms to fill with art. These pieces serve another purpose."

Lev lifted the bottom corner of a tarp thrown over a frame on casters that nearly touched the ceiling and shoved it aside. There was no door, or at least none anyone outside the Marks family would know of.

Asher laughed. "Where are you taking me?"

"If I told you, it would spoil the surprise. Stand back." Lev stretched to lift the latch hidden behind a candelabra, and the double doors nested in the wood paneling opened outward, revealing the dark maw of a hidden hallway.

"Creepy," Asher said.

"It's just wind caught in the walls." It was the positive pressure air control system. "This secret passageway is ancient." Lev plucked the electric lantern he kept on a hook and turned it on. "You may want to hold my hand." Lev was relieved when he felt Asher at the other end.

The hallway ended at the door to a vault.

"What the actual fuck?"

"It's a bit much, isn't it? Grandfather liked to keep his sterling and gold with him, like a dragon with a horde. Never trusted technology much."

"You should tell him about how our dear grandfather got locked inside," Silas suggested.

"Father was a dragon of a different kind."

Asher's eyes widened. "Wait. Are you serious? Your father's collection is here?"

The collection wasn't a secret, but the best way to prevent anyone from stealing it was if no one knew it was there in the first place. Father played into the air of mystery, but most people assumed his collection was kept in a high security archival storage facility.

Silas rubbed his fingers between his eyebrows like he had a headache, then threw his hand down. "I can't believe you prefer someone who gets this excited about an art collection over me. God, it's like Father is a celebrity." He stroked his chin then snapped his fingers. "Maybe he plans to lock you in the vault and take your art. A perfect death for you, don't you think? Sounds like something I would write."

Lev clenched his jaw and willed Silas from his mind. Vanquishing Silas was becoming more and more difficult.

"It's a big deal that you're showing me this." Asher squeezed Lev's hand.

"Good. I'm glad you understand that I care for you so much that I trust you to keep my secrets."

Lev spun the vault wheel and pulled the heavy door open.

The vault was empty aside from a pair of commercial grade double doors that didn't suit Lichenmoor at all. Lev unlocked the door and opened it. Fluorescent overhead lights clicked on automatically, one after another, illuminating row after row of archival drawers.

The windows had been boarded up, the rooms refurbished to be nearly fire and waterproof. Sensors and air-locked walls helped maintain the conditions required to preserve rare art.

Father had even hired someone to install a back up generator for power outages.

"Father's collection spans the entire floor," Lev said, holding the door with his back. "After you."

Asher hesitated on the threshold.

Lev cupped Asher's cheek and met his gaze. "You belong here. You deserve this. I want you here. Understood?"

"Yes, sir."

Lev kissed his forehead. "Shall we?"

They didn't make it very far before Asher stopped.

"Are all those chests full of art?"

"Yes. Would you like to see?" He guided Asher to Fenton Milieu's drawer and unlocked it with the second key on his ring.

Asher sucked in a sharp inhale and rushed forward, then paused to stuff his hands in his pockets as if he didn't trust himself not to touch the dark, moody portraits in the shallow drawer.

"Crafting color has always felt like alchemy to me, like magic. Like you said." Lev tipped his head in Asher's direction. "Milieu built his palettes with a hefty dose of black, darkening every color without losing their vibrancy, and embedded so much raw emotion in his art that each swipe of his brush was the warmth of a lover, a stab of betrayal, mourning in the shadows." Lev wrapped his arms around Asher from behind and kissed the side of his neck. "It reminds me of your work. Though no one could compare to you."

"You can't say things like that." Asher turned his cheek and met Lev's lips.

"But it's true." Lev reached around Asher to close the drawer.

"The art!" Asher yelped.

"The art will be perfectly safe while I kiss you." Lev turned Asher around to face him and did exactly that.

Asher moaned against his lips and kissed him back, hands dropping to free the button of Lev's trousers.

"What are you doing?" Lev asked, breathing fast.

Asher lowered to his knees and pressed his cheek against Lev's growing erection. "Thanking you."

Lev breathed through his nose, giving himself time to hide the anger and disgust from his tone. Asher was treating him like Ben, like their relationship was transactional. Did Asher really believe Lev needed that?

A dark shadow in Lev's peripheral vision was the only warning before Silas dropped to his knees beside Asher. "Come on, Levvy, give us a taste." Silas opened his mouth unnaturally wide, like his jaw had unhinged.

"No." Lev grabbed Asher's arm and jerked him up from the ground. Too fast. Too rough.

Asher winced.

Silas laughed. "Now you've gone and done it."

"I'm so sorry, darling." Lev hugged Asher against his chest, warily watching Silas climb to his feet. "Sometimes I don't know my own strength. Have I hurt you?"

"No." Asher pulled back, scanning Lev with an impassive face. "Are you okay?"

"I'm quite alright, thank you," Lev answered brusquely, cheeks flaming. "There's so much more I want to show you."

Silas materialized sitting on top of the drawers. "Nice save, but our boy is too clever."

"Let me lock this."

If Silas didn't fuck off, Lev was going to break all his teeth off with how much restraint it took not to call Silas a cunt.

Silas kicked his heels against the metal drawers with a rattling clang. *Kick. Clang. Kick. Clang.*

Lev inhaled deeply and clenched his hands into fists.

Kick. Clang. Kick. Clang.

"You fell right into my trap." Silas smiled until his lips

ripped into his skin. "Now you love someone the way I love you. I can't wait to watch you ruin him."

Silas was wrong. Lev wouldn't ruin Asher. He wouldn't—

"How long have you been staring vacantly having a conversation inside of your head, dearest Leviathan?" Silas shook his sleeve back from the black crew sweater and checked a nonexistent watch.

"Lev?" Asher curled his fingers around Lev's wrist and tugged him away from Silas. "What's wrong?"

"Nothing. Let's go."

Bless Blakely for accepting his answer, and allowing him to lead him forward without protest.

Silas did not follow. But he was always there. Always.

Lev played tour guide, ushering Asher down rows of paintings, pottery, rare books, and award-winning photography. The farther they waded into Father's collection, the more tension fled him.

Every few minutes, Asher stopped to exclaim in wonder, ask a question, or thank Lev profusely with a hug or kiss or an impassioned speech on why he was so smitten with one piece or another.

Witnessing Asher's joy warmed the chill Silas had left in Lev's heart. Sharing this vulnerable piece of himself was terrifying, but he wished he'd taken him sooner. He couldn't have planned a better first date—at Lichenmoor or elsewhere.

"Lucian collected everything," Lev said of a cabinet filled with rare antique chess pieces.

"Don't you think it's a little sad that they're all locked away here where no one can see them?"

Lev frowned. "I suppose you're right. I haven't given it much thought. We used to loan things out to museums quite often, but Father had grown so paranoid that he'd kept everything with him."

They paused in front of a particularly formidable portrait Lucian had painted of his own father—face draped in shadow, green eyes contemptuous, wrath rapping at the windows of his soul.

"When Father chose art over business, Grandfather was so furious he chucked all of Father's paintings off the cliff. The tide brought them back the next morning, utterly destroyed."

"Did he push your grandfather off the cliff?"

Lev laughed. "I'm afraid not. Grandfather lived long enough to imprint himself on my memories as a bigoted arsehole."

"Lucian must have hated him."

Lev nodded. "The last nail in the coffin was when Grandfather forbade Lucian from marrying my mum because she came from a middle class family in Ireland." Lev rolled his eyes. "The audacity."

"I didn't know that about your mom—mum."

"I suspect you wouldn't. Grandfather crafted a fictional family history." Lev laughed. "Whenever Lucian needed money or was feeling vindictive, he threatened to tell the tabloids. You sound adorable saying *mum*, pretty American."

Asher retaliated with an even more adorable look of irritation Lev couldn't help but plunder with a kiss.

"Who did these?" Asher paused before a row of life-size sculptures.

Lev didn't answer. The sculptures in that row weren't ones he cared to see. Father had sculpted Mum, Wendell, and made casts of their hands before they died, as if the ghastly stone replicas would keep them alive. He'd assigned Lev the punishment of making one of Silas too.

Asher reappeared, lips pushed into a troubled pout. "Lucian sculpted your mum and Wendell?"

"Morbid, aren't they?"

"I was going to say sad."

They passed a few more rows in silence. Asher lingered over glass art displays. Lev had collected an entire series of glass threads knitted into fabrics. Theo's Ophelia-inspired creation was there too. It was a brilliant bit of art, after all, even if its creator had been his romantic nemesis.

"I could spend days here and never finish," Asher said, some time later, after he'd pulled out half a dozen custom-built partitions carrying framed art for viewing like a rolling wall, before tucking them back in like a pocket door.

"You may stay as long as you wish and return whenever you like."

Asher stopped. "This is too much."

"Blakely, we've been through this. Gifts are to be accepted. Apologies are to be given only when absolutely necessary. Nothing is transactional." Lev covered Asher's mouth with his hand. "I could give you every penny I own, all of Lichenmoor, and it wouldn't be enough. Understood?"

Asher nodded.

"Use words," Lev commanded, keeping his hand in place. He wanted Asher's voice to resonate on his skin.

Asher rolled his eyes, but acquiesced, muttering a garbled "Yes, sir" against Lev's palm.

"Good lad."

Lev lowered his palm and kissed him before he could spout a snarky retort.

"There's one more thing I want you to see." Lev trailed his fingertips along the labels for each pull-out partition until they reached the last one. "Ah, here we are." He pulled the handle and dragged it over to reveal the final hidden room, the one that contained Asher's art, framed and displayed on each hexagonal wall of the turret.

Asher sucked in a sharp inhale.

"I used to display your paintings on the paths I frequented." Lev wrapped his arms around Asher from behind and looked over his shoulder. "I must admit, some days your art was the only reason I left my room."

Asher turned, eyes shimmering with unshed tears. "My art

comforted you and kept you company? I was there for you the way you were for me?"

Lev nodded.

"I don't know what to say." Asher shook his head. "I could retire now and be satisfied."

Lev kissed Asher's neck, then nipped. "I would be very cross if you were to deprive me of your future art."

"Ouch. You're always so bitey."

Lev laughed against Asher's skin.

"That tickles." Asher squirmed.

"So many complaints, little mouse," Lev whispered, relishing the resulting slide of Asher's arse against his cock. "Little did I know when I bought these pieces that one day I'd hold you in my arms."

"It doesn't feel real."

"No, it does not," Lev agreed and kissed him again. "I'd love to display them again if that's alright with you."

"Maybe a few. It's hard for me to look at something I made and not see all the flaws, all the ways I could improve it."

"We're all our own worst critics, aren't we? Imperfection makes you human and turns paint into art."

"Yeah. I mean, objectively, I know that. It's just..." He tossed his hair back from his face. "My brain is such a dick. Critiques are so much louder than the compliments."

"Tell your brain to remember my rule, or the next time you're unkind to yourself, I'll take you over my knee and massage your prostate until you come all over my lap like the good boy I know you are."

Lev would never punish Asher. Praise and pleasure were far more effective anyway.

"In that case, I hate my hair at this length."

"Very funny," Lev said, and sobered. "I've always felt similarly when it comes to critique. I needed Father's approval so much that I lost myself. It took a long time for me to shake it, and even now, I struggle with it on occasion. It's funny how the ones who raise us are the ones to hurt us most, even when they don't mean to."

Lev laughed without humor. "Lucian had never wanted to be like his father, but no child is untouched by the echoes of their past. It doesn't matter how far the apple falls if the roots are rotten and the trunk infected."

"What part of your father infects you?" Asher asked.

An incurable neurological condition that would carve out his soul until the only thing left was confusion, sadness, and rage. But Lev couldn't tell him that. Asher would leave, or worse yet, he'd promise to stay.

"My father wanted his father's approval too. He was lucky though. He accepted who he was early on and was unapologetically himself forever after. Meanwhile, I'm still haunted by his disapproval."

"It sounds like his expectations were so high, you never had a chance."

"Perhaps." Lev released Asher. "Well, aren't you going to ask me which of yours is my favorite?"

"You already told me. Falling in love through a painting is a pretty obvious declaration."

Oh. Right. The chain around Lev's heart loosened some. "The painting of the guilty man. Please tell me you still have it."

"I do, but the man wasn't guilty, Lev. He was grieving."

Lev blinked. "What? Sorry. I don't understand. You captured guilt so perfectly it's like a mirror."

"I never titled that painting. You're the only one who calls it the guilty man." Asher cocked his head. "Why do you see guilt instead of grief?"

"Because I'm guilty."

"Of what?"

Lev wanted to look away but he couldn't. He wasn't ready, but if he lied, Asher would put his walls back up.

"You could craft an alternate death for me that you wrongfully blame yourself for," Silas said behind Asher. "Perhaps I took a tumble down a stairwell? Or I got so high I threw myself off a cliff because I thought I could fly? You could always build on the old curse about the high tide's insatiable hunger."

"Enough!" Lev roared.

Asher jumped and dropped his hands from Lev's neck.

"Ash…"

"It's okay," Asher said, too eager to placate him. "I shouldn't have asked."

Silas cackled. "You should stop listening to me. If only you could."

Lev wanted to break something. Multiple things. A dangerous state to be when surrounded by art.

But he needed to focus.

"No. The fault is mine." He pulled Asher into a hug, only inhaling after Asher relaxed against him. "I'm knackered. I didn't mean to snap. I'm not angry with you."

"I know, Lev." Asher held Lev's face with his palms. "It's okay."

"He *knows*, Levvy. He *knows* you're crazy. He *knows* you'll hurt him."

Lev exhaled through clenched teeth. "I'm sorry. I'm tired. Maybe I'm coming down with something."

Asher's eyes narrowed, the muscles in his jaw twitching, then nodded. "I'm tired too." He attempted the most obvious fake yawn Lev had ever seen. "Let's go take a nap."

"For such a sulky black cat, you are so very patient with me. Thank you."

"First I'm a mouse, and now I'm a cat?"

"That's because you're everything to me."

Asher rolled his eyes. "Smooth."

Lev wasn't flirting. Asher *did* mean everything to him, and soon Lev would have no choice but to break his heart before he hurt him.

45

A SHRINE TO YOU

ASHER

Ghosts weren't real, and if ghosts weren't real, Asher couldn't deny it anymore. He wanted to be wrong. He could still be wrong.

But he knew he wasn't.

Lev's one-sided conversations, the intensity in his eyes as he disappeared inside himself, the responses that felt like they were meant for someone else...

All of it made heartbreaking sense, but Lev's forty was far younger than Lucian's sixty-two.

Did he know? He seemed lucid enough to at least suspect he was heading down that path. Had Lev been battling this alone? That poor man, trapped in this place, haunted by loss, tormented by the ghosts inside his head.

How long would it take until he was as lost to time as the chapel was?

That couldn't happen. Asher could no sooner lose Lev, or watch Lev lose himself, than wrench his heart from his chest.

But if Lev had Alzheimer's, Asher *would* lose him. He would watch Lev die twice—the slow death of who he was and the death of the body that housed him.

Adrenaline careened through his bloodstream. His pulse

sped. But he couldn't have a panic attack. He needed to be there for Lev.

He thought of Lev as he was now. Only now. Only him. The warmth of his hand, the way his copper hair glittered with the occasional gray hair as they passed each wall sconce.

"You're awfully quiet," Lev said. "Where's your head at?"

The question was casual, but Asher knew better. Lev needed to know they were still okay.

Asher squeezed his hand. "I still can't believe you collect my work."

Lev pulled Asher into a tender kiss that relaxed the fist around Asher's heart, and freed a flock of butterflies instead. When they parted, Lev tucked Asher's head under his chin. See? Nothing was wrong. Lev was fine. Asher melted into the safety of his arms.

"My love will be with you always," Lev said into Asher's hair, punctuating the sentence with a kiss to Asher's crown. "No matter how far you travel from Lichenmoor."

"I'm not going anywhere. The only reason I'll ever leave Lichenmoor is if it's with you."

Lichenmoor was Lev's cage, and Asher would do whatever he could to set him free.

Asher buried his face into Lev's soft sweater and breathed in the whisper of his cologne. "I can't lose you."

"You won't."

"I need you," Asher said instead of calling Lev's lie.

He clawed at Lev's clothes, pushed Lev against the wall, and kissed him again.

"What's gotten into you?" Lev asked, lips pink, face flushed, as he searched Asher's eyes.

"You, obviously."

Asher invaded Lev's space, leading with his tongue, and when their lips collided, Lev's groan rippled through his blood.

Lev broke the kiss. "You're not trying to repay me, are you?"

"No." Asher rolled his eyes and pulled off his hoodie then dove back in for another kiss.

"Not here," Lev said, voice gruff.

"I can't wait. Please." He needed connection.

A groan rumbled through Lev's chest, hands tightening on Asher's hips. "I want you in bed. You can be patient for me, can't you?"

The realization hit him. "Is Silas here?"

Lev's eyes flashed behind Asher and back to his face. "I... Why would you ask me that? I told you he's—"

"Do you see Silas like your father saw Wendell?"

Lev stilled, breath held in his throat.

"You do, don't you?" Asher's heart broke. "Silas is here, and he was in your father's collection earlier. That's who kept distracting you."

"Asher... No."

Tears glazed Asher's vision. "Tell me the truth."

Lev's face crumbled. He thumbed a tear from under Asher's eyes. He laughed so fucking sadly. "I should have expected this. My perfect protégé, always so observant."

"I don't want it to be true," Asher's voice broke into a sob.

"Nor do I." Lev swiped the tears from Asher's cheeks, tears that Asher feared would never dry. "Baby, please don't cry."

The request only made Asher cry more. "Are you sure?"

Lev gripped both of Asher's shoulders and dipped his head to capture Asher's tear-filled eyes. "Do you believe in ghosts?"

He'd asked Asher that the first night they met. Had Silas been there?

"No," Asher answered.

"Me neither."

Asher sniffed, a seed of hope sprouting through the earth. "Do you know for sure?"

"No." He held the back of Asher's head with both hands and kissed his forehead. "But it runs in my family." Lev's shoulders lifted, his beard twitched as he inhaled. "I never should have invited you here. I never should have asked you to stay. I let you fall in love with me knowing how tragic our end would be."

"You didn't let me fall in love. Come the fuck on. Give me some agency. I decide who I love. I decide to stay or go."

"I could have made you go..."

The hint of a threat was a knife to Asher's gut. How close had he come to losing his soulmate? Asher had never believed in soulmates, but he did now. Maybe one day he'd believe in ghosts too.

"Are you sure there isn't a different reason why you're seeing him? Maybe..." He didn't want to toss out mental health diagnoses.

"Trust me, I've investigated every avenue. A battery of tests and dozens of specialists found nothing wrong with me. I'm not schizophrenic or psychotic. We've tried medications and experimental therapies, but nothing can vanquish him."

Lev blew a shaking sigh through his lips.

"But you're so young. It's not fair."

"Sometimes I think it's exactly what I deserve."

"Because of what you did to Silas?"

Lev's gaze swayed from Asher to behind him.

Asher's skin crawled. A shiver shuddered through him. "What's Silas saying?"

"Hm?" Lev said without looking.

How much time had Lev spent talking to an empty room? Or arguing with the ghost of his guilt? It broke Asher's fucking heart—Lev alone, and yet never alone because Silas was there.

"Lev?" Asher forced Lev's gaze back to him, relieved at the sight of lucid bluebonnet eyes.

"Sorry. I try to ignore him, but he can be rather demanding." Lev pulled Asher's hands down from his face. "I don't want to discuss this here. Silas stays out of our wing. I'd rather speak there." Lev squeezed Asher's hand and tugged him forward.

Wait. Silas couldn't go in their wing? How did that work? Was that why Lev had roomed Asher with him? Why not the others? Had Lev worried Silas would hurt Asher specifically? Or was he afraid of what Silas would tell him?

Silence followed them down the hall and up the spiral staircase with arched windows facing the ocean. Beckoned by the wind whipping through the windows, Asher peered out at the fog swept horizon, wrapping his fingers around the cold stone frame.

The water around Lichenmoor had crept closer, slowly swallowing the rocky shoreline. Salt and the sour scent of rotting seaweed filled each deep breath Asher inhaled.

Come, the ocean called to him. *Dive into the abyss and I'll catch you.*

"Blakely?" Lev said, drawing Asher away from the ledge.

Asher turned away from the window and kept his eyes on the shallow path time had carved into the limestone stairs the rest of the way.

"He's gone," Lev said when they were halfway down the hall to their rooms. "There are only two spaces Silas will not go. Here and the church."

The church. Lev had asked why they always ended up in the church. Asher had always found it easily, almost as if Lichenmoor had led him away from Silas to a place they could be alone.

"I saw Silas for the first time after my father died. He appeared perched on the arm of a sofa, acting as nonchalant as if he'd never left. I thought I was dreaming at first, though I seldom ever dreamt of him. Once I realized I was awake, I reached for him automatically, but he slipped through my fingers."

"Are you in love with him?" Asher held his breath, waiting for the answer.

Lev stopped and gripped both of Asher's shoulders. "I loved him when he was alive, but he isn't the person he was before he died. He came back... well, wrong.

"Sometimes I almost recognize him, but this version of himself is crueler than I remember. Angry. Then again, he has every right to be. I hurt him, and now he's trapped here with me. I could hurt you too."

"You won't. I feel safe with you."

Lev scoffed. "You're delusional if you feel safe here. Lichenmoor is a death trap. I'm a—"

"It's not about Lichenmoor. If people were places, you'd be my home. I want to be here with you."

"You don't understand what you're committing to. Loving me is a curse. I'll steal your best years and leave you with my worst. I'll fade until I'm no longer the man you fell in love with. Until I'm only my emotions. Until I'm a burden." Lev buried his face in his hands. "Today is the best day we'll ever have and every tomorrow will be worse than the day before it."

"Then we'll make the most of every day we have left."

Lev lifted his head, eyes unguarded and vulnerable. "You still want me, after all of that, after bringing you here under false pretenses, after knowing how selfish I am?"

"You're not selfish."

"You'll be trapped here with me. You'll grow to resent me. Lichenmoor will become your cage too."

"Maybe." Asher leaned his forehead against Lev's. "But that isn't now. That isn't us. Let me take care of you for once." When was the last time Lev had allowed himself a moment's reprieve from his guilt? "Drop the past. It's just us now."

Lev nodded once. "Only now. Only us."

They traveled the remaining distance in a whirlwind, shedding their clothes, taking turns pinning the other against the wall, and when they reached their room, neither stopped to close the door.

Asher eased Lev down onto the bed with a palm against the center of his chest.

"My body is a shrine to you, and your bed is my church, and now I'm going to worship you."

OUROBOROS

LEV

Asher worshipped Lev exactly as promised, lavishing his cock with devotion until he exploded. When Lev tried to reciprocate, Asher declined.

"I want to sacrifice my pleasure and make our own ritual. I want you to fill my tattoos with color."

Lev understood the pain of watching someone he loved suffer, of bargaining his soul for another, of wanting to control his future. If Asher needed to make his own magic to make peace with their future, Lev wouldn't deprive him.

The living were nearly as powerless as Silas.

Asher was in heat by the time Lev finished, hands fisting the sheets, hips driving nearly imperceptible circles beneath Lev as he straddled him, hissing any time their cocks grazed, weeping so much precum, paint smeared. It was quite possibly the hottest thing he'd ever witnessed.

Lev layered the final details to the golden griffin over Asher's right pec. "Baby, are you sure you don't want me to take care of you?" He needed to put his poor lad out of his misery.

"No." Asher thrashed his head side to side, a shake of his head that surely meant yes. "Not until you're done."

"Lucky for you, I'm going to get carpal tunnel if I move onto your arms. We'll do them another time."

"You're lying."

Lev scoffed. "Wait until you're forty and see how long you can paint hunched over me." Lev blew against the golden griffin, drying what remained of the wet paint, raising the fine hairs on Asher's chest with gooseflesh.

Asher's nipple peaked. Lev couldn't resist fluttering the tip of his tongue over it. With a needy whine, Asher closed his eyes and tipped his head back, flashing an Adam's apple so delicious Lev longed to sink his teeth into it.

"You're a masterpiece," Lev murmured, stroking Asher's neck with his thumb, smearing it with glittering gold.

Asher licked his bottom lip and scraped his teeth against his tongue on the way back in, gaze dazed and glossy.

"Have a look, hm?"

The prospect of an art reveal cut through Asher's lust-induced delirium. He pressed his chin to his chest and gasped.

"I wish I could take credit for how beautiful these turned out, but I have only my muse and canvas to thank for it."

Asher gave a token roll of his eyes, before roving them back over Lev's art.

Lev scooped up the camera and snapped a few photos. They'd been taking photographs of each other over the last few weeks, and Lev couldn't wait to develop the roll of film. He planned to drag Asher to the dark room under the pretense of teaching him, then order him to watch the wicked images appear while Lev ate his arse and stroked his cock to completion.

Some of the photos would surprise him. After Asher had consented to somnophilia, Lev had taken photos while he slept to prove exactly how much he loved to sleep beside him, no matter how much he tossed and turned, to show him how beautifully his soft cock rested on his thigh, how hard and wanting he became when Lev played with him, teasing him into wet dreams before lapping up his cum.

"I wish you could tattoo," Asher said, trailing light fingertips over Lev's self-portrait.

"One day I will."

"*Okay*, Lev."

Lev lifted his chin. "I've been practicing."

Asher smirked. "When? We're always together."

He shielded his mouth with his hand and whispered, "All those times I retired to my father's studio or my study, I was actually in my secret tattoo room."

Asher grabbed Lev's wrist. "Wait. Really?"

Lev nodded, smiling like the besotted sap he was. "I bought all the equipment the morning after I saw your tattoos."

Asher's brow wrinkled. "You knew me two weeks."

"Yes, but learning takes time, and I've mastered so many techniques and mediums, the challenge of learning something new is a nice break from the tedium."

"You're always so humble."

Lev waved the joke away. "Without an apprenticeship, I fear it'll be a few years before I'm ready to test my skills on your arse—so no one will see if it's dreadful—but I've hired someone to instruct me virtually."

"Still. That's... Lev, that's a dream come true. Your art would be inside me, part of me forever."

Lev nodded gravely.

Asher's gaze turned hooded again, as if fanaticism blended with the submissive ecstasy of being claimed by Lev on a cellular level.

Lev swiped precum from Asher's slit with his thumb, and tasted it. "You like that idea, don't you?"

"Yes, sir."

"Good lad. I don't want anyone else putting my art on you from now on, understood?"

Asher's eyebrows curved with sincerity. "Thank you."

"Perhaps I'll cover your entire body with art drawn only by *my* hand, and only *my* ink bleeding into your skin."

"*Fuck.*"

Lev laughed. "I can't wait to make you beg for each one. For now, this will have to suffice." Lev nipped Asher's collar bone and sucked a hickey over the spot. "Trade positions with me. I want you to paint on me while my cock is inside you."

Asher pressed his lips together, so intent on hiding his smile.

Lev stroked the dimple at the corner of his mouth. "Is that a yes?"

"Yes, sir."

"Good." Lev kissed each of his dimples, then settled on the bed on his back, chilled skin warmed by the body heat Asher had left.

Asher hesitated, gaze darting between the palette Lev had already created, and the gunmetal toolbox filled with paint and art supplies on the desk.

"Use mine," Lev said.

Asher's color work was faultless, but watching his protégé paint with *his* colors felt like a blood bond in a way.

"What should I paint?" Asher asked, climbing onto Lev's lap.

"Surprise me. But first, I need you to come up here and sit on my face."

Asher's lips parted. "You were serious about that?"

"Gravely," Lev nodded. The mere suggestion had his cock lengthening. "I'm desperate to know what kind of art we can make when we're so connected neither of us knows where one ends and the other begins. An endless circle."

"An ouroboros."

"Precisely."

Asher crawled up Lev's body. Lev stopped him on the way, for a brief taste of Asher's cock before he ate him.

"Mm." All that wept precum tasted delicious.

Lev delved the tip of his tongue into Asher's slit, and hummed, cupping Asher's balls, heavy with cum. God, he wanted to drain them now, but he wanted inside Asher's arse more.

"Alright, love. Hold onto the headboard." Lev tipped his head back to watch him do exactly that. "Good lad. *Fuck me*, Blakely. You're so fucking sexy from this angle. You could suffocate me like this and I'd thank you."

Asher laughed. "I'd be pissed if you died, so don't."

"I'll do my best." Lev laughed, scooting down a smidge. "Have a seat now."

Lev wanted Asher to be in control, to actively consent rather than Lev pulling him downward.

"Lev," Asher said in a breathy sort of whimper.

"You are such a good lad, always pleasing me, worshipping me. It's my turn to take care of you."

As Asher lowered, Lev took a handful of each cheek and peeled him open with his thumbs until his tongue met his hole. Lev felt Asher's moan more than he heard it, so intently focused on kissing and coaxing him into opening, fingers mindlessly kneading his cheeks, toes curling at the sexual gratification of pleasing him. He could rim him for hours and still be famished.

Asher Blakely, the man he'd fallen in love with through a painting, was his, and he knew about Lev's terrifying fate, he knew he saw Silas, and he still wanted him.

"I'm ready," Asher said in a rush between panting breaths as he climbed off of Lev. "I can't wait."

Lev stroked the crest of Asher's hip bone. "Neither can I."

Asher pumped coconut oil onto his palm and slicked up Lev's hard cock with frenzied urgency, like it belonged to him, like Lev was just an instrument, a toy to use to get off.

Lev loved it.

With equal urgency, Lev stabilized his cock in one hand

and guided Asher downward. "Show me how well you can take me, how well you can paint on me."

"I will." Asher kissed Lev with tender adoration as he sank onto him in one smooth descent, fingernails digging deeper into Lev's pecs until he'd swallowed Lev completely.

"Bloody hell, Blakely." Lev's hands tightened on his hips.

Asher smirked, and raised a single eyebrow, the playful fire inside him rekindled. "What? I did what you asked."

"You listen too well." Lev grazed his fingers lightly over the place where his cock disappeared inside him. "How do you feel?"

"I feel like I'm yours, and like I want to come, but I want to be good more."

"You're always good, even when you aren't." Lev twirled his fingers through the forelock of dark hair that flounced down over his face. "I love you."

Asher pressed his forehead to his. "I love you too." He shifted his hips, and ground against him.

"Oh, no you don't." Lev stilled him with a hand on Asher's thigh. "Right now your only job is to keep my cock warm while you paint. The sooner you make me something pretty, the sooner I'll let you ride me."

"Let? We both know if I started riding you, you'd let me."

"That's true. But you want to please me, so I know you'll do as I ask." Lev palmed Asher's cock and squeezed. "I can't wait to reward you until you come all over whatever you paint for me."

Asher's brows darted together in agonized ecstasy, teeth sinking into his bottom lip, as his hole cinched tighter around Lev.

"Me too." He braced a hand on Lev's chest and reached for a fresh brush. "Close your eyes. I want it to be a surprise."

"You should cover my face with your boxer briefs so I don't peek."

Asher rolled his eyes, but acquiesced, fishing around in the sheets until he found them and draped them over his face, leaving his mouth clear.

"Heaven." Lev shivered at the first feathered caress of paintbrush bristles on his chest.

The sublime euphoria of serving as Asher's canvas turned Lev on even more, especially when paired with the degradation of his undergarment blindfold and Asher's scent surrounding him.

Lev's favorite artist, possibly one of the best modern artists alive, was painting on him.

What if Lev forgot this moment? The loss would be insurmountable. His heart ached in anticipatory grief. Tears stung his eyes. If only love could vanquish the hazy fog of dementia crawling closer every day. If only it could break the curse of his bloodline.

"Only now. Only me." Asher's slick, velvety cock slid over Lev's abs as he glided up Lev's cock and kissed him.

"How do you always know?"

Asher raked his hand through Lev's hair, scraping nails against his scalp. "Your art showed me your soul."

Was Lev's art really responsible for the strange way Asher read his mind? What if art really was as magic as Asher said? What if they'd built this bond and drew each other together? What if it wasn't divine intervention? What if they could make their own magic?

"I love you," Lev said.

"I love you too."

Asher sat back, seating himself fully on Lev's cock again.

"Only now," Asher said.

"Only you," Lev said.

Lev chanted the words like a spell inside his head as Asher's paintbrush returned to the space over his heart.

Wind wuthered across the moor. The gentle clink of a paintbrush stem rested against the plate. Bristles swirled in paint.

Like a Salvador Dali painting, time liquified into something intangible, measured by brush strokes and sensation—creamy paint, Asher's curled hand grazing his chest, bristles whispering against his skin, the tight heat enveloping his length, the occasional needy grunt as Asher adjusted his position.

Lev narrowed his attention down to only the path of Asher's paintbrush. Asher painted smooth lines arcing inward. A pair of half circles? Two crescent moons?

How had Asher lasted so long without breaking? Lev wanted to look, to flip Asher onto his back and topple their paint palette and make love that made art on the coverlet.

Lev released a low exhale and squeezed Asher's hips, holding him downward, lest Lev start fucking him on and off his cock.

"Ouch. Too tight," Asher said.

Lev relaxed his hands. "Shit. Sorry."

Asher laughed. "It's okay. I like it when you leave your mark on me too."

But Asher didn't like pain. Ben had ruined that. Part of why Lev was so committed to learning to tattoo was to help Asher reclaim the pleasure he got from pain—not because he wanted to hurt him in other ways.

Maybe tattooing his art would also help Lev repair his wounds. He'd never wanted to hurt Silas, but carving his art on Asher was different, because he wanted to be the one to put his art on Asher's body, even if it hurt him, and he knew how much Asher wanted that too.

The thought of it turned him on so much, some days he got an erection when he turned the tattoo machine on.

"Only now. Only me." Asher rocked back and forth in Lev's lap, shunting dopamine into Lev's bloodstream.

"Sorry. Would it help if you knew I was fantasizing about tattooing on you?"

"A little, but that's not only now, is it?" Asher stopped rocking after only a few tragic seconds.

"You're so mean to me, Blakely."

Asher scoffed. "You already got off."

"It would be easier if I could look at you. I promise not to peek."

"*Right.*"

"Did you roll your eyes?"

"Hush." Asher's paintbrush left him. A soft tink as he dropped it on the plate, then the swish of the bristles in paint. "I'm almost done."

Lev sighed theatrically. "I prefer instant gratification."

Delicate fine strokes kissed Lev's skin before Asher replied. "Any guesses yet?"

"Yes actually." The longer Asher had painted, the more sure he became. "An ouroboros."

Asher's brush paused.

"Close, but no."

Lev groaned as Asher's brush started up again. He clenched his abs, trying to stave off his desperation before he started begging.

Asher inhaled softly. His brush slowed. "Whatever it is you're doing, stop."

"You can't actually feel me flexing inside you." Lev's lips curled into a smile. He reached sightlessly until he found Asher's cock, and wrapped his hand around it, twisting as he stroked him.

"You're cheating," Asher said, sex seeping into his voice.

"All's fair in love and art."

Lev rubbed his fingers over Asher's glans, and lifted them in the vague direction of Asher's face. Like the good lad he was, Asher sucked them into his mouth and hummed, continuing to suck as he painted.

"You spoil me." Lev tightened his hand around Asher's cock, slowly increasing the pace.

The paintbrush clattered against the plate. Asher ripped his boxer briefs from Lev's face.

"Hurry and look before I come all over it."

"Don't you dare." Lev held Asher in place and looked down.

His vision blurred on vibrant raw sienna, goldenrod, and crimson before his eyes focused on hundreds of delicate feathers gracing a pair of phoenixes flying toward each other, long tails of plumage curling together to complete a circle.

A frisson of electricity lifted the hair all over Lev's body. Pleasure and aching need burned through his bloodstream. Viewing Asher's art while they were still connected, while playing his canvas, overwhelmed Lev's senses and broke down all his defenses.

"This is... Ash, I don't quite know what to say that won't be woefully inadequate. This is the most beautiful piece of art I've ever seen, and so much more impressive because you managed all of this while I was inside you, and doing my very best to distract you."

Asher smiled as a dusty rose blush bloomed on his cheeks. "Really?"

"You mixed your own colors, didn't you? That's why they're so much more striking."

Asher shook his head slowly, smile growing to a rare grin. "Maybe it's the canvas," he teased.

"How are you such a magician with color?"

"Sorry. It's a secret technique. That's why I blindfolded you."

Lev nodded, thumb stroking Asher's hip.

"It's a phoenix ouroboros," Asher said. "Sort of. Instead of a single phoenix devouring its tail, I chose two meeting in the middle because we're rising from the ashes together."

Lev's heart hurt in a good way, the kind of way that felt transformative, and whether Asher had intended to or not, his pair of phoenixes summarized precisely how starkly their relationship differed from the one he'd had with Silas.

Lev and Asher weren't codependent. They both took care of each other. They were a team instead of a single entity.

"You're a genius, Blakely. Do you know that?"

Asher snorted. "It's just a play on a cliche."

"What have I said about rejecting compliments?"

"I'm pretty sure you said you'd bend me over your lap and make me come over and over until I got dehydrated."

"Are you sure I said that? You know how seriously I take your hydration and food consumption." Lev peered down at the phoenixes again. "I'm so lucky."

"I'm lucky too." Asher arced down and kissed him, connecting them like the phoenix ouroboros that was theirs alone.

Asher reached for his sketchbook, the one he now openly left on his bedside table because Lev had earned his trust after months of good behavior. He wrote something on the page.

"What are you doing?"

"A new ritual." Asher tore the sheet of paper out and passed the book and pen to him. "Write down what's haunting you and fold it in half. We're leaving the past behind us."

"What did you write?"

Asher handed it to him. "It's supposed to be a secret, but I know you won't judge me."

I let him hurt me
and that makes me
weak

"You aren't weak."

Asher snatched the paper back. "I know that, but it still haunts me, and I want to leave that behind. I'm sure I'll disagree with whatever you write too."

If only you knew...

"But I'm not going to read yours," Asher continued. "I want

you to be honest. This is our ritual and it won't work if it's bullshit."

Lev tore a sheet of paper out and folded it in half, afraid to transfer an indent, and wrote:

I killed Silas because I was afraid.

He folded it in half again.

Asher held out his empty hand. "Give it to me."

Lev opened his mouth but no sound came out.

"If you don't trust me not to read it when I promised I wouldn't, then you have no business saying you love me."

"You can love someone you don't trust," Lev handed it over, "but I do trust you."

Clutching both pieces of paper in one hand, Asher climbed off of Lev's cock with a sexy grunt, and nearly fell off the bed. Lev lurched upward to catch him, but his knightly services weren't required as Asher righted himself and hopped down from the bed.

"Where are you going?"

"The fireplace in front of me, obviously," Asher said, dry sarcasm in full force.

Lev followed him. "What happened to my good lad?"

Asher shushed him and kneeled before the fire. "Now, we burn them."

"Mm. I like you all witchy like this, making your own magic."

"Take this seriously," Asher said, and shushed him again.

"Of course. Sorry."

Asher lowered his own confession to the flames, and Lev followed suit.

"I know this won't erase years of trauma and whatever villainy you think you're guilty of," Asher said, "but today we let it burn, and rise from the ashes."

As flames consumed Lev's confession, he almost believed forgiving himself could one day happen.

"I'm proud of you," Asher said.

"I'm proud of you too." Lev pulled Asher to his feet, and hauled him into his arms, kissing him on the way to the bed.

"Sit against the headboard," Asher directed.

"Mm. I love it when you're bossy," Lev said, assuming the position as requested.

All thoughts of art and rituals and coping with humor left his head as Asher crawled onto his lap, and crashed their lips together. Lev searched for the coconut oil without looking.

Asher found the oil and took over, slicking up Lev's cock again in that same dehumanizing manner as if Lev were a toy, except now their eyes were locked together and Asher had marked him with their sigil.

They fucked in a frenzy exactly the same way they'd kissed in the chapel, like they were afraid they were going to destroy each other but wanted to love each other more.

Using the headboard for leverage, Asher fucked himself harder, cock swinging in tantalizing synchrony.

Asher released the headboard, still riding his cock, and framed Lev's face in his hands, connecting their gazes until everything else faded. "Give me your fears, your regret. Show me your scars, your darkest parts, the side of you you're afraid of. You're my god and I'm your servant. I'll never stop worshipping you no matter how much you think you're a villain."

Such loyalty and forgiveness from a man Lev worshipped with equal fervor was too much for a mere mortal to experience. Lev's toes curled, his fingers scrambled to slow Asher's pace.

"I can't, Ash... I'm going to..."

"Do it," Asher gasped, muscles trembling beneath Lev's hands. "Come for me. I need you to. Fuck."

In a desperate attempt to get Asher off before he did, Lev took Asher's cock in his tight grip, dug his heels into the bed, and lifted his arse off the mattress, thrusting upward to drive his cock directly against Asher's prostate.

Asher fell forward with a long moan of anguished euphoria. His eyes rolled back. His hole bore down around Lev's cock, and rapturous bliss exploded across Lev's body, so powerful darkness bled into his vision and stars burst into existence.

Lev didn't slow, intent upon fucking every last drop of his come into Asher's hole. Asher cradled Lev's face and kissed him with such ardent devotion that tears blurred Lev's vision, and then Asher came too as if witnessing Lev's rapture was what he'd been waiting for, as if all along he'd still been worshipping Lev, not taking his own pleasure, and was only coming now because it was what his god demanded.

They both collapsed, catching their breath. Lev kissed the crown of his head and stroked his thumb over the pulse point in Asher's neck, joining his steady pulse with Asher's frantic one.

The tide rolled ashore as Lev held him, long after they'd both softened, unwilling to part them. Asher's breathing slowed. Lev would gladly stand vigil all night so Asher could sleep peacefully, still connected in their ouroboros.

"I wish you could see yourself the way I do," Asher said, lifting his head.

"You're awake."

"Not really. I'm sleep talking." Asher inhaled, shuddering like he'd just finished a long crying jag instead of fucking Lev nearly to death.

"Let's get you cleaned up then."

"No," Asher whined, eyes closed.

Lev clicked his tongue. "You wore yourself out."

Asher shushed him.

When Lev pointed out how uncomfortable sleeping with paint flake confetti would be, Asher soaked in the tub while Lev changed the sheets. Later, when Asher was safe in his arms and high tide whispered below, Lev finally did as Asher had asked and tried to see himself through Asher's eyes.

To Asher, Leviathan wasn't the wicked monster that was his namesake.

Asher saw beauty. But not like a landscape or a flower. Lev was a painting that showed him the world could be beautiful even when it was ugly as long as there was art.

Lev knew because he felt precisely the same way.

CATHEDRAL OF HIS CHEST

LEV

FEBRUARY 27

A steady downpour murmured through the window panes. Lev shivered. He should light a fire, but he'd burned through the stash of firewood in his study, and couldn't be arsed to pillage firewood from elsewhere, let alone risk waking Asher.

Lev pushed back from his desk, and rested against the cognac leather wingback chair. Speaking of cognac, he pulled out the bottle he kept in the lower drawer and refilled his glass.

He drank and swallowed, and drank again, then tapped the keyboard to wake his computer, and typed a missive to his neurologist and psychiatrist.

While Lev saw both physicians once per quarter, they hadn't evaluated him in person for some time. Given how quickly his symptoms were progressing, he thought it prudent to ask them to make a house call to Lichenmoor.

Lev had stopped searching for a diagnosis years ago, afraid that if he lost that last evolutionary shred of hope, he'd leap from Lichenmoor's cliffs.

There was no way to prove ghosts existed, and even if they

tested for every psychological and neurological condition in existence, he'd still always wonder.

But he had Asher now.

Not all cases of Alzheimer's were hereditary, but given Father and Grandfather's history, it was likely they shared a gene for familial Early-onset Alzheimer's.

If that was the case, Lev had a fifty-percent chance of inheriting the same gene. Asher deserved that clarity, and Lev needed to know if Silas was real.

Lev's mind kept circling back to the day Rebecca had spooked and taken Asher to the mausoleum. What if Silas had wanted to hurt Asher when Rebecca rocketed across the field?

What if Silas *could* hurt Asher? What if Silas had lured Asher out during high tide the day he nearly drowned? What if Silas had caused Father's death?

God, he sounded mad, but no harm could ever come to Asher. Lev would send him away if he had to in order to keep him safe.

Next, he emailed his therapist to inquire about more aggressive agoraphobia treatment. While he and Asher's daily jaunts had helped, his progress had stalled.

Asher's suggestion that Lev leave on horseback had nearly worked. Lev *had* been able to leave, but only if Asher rode in the same saddle with him, and while Lev *had* traveled farther than he had on foot, that was only because a horse covered more ground. His agoraphobia had chased him and Asher right back inside in about the same amount of time.

Silas's snide and gleeful commentary upon Lev's return amplified the humiliation and impotency Lev already felt.

Lev needed to hurry. One day, Asher would feel as trapped as Lev had with Silas. Not to mention, if Asher *was* in danger, perhaps Lev could leave with him.

Silas materialized in front of the fireplace. "Our Asher certainly has a type—older, prone to fits of anger, sketches younger men when they're naked."

Asher had begged Lev to paint him in the nude to reclaim the sensual blend of his passion for art and his passion for Lev. But Lev had only acquiesced after Asher agreed to let Lev burn the painting after. While Asher's trust humbled Lev, he never wanted Asher to fear it falling into the wrong hands as it had with Ben.

Lev shifted his attention back to Asher, asleep on the sofa, dressed in nothing more than the jacket Lev had insisted he wear after they'd made love in front of the fireplace.

"Poor Asher fell in love with his hero only for his hero to be the villain," Silas said.

Lev didn't want to be a villain anymore.

Asher was so young, his life a sketch waiting to be filled in. What if Lev could live like that with him? What if he could start over with a blank canvas, one not marred with blood stains, scribbles, and scratches? What if he could have a second chance?

Silas dragged the pad of his index finger along the mantle and frowned, rubbing his finger and thumb together as if checking for dust. Had he left a line in the dust? Lev stifled the urge to rush across the room and look.

"Lie to yourself all you like, Levvy, but I'm the dark truth, the proof of your villainy, no matter how much you try to ignore me."

Adrenaline and fury spiked in Lev's bloodstream. He gnashed his teeth together, quite literally biting back his words.

Starving Silas of attention was the only tool he had left.

Silas pushed off the mantle and sauntered over to the desk.

"I've had a lot of time on my hands while you've been so preoccupied. I can't wait to show off my new skills." Silas hopped on the corner of the desk, leaned close, and whispered, "Careful Levvy. One day, I'll learn how to manifest myself physically. Then what will you do?"

Silas's threat echoed Lev's own growing fears that with

each passing day, he wasn't losing more of himself to Alzheimer's, but feeding his soul to Silas.

Lev drained the rest of his glass and scrubbed his face with his hands.

He closed his laptop and picked up the sketch he'd finished while Asher slept.

The watercolor palette he'd mixed and left to dry was ready to work with. Art was his only reprieve from Silas's haunting.

He plucked up his brush and began with the base tone of Asher's skin, searching for ripples in his glass of water each time Silas repositioned his perch on the desk.

"Lev?" Asher sat up, blinking blearily.

"I'm here, baby. Did I wake you?" Lev darted a glance to Silas, but he wasn't there.

Lev couldn't quite remember the last time he'd seen him. Had art banished him, even if temporarily?

Asher's dimples flashed with a soft smile as he pushed his hair out of his face. Lev's barber visited Lichenmoor once each month, but Asher's hair grew faster.

Shampooing and conditioning his lad's hair, then trimming it between visits, had become one of Lev's most treasured memories.

He'd painted each occurrence, focusing on the delicate details he couldn't bear to forget—the shade of near-black that warmed into dark chocolate under bright light, the soft swirl of the cowlick hidden beneath his luscious waves, the bottom right corner of his hairline on the back of his neck that Lev loved to kiss.

Asher crossed the room, swimming in Lev's coat and leaned his hip against the desk. He lifted the drained glass of cognac, and sniffed. "Couldn't sleep or breakfast of champions?"

"The latter. That's how I still have all my hair. It's a secret recipe."

Asher rolled his eyes, and unzipped his jacket, gooseflesh

pebbling over his tattoos, cock already hard. Had the caress of Lev's coat on his bare skin turned him on, or Lev himself?

"Mr. Blakely, whatever happened to your clothes?" Lev tugged Asher's sleeve, coaxing him closer, and exposing one shoulder.

As an artist, Lev had always appreciated the beauty of the human body, the sensuality of every frame and shape and texture, but Asher's shoulders were equally salacious and architectural. Lev wanted to latch his mouth on the curve of the joint and suck.

Asher swallowed, drawing Lev's eyes down the line of his sternum and around the ouroboros encircling his navel to the cock he longed to suck.

"Mm. You wear this far better than me, but I think I need to see your other shoulder to be certain." He tugged the other sleeve, and his smart lad caught on, shrugging the jacket down to his elbows.

"What are you painting?" Asher asked.

Lev shifted his palette and glass of water to the side. "You, of course."

"This is how you see me?" Asher asked, peering closer.

"Your beauty is otherworldly, but I'm only human."

Lev added a flush of scarlet to the Asher's cheeks, a mirror image to the blush he sported now.

Siphoning inspiration from reality was a well-worn tool in any artist's arsenal, but when the muses favored him, Lev traded his cage for a place outside of Lichenmoor where art and life bled together, and reality and fantasy shared the same bed, where a single drop of paint bloomed into an ocean and brushstrokes grew mountains.

"What are you thinking?" Lev said, drawing closer, disturbing dust motes that sparkled in the firelight like fireflies.

"You stole the blush in my cheeks and turned it into art."

"Yes. Well, you are, after all, a live portrait, my model, my muse since I met you."

Asher trapped his bottom lip between his teeth.

"You like it when I call you my muse, don't you?" Lev pressed a thumb against Asher's bottom lip, slowly freeing the delicate tissue from between his teeth. "Hm?"

Asher shivered, sexy eyes almost shutting as he blinked slowly. "Yes."

"I thought so." Lev leaned forward and whispered against the shell of Asher's ear, "I wish you could trap me inside a painting and take me away from here."

A tantalizing flush crept down his chest, the kind he ordinarily had only after he climaxed.

"Lev..."

Silas reappeared behind Asher, hands gripping his shoulders.

Lev flinched. "Blakely, be a good lad and come here." He extended his hand.

Asher's brows darted together, sparing a single glance to where Silas stood, where Asher couldn't possibly see him.

Lev dragged Asher closer, nipped the parka back over his shoulders and pinned him safely between his widened knees and the desk.

"He's here, isn't he?" Asher asked.

"Tell him, Levvy." Silas leered over Asher's shoulder. "Let's see what he says. Maybe that will send him away. Maybe then you'll pay."

"He is," Lev answered after a damning amount of time had passed.

Asher looked over his shoulder and shivered. "What does he want?"

Lev planted his hands on Asher's hips and bowed his head against his chest.

"He wants me to suffer. He wants me to lose you."

Asher clutched Lev's head to his chest. "You won't lose

me." Asher's jaw hardened. His spine straightened. He lifted his chin. "Fuck him."

Silas feigned a gag. "No, thank you."

Asher ran his fingers through Lev's hair absently, as if they were so close, comforting the other comforted them both.

"You've suffered long enough, Lev."

"Thank you for trusting me when I say he's there, and for not treating me as insane as I feel."

"I'll always trust you, and you can trust me to take care of you. Whatever Silas is, we'll fight him together. If he's a ghost, we'll haunt him with our happiness, and if he isn't..." Asher's countenance turned troubled. "Sometimes the monsters in our heads are the most difficult to defeat, but we will win."

If Silas was Alzheimer's, there was nothing to fight; only memories lost with the passing of time.

"I've messaged my medical team asking them to examine me here. Perhaps I could try another round of medications."

"I think that's a good idea."

"Which way are you leaning?" Lev asked. "Ghost or hallucination?"

"I don't know..." Asher trapped his bottom lip between his teeth again. Color flooded the blanched crescent indent he'd left as he said, "Sometimes I think I see him in the shadows, or even feel him."

Lev's head snapped up as if he expected to find Silas touching Asher now, perhaps quietly curling his fingers around his throat. But Silas had disappeared again.

"Feel him, how?"

"I don't know," Asher repeated, and looked down at his hands. "I feel watched, or like I'm not actually alone. Before I knew you saw him, when you gained that faraway daze, I often *felt* a strange sense that someone was there. Maybe it's just wishful thinking."

"Wishful?"

Asher met Lev's gaze with doleful eyes. "I want Silas to be a ghost so badly that I don't know if I'm just reaching for proof that isn't there because I don't want you to have Alzheimer's."

Lev's heart rended in two. He thought he'd come to terms with the fact that he'd die an agonizingly slow death lost in the catacomb spiderwebs of his fucked up head, but witnessing Asher navigate the same path to acceptance rekindled his grief.

"I understand, and I'm so very sorry," Lev said.

Asher cradled Lev's face between his hands. "I'm not sorry. I'll never be anything other than grateful that you brought me here so I could love you."

"I'm afraid I'll always be sorry for the pain I may one day cause you, but to love you and be loved by you is the only time I've ever been truly happy, and I'm grateful too."

Grateful *and* guilty. Lev didn't deserve to be happy after what he'd done.

"Did Silas leave?" Asher asked.

Lev nodded gently, face still cradled in Asher's hands. Vanquishing Silas, even temporarily, was too precious to acknowledge aloud.

"I felt him before, and now I don't," Asher said.

"Good. That's..." Lev's composure collapsed under the weight of his relief and grief, and something he hadn't felt since Father had died—hope.

Asher curled over Lev, cocooning him beneath the cathedral of his chest, and in that sublime sliver of liminal space, Lev vowed to sacrifice his soul, shackle himself to Silas, and spend an eternity walking circles in the mist, if only to remember him.

When Lev later checked the mantle, there was no line in the dust to prove Silas's existence. There was no dust at all.

PASSION TO DOLDRUMS

ASHER

MARCH 2

Asher woke in the dark, dazed, heart racing from a nightmare of being trapped by high tide, unable to move, waiting for the ocean to consume him.

It didn't help that the sea had surged while he'd slept and sounded even closer than it usually did. At least the weight on his chest making each craven breath more difficult was Lev's arm, rather than a sleep paralysis demon.

The slow, fluttering pulse of Lev's heart pressed against Asher's side felt like the wings of a butterfly in his palms, each beat washing away more of his nightmare and replacing it with blissful scenes from the night before.

Asher had spread himself flat on his back and begged Lev to reward his good lad with his cum until Lev braced his hands on the headboard, and fucked Asher's mouth the way he fucked his hole. Lev hadn't let Asher swallow until Asher had come all over himself with only a few jerks and Lev's filthy words.

Wind whistled down the chimney with a puff of ash

scenting the air before it slipped between the gaps in the sheets, lifting them like a parachute. An unlatched gate screeched and slammed shut with a metallic clamor that rattled his teeth.

Asher rolled onto his side with his back to Lev, who even in sleep, pulled Asher into his arms, until they were skin against skin.

Lightning flashed. Asher tensed. He hated waiting for thunder to follow. Lev, on the other hand, regularly slept through soul reckoning thunderstorms that kept Asher up all night. The clap of thunder wasn't very loud, but it took Asher by surprise and startled him all the same.

The next stab of lightning lit up the room. Asher's skin prickled, not with electricity or cold, but fear because someone was standing in the corner by the door, eyes glinting obsidian in the dark. Asher's heart leapt to his throat, but the next flash of lightning revealed an empty corner.

What the fuck?

A floorboard creaked in the hall outside their door. The thin gap of dim lamplight under the door shuddered as if someone had walked by. No. It was much more likely that the electricity had flickered than an intruder was taking a midnight stroll down the hallway.

Unless it was Silas.

The doorknob rattled, but that could have been wind flitting through the keyhole. Right? Or it was someone trying to break in. Maybe Asher was hallucinating, scaring himself with his flight of fears.

But what if it was Silas?

Asher carefully inched out of Lev's hold and pulled on a hoodie and sweatpants over his bare skin. He carried his shoes to the door. If Asher had been sneaking out of his own room, he'd never have had a chance with how loud the hinges were, but Lev's door was silent, or at least silent against the drumroll of raindrops as Asher slid through the door and closed it behind him.

The hall was empty.

Asher would have turned around and climbed back in bed were it not for the tapestry at the end of the hall flapping with the wind, lifting up just enough to reveal the secret door to the east wing was open.

Okay, maybe Lev had forgotten to lock the door. Maybe the wind had pushed through the centuries-old lock so fiercely the door unlatched. Or maybe, just fucking maybe, Lev wasn't going to forget everything about himself and Silas was a ghost leading him to that forbidden hall.

Asher ducked his head under the tapestry. His love for Lev was the only thing that gave him the courage to close the secret door shut behind him and walk into the dark.

The east wing was dusty, but otherwise untouched, and the long, abandoned hallway was far less menacing than the passageway. Asher flicked the light switch, illuminating stone walls lined with dull moth-eaten tapestries and ceilings held up by arched wooden beams, details he hadn't noticed, or remembered before.

His footsteps were overloud as he followed the prints he and Lev had left, careful not to leave a single fresh print to betray him over what felt like hallowed ground toward the locked door at the end of the hall.

If Silas had led him there, he was hiding. The only footsteps he heard were his own. What if he'd chased nothing more than his imagination down that passageway?

The skeleton key fit easily into the lock, but the door was stuck. Was something blocking it? He shoved his shoulder against the door, and with a creak that sounded like a scream, the door opened.

Dust stung his eyes. He sneezed twice. When his vision cleared, he jumped back into the hallway like a startled cat. A man stood in the corner, nose pointed toward the wall. Asher's heart hammered in his ears. The primitive part of his brain yelled it was time to run.

What. The. Fuck?

Wait, was Silas real? Had Lev locked him inside? Had Silas never died? Asher's panic-addled brain suggested a dozen absurd outcomes before his brain turned off completely, and Nonna's lessons about manners took over.

"I'm sorry. I didn't realize this room was occu..." he trailed off.

The man was too still.

"Oh, for fuck's sake." Asher strode into the room and flipped the light switch.

Lichenmoor was creepy enough already without Lev stashing a life-sized statue inside a locked room to jump-scare trespassers. He slipped around the steamer trunk beside the statue to confront Lev's lost love head-on.

Who else would Lev have kept under lock and key, hidden away like he'd hidden the truth about why he'd invited Asher here?

Silas Morrigan looked exactly as Asher had expected him to. Even in stone, Asher's stomach plummeted with jealousy. Milky marble matched Silas's skin tone, and large eyes made him spritely.

Asher touched Silas's cold lips, trailed his fingers down his neck, along the sharp collarbone like he had in Lucian's studio. His hands roamed over Silas's shoulders, down slender arms to the dead man's hands. Each finger was highly detailed, from wrinkled knuckles to the prints etched onto the pads of his fingers.

Lev must have started the sculpture when Silas was alive.

Or used photos. Fingerprints, maybe? Lev wouldn't have forged them. Then they'd be meaningless. The lower half of the statue was still in progress, thank fuck. Asher had no interest in comparing dick lengths.

The scent of fresh oil paint dragged his attention to painted canvases on a rack. More were stacked against the longest wall, backs to the room, like the statue had been.

"Why doesn't he want to see you?" Asher asked the statue.

Maybe because he saw Silas all the time against his will... But then why would he spend countless hours painting him?

Asher sidled out from behind the statue and flipped through the paintings on the rack. The first was a portrait that hurt to look at because Asher would never be able to paint something so beautiful.

Most of the paintings were unvarnished, some still tacky. All of them were of the man with an elven face and raven hair so black it was nearly blue. The twin to the statue, the rightful owner of the ouroboros encircling Asher's navel.

Silas.

Loose plastic sheeting prevented the canvases against the wall from sticking together. He tilted one away from its neighbor. Silas's blue eyes glared from the painting, glossy and rimmed red, like he'd spent all night crying. The longer Asher stared, the more convinced he was that Silas wasn't sad. He was fuming.

"What happened to you?"

He wedged his fingers between the next pair of canvases. Another of Silas, this time with a small smirk of pleasure. The next was Silas too. On and on it went. Lev had cataloged every manner of emotion, varying perspectives, positions, angles of light. He'd studied Silas in shadow. In firelight. From the throes of passion to the doldrums of depression.

The realization that Asher stood no chance against the object of such adoration and obsession hit him square in the chest and froze his marrow. Lev was lost in the past, in love with a ghost. Meanwhile, Asher had a fanatical celebrity crush. He swallowed back salty tears and blinked before they fell.

Thunder boomed. Asher scarcely noticed, too engrossed in Silas. He turned away from Lev's art with dull resignation. Someday Lev would forget Asher, but never Silas.

A love like that transcended death.

Lightning slipped through the gaps in the curtains and caught on an open steamer trunk. Was it open when he'd first entered the room? Asher looked back at the statue. Of course it hadn't moved.

Asher almost skipped the trunk. What was the point? Lev didn't seem like the kind of person to stuff his ex's body in a box, but Asher should at least check that Silas's mummified body wasn't inside.

He pushed the trunk open wider. Neatly folded clothes were stacked in a row like books on a shelf. He pulled a collared shirt out. A cross was embroidered on the left side of the shirt with HALLOWED SAINTS in script beneath it. The shirt was smaller than Silas's statue suggested.

Asher had imagined Silas as a much less intimidating teenager just out of high school. But maybe not. How long had Silas lived before he died? Asher knew so little. He unfolded a knit sweater, and stopped just short of holding it up to the statue, afraid to embarrass himself in front of Lev's dead ex in the off chance ghosts did exist.

Had Lev kept Silas's clothes so he could hold them to his chest, knowing that was the closest he'd ever get to touching Silas again? Asher's heart broke twofold, for Lev's loss most, and for himself. Asher couldn't compete with a ghost—metaphor, or not.

He carefully shifted the clothes to the side, and found stacks of paperbound notebooks. Silas had been a writer. That made sense. The faded black notebook on top stood out from the ones beneath. The pages didn't lay flat, but fluffed up, wrinkled, not from water damage, but like they'd been referred to again and again.

On the top right corner of the cover, someone had drawn a simplified ouroboros the size of a wedding band. Inside the circle was the letter 'L'. He shouldn't read it, especially if it was Lev's diary. Then again, Lev had stolen Asher's notebook without hesitation.

Asher peeled the cover back.

SALT AND DAMP EARTH

ASHER

If it was a diary, it didn't belong to Lev. The delicate, slanted script inside bore no relation to Lev's bold, artistic scrawl.

Lev,

I miss you desperately.

I can't eat, I can hardly sleep, but I can write and so I will. First, I tried writing you a letter, but then how would I send it?

Wouldn't it be romantic if we wrote letters in notebooks and swapped them like we did when we were younger? I'll give this one to you when I return to Lichenmoor.

If I return.

Silas

Lev,

Do you know what I miss the most, Levvy? Not your touch, surprisingly enough.

I miss the safety of being known. Because you see me. All of me. You understand that I'm a row of dominoes that have started to fall and I keep racing to add another domino in front, knowing the next one will fall, and the next and the next.

All my life I didn't know why I kept racing to add another domino, why I didn't let the last one fall. But then I met you, and now each new day is for you.

If I think too long on it, I'll cry, and I know you hate when I cry, so I suppose I'll end this here.

Silas

ASHER FELT like he'd just met the man behind the statue.

"What happened to you?" he asked Silas again, in the empty room so full of him.

He flipped the page. Silas wrote every day, adding dominoes for Lev like he'd said.

Some entries were short:

Lev,

Last night it rained and I dreamed I was at Lichenmoor. I could scarcely get out of bed. I wish I never woke up.

My only motivation? Avoiding Sister Agatha's
ire.

Silas

Other entries contained poems, some of them surprisingly
good. Others, a moody teenager's attempt at being profound.
His tone grew more dreary with each page turned.

Lev,

I no longer like the color orange.
Or the cinnamon sprinkled on my toast.
When I go outside I don't look up.
A single salt crystal tastes like the ocean on your
lips.
Everything reminds me of you.

Silas

Hello Snake,

Mum visited today.
I refused to speak to her. I wish she'd died
instead of my father. She said I was being melodramatic when I informed her.
Of course I'm melodramatic. I'm a poet!
Where do you think I learned it from?
Next, she shared the most delightful revelation
that she found one of your letters in my room. I
didn't believe her until she showed it to me.

She spent the rest of the visit praying for my tarnished soul. Next time I'll pretend I'm a good Catholic boy, if only to avoid the headache.

I'm told you're doing well without me. Mum says you've moved on, and I should too. Again, I didn't believe her, but she anticipated that too and brought news clippings.

Rugby team captain. Lauded for your new art series. Photographed all across university with heiresses more in line with your breeding than me.

Of course my hag of a mum thinks I'd actually believe you'd moved on to women, and that if I learned you were behaving so sensibly, I'd outgrow this silly little phase too.

But that's not how it works, Mummy. Sexual orientation isn't something I can solve with piety and a rosary. I have as much power to choose who I love as I have power to return to Lichenmoor. None.

Then there's you, Brother. You think you have no choice but to be perfect, but you're simply too afraid to choose me.

Perhaps if you weren't doing so well, Father would try harder to bring me home.

I resent you for that too, for mattering more to him than me, for being born by him, for having a life outside of me when the only thing I have is you.

I just have one question:
Did you move on?
Please tell me how. I'd like to move on too.

Silas

SILAS'S next entry came a week later. He'd broken his daily streak.

Lev,

The sisters have taken issue with me. Maybe God told them I'm hell-bound. More likely Mum.

Beating me over the head with a bible has done little to cleanse my soul, and I can't tell you how many hours I've spent on my knees with my rosary to no avail.

Instead of praying, I bite my tongue until it bleeds, and when the bleeding stops, I bite again.

Silas

Lev,

For the first time in my life,
I don't want to write.
It's like my words no longer belong to me.
Every line is clumsy as if someone

turned my prose into mockery.
God has deemed me unworthy.
And now I've lost my poetry.
Yes, Levvy, I know that rhymed,
but that's the point I'm trying to make.
Rhyming doesn't turn tangled words into poetry.

Silas

Lev,

Without you, life is starved of all meaning. You
were the only star in my wretched solar system,
and now I'm lost in an endless black abyss, and
I fucking hate astronomy and overwrought cliches,
but as I've said, my words have left me.
Like you did.

Silas

Lev,

Mum visited again, and when she saw how
skeletal I've become she threatened to have me
institutionalized.

I can't go back there.

Good thing she didn't see the cuts I've been
carving.

Don't worry. I'll be careful. I leave my
marks where only you can see.

You're disappointed. I know. You'll be so

angry when you find the fresh scars over my old ones. If you care to look at all.

Silas

Lev,

I hate you for showing me what I was missing, for giving me what I now can't live without.

There's a beam over my bed. Sometimes I look at it and think all I'd have to do is sling a rope around it and leap.

I think I'll try to run away first.

Silas

Lev,

I didn't make it far. I didn't have change for the phone booth, or coins for the bus toll.

The sisters delight in doling out my punishment. Yardsticks on knuckles. Caning and the like.

Who gave them the authority? God?

I could overpower them.

Would it be melodramatic if I strangled them with my rosary?

Silas

Lev,

I don't know what I expected. Instead of dying, I panicked, and kicked the lamp off of my night stand, just before my bedsheet-rope broke.

The sisters were mad about the lamp I'd broken. They made me kneel on the broken glass, but they couldn't break me.

Losing you did that.

Silas

EACH PAGE BECAME HARDER to turn. Heavier. Like the paper pulp had been laced with lead.

Why had Lev saved this? Why were the pages so worn? Why was Lev punishing himself?

Lev,

I refused to kneel for my last punishment. Sister Agatha beat me but I wouldn't bend. She was furious.

The victory was intoxicating. I'd finally stopped letting things happen and made them happen instead.

But that didn't last long. Never underestimate Sister Agatha.

I hate you so much.

I've already opened my chest, wrenched my

ribs apart, and showed you what hurt. You know why I don't believe in God, why I can't step foot in Lichenmoor's church.

I've been banished here because of you. And now you've just moved on?

There's a small statue of the Virgin Mary on Sister Agatha's desk. I think I might bludgeon her to death with it.

Don't worry. I won't actually do that, but only because I have to see you again, even if I have to wait until I'm seventeen.

Even if I hate you.

Silas

Lev,

This time when Mum visited I told her I'd changed. Satan no longer slithered through my veins. Then I asked if I could leave.

She said she'd pray for me.

I found a shard of glass under my bed from when I'd been made to kneel after my failed suicide attempt.

Almost as if God has given me His blessing.

Silas

Lev,

You didn't visit me at the hospital.

I suspect Father didn't want you to know, lest it distract you on the rugby pitch or steer you off course from your perfect future.

But I still hate you for not coming for me. Why haven't you come for me?

Silas

Lev,

I wish you would have called sooner, but apparently it takes two suicide attempts for my mum to let us talk.

Silas

Lev,

Father called. Not mine, of course since he's dead. Yours.

I'm to pack my bags, but I won't until he gets here, and I won't believe I'm coming home until I step foot in Lichenmoor's foyer.

I won't even let myself remember the scent of salt and damp earth, the taste of the ocean, the wind howling across the moor.

Even if I come home, I don't think I'll ever feel at home again.

Anywhere.

I'm disposable. Sent away and forgotten. I could spend a night, a week, a month at Lichenmoor only to be put out with the rubbish bins.

What if you don't want me anymore? What if you never did?

I'm afraid there's no happy ending for us. Or at least not for me. You, however, will land on your feet, just like you always do.

I should destroy this notebook, but instead I think I'll give it to you, so you know everything I've been through because I loved you.

I suffered while we were apart.

Did you?

Silas

ASHER RETURNED the notebook to the trunk. When had he started crying? He wiped his cheeks with the inside of his hoodie and looked around the room, almost expecting him to be there.

Silas.

The man who'd left his mark on every inch of Lev's heart, who, even in death, felt so alive, Asher almost heard him breathing in the silence. Or maybe Lev had poured so much of his own soul into resurrecting the lover he'd lost that he'd left a sentient presence like a poltergeist.

Asher stood before the cold statue. The rungs of his ribs stuck out too much, even on a frame as lithe as Silas's was, and his fae-like features had taken on a sinister sharpness, his large eyes too sunken and owlish. Had the tips of his lips been curled into a smirk before?

Lightning flashed and the resultant thunder shot chills down Asher's spine. He felt dizzy, the air stifling.

Asher was overcome with the strangest compulsion to kneel at the statue's feet and weep. He wanted to atone, to trade his life for Silas's own, to give Lev the man he'd lost, the man who'd survived so much.

He pressed his palm against Silas's hand, smaller than his own. How many times had Lev done the same, wishing the hand he held was warm? He said goodbye to the multitudes Silas had once contained, goodbye to the shards of Lev's heart trapped inside his art.

Dust stung his eyes again. He sniffed. Fine. Maybe it wasn't the dust.

Asher closed the door on Silas and locked it, knowing he'd never know Lev as well as Silas had, and Lev would never love him as much as he'd loved Silas, knowing a lock would never keep Silas out.

TEMPEST

LEV

MARCH 2

Lev woke to an almighty crash, followed by ricochets of shattering glass, and a cacophonous squall. Dazed, dusting the cobwebs from his dreams, he reached for Asher. The poor lad would be freezing. The bed was empty.

Lev bolted upright and pulled the string of the bedside lamp, blinking like a nocturnal animal forced into daylight. A frigid gale wailed across the moor, a sound far from foreign, yet this time it carried an ominous warning. Fistfuls of hail hurtled at the windows, so loud it was like a firecracker in a kettle. A different storm was coming.

Surely Asher was in the bathroom. He hated high tide on full moon nights when the gravitational pull dragged the ocean even closer to the castle. He wouldn't have gone far. But Asher wasn't there. Or in the room next door.

With rising worry, Lev rushed back to their room, dragged the bedside table away from the wall with a groan of wood against wood, and pressed one of the dozens of roses carved into the points of each square of wood paneling. The false wood panel fell into his waiting hand.

Reaching past the bag of photographs, the silver jewelry box, and a handful of spare skeleton keys, Lev pulled out the GPS tracker that paired with the wristwatch he'd made Asher promise to wear.

Asher would disapprove if he knew Lev was tracking him like a pet with a microchip, but he wasn't meant to know. The last thing Lev wanted was Asher to leave it behind before going off on his own and running afoul of the tide or falling off a cliff, or the multitude of other ways he could die.

The map on the screen wasn't accurate enough to narrow down his location to a position in a room or floor level, but it had given Lev a good estimate of where he was in the castle. The pin on the map was right on top of the transmitter.

Good. Lev exhaled. Maybe Asher was out in the hall or on his way back from the kitchen.

He plucked a down parka from the back of his closet and slung it on in case Asher was cold when he found him, stepped into his boots, and stopped. The watch in question, the one Lev had leveraged his father's death to ensure Asher would wear, rested on top of the eternally boring and niche art history book he'd read before bed.

That obstinate, insolent, beloved lad was going to be in so much trouble when Lev found him. He grabbed a torch from the drawer beside his bed, and hurried out into the hallway.

"Asher!" he roared, words stolen by the storm.

It was even louder in the hall. Fear roared in Lev's ears at the realization that Asher stood no chance of hearing him. Nor would Lev be able to hear him in turn.

Lev's hair stood on end. Electricity itched across his skin, and the metallic taste of ozone bloomed on his tongue. The sky lit up like an atomic bomb, dispatching rainbow shards through the stained glass windows, terrifying and beautiful, as he dove to the ground, flattened his front on the floor, and guarded his head with his hands.

Thunder cracked with an otherworldly, guttural growl that

could only have come from the depths of hell. He hadn't heard the windows explode over the storm, but the blast of glass shrapnel pelting his body was all he needed to know.

Lev leapt to his feet and ran down the hall. What if Asher had been struck by the lightning? What if he'd been standing by a window? What if a fallen tree had caved in Asher's head, or suffocated him with the weight on his chest? What if Asher was on the moor? What if he'd gotten lost in the fog? What if he was already dead?

Lev took a deep breath. He needed to remain calm. He couldn't let fear tangle his thoughts. Asher needed him. He chanted their mantra like a spell inside his head.

ONLY NOW. Only Asher. Only him.

"ASHER!" Lev called again, straining to listen over the storm.

He ran down the hall toward the staircase. Silas waited at the landing, scowling with hands pressed on his hips, saying something Lev couldn't hear, punctuating it with a frustrated shake of his head.

"You're going the wrong way," Silas yelled, too loud, too clear, unaffected by the storm, almost as if he was coming from inside Lev's head. Was he?

Intent on charging around Silas, ignoring his advice and existence, Lev took a few steps forward and stopped. What if Silas was more than a monster inside Lev's head, a monster born from guilt and armed with sharp claws of regret? What if Silas had led Asher somewhere?

Lev spun around. The secret door at the end of the hall was open. Lev's suspicion multiplied. Why would Asher have gone down the claustrophobia-inducing secret corridor in the middle of a storm? He barreled back the way he came, running in slow motion like he was locked in a nightmare, shackled by sleep paralysis, trying to save Asher as he drowned.

The lights flickered, dimmed, and went out. Chills cascaded down Lev's spine, squinting in the darkness as he charged toward the even darker rectangle of the door, skidding on the scattered glass and nearly slipping on the wet hardwood.

The open door at the other end shunted wind down the hall with the force of a hurricane trapped in a jar. Dust showered down from the rafters with each gust. This wasn't just a storm. It was the storm of the century, an apocalyptic cataclysm that would have any atheist doubting their convictions.

Wendell had written of Lichenmoor during a storm much like this. Lev had been seven or eight and the storm was too loud for him to sleep. He'd knocked on the secret door connecting his room with the one Wendell stayed in while Mum was sick, and found him writing in bed.

"Let me finish this page," Wendell had said, then pulled the covers back without stopping his pen.

Consoled by the weight of Wendell's hand on his head, Lev's vision had blurred on Wendell's words as the scratch of pen against paper lulled him to sleep. Wendell had never published the piece, and Lev could only remember a few paragraphs, incomplete and unsatisfying, like a page torn out of a banned book before it was tossed in a bonfire.

A blood-red harvest moon hung in perigee, and a hornet's nest of a tempest summoned a beast that slithered over jagged rock and sloping moors, and devoured the land around Lichenmoor, then opened its mouth and unhinged its jaw.

Silence fell over Lichenmoor, but it was nothing more than a false retreat while a monstrous wave crested, crescendoed, then began to fall, crashing into Lichenmoor Hall and feasting on every soul.

Once the ocean was finally sated, it left behind a curse dooming anyone unfortunate enough to die at Lichenmoor to an eternity walking through fog.

Grief washed over Lev like the sea, unexpected and yet inevitable, slamming into his stomach and punching the wind from his lungs, as strong as when Wendell had died.

Lev's grief wasn't a spectrum, a road that led from denial to acceptance, a journey some completed in one go while others took a few wrong turns before finding their path. His grief was a car with no brakes smashing through a barricade at the top of a cliff tumbling into a free fall that never ended.

Sometimes he could almost forget he was falling, but he could never forget what he'd lost to death, and then he'd start back at the top of the cliff, drive straight off, and fall again. He couldn't lose Asher in a moment of violence the way he'd lost Silas, or the protracted way cancer had claimed Wendell and his mother. He couldn't lose Asher. Full stop.

Lev emerged from the passageway and nearly slammed into Silas.

"I wonder where Asher is," Silas said in a way that had the hair rising on the back of Lev's neck.

Lev strode toward Silas's door and unlocked it. Asher wasn't there. But Silas was.

"You shouldn't have let him keep the skeleton key," Silas said, leaning against the statue of himself. "Our little Sherlock simply couldn't resist."

"Mine. Not ours."

Silas wasn't wrong, though. Lev suspected Asher had stolen the skeleton key when it went missing, but he hadn't asked Asher about it, or searched for it. Trusting Asher to use it wisely and stay out of the east wing had been a grave error in judgment. Hopefully not a fatal one.

Lev turned on his heel with increasing fear. He needed to

hurry downstairs and out into the storm before the tide surged over the seawall.

"Perhaps you should finish carving me below," Silas called after him with a cackle that scratched at Lev's ears drums. "Give Asher something nice to look at instead of an old man."

Lev's dread mounted. Silas was too smug. What had he done?

"Be sure to confiscate the key when you find him. If you find him." Silas blocked the top of the corkscrew staircase that wound around the outside of the tower on the precipice of the cliff, the quickest shortcut to the ground.

"Move," Lev growled.

"But what if he's not down there, Levvy? What if I killed him with a candlestick in the attic?"

"If you had something to do with this... If you've hurt him—"

Silas snorted. "You can't even vanquish me from your thoughts, let alone punish me for whatever I have or haven't done. Not to mention, I have an eternity to wait for you to hurt him all by yourself."

"Tell me where he is or get out of my way."

When Silas didn't move from the first step, Lev pushed past him—and slammed his shoulder into something hard. Silas teetered on his heels. His powder blue eyes flew wide, his mouth a perfect 'O' of shock.

"What the fuck?" Lev reached a shaking hand out and recoiled when it didn't sink through the dead man's sternum, and instead met resistance. A shiver scuttled across his body.

"What the fuck, indeed," Silas said with a sinister grin.

No. Silas was just a constellation of misfiring neurons. Lev's hallucinations were growing stronger, turning tactile. Silas couldn't hurt Asher, unless the storm had ripped a stitch in the veil between living and dead and Silas was the one growing stronger as the tide crept in.

The tide. He had to find Asher.

He shoved Silas against the wall with his forearm, and leveraged Silas's chin, pushing him up the wall until his heels dangled, which didn't take long. He wasn't nearly as tall.

"Mm. I missed this," Silas purred, black lashes falling against skin no longer pallid, peach suffusing his cheeks in real time like ink drops blooming in water, the first splotch of color on Silas's skin since Lev had killed him.

Silas licked his lips, now cherry pink, drawing Lev's eyes lower, not because he was tempted to kiss him, but with donning horror. On the side of Silas's neck, an artery fluttered like a moth trapped beneath silk. The storm faded until the only sound was Lev's heart beating in lockstep with the pulse in Silas's neck.

What the fuck was happening? Lev loosened his grip.

Silas slid down the wall, landing on his feet with feline skill. "Why did you stop?" Silas whined, cocking his head to the side, teasing Lev with the column of the throat he'd once loved to bite.

Lev's hand shook as he pressed his fingertips against the side of Silas's neck. Warmth radiated back with proof of life. The last time Lev had checked his pulse, he'd been lifeless.

"I told you this would happen," Silas said, sliding one hand under Lev's shirt.

Lev felt him and his stomach nearly revolted. "Don't touch me."

Silas pouted. "That's not very fair. You're the one who touched me first." He withdrew his hand, and cupped his chin, scanning Lev head to foot. "I wasn't sure before, but I quite like you like this—sexy in a vintage sort of way, softer around the middle, and the wrinkles are patina. You remind me a bit of Father."

"Fuck you," Lev spat.

"Oh, I'm afraid not. You'll have to grovel for years before I let you fuck me again." Silas stroked the scars he'd left on Lev's forearm. "There's simply so much to atone for."

Instead of telling him to sod off, Lev lowered his voice and leaned closer. "Do you want to know what I think, *Si*?"

"Not particularly," Silas said, affecting a bored tone.

Too late. Lev had caught the way he'd winced at the long lost pet name. His mask had slipped. Interesting.

Silas yawned theatrically and checked a nonexistent watch. "Don't you have a soon-to-be-ex-boyfriend to find?"

"Why play hide and seek when you know exactly where he is?"

Silas splayed a hand on his chest. "Me? I'm just a figment of your imagination. Or are you so far gone you think your hallu-cination is off mopping the floors or haunting the moors while you sleep?"

The cruel laugh that followed snapped what little remained of Lev's control. He gripped Silas's black jumper in both hands and slammed him against the wall. "Tell me where he is!"

"Careful, Levvy. You know how much I like it rough, but you don't want to kill me again, do you?" Silas arched his back, pressing his lower half against Lev. "You were so very sad the first time."

Lev dropped him. Silas only ever initiated sexual contact when he had an ulterior motive. What was it this time? He would never have come back from the dead just to fuck him.

Jesus fucking Christ, why was he wasting time on some-thing so preposterous when the motive was stalling him.

Lev fled down the steps, one hand gripping the slippery stone railing, lest he fall to his death.

"Leviathan!" Silas shouted after him before the wind stole his voice.

Lev spiraled down the tower as wave after wave hammered the shore. The ocean would spill over. There was no stopping it.

What if Asher was out there?

He stopped at a window and leaned over the railing. Visibility was near zero, save for the scattered emergency floodlights he'd installed after Father had died.

Lichenmoor was under siege, the ocean battering the seawall, slamming wave after wave into the stone barricade, spitting walls of froth, moments away from turning Lichenmoor into an archipelago of gardens, guest houses, stables, and other outbuildings.

If Asher was out there, his chance of survival was fleeting. If Asher had strayed beyond the seawall and been caught by the tide, he'd most certainly already died.

Lev locked the thought inside a box, and descended as fast as he dared, promising the ocean he'd trade his soul for Asher's.

At the end of the stairs, Lev sprinted through the downpour, relying on memory to take him to the stables. He spared no time to saddle Rebecca, pausing only long enough to bridle her and vault onto her back.

Outside, Lev urged her into a gallop, racing faster when the water started to spill over.

Asher was nowhere to be found.

Lev checked everywhere, and bellowed his name until his voice broke, and waves snapped at Rebecca's knees, and he had no choice but to return her to the stables. He only had enough time to open the barn door and lock her inside, then ran for the castle, sloshing through ankle-deep water, rip current threatening to knock him off his feet and drag him out to sea.

When he finally made it to the castle he slammed the door behind him and leaned his back against it, trying to catch his breath.

"Lev?"

ART WILL REMEMBER

ASHER

Rain ran in rivulets down Lev's pale face from the soaked red hair plastered to his head. His eyes were red-rimmed and vacant. Haunted.

Asher rushed down the staircase, and across the foyer.

"What happened? I was so worried." Asher slammed into Lev's arms, hugging him.

Lev grunted on impact, but didn't return the hug.

"Are you okay?" Asher reached for the zipper of his jacket. "You must be freezing."

"Don't touch me!" Lev shouted with an acrid venom Asher had never heard before.

Asher flinched, dropping his hands, and took a few stumbling footsteps back. "I'm sorry."

Lev advanced on him. "What did you do? I swear to fucking God, Si, if you hurt him, I'll make sure you suffer."

The realization rippled through Asher and cracked his heart in half.

"Lev, I'm not Silas. I'm Asher."

Thanks to Ben, Asher had a lot of experience deescalating an angry man, but he had no idea how to deescalate a furious confused one.

Terror took hold. Asher turned and ran toward the staircase. Lev gave chase, but slipped on the wet floor—Asher shouldn't have looked back to check on him, but he couldn't help himself.

"I'm not Silas," Asher tried again, stopping at the top of the landing.

Lev hadn't slowed and still looked as murderous as he'd threatened. Three more steps and Lev would be on him, but Asher stood his ground.

"I'm Asher, Lev. Asher, and all of the terrible nicknames you've given me. Blakely. Dormouse. Pretty American. Your good lad. Asher. It's only me. Only me."

Angry suspicion turned wary. "Asher?" Lev blanched down to his freckles. "Oh my God. I thought you were gone. I thought you were *him*."

Asher's heart shattered completely. Was this what fate awaited them? Lev confused and frightened, fighting with a Silas that wasn't there, thinking he'd lost Asher?

Lev raced up the remaining steps and held Asher's face in his hands. "Are you alright? I haven't hurt you, have I? Did someone else hurt you?"

Asher shook his head. "Lev, is Silas here?"

"No, lad." Lev caressed Asher's jaw with his thumb. "Only you."

Asher rested his forehead against Lev's. "Only us."

"Only us," Lev agreed and kissed Asher in a slow burn, lovemaking pace, easing them both down from anxiety and urgency into something safe and unhurried and adoring.

Their kiss continued uninterrupted as Asher unzipped Lev's coat, and Lev shrugged out of it.

Without words, Asher promised Lev that he'd always love him, even if he became unrecognizable. Even if Lev couldn't recognize himself. He'd take care of him and keep him safe and kiss away his fear and pain.

"I thought I'd never see you again," Lev murmured against his lips. "Silas made me think—"

"Silas lured you out there?"

Lev nodded grimly.

The realization of how close Lev had come to dying tightened a chain around Asher's chest.

Lev couldn't die. He was as strong and reliable and eternal as the tide. He was Asher's hero. He was his everything.

But ghosts weren't real and the diagnosis Lev faced could have killed him.

"You could have died." Asher's voice broke into a tearless sob. "I don't want you to have Alzheimer's. I don't want you to forget me. I don't want you to die like your father."

Anguish aged Lev as his brows twisted, and the wrinkles around his eyes curled down. "Neither of those things will happen for a very long time." He kissed Asher's forehead and left his lips there. "I know how bleak it seems, but I could never forget you. My soul will recognize you and my art will remember."

"Like with Silas?"

"No, love. Not like that. While I did paint Silas partly to preserve and honor his memory, painting him was a punishment that started with Father. I choose to paint you because I could look at you every day for the rest of my life, dream of you every night, and still never tire of you."

"I love you," Asher said and it wasn't as devastatingly beautiful as what Lev had said, but it must have been good enough because Lev's arms enveloped him.

"I love you too," Lev said into his hair. "I do have a question, though. Why did you get out of bed?"

"I heard something, and left to go check..." Asher tensed. "Then I went somewhere I shouldn't have."

"To Silas's room?"

"How did you know?"

"Lichenmoor has a way of spilling secrets."

"How unhelpfully cryptic," Asher said.

Lev laughed. "The door of the passageway was open."

"I'm sorry I didn't listen to you."

Lev waved the apology away. "I'm sorry you saw what you did, especially without me there to explain. Do you understand now why I didn't want you in there?"

Asher nodded. "Because it's private and..." He breathed through the stab of jealousy. "It shows how much you love Silas."

"You're partially correct. At first, yes. I wanted to protect that secret wound inside of me, but my reasons changed over time. After I fell in love with you, which wasn't very long after meeting you, I didn't want to hurt you."

Asher's thoughts detoured down a different path. He'd betrayed Lev's privacy when all Lev had wanted was to protect him. Asher was an asshole. No, he was a terrible person.

"I'm so sorry," Asher repeated, interrupting Lev's reverie.

"Baby, please stop apologizing."

"No. I fucked up and put you in danger. You were terrified and you could have died." He sucked in a breath and rested his hands on the button of Lev's pants. "Please let me make it up to you, let me show you how sorry I am. Please."

Lev grimaced. The rejection stung. Asher had lived with Lev's praise for so long, and now he no longer deserved it.

"Our relationship is not transactional," Lev said evenly, but it felt like an admonishment.

"I know. You taught me that. That's not what I meant."

"I'm listening," Lev said with so much sincerity and patience, Asher felt even more unworthy.

"I wasn't trying to offer payment. I need to make this right with *me*. Me." He slapped his hand over his heart. "But that's only part of it. I almost lost you. One day I *will* lose you." Saying it aloud sent his heart rate skittering and pierced holes in his lungs.

"I'm scared, Lev, and I don't want to be scared. I want to be good."

Lev's brows darted together. "Ash..."

"But maybe you don't want that right now, or maybe you never wanted that and were only doing it for me." His chest tightened. "Fuck, if that's true, I'm so sorry. I never wanted to pressure you. Forget what I said. You just came in. You must be exhausted. And cold. Are you sure you're not hurt? We should go upstairs."

"I'm perfectly fine," Lev said in a soothing tone that didn't soothe him at all.

Lev could have died and he *would* die and he would suffer and...

Lev frowned. Why was he frowning? Was he upset? Asher had forced him to be his dom before, hadn't he? Asher was no better than Ben.

"Asher, I'm safe. Slow your breathing." Lev gripped his shoulders. "You're going to make yourself lightheaded."

But Asher couldn't slow down. He couldn't keep Lev safe. He couldn't watch him every hour of every day.

A beehive buzzed inside his head. His skin itched. He was going to be sick.

"Inhale slowly," Lev said from far away like he'd talked down a plastic cup on a string.

Asher tried. He wanted to be good. He inhaled.

"Good. Now breathe out slowly."

Asher couldn't. In fact, he'd breathed at least five times before Lev finished his sentence. He inhaled and exhaled faster than his lungs could empty, and hyperventilated until his lips felt fuzzy and his hands turned splotchy.

"I'm not going to die and neither are you. You're having a panic attack."

Asher knew it was all in his head. That's what Ben had said. He could breathe, but his mind was weak. *He* was weak.

Lev pressed Asher's palm to the center of his chest. "Try

following me." Lev's shoulders lifted on a long inhale. "Only now. Only me."

Asher tried. He tried so hard to breathe.

"It's okay to be scared." Lev guided Asher into a seated position with his knees bridged and sat across from him. "I'm scared too, but I feel brave when I'm with you."

Lev gently parted Asher's knees and rubbed circles on his back. "Let's try putting your head between your legs, hm?"

Asher nodded and bowed his head.

"Good lad."

But Asher was too far gone for a simple *good lad* to fix.

"You never forced me to do anything," Lev said. "You were right to suggest submitting to me. Comforting you like that comforted me too, and I think that's precisely what we both needed."

When that didn't work, Lev said, "All panic attacks come to an end. I promise you'll feel better very soon."

Asher lifted his head from between his knees. "Mine." Inhale. "Don't." Exhale. "Stop."

The last time he had an attack this bad, he'd panted for four hours before asking his dad to take him to the emergency room.

His dad was the total grizzled cowboy type who never went to the doctor unless Asher's mom made him. Meanwhile, Asher needed medical intervention because he was too sensitive, too easily triggered, too broken by Ben.

Asher had no idea how far away the closest hospital to Lichenmoor was, and the roads were flooded anyway. He was surrounded by water and he couldn't breathe.

"Let's try something else," Lev said calmly and cupped his palms together in prayer, opening only enough to place them loosely over Asher's nose and mouth. "Breathe into my hands as you would a paper bag."

Asher tried, but Lev's hands smelled like the saltwater he could have drowned in.

What if the ocean flooded the castle? How could he protect Lev when he couldn't breathe?

Asher shook his head and batted Lev's hands away.

Lev clucked his tongue. "I'm so sorry. I hate watching you suffer like this."

But Lev was the one who would suffer, and Asher couldn't do anything to stop it. How could he breathe when he knew he would lose him?

Asher inhaled and exhaled and inhaled and exhaled and inhaled and exhaled until he tasted tears as salty as the ocean on his tongue.

When had he started crying?

"Asher Blakely, that is enough." Lev cut through Asher's thoughts with a sharp clap of his hands.

Asher paused. Not long. Maybe a second.

"There you are, darling. Tell me what you can see."

Asher only had time for a one-word answer between breaths. "You."

"Very good. Anything else? Don't talk, just think." He took Asher's hand and held it to his chest again, breathing slow and steady like waves ebbing.

Ginger lashes. Ocean eyes. Freckles like stars. What else?

"You're doing so well. What do you smell?"

"Saltwater," Asher said aloud.

"Let's skip scent then, shall we?"

Thunder rumbled overhead. Lev narrowed his eyes at the window as if the storm was responsible for the unfortunate timing.

"We don't need sound either. Tell me what you feel."

The rise and fall of the palm Lev still held to his chest. Lev's legs, now bent at the knee, walling Asher in. Lev's hand rubbing circles on his back.

Lev leaned in and kissed Asher's cheek, grazing Asher's skin with his beard. "In case you need more tactile sensations for your list." Lev kissed Asher's temple, then forehead. "I'm simply trying to help."

"Right," Asher said with a laugh.

"Was that sarcasm *and* a laugh?" Lev kissed Asher's lips as gently as if they were butterfly wings. "What do you feel?"

"You. Only you."

Lev pushed Asher's hair back from his face. "I'm so proud of you."

Asher's first impulse was to reject the compliment, but that was against the rules, so he focused on Lev and breathed.

And breathed.

And breathed.

"I'm so relieved I didn't have to carry you to the kitchen for a paper bag." Lev flashed a playful grin that was so charming and contagious, Asher smiled too.

Asher inhaled deeply, then exhaled everything.

"Good lad. Let's go upstairs and if you still want to play, I'll gladly take you in hand."

Warmth spread through him at the suggestion. "Yes, sir."

5 2

THE CLOSED DOOR

ASHER

Lev pushed open the door to their room with his back after he'd insisted on carrying Asher over the broken glass in the hallway.

"How are you feeling, baby?" Lev asked, lowering Asher to the ground, one hand still curled around his waist as if Asher had forgotten how to stand when he'd forgotten how to breathe.

"I can't believe you didn't think to tell me you almost got struck by lightning."

"It would have been counterproductive to share it while coaching you out of a panic attack—*Try to slow your breathing. Say, have I told you about that time I was almost struck by lightning?*"

The joke took Asher by surprise, and he burst into laughter.

Lev smiled slowly. "Lichenmoor is the tallest thing around for miles and miles. It gets struck by lightning all the time. Why do you think there are so many windows without panes? Father couldn't be arsed to replace some of them. Honestly, I find it far more shocking that the power is back on already."

Asher narrowed his eyes. "Shocking?"

422

"It was a slip of the tongue. I'd never make such a dreadful joke, unless you thought it was funny..."

"No." Asher rolled his lips inward to hide his smile.

"You can try to look cross all you want—particularly because I find it adorable—but you can't hide your dimples."

"If Lichenmoor gets struck by lightning all the time, shouldn't you have put a disclaimer in your invitation?"

"That was rather careless of me, wasn't it? I'll be sure to add that the next time I invite you, but seeing as you're already here and I've no intention of letting you leave..."

Asher rolled his eyes and took off his hoodie.

The muscles in Lev's throat flexed as he raked his gaze over Asher's bare skin. "Why don't I nip to the loo and start a bath for us?"

"Okay."

"Splendid." Lev took a few steps and stopped when Asher didn't join him, pointing a far too casual thumb toward the bathroom. "Do you need to use the loo?"

"No."

"Very well." Lev stepped into the bathroom. "Are you sure you don't want to join me?"

"No, thanks." Asher bent beside the unlit fireplace. "You can leave the door open if it makes you feel better."

"Ah, I've found the candles," Lev called. "I'm going to light a few in case the power goes out again."

When Asher didn't answer immediately, Lev called, "Asher?"

Poor Lev. "I'm still here."

"As you bloody well should be."

Asher smiled and lit a match, igniting the crumpled up rejected sketches Lev kept in a trash can for kindling. The log caught quickly, coaxed by the wind wafting down the chimney.

He brushed the dirt off of his hands, and moved to stand, then stopped. The end table had been moved to the side. A small wood panel rested on the floor, a little bigger than a sheet of paper, a perfect match for the empty space in the wall above it.

What the fuck?

Asher looked over his shoulder, but Lev was still bustling around the bathroom lighting candles.

Dread filled him as he kneeled in front of the hidden compartment, bracing for a rat to leap out and scare him. There wasn't a rat, but something was inside. Multiple small shadowy somethings.

Lev had insinuated that he'd hurt Silas, and was the reason why Silas had died. Was the evidence inside? Had Silas opened it for Asher or had Lev forgotten to close it in his haste to find him? Maybe he stored emergency equipment there.

The first thing Asher's hand touched was a brown paper bag stuffed with what felt like a thick stack of cards or cash. Asher pulled out a tarnished silver box no bigger than his palm, etched with thorny rose vines.

Inside, he found a thick lock of silky black hair a few inches long tied together with powder blue ribbon. It was the same color as Silas's eyes.

Asher rubbed the hair between his fingers, soft and slippery as a spider's silken threads. Okay, so that was creepy as fuck, but it could still be explained. Maybe Lev had saved a neat clipping of Silas's hair, and stored it reverently beside his bed to stroke like a stalker while he and Silas were apart. Or he'd clipped it from Silas's body.

Asher closed the box and pulled out a stack of photographs with Silas's passport on top. Someone had stashed a photograph of the two of them inside.

They must have been teenagers or a little bit older, and the pose they shared projected innocent brotherly love. Lev smiled at the camera, fair skin and freckles stained sepia with sunkissed skin, one long arm slung loosely around Silas. Silas smirked more than smiled, staring into the lens so intensely it was like he knew one day he'd be dead and his replacement would try to fill the space he'd left.

The arched window behind them looked like one from the ballroom art studio. Sun sparkled off the ocean and in through the window, transforming Lev's ginger hair into strands of sunlight. He was beautiful. At first glance, Lev looked happy, but there were signs of strain in the tightness of his lips, in the way his other hand hung clenched against his side, in the shadows underneath his eyes.

The washed out passport photo couldn't have been more different. That version of Silas glared at the camera with a sullen pout.

Wind tousled the hair at the base of Asher's neck. He shivered, imagining the passport version of Silas standing over him as he snooped, and cast a paranoid look over his shoulder, but no one was there.

The snippet of Silas's hair was suspect. The passport could be rationalized away, but Asher couldn't lie to himself about the thick stack of photographs taken from every angle and distance. Some of the photos were so zoomed in, they framed only a single fingertip or the arch of an eyebrow, the soft shell of an ear, all of which belonged to a single person.

Silas.

Silas, the man from Lev's paintings, the sad specter of himself in his passport photo, not the brother Lev had posed with. His eyes were flat, no longer fae-like, his skin taut over sharp bones. Worst of all, the flushed cheeks and red lips that had given him a Snow White appearance had faded to a pallid grayscale.

This was Silas *after* he'd died.

Lev should have chosen a better place to hide his murder evidence—if it was murder evidence. Photographs of Silas's corpse didn't mean Lev had actually killed him, right?

Lucian was known to take hundreds of reference photos to master every detail and angle. He'd probably done the same with his wife and Wendell. Lev used reference photos too. Maybe Lev had found Silas and he or Lucian had taken the photographs.

Asher rolled his shoulders, shrugging off the bug-crawling sensation.

The last item in the paper bag was a piece of old paper folded into a square. He opened it carefully to reveal Lev's original self-portrait, the one with the eyes scratched out all the way through the paper, the one Asher had tattooed over his heart.

Why had Lev kept it? Why had he kept any of it? Asher shoved everything back into the bag. He'd seen enough.

"What are you doing?" Lev asked.

Asher jumped. A violin string of fear from a horror movie sliced through his thoughts. He dropped the bag with a loud clatter of the silver box striking the floor, and turned.

Lev stood in front of the bathroom door. A muscle in his jaw ticked. How long had he watched? How much had he seen?

"You scared me." Asher rushed to his feet. "I was just starting a fire for us and found that piece of wood on the floor and tried to put it back, but then the bag fell onto the floor and well... You saw the rest."

Lev pushed off the door, exuding danger. "You must think I'm stupid."

"No, sir."

"Don't call me that," Lev snapped.

Asher's eyes darted to the exit.

Lev followed his gaze. "You're not thinking about leaving already, are you?"

"No. Of course not."

Lev prowled closer, putting himself between Asher and the door. "The water is still rising."

"I know." Sweat trickled down the back of Asher's neck. He breathed slowly through his nose, and begged his panicked pulse to slow. He didn't dare look at the secret door to his right, the best chance he had at getting out.

"Well, what do you think now that you've seen my most treasured possessions?"

"I think you loved him very much, but I already knew that."

"Come now, Blakely. I know you saw the photographs."

"I didn't look, but if I did, I'm sure I wouldn't find any evidence of wrongdoing," Asher said slowly, buying himself as much time as he could, down to the milliseconds between words.

If he threw the end table at Lev would it slow him down enough to get out?

"You wouldn't kill him unless you had no other choice," Asher continued, slower still.

"Nice sentiment, but you're wrong," Lev said. "He always had a choice, and he chose to hurt me."

Wait. What?

"Lev..." Asher oozed empathy he hoped was convincing, and didn't acknowledge the mistake that had slipped into his speech.

Because that wasn't Lev. It was someone else.

"I'm so sorry he hurt you," Asher continued, then grabbed the end table and hurled it at him.

The lamp fell. Glass broke. Lev roared.

Asher flipped the tapestry up, and hurried through the secret doorway.

"Oh, no you don't." Lev snatched Asher's ankle and yanked him off his feet.

Asher hit the ground with only his knees and chin to break his fall. His teeth sank into his tongue. At the taste of blood, the room started to sway.

Pushing through the pain, and nausea, and mounting panic, Asher scrambled to find something to use as a weapon. But Lev was too fast and too strong, and ripped Asher back by his ankles, while Asher could do nothing more than leave a trail of fingernail marks in the floorboards.

"Where do you think you're going?" Lev laughed cruelly.

No. Not Lev. Dr. Jekyll had left, and Mr. Hyde was home. Silas was in control.

Asher was sure of it. He'd worry about the why and how later.

"Lichenmoor is an island, and I know every secret hiding place," Silas said through Lev. "You're trapped here, just like me."

Silas flipped Asher onto his back, and straddled him. The abrupt change in position combined with a mouth filled with blood amplified Asher's nausea. He turned his head and spat blood. On the plus side, maybe if he vomited it would distract Silas long enough or snap Lev out of whatever the fuck was happening.

Struggling to slow his frantic breathing, Asher tried to focus on his senses. He saw a fire poker too far away, a shard of broken porcelain under the bed. The vein bulging in Lev's neck. He heard the crackle of flames, the relentless rain.

"You poor dear," Silas said in a sickly sweet simpering tone. "All that blood must taste dreadful. Try not to dwell on it. We can't have you fainting."

"I'm sorry I scared you. I know you just want to keep me safe," Asher tried.

"Oh, sod off. I've gone mad, not daft."

"You haven't gone mad."

Silas arced down and kissed Asher, invading his mouth with Lev's tongue. Asher's vision swam like he was floating on the waves flooding Lichenmoor. Saliva filled his mouth.

"Mm," Silas hummed. "You're delicious. Now I see what all the fuss was about."

"Get off!" Asher shoved Lev's stomach and bucked his hips, trying to topple him.

"Keep writhing around like that. I quite like it." Lev's dick thickened against him.

Disgust and renewed panic surged through him. Asher fought like a cat trying to avoid taking a bath, and sank his teeth into Lev's arm, probably right on top of those fingernail scars.

Silas rolled Lev's hips, rutting his cock alongside Asher's. "I do love a bit of pain with my pleasure."

"Well, I don't. Red. Lev, I said red. Lev, stop."

"What on earth are you going on about?"

With a sympathetic wince, Asher reeled back his fist and aimed for Lev's balls. Silas caught Asher's hand before it connected.

"I'd like to keep my bollocks intact, thank you very much."

Asher gnashed his teeth together. His options were dwindling. Asher widened his eyes in fear and pointed over Lev's shoulder.

"Lev, look out. It's Silas!"

"That's not poss..." Silas followed Asher's gaze.

Asher reached for the shard of porcelain under the bed. His fingertips slipped on the sharp edge—

"Careful. You don't want to cut yourself, do you?" Silas shackled Asher's wrists, and pinned them by his head. "I must say, you're exactly as sharp as I hoped you would be."

"And you're as self-absorbed as I guessed, distracted by your own ghost. Silas." He'd said the name like a curse.

"Aw. What gave me away?" Silas pushed Lev's lips into a pout that didn't suit Lev at all. "I wanted to play with you more, but now that you've guessed, I might as well get rid of you."

"Lev won't let you hurt me."

"I'm afraid Lev won't be able to stop me until the tide recedes. Don't worry. I'll tell him you said goodbye." Silas patted Asher's cheek. "I can't wait for him to lose you. Killing you will be the perfect revenge."

"Wait. Are you seriously still hung up on your ex? Hasn't it been twenty years, or something?"

"Lev is not an ex. He's my brother. Our bond is something you can't understand because you don't have that with him."

"*Okay*, Silas," Asher said with a sardonic roll of his eyes. "That's not what Lev said."

"I know everything Lev has said. I know when he's serious and when he's just trying to fuck someone."

"I don't know, man. You sound kind of insecure to me."

Silas scoffed. "Please."

"You don't go in the church. You don't come here either, so no, you don't actually know everything he's said about you." Asher chewed on his lip. "I wonder why you're in here now. Probably because you aren't real."

Silas lifted Asher's hands and slammed them back against the ground.

Asher hissed.

"Ouch. That sounded like it hurt," Silas said.

It had hurt, but if Silas wanted to cause him real pain, he'd have to try a lot harder. Between his tattoos, and Ben's mistreatment, Asher had a high pain tolerance.

"Do you know what I think after reading through that pining notebook of yours?" Asher asked.

If Silas hadn't threatened to kill him, Asher might have felt guilty. Of all people, he knew how painful pining and rejection could be. But since Silas *was* trying to kill him, he might as well put all the snarky shower arguments he'd had with Ben in his head to good use.

"I had no idea you knew how to read," Silas said.

Asher understood why Lev had been attracted to Silas. Aside from his envy-inducing beauty, he was witty and sharp-tongued. Fighting with him was fun.

"I know, right?" Asher said. "I can read and write and do something you can't do, something only Lev and I can."

"If you're going to make a crude joke about some strange American sex act, spare me."

"It's not a sex thing," Asher told Silas. "I can make art so powerful, Lev fell in love with me through a painting."

Silas snorted. "That's it?"

"Nah. But I don't need to prove anything. You can keep trying to change my opinion though if you want." Hopefully until Lev became Lev again.

"I'm tired of talking," Silas said as casually as if killing Asher was nothing more than ripping a page out of a book.

"Lev will hate you."

"Oh, I know. He's hated me since long before I died, but there's freedom in being hated. When people have already made up their minds, I can do whatever I want."

Lev's legs tightened around Asher's hips as Silas released Asher's hands, wrapped his own around Asher's neck, and squeezed. The first thing Asher did was punch Lev in the balls like he'd intended. This time he connected.

Silas winced. "Poor Levvy is going to be so sore tomorrow."

Asher and Ben had done breath play. He was no stranger to the sensation of being strangled, but for all Ben's crimes, he'd never fucked around with Asher's life. Safe breath play was one of the few kinks he still liked. The soft rising pressure in Asher's head was so familiar it almost soothed him.

Maybe that was why Silas had let his guard down and gave Asher the chance to punch Lev in the kidney.

"For fuck's sake, Blakely!"

Asher's heart lifted with hope. Had Lev come back? But Lev didn't release him. Silas tightened his grip, and Asher's vision dimmed like a fire slowly burning out.

Lev would be so alone and heartbroken if Asher died. Asher had to stop Silas.

"I do wish you'd put up more of a fight," Silas said. "This is rather anticlimactic."

"Maybe you're not doing it right," Asher tried to say.

"Sorry. I'm afraid I can't understand you, but no matter. Let's not pretend you have anything profound to share."

Asshole. Channeling all his rage, Asher kicked his legs and tried to pry Lev's fingers from his neck.

"See, isn't this more fun?" Silas asked.

When that didn't work, he tried to scratch Lev's neck, maybe punch him if he was lucky, but his arms were so hard to lift, each attempt slower. Lev was just too far away. White spots drifted in his vision like snowflakes.

The room darkened, tightening into a hallway with Lev standing at the end. Asher called to him. Lev's name echoed down the hallway but he didn't answer. Asher tried again and again but the hallway stretched longer and longer each time he sent Lev's name echoing down the line until he said Lev's name for the very last time and Lev disappeared.

The hall didn't seem so long anymore. Lev had been blocking a closed door. A rectangle outline of bright light beamed through the gaps around the door. The light reminded him so much of lightning. Too white. Too blue.

But then the light turned off.

The hall went dark.

And Asher's flame burned out with a final thought—he hoped Lev would forgive himself.

NO MORE SECRETS

LEV

22 YEARS OLD

"What are you doing here?" Lev hissed, and pulled Silas into his room, then ducked his head out to check the hallway was empty.

Silas staggered inside as if Lev had manhandled him, which he most certainly had not. Lev had long-since learned to handle Silas with care. Anorexia had ravaged his body on and off through his teens, and while Silas had hovered at a healthy weight for the last two years, it would take a lot longer than that for his bones to be as sturdy as Lev's.

"You can't do this. You love me. We're family," Silas wailed, tears spilling without shame down delicate cheekbones smattered with purple petechiae like they'd been flicked from a paintbrush.

Silas had always bruised easily. If he cried or screamed hard enough, burst blood vessel freckles peppered his skin. Pleasing him without bruising him had always been a delicate line to navigate.

Pain and sex were the only things that took the edge off of

Silas's suffering, and Lev had never denied him, even if he hadn't wanted to.

"I do love you, Si." Lev pulled him into a hug, partly to muffle the infernal racket he was making. "We'll always be family. I just can't love you the way you want me to."

Twisting the knife in Silas's back deeper with the same truth he'd already told him earlier was excruciating, but if he surrendered to Silas now, he'd restart the same broken clock, and he couldn't do that again. He'd already sacrificed far too many years of his life to Silas.

Silas pushed out of Lev's arms. He stopped crying mid-sob, stymying his tears faster than turning a faucet off. His face transformed from agony to a hateful scowl that lifted the hair on the back of Lev's neck. When would Lev stop falling for his theatrics?

"Sorry. Forgive me for not understanding, but are you telling me you only love me as a brother?" Silas pushed his lips into a masquerade of a pout. "The goodbye sex we had before you dumped me certainly wasn't a brotherly game of croquet."

"It wasn't goodbye sex," Lev said through clenched teeth, balling his hands into fists. "You needed me and I took care of you, and then I broke."

Every time Silas had asked Lev to hurt him, he'd stacked another boulder on Lev's chest, and they'd been doing it for so long that Silas had buried him, and Lev hadn't noticed until he could scarcely breathe against the weight of it. Lev hadn't realized that last time was the last time until he'd tried to breathe and couldn't.

If Lev stayed with Silas, he would suffocate.

"You literally shagged me, then dumped me. It's like you did it on purpose just to take advantage of me and then hurt me," Silas said.

"No. What you're not going to do is cast me as the villain taking advantage of you. Trust me, if I'd had any choice, I wouldn't have fucked you at all."

Silas's jaw dropped with the most scandalized gasp. "What a terribly cruel thing to say."

"I'm not finished!"

"Lower your voice," Silas said, as if he hadn't brought an argument to Lev's room on purpose to hold him hostage under the threat of waking Father.

Lev screamed inside his head.

"If I'd ever planned to *shag you and dump you*, I would have checked the tide charts first, because nothing is worse than being trapped by high tide at Lichenmoor with you."

Silas's mouth closed, then opened, and closed again.

Lev shouldn't have said that last part even if it was true. "I'm sorry. Why don't we pause this for now and get some rest before we say things we regret? We can talk more after we've both slept."

"How?"

Lev stroked Silas's hair behind his ear. "What do you mean?"

"How can I sleep when I'm the worst thing that's ever happened to you? What about losing your mum? What about Wendell? Is staying with me really that terrible?"

Lev clicked his tongue "Silas, no. Not at all. I was angry and meant it in a dramatic cliche sort of way. Understood?"

Silas nodded.

"Good." Lev hugged Silas, this time not to silence him, but to comfort them both. Lev tucked Silas's head under his chin and hugged him tighter.

Silas melted against him and inhaled a shuddering breath as if his tears had been real all along and he'd finally settled himself in the safety of Lev's arms. Silas had loved Lev for more than a decade, for more than half of his life, for nearly all of his memories.

While the same could be said for Lev, there was one astronomically important difference—Lev had a life outside of Silas, and Silas did not. When the tide receded, Lev would leave, and Silas would be alone.

Lev and Silas would both start a new chapter tomorrow. It was terrifying, and perhaps the tiniest bit exhilarating, which made him feel like the world's biggest prick, because Silas was staring down a future of blank pages without Lev to fill them with.

But maybe Silas could learn to be happy on his own, and then after that, maybe he could find someone else. Lev had to tell himself that, he had to believe it was true, because if he let his mind wander to how Silas would suffer, he'd never be able to leave.

"How can I sleep without you?" Silas asked, tugging Lev back to the present.

"You don't have to."

Silas tipped his head back and looked at Lev with powder blue eyes so devastatingly vulnerable. "How would we sleep? Like lovers or brothers?"

"We'll sleep like we always have, because whatever label we fall under, we'll always be Lev and Silas, and I'll always love you."

Silas's muscles tensed. His eyes shuttered. "What does that mean?"

"It means I love you and I want to hold you while you sleep, but I still can't love you like that anymore."

Some of Lev's scratches hadn't stopped bleeding, so he gradually released Silas and stepped out of fingernail range just in case. There was nothing he could say because he'd already said it, and then he'd said too much.

"Perhaps we should tell Father... Maybe without the pressure to keep us a secret, you'll feel better?" Silas said quite sensibly, as if he actually thought it would help.

Lev wanted to believe him, but he knew Silas as well as he didn't know him at all—it was the same manipulation tactic he'd paraded around since they'd started dating.

"Maybe we *should* tell him." At this point, he'd rather disappoint Father than fight with Silas again. "You can't blackmail me into staying with you, Si. That's not love."

"It could be if you tried."

Lev shook his head. "I wasn't talking about myself. If *you* really loved me, you wouldn't do this. You'd let me go."

"It was supposed to be only me and you."

"It never was, though, Si. I was so young. I wasn't equipped. What happened to you was terrible, but I didn't steal Wendell from you, or send you to that school, nor did I bully you. I shouldn't have carried all of your darkness for you as if I was the one who'd hurt you. Maybe if I'd told someone, they could have helped you."

"You act as if I haven't been carrying you too."

"If you have, then I'm sorry. We should have been kids. We should have run amok in the fields, and played in the ruins, and swam for hours in the summer, instead of sharing secrets in the shadows."

"I could leave with you. Maybe we can start fresh somewhere else."

How many times had Silas promised that only to change his mind at the last minute with a slash of his wrists or an overdose to delay Lev's departure?

"You won't. Even if you did, it's too late for that."

"Perhaps I'll tell Father the truth myself, then. No more secrets."

What was Silas playing at? A thousand horrifying suggestions cartwheeled through his head.

"You must remember the first summer we were together, Levvy? You touched me and I said it felt funny, but you were older and I looked up to you, so when you said it should feel good, I pretended that it did, but it never felt good. It only ever hurt."

The suggestion of a false accusation like that was a fatal fucking blow to their relationship, but he could be upset about that later, after he found out if someone had hurt Silas.

"Did someone do that to you?"

Silas shrugged one shoulder. "If they had, would you stay?"

"Have they?"

Silas snorted with derision. "No, but words can do so much damage, especially when given a pen." Then the little narcissistic twat lifted his nose and sighed like ruining Lev's life was all such a bore.

"You're disgusting."

"Yes, *Brother*. You've already made your opinion about my appeal quite clear."

Silas barely spared him a glance, looking around Lev's room like he was a guest who wanted to leave but couldn't find his hat.

"Father won't believe you."

"What about the defensive wounds I left on your wrist? You were so kind to fuck me. I'm sure I'm just swimming with evidence."

Claustrophobia curled around Lev. Had Silas anticipated Lev's departure before Lev himself had? Was all of this a plot to steer Lev back to Lichenmoor?

"I don't recognize you anymore," Lev whispered.

"I think you've never seen me more clearly. Ever since you met me, you only saw what you wanted to see, and you only loved who you wanted me to be."

"No, Si. That's not true." Fuck. Lev sniffed back tears and pressed his hands to his eyes.

What was real and what wasn't? Was this Silas the same Silas who'd sung lullabies when Lev had missed his mum? Had he ever been the precocious boy who had talked his way into Lev's home and his heart?

Or had Lev wasted the last twelve years of his life, the twilight of his childhood, the dawn of his adulthood, loving someone who was incapable of loving anyone but himself? Lying to himself was easier.

"You're just trying to hurt me," Lev said.

"Of course, I'm trying to hurt you," Silas shouted, giving no fucks for Father at all. "You want to leave me here to rot."

Lev forced his fear into patience like he'd been taught to do with horses. "Silas, we can always try again, but we can't do that if you tell Father those lies."

"I don't think I want to try again. I think I want to destroy your life the way you've destroyed mine."

"But I didn't—"

"And then, I'd like to try with someone new. I can be the sad half orphan instead of you. I can be the golden child, the one who persevered in spite of your abuse."

Silas crossed to the door. Lev couldn't think beyond stopping him as he erased the distance between them and grabbed him by the shoulders—and even then, he'd been gentle, even when Silas was trying to put him in prison.

"Silas, wait. We can fix this. I still love you."

"Let go of me." When Lev didn't, fear snuck into Silas's voice. "Strength is nothing without wit. Besides, you'd never hurt me." A wicked gleam twinkled in Silas's eyes as he opened his mouth wide and bellowed, "Father—"

Lev slammed his hand over Silas's mouth.

For a fleeting, fractured millisecond, Silas's powder blue eyes shot wide with fear. Then his head flung backward, bounced off the wall at his back, and came to rest, hanging limply over his chest.

It had all happened so fast.

54

SWIMMING IN THE SHALLOWS

LEV

22 YEARS OLD

Fuck. He must have given Silas a concussion. Lev fought gravity to keep Silas upright. He was much heavier when unconscious.

"Si?"

No answer.

Lev shook him gently, but his head listed and lolled on his neck.

"Silas?"

Lev wedged his knee carefully between Silas's legs and stepped closer to press him against the wall so he wouldn't fall as Lev lifted his head. He'd never seen him so peaceful, not even while he slept—lips parted softly, the muscles in his face relaxed, ordinarily so tight against his sharp cheekbones. His eyes were closed, but not completely.

Lev cradled Silas's head and neck in the crook of one arm like he was a newborn, and when his head lulled back, his mouth opened, and his eyelids lifted slightly.

Was he waking up?

But he wasn't moving, and when Lev used one hand to part

Silas's eyelids, something about his eyes made Lev feel like he was looking into a mirror, like the only life he saw was his reflection staring back.

No. That wasn't right. Silas was stunned. That's why his body dangled limply. But Silas reminded him of a crow that had crashed into the window and snapped its neck, and his chest was too still.

Guarding Silas's neck, Lev eased them both down to the floor.

"Father!" Lev screamed until his voice cracked.

Where was he? He couldn't be in his room. He would have heard too much not to check on them.

Lev held Silas's head in his lap and called for his father by any and all names, even Dad, because Lev was a boy who needed his father after he'd hurt the boy he loved. He even tried calling for Lucy, a pet name Wendell had used.

Wendell. He'd hurt Wendell's son. Lev called for Wendell too and his mum and Luna.

Why couldn't anyone hear him?

Lev sobbed and screamed Silas's name. How cruel that he'd wanted to scream at Silas earlier, and now he'd do anything to whisper to him one more time and know Silas could hear him.

But that could still happen. Silas wasn't dead. He couldn't be dead.

"No, Si. No," Lev sobbed, pulling Silas closer so he could hold him. "Please don't go."

Lev knew how fragile Silas was. He should have been more careful. He shouldn't have tried to stop him.

If he hadn't been so afraid to disappoint Father, if he'd sacrificed more, and tried to love Silas more, opened a window when he felt like he was suffocating instead of trying to leave, maybe none of this would have ever happened, and Silas would still be here.

"Leviathan?"

The door pushed open, but Lev's legs were blocking it. Why bother? Father couldn't fix this.

Lev knew the truth. Silas was dead, and while he was still warm, he'd been dead far too long for there to be any hope of reviving him.

"Leviathan, what's wrong?"

"It's Silas. He's dead. I killed him. I killed him. I killed him."

Lev sobbed anew and rocked Silas gently in his lap until he couldn't see Silas's face through his tears. But that was probably for the best. He didn't want to remember Silas like this. He didn't want to remember any of this.

"Let me in, Lev," Father said so gently. He never called him Lev.

But the gentle way Lucian had called him Lev wasn't real. It was a diversion. Lucian slammed into the door with a shocking smash that sent Lev's broken heart racing into a gallop.

Could he give Silas his extra heartbeats? Why was he allowed so many when Silas had none? Why couldn't he share them?

The door swung wider and crashed against Lev's leg. He didn't care about the pain, but he didn't want any more of Silas's bones to break like he suspected his neck had, so he scooted back and dragged Silas out of the way.

Father swept in, and swung his gaze down to Lev holding Silas to his chest like a porcelain doll with a chipped face, then sucked in a sharp breath.

"What happened?" Father asked quietly.

He wasn't cross. He was calm, but it was a mask. Lev knew what his father looked like when he knew he would lose a person he loved. He'd witnessed it twice.

Father was scared. Lev was too, because what was more terrifying and primitively dread-inspiring than the black nothingness of death, knowing that there was no afterlife, that he'd never see Mum, or Wendell, or Silas ever again?

They were just gone.

His mum would never stroke his hair and sing to him until he fell asleep. Wendell would never tell him another story, or write a single word, or say, *I love you* again, and Silas...

Fuck.

Silas would never slip through the secret door, and come to Lev for comfort, and ask Lev to fight his monsters for him, or look at him like he wanted to crawl inside Lev's marrow and live there forever.

Lev would never draw his sigil on Silas's skin to protect him.

Only now, only you had died with Silas.

There was *only then*, when Silas had been alive, and now *only Lev.*

Only Lev.

Only Lev.

"We were fighting," Lev sobbed, too devastated to be embarrassed of crying like a child in front of him. "I didn't want him to t-t-tell you about us. I didn't want to disappoint you. I tried to stop him. I didn't want to hurt him. He's just so easily broken."

"It's alright, son. Let me have a look at him. It's probably just a wee bump on his head and tomorrow he'll be whinging at breakfast."

"He won't. His neck is too fragile. It cracked like a branch— no, like a twig, and he can't hold his head up."

Lev dissolved into tears again. He couldn't breathe. Was that how Silas had felt during that nanosecond of shutting down synapses?

Or had he been relieved? He'd been dancing at the edge of the cliff between life and death for so long, and he'd finally leapt.

"Leviathan, you need to let him go so I can have a look at him. Now."

"How?"

How could he let Silas go? He had to make sure Silas knew he was loved, had always been loved, tell him how sorry he was and...

What if Lev lost him and never found him again? What if Silas slipped beneath the surface of the ocean, hollow eyes staring unseeingly at Lev as he slowly sank into the depths of existence?

No. Lev wouldn't let him go. He'd carry Silas in his arms until they were nothing more than shadows and stars.

"I have an idea. Why don't you hold his head in your lap while I look at him? I'm sure Silas would prefer it. Just try to breathe so you can be strong for him."

Lev could do that. He loosened his hold and ushered Silas out of his arms and onto the pillow of his lap.

"Well done," Lucian said as if they were in the art studio, and Lev had finally earned his approval.

Lucian pressed his fingers to Silas's neck, searching for the pulse Lev already knew had fled. When he couldn't find it, his shoulders slumped, but he put on a brave face, which was very kind of him. Fatherly even.

"Let's get him on his back. There's still a chance. You can do that for him, right?"

Lev nodded and let Father take him. He'd never felt more powerless and alone than when he let Silas go.

Silas wasn't his to hold anymore.

Father was careful, but gravity was violent. Silas's head rolled on his broken neck, face drifting toward Lev, to stare with pale blue irises eclipsed by dilated pupils.

Lev climbed to his feet and backed away, watching outside of his body as Father bent over Silas and breathed air into his lungs, and pushed on his chest, trying to pump blood from the heart Lev broke, growing more panicked as the last connection he had to Wendell vanished, and he arrived at the same conclusion Lev already had.

Silas was dead.

The balcony door was open. Lev wasn't sure if he'd opened it or Silas's soul had left through it. Wind whispered into the room, swirling and swishing the white curtains like a current coaxing waves into churning. The ocean called his name on a crashing wave, summoning him away from the body Silas no longer lived in.

Wind snatched the tears from his cheeks as he followed Silas's soul out onto the balcony. He gripped the thick stone parapet and hoisted himself onto it, then climbed to full height, and stood at the precipice of death.

The tide had retreated. Only jagged, craggy rocks would catch him, but the ocean promised to return for him, and he saw Silas swimming in the shallows. Lev didn't hesitate. He listened. With Silas's name on his lips, Lev took his last breath, and leapt off the ledge.

"Leviathan, no!"

Father caught Lev around the middle. His horizon tilted sideways. Father carted him kicking and screaming away from the balcony and tackled him to the ground. The only man stronger than Lev at Lichenmoor was his father, but Lev had grief on his side, and he fought to free himself. He had to get to Silas.

"Fetch the horse's kit!" Father roared.

The kit? What for? Had Silas survived?

"Let me go! Silas needs me."

"Silas needs you *inside*," Father shouted, then lowered his voice. "He was so upset when he woke up without you. Come and I'll show you."

Lev sniffed and nodded. Father was right. Poor Silas must be furious with him. Lev would comfort him.

"He'll be so pleased." Lucian released Lev and lifted him from the floor. "Take care and enter slowly so you don't frighten him."

Lucian steered him into the room. The door clicked shut behind him, locking out the wind.

"So Silas isn't cold," Father explained.

"Of course."

Lev scanned the floor for Silas and found him in the center of the bed on his back, face turned toward the balcony, eyes closed like he'd fallen asleep while waiting for him.

A crown of silken hair as shiny as crow feathers spilled out on the pillow cradling his head. Father had covered him with the fluffy cloud of Lev's duvet.

"The floor wasn't very comfortable, so I carried him to bed and tucked him in."

"Was he upset?"

Father pressed his lips together and shook his head. "He knows it was an accident."

"Thank you." Lev crossed to Silas's side.

"He's still not quite himself."

"Si? It's okay. I'm here," Lev whispered and lifted Silas's hand and pressed it against his cheek. "He's still so cold."

"He'll warm up under the covers soon."

Lev would help him. He'd share his body heat. He peeled the covers back.

"Christ. Leviathan, don't wake him!" Father yanked Lev back from the bed. "Wait until the doctor examines him."

No. Lev shook him off and ripped the duvet back. Silas didn't flinch, and he wasn't breathing, and his eyes were as empty as when Lev had last seen them.

Losing Silas all over again eviscerated him. Lev collapsed over Silas's chest and sobbed into his shirt.

"No. Silas, please. I'm so sorry."

Lev took Silas's hand and curled his limp arm over Lev's back. Silas couldn't be dead; he was comforting Lev, stroking his back, saying he forgave him, and Lev would promise to love Silas the way he needed him to.

Then they'd leave Lichenmoor, and Lev wouldn't feel claustrophobic anymore, and Silas wouldn't be sad anymore.

The floorboards creaked. Lev lifted his head. Father nodded

at someone in the doorway. Silas's arm rolled off Lev's back and landed on the bed sickeningly.

"Luna, the box," Father snapped.

What box? Lev couldn't let them take Silas and put him in a box all by himself. Silas would be lonely. He needed Lev and Lev needed him.

Silas couldn't leave him.

"Oh love, please don't cry." Luna stroked Lev's back the way he wished Silas could have.

"I can't lose him. I can't live. I can't—" He choked on a sob.

Lev cried and cried into Silas's neck until he couldn't breathe. How could he breathe without Silas? How could he breathe when Silas couldn't?

A sharp pain lanced his thigh. He clutched Silas tighter. His pulse slowed, and his vision blurred, and he didn't care about breathing anymore.

The bed swayed over gentle waves and carried Lev and Silas out to sea. Lev wasn't afraid.

The tide would return them.

55

THOSE FORGOTTEN

LEV

MARCH 2

Silas's laugh skittered across Lev's eardrums like a spider.

"You're doing it again, Levvy."

Lev followed the laugh to Silas jumping on the bed in pajamas. "What? How did you..."

The past and present blended. Time was moving in circles again, wasn't it? The characters changed but the end remained the same.

Lev looked down. Below him, Asher's eyes were open. Not dull and glassy. Not scared. Tears had escaped the corners of his cheeks and he looked so very sad, but loving.

"Asher!" Lev released Asher's neck. "I'm so sorry."

Asher sucked in a long breath through bloodstained lips. Lev peeked inside his mouth to check for a busted lip, but Asher had a painful gash on his tongue. What a nightmare that must have been for him.

"Are you alright? Why did I ask you that? Of course you aren't. I nearly killed you."

Lev helped Asher sit up and turned his chin from side to

448

side. His head didn't roll limply on his neck. Lavishing apology after apology, Lev checked his head for injuries, and then the rest of him, but the only marks he found were the marks on Asher's neck.

"Blakely, can you please confirm I haven't killed you?"

That entirely serious request earned Lev the most pitiful attempt at a laugh.

"Don't talk, darling. Just breathe."

Lev pressed his ear to Asher's chest, and the sound of his heartbeat and the air whooshing through his lungs and the way Asher hugged his head was exactly what Lev needed after the memories he'd been locked in.

"Say something so I know I haven't broken anything."

Lev looked for Silas. He was still a threat, but wherever he was, he was hiding.

"Stop apologizing," Asher answered with a tragic rasp.

Lev pulled back to inspect him again. Asher had fought hard. Lev's arms were covered in scratches and he felt like he'd taken a few punches.

"Are these all from you?"

"Sorry," Asher whispered.

"Thank you for stopping me." He pressed his forehead against Asher's. "I almost killed you."

Asher cupped Lev's cheek. "But you didn't. Don't cry."

"Am I crying?" Lev wiped his cheeks. "Oh. I guess I am."

Asher coughed and cleared his throat. "You were crying before, too."

"You already sound so much more like yourself instead of a very sad frog, but does it hurt?"

"I'm fine. Why were you crying?"

"I don't remember. I hurt you, and I don't know how or why."

"It wasn't you. It was Silas."

"Silas doesn't exist. He lives inside my head. I did this."

Lev trailed his fingers down the side of Asher's neck, cataloguing each of the red fingerprints that would become bruises. Maybe the visceral pain in his gut was guilt, rather than an injury from Asher fighting him off.

"Lev…"

Lev climbed to his feet and scrubbed his face with his hands. "I don't know what to do. You're not safe with me, but I can't leave you because what if Silas comes back, but what if I disappear again?"

Asher tried to stand.

"No. If there was ever a time to listen, be a good lad and stay far away from me."

"Where did you go when you left?"

"I beg your pardon?"

"Before you…"

"Tried to strangle you?"

"I was going to say something less dramatic."

Lev cocked his head to the side. "Oh? What sort of spin would you have given it?"

"A neck massage." Asher laughed.

"It's not funny."

Asher made another move to stand.

Lev rushed forward. "Let me help you."

Once Asher was in bed with his head perched atop several pillows, Lev backed away toward the bathroom.

"Wait here. I'm going to grab a sword from my closet."

"Fuck no." Asher snagged Lev's wrist. "You tried to kill me the last time you went into the bathroom by yourself."

"Precisely! How do you plan to stop me without a sword?"

"We'll go together, and you can tell me where to find it. The last thing I need is for you to turn all Silas-shaped with a sharp object."

Asher hopped down from the bed far too carelessly for someone who'd recently been strangled and dragged Lev toward the bathroom. Lev had worried Asher had other injuries, but he had no limp and needed no escort.

Christ. A few minutes longer before he'd snapped out of it and Lev would have been crying over Asher's corpse like Silas.

"Are you going to explain why you have a sword in your closet?" Asher asked.

"In a word, ADHD. I'm afraid the story is terribly boring. It's not even an impressive sword. Not much longer than a bread knife."

It took Lev the entire trip to the closet and back, including changing out of their bloodstained clothes, to explain how he'd been reading while walking and crashed into a suit of armor, which then fell down a seldom-used stairwell, making a colossal racket.

"I had no choice but to close my book and go down the stairs after it—"

"Why?"

"Blakely, you can't just leave swords at the bottom of stair-cases. Imagine if you tripped and somehow survived cart-wheeling head over arse all the way to the bottom only to land on a sword."

Asher exploded into an uproarious round of laughter that sounded like the quack of a duck with a head cold. Lev almost smiled, but not even the reward of making Asher laugh could boost his spirits. He'd been so close to never hearing him laugh again.

"I took the sword and left the armor with the limbs askew and completely forgot about it. At least until Luna stumbled upon it later and screamed like a kettle."

"Poor Luna."

"Indeed." Lev helped Asher into bed and handed the sword back to him before sitting against the headboard beside him. "Promise me you'll use this if I start to look murderous?"

"Yes, sir," Asher said in a solemn whisper.

"Good lad." Lev kissed his temple. "Now that you're armed, where were we?"

"Do you remember catching me looking at the things you hid in the wall?"

Lev wracked his mind for the memory and shook his head. "No. Did you look inside the bag?"

Asher nodded.

"What a horrifying thing to discover. Ordinarily, I'm very good about keeping everything locked away, but when I couldn't find you, I was frantic." Lev dropped his gaze, and forced what he hoped were very repentant and alluring eyes back to him. "Please don't be angry. The watch I gave you has a GPS tracking device, and I hid the transponder there. I pulled it out to search for you, but as you may have noticed, your watch is still on the table where you left it."

Asher lifted a single incredulous eyebrow. "Excuse me, what the fuck?" He'd said it at a normal volume, which meant he was definitely yelling.

"I know how it sounds, but I was only trying to keep you safe. I trust you to go wherever you care to, and if you ever want to leave, I'll let you."

If he had any say in the matter, he'd chase Asher back to America right now, but he'd settle for as soon as the roads were passable.

"I don't know if Lichenmoor is cursed, or if maybe Silas..." Lev shook his head. He was Silas. "Regardless, I can't bear the thought of you lost out there, and you simply have far too much confidence for someone with such a dreadful sense of direction."

Asher held out his left arm. "Put it on."

"You're taking this remarkably well." Too well.

"Silas told me about the curse."

Lev nearly dropped the wristwatch. "What? When? How?"

"We talked a lot before he strangled me."

"*I* strangled you." Lev finished fastening the watch and kissed Asher's hand.

Asher shook his head with a dismissive frown. "No, you didn't." He looked at the watch. "Is this custom or do luxury secret GPS tracking watches exist?"

"They're intended for unfaithful husbands, as it were."

Asher silently watched several seconds tick by.

"What are you thinking about?" Lev asked.

"Marriage," Asher said.

The single word pierced Lev's heart like a sword, because that would never happen for them. "I don't know what to say except that I quite like the idea of you as my husband."

"I didn't say I was thinking about marrying you," Asher said so convincingly, only the flash of his dimples made Lev believe his joking smirk.

"Words hurt, Blakely." Lev placed his hand over the spot where his heart hurt so acutely, he hoped he wasn't having actual chest pain.

"When I asked Silas how he was in your room, he said he was only strong enough because of the storm, and he could only hurt me until the tide retreated."

"That's just a story Wendell wrote. Silas wasn't in our room. I was."

"But where did Wendell get the idea from?"

"The aether? I've no idea."

Asher took Lev's hand and knit their fingers together. "Where did you go while Silas strangled me?"

"A memory."

"Of when you killed Silas?"

"Yes, but I didn't strangle him, if that's the theory you're testing."

"How did you kill him?"

"Why aren't you afraid of me? Are you actually this reckless with your safety?" Lev snapped and pulled his hand free from Asher's. "I promise you, there's no redeeming revelation. I murdered him and I was too much of a coward to confess. I don't even know where he's buried. He's just out there somewhere all alone when the only person whose company he needed was mine. I killed him with my own two hands, and the closest to a prison sentence I've served was the last five years locked at Lichenmoor. That's nothing compared to all the years I robbed Silas of."

Lev buried his face in his hands and filled them with tears, all while Blakely, in his fucking unending benevolence, tried to reassure him. When that didn't work, Asher climbed onto Lev's lap and held Lev's head to his chest the way Lev had done to Silas after killing him.

Lev lifted his head. "I don't deserve your faith in me. I don't deserve your leniency. I don't deserve your love. I never should have invited you here, and I should have sent you home immediately. Murderers don't deserve happy endings."

Asher wiped his tears. "I believe you when you say you're guilty, but if you never confessed, maybe you should confess to me."

Lev nodded. That was an excellent idea. Perhaps Asher would finally realize how dangerous he was. So Lev told Asher everything he remembered, which was everything that had happened, because of all the things Lev had forgotten, he would never forget Silas's death.

Asher listened without comment or judgment until Lev sobbed the ending into Asher's poor battered neck.

"When I woke, Silas was gone."

Lev straightened and allowed Asher to blot his tears even if he didn't deserve it. How could he deny him when he looked at Lev with such pained devastation?

"Father had disposed of him, and I was so distraught, a doctor sedated me again, this time with human medicine instead of horse tranquilizers. I kept trying to turn myself in, but Father was willing to spend a fortune and commit whatever crimes were necessary to stop me.

"He refused to tell me what he'd done with Silas's body, and without a body, there was no murder to confess to. Father may have tried to shield me, but I've always been guilty, and I never stopped looking for him."

"Silas doesn't know where he was buried?"

"No, probably because I don't know, and he's me."

"What about Luna?"

Lev groaned. "God, the hell I put her through between Silas and how much she feared for me in the months after. She seldom left my side and watched over me while I slept. I believe her when she says Father never told her either.

"Personally, I suspect Father incinerated Silas's body in the forge, then pulverized his bones, and tossed his remains into the sea."

"Because Lucian requested to be cremated and buried at sea?"

"Clever as ever, Mr. Blakely."

Asher grimaced. "Don't call me that like you're going to make me leave."

He was going to. That was true. "We still have until the ocean recedes."

"Fuck that. If you want me to leave, I'll fight a hell of a lot dirtier than when you were strangling me."

Asher took the sword and pressed the blade to the unprotected flesh between the bottom of Lev's sternum and his ribs, ready to plunge it into his heart. Lev had always known Asher was strong, but now Asher knew that too. Lev's job was done. Asher would be safe after he left Lichenmoor.

Lev stroked the side of Asher's neck again. "I know."

"You could leave with me."

Lev shook his head. "Even if I could, I wouldn't. I won't let you suffer so many years alongside me only for me to die decades before you."

"You don't know that. What happened to only here, only now, only you?"

"You told him!" Silas hissed, appearing behind Asher on the bed. "That was ours."

Asher didn't notice. More confirmation that Lev had been the one to hurt him. He was so grateful Asher already had the sword prepared.

"I'm so sorry, but I love you too much to hurt you."

"That's what you'll be doing if you make me go. Do you think I could ever be happy, that every breath wouldn't be agony, if I knew you were haunted by him and your guilt, alone at Lichenmoor with no one to care for you if there's really..." Asher's words were lost to a sob. His eyes hardened with resolve. "You won't let yourself have me because you think you don't deserve to be happy, but you've put yourself in solitary confinement for five years. You can't send me away. You can't."

Lev swept Asher's tears away. "You'll be sad at first, but you'll think of me less and less, you'll find someone to love you like I..." Lev pinched the bridge of his nose and turned his head.

"You can't even say it. You can't even finish the sentence and look at me when you say it. I won't go. You'd be better off killing me than sending me away. I'm your good—" Asher's own sob interrupted him; he pressed the blade deeper, though not through Lev's skin yet. "Please."

Lev didn't know what to do. He couldn't leave him and he couldn't look at him. He needed to keep him safe and then escort him to the gates.

Silas was too quiet. When Lev lifted his head, Silas was still behind Asher, but he mirrored Lev's motion in perfect synchrony.

"You think you deserve to be alone, Lev. You think you deserve to suffer, that you need to be punished, but you don't."

"Asher..."

"He's lost the plot, hasn't he?" Silas said, dropping his little mirror act. "You, of all people, deserve to suffer most. Don't worry. You'll kill him next time. We've got hours until low tide.

If the tides can be trusted with such a storm afoot. It reminds me of the night I killed Father."

"Shut up!" Lev snapped.

"Lev?" Asher looked over his shoulder and back at Lev.

"I do wish I hadn't killed him." Silas grinned smugly. "After all, I'm not a murderer like you, but how else was I supposed to summon you?"

That wasn't true. It couldn't be true.

"I thought you'd return on your own, but you're not Father's lapdog anymore."

"Lev, what's not true?" Asher asked in a brave voice that was clearly bravado.

Damn and fucking blast. He'd said that out loud?

"Oi!" Asher said in an American-attempting-a-footballer sort of way. "Look at me. Only me."

"He can't be serious," Silas said.

Lev ignored him and did as Asher asked.

Asher took Lev's face in his hands. "Only now. Only me."

"The sword, Asher." Lev pulled Asher's hands down.

Asher groaned and picked it back up.

"Good lad." Lev leaned in until the bite of the blade pierced through his shirt. "Only now. Only you."

"Is he still here?" Asher asked.

"Yes."

"Good."

"Asher..."

"No. We're only here and now with your asshole ex in the cuckold chair."

"The cuckold what?"

"Oh come *on*. You're not that old."

"I know what cuckolding is, but I'd no idea there were chairs. I'm simply too soft and sensitive and terrible at sharing."

Asher laughed, and this time it sounded like his own laugh

instead of a quack. It was the most beautiful sound Lev had ever heard, so beautiful he wished he could paint in sound.

Asher sobered. "I have something to say, and I want you to listen and not interrupt me. That goes for both of you."

Lev nodded. Silas rolled his eyes in a way that projected deepest loathing.

"I know Silas suffered. I know what it's like to be bullied and have no friends at school, and while my mom does accept me, not everyone in my family does. It was so difficult. Sometimes it still hurts. But I've never lost a parent or battled an eating disorder. All of that must have been so heavy for you both. You were right to break up with him, though."

Silas said nothing, but he'd gone eerily still, not in the way he had when he died, but in the way a predator would.

"There's no excuse for murder, but it was an accident. You didn't premeditate it. In America, you'd spend less than a few years in jail, especially if you pled guilty, and when I tried to look up English law, I got a little confused by the lords and whatnot, but the sentence seems similar. When you throw in that his bones were so brittle, I don't know if a jury would have convicted you."

"You researched English law?"

"Yeah. I've researched all kinds of things on your computer during your morning jogs. You wouldn't stop telling me about how you were basically an axe murderer, and research helps my anxiety. To be informed is to be armed."

"You were more anxious about my prison sentence than the axe?"

"I worried a little at first, but I know you, and you would never kill me."

"Asher, I nearly strangled you to death. The only reason you're even alive is pure luck or some god reaching down from the heavens."

"No. It was Silas."

"Silas is dead," Lev shouted.

Instead of looking afraid, Asher looked amused, which only aggravated Lev more, but he'd already raised his voice once, so he took a deep breath before continuing. "I'm sorry I shouted. I'm not angry with you. I just wish you would accept that there is no Silas for you to blame."

"Are you done?" Asher asked with so much bloody sass. "Good, because I wasn't even talking about Silas killing me. I'm still alive because Silas saved me. Side note: I love that for him because I know how much he wanted you to kill me."

"Asher…"

"No, Snake. Let him finish." Silas appeared at Lev's side with his chin perched on his palms. "I'd love to hear more of the mental gymnastics our Asher has twisted himself into to excuse any time you've tried to kill someone."

"Listen to me, Lev." Asher cupped Lev's cheek with his free hand. "Only me."

"Sorry."

"Silas didn't want to kill me. He wanted you to remember killing me. He just got the timing wrong. I don't know shit about ghost physics."

"Ghost physics?" Lev and Silas both said, though Silas added a derisive snort.

"Do you mean the *paranormal?*"

"Don't be pretentious about vocabulary when I just lost a ton of brain cells."

"That's not funny."

"Silas kept bragging about how sweet his revenge was going to be while he strangled me. I must have closed my eyes or passed out because when I opened my eyes again, you were crying and then you finally looked at me."

"I'm so sorry for what I put you through, but your version of events doesn't exculpate me."

"You're not listening!" Asher took the sword and threw it at the wardrobe. "Silas is your Ben. He fucked with your head and hurt you, maybe in a different way, but he trapped you. He forced you. I hate him for that and I hate him for torturing you for decades."

"The feeling is very mutual," Silas said.

"He's worse than Ben," Asher continued. "Because he knew you the way only family could, and he used it against you. I know you killed him, but it sounds like he was so fragile to begin with."

"I should have been more gentle."

"You were a victim, Lev, even if he was too."

"When he went away to school, I was happy."

"You were happy because you were free, and still he's trapped you here."

"No. I trapped myself here. All of this is in my head."

"Even if you hallucinated him for the last five years, he manipulated you as long as you knew him."

"What if deep down I chose to kill him?"

"You can't hold yourself responsible for subconscious thoughts you never had."

Lev shook his head and looked at Silas who was trying very hard to look unassuming, something he never did.

"Only me." Asher forced Lev's face back to him, then removed his hands from Lev's cheeks.

"Sorry," Lev said.

"You say sorry too much."

"I could say the same about you."

"You can't say shit because you say sorry as a question."

Lev smiled in spite of everything.

"Silas made you do things you didn't want to do, Lev, and then he used it against you. That false accusation would have ruined your life and put you in prison longer than if you'd pointed the police to his body. I didn't see how much I'd been harmed by Ben, how little of it was my fault, until you showed me. Silas hurt you."

"But you didn't kill Ben."

"And if I'd had to escape?"

Bloody hell. Asher was right. The parallels were there. Ben may have used BDSM to control Asher, but Silas had controlled Lev with sex and secrets too.

"I'd have praised you," Lev conceded.

"Exactly. You've been grieving Silas all this time and thought it was guilt, and I think it's time to stop."

Asher kissed Lev gently and continued. "Silas's epitaph said, *True death only comes for those forgotten.* It's a comforting thought. When people die they live on inside your memories. But what if some people should be forgotten? What if you've kept Silas's memory alive for so long that it's hurting you?"

PAPER BOAT

LEV

The crackling fire and light drizzle outside was the only sound in the room. The storm had passed and when Lev looked to his right, Silas was absent.

Asher slipped out from under Lev's arm.

"What are you doing?" Lev asked.

"A new ritual." Asher crossed to Lev's desk and returned with his sketchbook. He found a blank page, then passed the sketchbook to Lev with a pencil.

"Draw Silas how he was before he died."

And so Lev drew Silas as he was, as he'd always been, because he hadn't come back all wrong. He'd been that version of Silas all along. In a way, Silas had been right—Lev had never loved all of Silas, and when Silas died, Lev put him on a pedestal, and forgot the bad parts on purpose.

Lev honored the Silas that was real, sketching the shards of light in his irises when he was playful, the slender fingers that had written love sonnets, the sharp cheekbones that flushed when Silas had fiercely insisted that Lev was more than Father's expectations.

And as he layered shadows in the hollows beneath Silas's sunken eyes, he filled in the dark parts he'd left out of all the paintings he'd punished himself with, the mind games, the clinginess, the cruel accusations. Each strand of graphite hair marked the days he'd spent in the dark with Silas.

Lev hid the bars of the cage Silas had trapped him inside in the slight upward tilt of the nose Lev had once kissed, the contempt in the subtle curl of his upper lip, the cruelty in the corner of his smirk, and lastly the envy projecting from his pupils.

He blew the excess graphite off of the paper like the magic dust in the bedtime stories Wendell had told him, and with that last breath, and a gust of silver dust, a teardrop splashed onto the page, and Lev said goodbye to Silas.

In that vaguely supernatural way that Asher sensed the murky contents of Lev's mind and heart, Asher caught Lev as he collapsed into his arms.

"You're so brave, Leviathan Marks."

For the first time since Silas had died, Lev liked the sound of his full name, especially when it was spoken from Asher's tongue. Lev wasn't the monster of his namesake anymore.

In a clumsy clash of need and impatience and the holiest devotion to whatever god had destined them for each other, their lips slammed together.

This kiss was different—it felt like a vow, like they were consummating their fated connection, locking their souls together forever with a bond so strong, neither time nor distance, or the slow death of lost memories, or even the soft exhale of Lev's last breath would part them.

Lev tasted copper. Asher's split tongue must have broken open. Asher pulled back and Lev was about to reach for the waste bin in case he vomited, but Asher took Lev's hand, and gently unfurled it, then spat blood onto the drawing of Silas with a protective rage that made Lev want to fuck Asher and be fucked by him until they both cried in rapture instead of regret.

"Fuck him," Asher said, slightly slurred, and wiped his mouth.

"Shall I chuck the drawing in now to complete whatever ritual you're up to?"

Asher stopped him. "Not here."

After collecting all of his *Silas mementos*—as Asher called them—they ventured into the hall.

Asher slowed. "You never moved out of the room Silas died in, did you?"

Lev shook his head. "I didn't want to leave the last place I'd seen him. Luna tried to convince me, and Father's attempts to command me didn't work outside the art studio. In the end, they couldn't force me. Not when my mental health already teetered on the edge of sanity. After Father died and Silas appeared, I realized he couldn't bother me in my old room, so I moved back in."

"We're never sleeping there again," Asher said, jaw tight.

"Please don't be angry."

"I'm not mad. It's just really fucking sad."

"Does it help to know I roomed you in Wendell's room so he could watch over you? Some might say it was almost romantic."

"No one would say that. It's creepy. You don't know how many times I jacked off in there."

Lev laughed so loudly it echoed throughout the entire stairwell.

"It's not funny either."

"Yes. You're right. Poor Wendell must have been so uncomfortable."

Asher rolled his lips inward, but he never could hide his dimples.

The lower levels of the castle hadn't flooded, aside from the dungeons. Lev built a fire in the forge.

"Are you sure you want to get rid of all of them?" Asher asked. "You could keep the photograph of when you two were happy. I don't think burning everything matters if we're making our own magic."

"I wasn't happy." Lev tossed the photo and passport in, then the first handful of photos Asher passed him, watching the small details of Silas's fingertips, the hair beneath his belly button, and the curve of his ear warp, and fade, and disappear. There were hundreds of photos, and more and more of Silas died as Lev tossed the photos Asher dealt to him.

At some point he found himself on his knees in front of the forge with empty hands. Asher passed him the self-portrait with the scratched out eyes, the art Father had said was finally honest. The real truth, however, was that Father never should have pushed Lev to punish himself through his art.

Art should have been his respite. Painting could have helped him process his emotions and provide catharsis, but the only thing he'd painted since Silas died was his guilt.

"I wish I could erase the tattoo over my heart and replace it with something that won't remind you of Silas every time you take off my shirt."

Lev slid his hand under Asher's shirt and placed it over his heart, soothed by his warm skin and the vibration of his pulse. "Your tattoo will remind me you saw the truth before I did, and helped me see it too." He dropped the self-portrait onto the fire. The flames devoured it the second they tasted paper. "I can paint my eyes over your tattoo every day for the rest of time if that would please you."

"That sounds a lot like punishing yourself, and I'll never let you do that again."

Lev smiled thinly. "Thank you for that."

"Are you okay?" Asher brushed Lev's hair back from his temple.

"I am. Let's finish, hm? Then we can go bedroom shopping."

They didn't have to travel very far with the paper boat Lev had folded from the bloodstained sketch of Silas. Lev rubbed Silas's raven hair between his fingers one last time, then placed it gently in the paper boat and carried it to the mouth of a shimmering riptide.

"Any second thoughts?" Asher rested his head against Lev's shoulder and wrapped an arm around his waist. "Remember, it's our spell."

"I know, love."

Lev bent and held the paper boat just above the water. "I'm ready."

Asher lit a match and dropped it into the boat, and as soon as Lev was certain the wind wouldn't blow it out, he released the boat, and delivered the last of Silas to the sea.

Flames engulfed the paper boat as it sailed beyond the shore break, bobbed over the gentle swell of a building wave, and disappeared, laying Silas Morrigan to rest in the arms of Lucian Marks, who'd sacrificed an eternity beside his two soulmates to ensure Silas would never be alone. If only Silas had known.

A weight lifted from Lev's chest and when he inhaled, he breathed fully for the first time in decades. He was free.

By the time the ocean relinquished the land three days later, Lev was ready to leave Lichenmoor, but it took one week, and several failed attempts to succeed.

They stopped at the gate where he'd first seen Asher through the fog.

Asher took his hand. "Only now. Only me."

"Only us," Lev agreed, and this time when he lifted his foot, all the years of agoraphobia therapy finally worked, and he stepped over to the other side and left Lichenmoor behind.

He looked back at the castle high on the bluffs and knew

Silas was no longer there, just like he knew he wouldn't see him again. He wasn't sure if it was the ritual that had worked, or if Silas was a ghost, but Lev had his own theory.

Life and death weren't separated by a veil, but a window. Some could see through it, even press their ear to it, but they couldn't open or climb through it. He and Silas had been trapped on either side until a rare thunderstorm fractured the window between life and death, and lightning was the afterlife bleeding through the cracks.

Some questions would never be answered, perhaps shouldn't be answered. Questions like how Silas had been able to stay after he died, or why he'd decided to trap Lev in his web, and what if banishing Silas was only a false high, and Alzheimer's still roosted in the rafters of Lev's mind, waiting until the right moment to strike?

But he'd take his own advice and live only now. With him.

EPILOGUE

ASHER

The storm that brought Silas's memory to life had destroyed what remained of him, flooding several rooms in the east wing, including the one behind the locked door. The room had never been Silas's, but a place they'd met to have the rough sex Lev hadn't wanted.

Lev had tried to paint his pain as punishment, and lock it away with the notebooks Silas had filled with loneliness, but pain didn't listen to locks, and penance without forgiveness was just purgatory.

Unfortunately, they hadn't discovered the mess until after their trip to Berlin where Lev had undergone a series of tests and treatments at a world-renowned hospital. They were still waiting on genetic testing results for hereditary Early-onset Alzheimer's and several extremely rare conditions, but everything looked reassuring so far.

Stewing in six weeks of damp had destroyed Lev's paintings of Silas, and the leak in the ceiling had turned the trunk into a vat of disintegrating paper. They'd tried to salvage Silas's notebooks, but it was like trying to catch the wind. Lev had lost it, searching the water for any shred of Silas to cling to, until Asher had dumped bucket after bucket of water out of the window and Lev accepted that Silas's words were gone.

While Asher held him, Lev had cried the cathartic tears he hadn't when the ocean swallowed the paper boat, because no matter how much Silas had haunted him, Lev had still lost the man he'd loved for three decades.

Luckily, Lev hadn't lost all of Silas's words. Wendell had compiled a thick anthology of Silas's short stories and shelved it beside his own books in Lichenmoor's library.

Inside the book, Wendell had left a handwritten message above his signature.

If you miss me when I'm gone,
find me in the library.
If you ever feel alone,
shelve your book beside my own.
If you forget what I sound like,
listen to the voice I write with.
If you feel like an imposter,
look at the book in your hands.
If you wish you'd had more time with me,
spend time inside my head.
If you ever doubt my love for you,
open any of my books and read the dedication:
For Silas, with love

For all Silas's faults, he'd deserved to be loved. Hurt people hurt people. Silas's tragic history put his actions in perspective, and Asher no longer demonized him.

Lev had insisted on burning the art he'd created to punish himself, even the painting in Lucian's studio. While the paintings burned, Asher had encouraged Lev to relinquish what he could of his guilt, but forgiving himself would probably take years more of therapy.

Disposing of the life-size statue of Silas had been a more difficult task, but with Hector's help, and his tractor, the statue now resided on the ocean floor off the cliffs of Lichenmoor.

The tide did not return him.

Asher's road to forgiveness was still ongoing. He'd rejoined his virtual support group, and been surprised by how many of the men had remembered him. There were new faces too, and he found comfort and kinship in their shared struggle and growth.

With the help of a therapist specializing in men's sexual assault and abuse in the kink community, Asher had rearranged the jumbled puzzle pieces of his experience into a clearer image. Whether he'd said no to Ben or not, he never could have consented freely when Ben had groomed and black-mailed him.

Ben had died in May. Regardless of the pain he'd caused, Asher had still grieved him, though not as extensively as Lev had grieved Silas.

Enduring Ben's abuse didn't have a silver lining. It wasn't some character-building exercise, and it sure as fuck wasn't God's plan as Nonna had suggested when he'd left Watson. But Asher didn't blame himself anymore. He knew his own strength. Ben hadn't broken him, and Lev hadn't fixed him, because he'd never needed to be fixed to begin with.

But that was the past. It wasn't now, and it wasn't them.

He and Lev had collaborated on a series of paintings on grief, guilt, and forgiveness. The art they'd made was honest, and beautiful, and hurt in all the right ways.

Free from Lucian's expectations and punishments, Lev had

stepped into his own renaissance age, creating masterpiece after masterpiece that differed so starkly from Lucian's style, no one would ever compare them again.

Asher's solo exhibition of The Seven Sins and the Bolton Strid had achieved higher critical acclaim than their own joint exhibition, but Asher already had the only approval he needed —his own.

SEPTEMBER 17

Lev sifted through the mail they'd picked up from the post office as they walked up the front steps.

"It's here." Lev stopped mid-stride and passed him a nondescript white envelope that looked more likely to contain an electricity bill than a life-altering revelation.

Asher's stomach dropped with dread. The envelope weighed nothing but might as well have been packed with lead.

Lev's face blanched before Asher's eyes. "Let's read it inside."

"Okay." Asher took Lev's hand and led him up the steps.

The front door screeched open as they entered, more unnerving than usual.

"Do you want to sit down?" Asher asked.

Lev shook his head. "I need to know straight away, but... Might you read it to me? I don't know if I can."

Asher's heart ached. "Of course, Lev."

"Thank you."

Asher slipped his finger inside, and tore it open. "Whatever it says, remember we live in the now, okay?"

Lev nodded solemnly.

Asher's heart somersaulted inside his chest as he pulled out the letter and unfolded it, promising himself he'd be strong for Lev, no matter what it said.

"Leviathan Marks," Asher read aloud. *"The results of your whole genome sequence were negative. Please see the attached pages for the full report, and consult your practitioner for explanation and follow-up. Wishing you continued good health, Calista Falk, Genetic Counselor..."*

"It's negative?" Lev asked in an even voice.

"Yes. *The results of your whole genome sequence were negative,"* Asher read a second time, and held the pages out. "Look for yourself."

Lev donned a pair of reading glasses that made him even sexier, lips moving as he silently read the first page and the lab results. A smile teased the corner of his lips. "It's negative."

"It is." Asher burst into tears, the months of dread escaping him so quickly he almost felt dizzy.

"Baby, don't cry."

Asher sniffed. "I'm sorry. It's just... We get our happy ending."

"We do." Lev grinned and pulled Asher into a hug.

Asher looped his arms around Lev's neck and kissed him, pouring endless depths of devotion and gratitude and everlasting love into Lev's soul.

Salty tears erased any memory of the sorrow they'd shed, painting over the pain and turning it into relief.

Lev hummed against Asher's lips and deepened the kiss, gripping Asher's ass and lifting him off his feet. With a needy whimper, Asher tightened his hold on the back of Lev's neck and wrapped his legs around Lev's waist.

"I love you," Asher said, breathless, tears still falling, when they parted.

"I love you, too." Lev eased Asher back down onto his feet and wiped Asher's tears with his thumbs. "You're still crying, hm?"

"Yes, sir." Asher nodded and bit into his bottom lip.

Lev's eyes darkened. "You're such a good lad, crying for me because you love me so much. What's your color, Blakely?"

"Green," Asher said on a long exhale, and licked his bottom lip. They could both use some decompression.

Lev caressed Asher's cheek. "Kneel for me."

The command injected heat into Asher's veins as he lowered to his knees right there on the wood floor, sat back on his heels, pressed his palms against his thighs, and looked up the length of Lev's decadent body.

"Mm. Look how obedient you are, how sweetly you listen. You're so pretty down there on your knees for me."

Surrendering to Lev was a far more honest and vulnerable submission than when Asher was with Ben, because Lev was stronger than him, and because he trusted Lev to take care of him, and because he wasn't submitting out of fear or desire for acceptance. He submitted because it soothed him, and pleasing Lev pleased him too.

"Unknot my bootlaces, Blakely."

Asher rushed to comply, bending his head. A belt jingled above him. Asher froze, muscle memory tensing his body as he braced for the sound of a strap whipping through the air. Battling his PTSD would always be a challenge, but it was easier to stop the cycle because he'd reclaimed his strength and trusted himself.

Fingers carded through Asher's hair, stroking his scalp soothingly. "Look at me, baby."

Asher did.

"Keep your eyes on me always." Taking Asher's chin in hand, Lev stepped out of his boots and kicked them aside. "Unbutton my trousers."

"Yes, sir." It took Asher a second to find the button with jittery hands and eyes on Lev, but he managed.

"My zipper next."

Asher looked down.

"Eyes on me," Lev reminded sweetly. "I know you'll be careful. You have a vested interest, after all."

Asher rolled his eyes, but suppressed the urge to debate Lev's vote of confidence. He wanted to be good for Lev. He wanted to serve him, so he slipped one hand inside Lev's pants to guard his cock and slowly dragged the zipper down.

Lev stroked Asher's chin with his thumb. "Thank you, baby."

Asher's cheeks flushed at his praise.

"Now, pull me out."

Lev wasn't fully erect yet, but Asher would get him there.

"Such a good pet." Lev stroked Asher's scalp with nimble fingers as his cock bobbed higher. "Hold your hands in your lap and get me ready with only your mouth."

Precum wept from Asher's cock and seeped into his boxer briefs as he leaned forward and nuzzled his cheek into the ginger hair at the base of Lev's cock. Humming, Asher ran his lips up and down Lev's length, and licked him broadly with his tongue, teasing his glans out from his foreskin, lapping each fresh drop of precum while Lev rained praise down on him.

"Color?" Lev asked in a sexy rasp.

"Green," Asher murmured against his cock, then sucked Lev into his mouth, and gave everything he had, fucking his throat on Lev's cock until tears from the intrusion blended with the tears of relief that hadn't stopped falling.

Lev moaned, hand falling to Asher's head in ownership and rapture. The sight of his hero succumbing to pleasure turned Asher feral as he swallowed against the head of his cock.

"Wait. Slow down." Lev gripped his cock and stepped back, withdrawing from Asher's mouth.

Asher whimpered, leaning forward, tongue stretching toward him, knees still rooted to the spot.

"Mm. I like you like this, so eager. But you'll have to wait a little longer. Stay." Lev took a single step backward.

Asher huffed. "Don't tease me."

Lev laughed darkly. "I would never tease you. If there's something you need, tell me and I'll give it to you."

Now wasn't the time for playing coy. "Please fuck my mouth until I can't breathe and use my tears as lube when you fuck me."

Lev's brows lifted and the muscles in his forearm flexed. "My, my. What a filthy mind you have." He mocked a pout and stroked his chin. "But, I'm not sure I'm convinced." He took another step back. "If you really want me to do that, lock your hands behind your back and follow on your knees."

Asher did as he was told, shuffling forward on his knees, turned on by the light degradation, willing to debase himself to the depths of humiliation. Lev would have done the same if the roles were reversed. They loved each other with equal shamelessness.

Lev backed away, leading Asher across the foyer, until he bumped into the wall. Asher toppled forward, so deep in subspace, he didn't try to catch himself, because Lev had told him not to use his hands.

Lev caught Asher and stroked his shoulders with his thumbs. "I've got you, darling."

"You always protect me."

"You protect me too." Lev's hands tightened around Asher's shoulders. "Now, no more talking. Tap my thigh twice if your color changes, and I will stop immediately. Show me."

Asher tapped his thigh as directed.

"Good lad. Open your mouth."

"Yes, sir." Asher opened wide and displayed his tongue, begging with his eyes.

Lev took his cock in hand and jerked himself lazily, exposing more and more of his glans with each tug, torturing Asher with the tantalizing image.

Asher whimpered, desperate for Lev's low gasps, and harsh curses, the long moans that reverberated inside his chest. He needed Lev to stuff his throat with his cock and fill his stomach with cum, and then fuck his ass until he fed cum into his guts.

"Ah-ah." Lev tapped his cock on Asher's lips. "Whimpering is too close to talking."

Lev rubbed his cock over Asher's face, painting precum on his lips and cheeks. Asher had never felt so adored by something so disrespectful. If he'd been allowed to talk, he would have thanked him.

All thoughts of anything else scattered to the four corners of the earth only he and Lev inhabited as Lev plunged back into Asher's mouth and slid down his throat. Asher submitted, even as he gagged, even as tears flooded his vision, and saliva drooled down his neck.

"Show me you can breathe," Lev said in a gravelly grunt, glacier gaze alert and inquisitive behind the veil of lust, cheeks flushed down to his freckles, jawline sharp with agonized pleasure, lips parted on a gasp as Asher swallowed his head and inhaled through his nose.

"Good lad. Again."

Asher exhaled and inhaled again, falling deeper into subspace, so safe in Lev's hands, he'd handed him control over his breaths.

"Look at you listening so well, holding me in your throat." Lev's voice broke into a moan. "*Fuck me*, Blakely. Your mouth is ecstasy." His hand tightened in Asher's hair, stinging Asher's scalp and spilling more tears down his face. "You're so fucking beautiful like this."

Lev cupped Asher's cheek and pulled his cock back, leaving a thread of spit connecting them as Asher caught his breath. "What color are you? You may speak."

"Still green," Asher gasped, throat raw. "Please fuck me."

"Oh, I'm afraid I'm not finished with you yet. I'll need a great deal more tears before I can fuck you."

Asher didn't answer, only opened his mouth wider and waited like the good boy he was. Lev pushed his cock back in and fucked his mouth in earnest, filling the foyer with the *gluck-gluck* of his cock wedged in and out of Asher's spasming throat.

Tears and drool spilled down Asher's front, saturating his shirt as he cried with relief and love and getting his throat fucked to within an inch of his life. Lev's head tipped back, exposing his neck. He was close.

Lev pulled out roughly, and dragged his cock over Asher's face, bathing himself in Asher's tears. Asher extended his tongue and lapped at Lev's balls.

"You're so perfect, baby," Lev said, awe-laced pride projected in his tone. "Turn around and get on your hands and knees for me."

Trembling and breathing through silent tears, Asher nodded and did as he was told. Lev pressed between Asher's shoulders until his cheek rested on the floor, then pulled Asher's sweatpants down only enough to bare his ass.

Lev scanned Asher's face. "I'm going to fuck you now. Do you want me to do that?"

Asher nodded.

"Words, Blakely. I need to hear your consent."

Asher rolled his eyes. "Begging for an aggressive throat fucking wasn't consent enough?"

"What happened to my good lad?" Lev teased.

"Your good lad is going to be very bad if you don't get inside of me right now."

Lev clicked his tongue. "As tempting as that sounds, I'm afraid I must get lube first."

"What?" Asher glared over his shoulder.

"Tears and spit is hardly enough lubrication to take me. I told you, I don't like to break my toys, but please do continue to run your bratty mouth as much as you wish."

Asher would have, but Lev reached into Asher's sweatpants pocket and pulled out his wallet.

"I stashed lube packets in here for just such an occasion."

"That's almost as bad as the stalker watch."

"You should thank me. I was only anticipating your greedy, impatient hole." Lev rubbed the packet between his hands to warm it, tore it open with his teeth, and worked the lube around and inside Asher's hole with one perfunctory caress of his finger.

"Fuck, Lev."

Lev laughed sinfully, and spat on Asher's hole, then pushed his cock inside in one long, slow thrust until his hips were flush. A cold sweat broke out across Asher's skin, goosebumps running like wildfires, every hair in his body lifting, his muscles tensing, his toes curling.

"Ready to come already?" Lev teased.

"Lev," Asher growled.

"*Ash.*"

Before Asher could say something snarky, Lev pulled back slowly, and buried himself back in with a roll of his hips that dragged his cock against Asher's prostate. Asher mewled, a sound he'd be embarrassed about later, but gave no fucks about now.

Pleasure crashed over him like the waves outside, giving him no chance to bob above the surface as Lev took his pleasure too, curling over him, whispering how much he loved him, how he'd live in the now with him for as long as the world existed, how he'd follow Asher in death, haunting him for the rest of his life in a way that didn't hurt, in a way that kept him safe, and loved, and cared for until he joined him later in the afterlife.

At some point his promises turned to prayers, to whatever gods had brought them together, and then his prayers went quiet and Lev's thrusts turned frantic, charged and electric, raining down pleasure so powerful it pushed Asher off the cliff into nirvana. Lev dove in after him on an ardent moan, thrusting with erratic abandon as his cock surged.

A surprise second orgasm rumbled through him, but it wasn't Lev's climax that got him there.

It was the call of the void in their connected gaze, asking, *What if?* It was Asher's answer as he leapt into the depths of Lev's soul. It was the realization that their love was as powerful as the storms that battered Lichenmoor, as the endless tide and vengeful ocean, as two phoenixes immolating and born again in the ashes of their suffering.

AFTERWORD

Thank you so much for reading *What Death Forgets*. I treasure each and every one of my readers and I'm so grateful you took a chance on my book.

Your review can help others find Asher and Lev's story, so please consider leaving one on Amazon, Goodreads, social media, or wherever you normally recommend books.

Like Lev and his art, I believe a story is no longer mine alone once I share it with readers. I wanted to give you the freedom to come to your own conclusions about the supernatural elements of the story, but I'm happy to talk about my theories and would love to hear your own!

You can connect with me @theaverdone on Instagram, TikTok, and Facebook, or email me at thea@theaverdone.com.

If you'd like to be the first to learn of new releases and receive exclusive bonus content please subscribe to my mailing list, or visit www.theaverdone.com.

With love and gratitude,

IF YOU NEED SUPPORT

YOU MATTER TO ME.
If you're thinking about hurting yourself please reach out to someone you trust, a healthcare provider, your country's suicide prevention hotline, or go to the emergency room.

Dial 9-8-8 in the US for the US Suicide & Crisis Lifeline or visit https://988lifeline.org/

YOU ARE NOT ALONE.
At least 1 in 6 men have been sexually abused or assaulted.

If you are a man who has experienced sexual abuse or assault, visit https://1in6.org/ for confidential support and resources

LGBTQ+ KINK COMMUNITY ABUSE SUPPORT
Dial (800) 832-1901 or visit https://www.tnlr.org/en/24-hour-hotline/ for The Network/La Red's 24-hour hotline

RESOURCES THAT WON'T CALL THE POLICE.
For an excellent list of mental health, sexual assault, and abuse resources that won't call the police, visit https://dontcallthepolice.com/national/

ACKNOWLEDGMENTS

I am endlessly grateful for...

My husband and my family
The friends who know my heart
My PA Sabrina, for whom this book may not have happened
without.
My agent, Eva Scalzo
My street team
The early readers who helped me perfect this story
The artists who inspired me and brought my vision to life
And the person holding this book,
Thank you for reading this story of my heart.

ADDITIONAL THANKS TO:

Amy, Alona, Ash, Tony Belpedio, Brenna, Cait, TA Caldwell*,
Dana, Ezra, Jillian Hartle, Jeannine, Kitty, Lilian, Adrienne
Lothy**, Milo, Ren, Sabrina

Your help was instrumental in improving this story.

* Without your special attention to light fixtures, Lev and
Asher would bumble about in the dark for half the book.
** Thank you for giving me the confidence and support I
needed from the first page to the last.

ABOUT THE AUTHOR

Thea Verdone writes MM modern gothic romance about imperfect people haunted by inner demons and dark histories.

Whether it's a crumbling gothic castle, the ocean at night, or a mansion with a piano, her settings are as alive as any other character.

She writes her books from a desk that faces a forest in the Pacific Northwest, which is all she's ever wanted.

THEAVERDONE.COM

ALSO BY THEA VERDONE

- MM modern gothic romance
- Pianist with synesthesia
- Relationship in crisis
- Hurt/comfort
- Depression representation
- Toxic relationship turned healthy
- Villain redeemed

Alek and Ian's relationship is built on lies and the cracks are starting to show.

A pianist gifted with synesthesia, Alek sees sounds and hears colors and transforms all of his emotions into music. But no matter how hard he tries to hide behind a facade of apathy and seduction, he can't escape the dark past that haunts him.

Contractor Ian sees the beauty in something destroyed by neglect and his obsession with fixing extends beyond historical buildings. But when Alek's self-destructive tendencies turn their relationship to ruins, Ian fears Alek is the first project he'll have no choice but to abandon.

Now the Gothic Victorian mansion they're renovating is the only thing connecting them. Alek will do anything to keep Ian with him.

Except tell the truth.

Because Alek is lying about everything, starting with his name, and when Ian learns the truth, their house of cards will collapse.

Find it in paperback, audiobook, and ebook at

books2read.com/nlnl

CONTENT WARNINGS

- Abuse of power by college teacher *
- Abusive BDSM relationship *
- Alzheimer's
- Blood phobia
- Brief mention of cattle slaughter
- Brief mention of CSA *
- Broken bones *
- Bullying *
- Cancer
- PTSD
- Dubious consent
- Eating disorder - anorexia *
- Homophobic parent/family
- Liver failure
- Loss of parent/s and loved one/s
- Nausea/vomiting
- Murder/attempted murder
- Non-consent *
- Overdose
- Panic attacks
- Religious homophobia
- Religious trauma
- Self harm - briefly mentioned
- Sexual assault *
- Strangulation
- Suicide attempt

Please Note: while I took great care to show enthusiastic consent and safe and sane sexual acts between the love interests, there is potential dubious consent because of power dynamics.

There is a happily ever after

* = does not occur between love interests